The Gregor Demarkian Holiday Series
by Jane Haddam

Not a Creature Was Stirring
(Christmas)

Precious Blood
(Easter)

Act of Darkness
(Fourth of July)

Quoth the Raven
(Halloween)

A Great Day for the Deadly
(St. Patrick's Day)

Feast of Murder
(Thanksgiving)

A Stillness in Bethlehem
(Christmas)

A STILLNESS

IN BETHLEHEM

jane haddam

Bantam Books

new york   toronto   london   sydney   auckland

A STILLNESS IN BETHLEHEM
A Bantam Book / December 1992

BOOK DESIGN BY MARIA CARELLA
MAP BY LAURA HARTMAN MAESTRO

Library of Congress Cataloging-in-Publication Data
Haddam, Jane, 1951–
A stillness in Bethlehem / Jane Haddam.
p. cm.
ISBN 0-553-09024-0
I. Title.
PS3566.A613S75   1992
813'.54—dc20   92-18574
CIP

Published simultaneously in the United States and Canada

Bantam Books are published by Bantam Books, a division of Bantam Doubleday Dell Pub-
lishing Group, Inc. Its trademark, consisting of the words "Bantam Books" and the portrayal
of a rooster, is Registered in U.S. Patent and Trademark Office and in other countries. Marca
Registrada. Bantam Books, 666 Fifth Avenue, New York, New York 10103.

PRINTED IN THE UNITED STATES OF AMERICA
BVG   0 9 8 7 6 5 4 3 2 1

a stillness in bethlehem

PROLOGUE

O little town of
Bethlehem
How still we see
thee lie...

1

LIKE DOZENS of other small towns scattered across the White Mountains and the Green Mountains and the Berkshires, Bethlehem often got its first dusting of snow just after Halloween and found itself hip-deep in white by the first of December. This first of December had not been that bad. It had been a mild season from the beginning, causing squeals of panic and indignation to rise from the flatlanders who had bought up the ski resorts to the north. The squeals and panic were noted with a certain amount of satisfaction by the natives, who didn't much like the flatlanders in spite of the money they spent. Then, in the middle of everything, there had been a quick-mud thaw. The temperature had dropped far enough to freeze that over only on the first of December itself. It was now December second, the official opening day of the Bethlehem Nativity Celebration, and everything looked a little skewed. Peter Callisher thought that what it really looked like was haphazard. The people of Bethlehem, Vermont, had been putting on their Nativity Celebration since 1934. The Celebration had grown from a small collection of rough sheds propped up with two-by-fours around the gazebo in the town park to a kind of psychic delusion that possessed the whole town three weeks out of every year. Each cycle of the Nativity play now took a full week, starting on Monday and ending on Saturday, bringing new and bewildered bevies of tourists into the inns around Main Street every Sunday afternoon. The Holy Family had taken up residence in the gazebo itself, and the cow and the donkey and the sheep that surrounded them were all real enough to cause difficulties in managing their manure. It all looked eerily authentic, in spite of the fact that Palestine rarely got this much snow—or any snow at all.

For Peter Callisher, standing at the window of the living room in the apartment he kept over the offices of the *Bethlehem News and Mail,* it all looked depressing, as if they were trying to hold on to something they should have let go of long ago. Peter wasn't a flatlander, but he looked like one. He was tall and angular and bookish, complete with wire-rimmed glasses and a parka from L. L. Bean, and there was something about the way he moved his hands that spoke very strongly of Away. It should have. Peter Callisher was forty-four years old. He had been born and raised in Bethlehem, in the small brick house on Dencher Street his father had built around the time he took over the *News and Mail.* Peter had sold that house exactly six years ago, when his father died and he had taken over the *News and Mail* himself. In the time between, he had been about as Away as anyone could get. At first, there had been the usual things. He had gone south to Yale for college and then to New York to take a master's degree at the Columbia School of Journalism. After that, he had gone to work for *The New York Times.* It was what happened after that that got to people, because they found it inexplicable. Running away to Boston or New York or the Ivy League: That was all right. That was about sex. Running away to Pakistan, even if *The New York Times* was paying you to do it and calling you a foreign correspondent: That was something else again. As for coming back to town with a bullet in your hip when you hadn't even been in a war, and trailing rumors about Afghanistan and the mujahadeen—that was enough to put an end to conversations all over town, even down in the basement of the Congregational Church, where the old ladies made holiday baskets for the poor in Burlington and talked about the children of friends of theirs who'd died.

From where he was standing, Peter Callisher could see most of the town park and the south end of Main Street. As usual on the first day, before the serious tourists had begun their serious tramping about, people were milling around, trying themselves out, wondering how they'd gotten themselves into this fix. The three wise men had new robes this year, brightly colored and sewn over with paste gemstones. They even had camels sent up from a theatrical-animal supply service in Boston. The child Jesus had swaddling clothes shot through with gold thread. The angel of the Annunciation had wings wired to glow with incandescent bulbs. According to *The Boston Globe,* Bethlehem was likely to realize over three hundred and fifty thousand dollars from this Celebration, spread out across viewing tickets, room rents, restaurant checks, parking fees and souvenirs—of which there would be plenty, on sale twenty-four hours a day from the old horse barn in back of the Town Hall. According to *New York* magazine, Bethlehem's take was going to be closer to half a million, due at least in part to the fact that *New York* had been hyping the Celebration vigorously for every one of the past five seasons. Whatever the final count, the money would more than come in handy. Like too many of the towns on the edges of the rural backwaters of northern New England, Bethlehem didn't seem to have any money of its own.

Peter had left a cigarette burning in his only ashtray. He put it out—unsmoked; he had started smoking in India, out of polite necessity, and never really developed a taste for it, only a habit—and headed for the door that led to the stairs on the first floor. Those stairs ended in a landing fronted by two doors, one to the outside and one to the newsroom. Theoretically, this ensured his privacy. If he didn't want his employees to know what he was doing, he could use the outside door and not have to pass through the newsroom at all. In practice, privacy was an illusion he didn't waste his time worrying about. Everyone in town knew precisely everything he'd done since he'd first come back from God Only Knew Where.

He reached the landing, opened the door to the newsroom and stuck in his head. He had one or two truly local people working for him, but most of his employees were from Away. They were smart kids with rich parents, who'd been sent proudly through Groton and Harvard—only to decide that what they really wanted to do was to Go Back to the Land. They worked hard, demanded little money, and grew alfalfa sprouts in big white plastic tubs in the ladies' room. Not a single one of them had the least idea of what it really meant to belong to a place like this.

Peter squinted across the piles of paper that never seemed to change position and found Amanda Ballard, his best, checking type sizes on a font chart. Amanda Ballard was not only his best: She was his prettiest. Thin, blond, even-featured, straight-haired and blue-eyed, Amanda was a vision of cultural perfection, circa 1968. She was a lot of other things circa 1968, too. She seemed to think and speak in staccato bursts of discarded clichés, apparently unconcerned that even the politics of her beloved New Left had passed her by. If it hadn't been for the odd deformation of her right ear, with no earlobe at all and a stunted little nub at the bottom that looked like a pierced earring in the wrong place, she would have been indistinguishable from a doll. She was thirty-six years old and looked sixteen—and would look sixteen, Peter thought, when she was eighty. In that way, she was very different from Peter himself, who had weathered in body as well as in mind. His skin was creased into folds at the corners of his eyes and along the line of his jaw. Sand and wind and worry had marked him. His mind had tied itself into knots in its attempt to hold on to a belief in the essential goodness of human beings, and been defeated.

Amanda put down the font chart, picked up what seemed to be an Associated Press tear-off and frowned. Frowning, she looked very much the way she did in bed, after intercourse, when she tried to explain to him why his attitude was all wrong. Peter watched while Timmy Hall, their great overgrown copy boy, came up to ask Amanda a question. Seeing Timmy around Amanda always made Peter nervous, as if that great tub of lard might suddenly turn lean and mean and lunge with sharpened teeth. It was a ridiculous image. Timmy was strange, but not that kind of strange. His peculiarities ran to eating Marshmallow Fluff with his scrambled eggs. Amanda was fragile, but not that kind of fragile. Peter could never put a finger on what kind of fragile she was, but he was attracted to it. Besides, Amanda had known Timmy forever, as far as Peter could tell. She'd even gotten Timmy this job. Timmy was mentally retarded and had been brought up in the mental-health complex in Riverton. Amanda had met him there while she was doing something Peter had never been able to pin down, but that he secretly suspected was getting straight from drugs. That was the kind of trouble Amanda would have, heat prostration from an attempt to resurrect the Summer of Love.

Peter shifted on his feet, nodded to the two or three people who had noticed him standing in the doorway, and said, "Amanda?"

Amanda put the Associated Press tear-off down, shook her head at something Timmy was saying and came toward the door. "We can't play tricks like that on our readers," she said over her shoulder—to Timmy, Peter supposed. Then she came up to him and sighed. "If we're going to deliver to the printers by three o'clock, we're going to have to get a lot more done than we've been getting done. How are you?"

"I'm all right. I came to find out how you were. Everything quiet?"

"Absolutely," Amanda said.

"Not a squawk out of our usual troublemakers? No hunters shooting game wardens? No Sarah Dubay marching up and down Main Street saying the end of the world is at hand?"

"Sarah doesn't say the end of the world is at hand," Amanda said, "she says Christ was really an alien."

"Whatever."

"You shouldn't be so worried." Amanda stretched her arms. "I've just been looking at the numbers. We're going to print them on page five because everybody in town wants to know how well we're doing, but you know how the tourists feel when they think we're being mercenary. Anyway, the inns are booked solid for all three weeks, and the tickets are sold out for every performance, and there's even some special arrangement with a school in New Hampshire where they're going to bus the kids in every night. It's going to be fine. The town's going to make a pile of money."

"I hope," Peter said. "No word from the mountain? Nothing from Jan-Mark? Nothing from Tish?"

"Not a peep."

Peter came all the way into the newsroom and shut the door behind him. The windows that fronted the street on this level were mullioned, but the mullions were new and modern and large. Peter could see the short paved stretch of Main Street that ended at the gazebo and the town park. The windows of the stores were full of evergreen branches with twinkly little lights implanted in them. People came to see a six-day-long Nativity play, but when they weren't watching it they wanted their Christmas American Traditional. Over on Mott Street, Jean and Robert Mulvaney had turned their little dry-goods store into Santa's Workshop and ordered a stack of toys to sell to outlanders with too much money and not a lot of sense.

"I don't know," Peter said. "It's been much too quiet. Don't you think it's been much too quiet?"

"I think I've got much too much work to do to worry about whether it's been much too quiet."

"I don't know." Peter sighed. "It's opening day. Every year before opening day, we have a crisis. Where's the crisis?"

"Maybe Dinah Ketchum will finally shoot that daughter-in-law of hers dead, and we can all get ready to listen to another lecture from Montpelier about how we have to bring Vermont into the twentieth century. Are you going to let me get back to work?"

"Sure."

"You ought to do something yourself," Amanda said. "At least look like you're doing something. If you don't, Timmy Hall is going to come up and give you five awful ideas for the paper."

7

Timmy Hall was nowhere to be seen, which was par for the course for Timmy. Their copy boy always seemed to be either underfoot or invisible. He always left Peter wondering how old he really was.

Peter shook that out of his head, watched Amanda go back to her desk and turned to look back out at Main Street again. He was being an old Nelly, of course, but he couldn't really help himself. Small towns like this were full of people whose deepest wish was to have a television camera aimed at them. There would be a lot of television cameras on hand for the opening of the Celebration, and the nuts should have come out of the trees by now. So where were they?

Peter considered the possibility that this year there would be no nuts at all, and no trouble, either, and dismissed it out of hand. He had been around the world and back. He had been born and brought up in this very town. He knew better.

He decided to take his mind off it by looking at the mock-up for the front page, which was always news from Away and always amusing. It was a front page he was particularly proud of, because it had everything—as far as Bethlehem, Vermont, was concerned. In the first place, it was about violence in the flatlands, which allowed the citizens of Bethlehem to congratulate themselves on how intelligent they had been to stick around *here*. In the second place, it was violence with style and a kind of Agatha Christie twist, which made it fun to read. There was even a picture, a great big smudged-looking thing of a thick tall man with a Middle Eastern solemnity to his face. The headline read:

HIGH SEAS MYSTERY: DEMARKIAN NABS MURDERER
ON BILLIONAIRE'S BOAT

Then there was a subhead, one he'd written himself:

THE ARMENIAN-AMERICAN HERCULE POIROT SOLVES ANOTHER ONE

It was too good to be true.

It was so good, in fact, that Peter Callisher used it as one more proof positive that a disaster was about to befall them.

2

TISHA VEREK had been the wife of a notorious man long enough to know how to behave, and on this morning of December second—with a thin mist of snow falling on the barren ground of her summer garden and the half-light of a cloud-occluded dawn making all the world look gray—she was behaving herself with a vengeance. It was eight o'clock in the morning, much too early to get anything done in New York— but this was not New York. This was Bethlehem, Vermont, where Tisha and her husband Jan-Mark had moved five years before, during one of Jan-Mark's counterphobic fits. Tisha often had trouble believing that Jan-Mark was really *here,* in Vermont, in the country, and that he hadn't vanished into smoke as soon as the carbon dioxide began to thin in the air. Jan-Mark was that quintessential urban invention, the contemporary artist. He smoked too much, drank too much, swore too much and snorted too much cocaine. He hand-stretched custom canvases to forty feet in length and pasted them over with twice-washed trash. He painted red-and-black acrylic swirls on conventional four-by-eights and called the results "Cunnilingus." Most of all, he met other men like himself, and women, too, in heavy-metal bars where the air was thick with marijuana smoke. Back in the city, all but one of his friends had AIDS. The one had made a vow to Buddha in 1972 and lived in an apartment filled with joss sticks and chimes.

Tisha had never made a vow to anyone, anywhere. She hadn't even made a vow to Jan-Mark at their wedding. She'd written the ceremony herself, and she'd been very careful about all that. Tisha had been very careful about almost everything in her life. She was forty years old and looked thirty, the result of decades of patiently taking care. Her thick red hair was the color of flame and only barely touched up. It floated out from her skull in the tight crimps of a natural wiriness. Her skin had the hard smoothness of good porcelain. In the winter it grew faintly pink with cold, but in the summer it wasn't allowed to tan at all. She weighed ten pounds less and wore jeans two sizes smaller than she had at seventeen. The refrigerator was full of crudités and the basement was full of dumbbells to take care of that. Once upon a time, she had been a lumpy girl named Patty Feld, growing up unpopular in Dunbar, Illinois. She had made a promise to herself then about what she would become. She had made meticulous plans for taking elaborate revenge. In the years since, she had made herself into exactly what she had promised herself to make herself into, and every once in a while, she had indulged herself in a little revenge. Patricia Feld Verek had never been the sort of person it made sense to cross, not even as a child. At the age of five, she had put a snake in the lunchbox of the only mentally retarded girl in her class. At the age of twelve, she had told twenty-six people that Mary Jean Carmody was going all the way with Steven Marsh, which wasn't true. The fact that it wasn't true hadn't helped Mary Jean Carmody any, because Steven was hardly going to deny it. Tisha had wanted Mary Jean off the junior cheerleading squad, and Mary Jean had been thrown off. Now what Tisha wanted was something definitive, a token of power, from the people of Bethlehem, Vermont. This was the morning on which she intended to get it. After all, it only made sense. This was a terrible place, a prison, a cesspool. This was the pit of hell dressed up to look like Santa's Workshop. Tisha had been around long enough to know.

The house where Tisha and Jan-Mark lived was not an old farmhouse but a new log one, four levels high, stuck halfway up a mountain and surrounded by trees. The second level was a loft that served as their bedroom, screened from nature and the living room only by a thick built-in bookcase that acted as a headboard for the bed. Standing on this level, just past the bookcase on either side, Tisha could see down into the living room with its massive fieldstone fireplace and chimney. She could also see back into the bedroom, where Jan-Mark was lying fetuslike in the bed, smothering himself under four Hudson Bay point blankets and a down quilt. He was dead to the world, and Tisha didn't blame him. He'd been up until two o'clock in the morning, drinking blended Scotch whiskey and singing along to ancient Beach Boys records.

There were a pair of cedar chests at the foot of their oversized, custom-made bed. Tisha opened one of them, pawed through the sweaters until she found one dyed a bright lime green, and pulled the sweater over her head. Tisha liked colors like lime green. They clashed with her hair and made people nervous. She liked Jan-Mark being asleep, too. Jan-Mark liked to *épater la bourgeoisie,* but only for Art and only when he started it. He hated it when she went off on her own, doing all kinds of things he didn't understand, making people upset for no good reason he could see. Tisha didn't care about that—in her opinion, Jan-Mark didn't see much—but she didn't like to argue, and if it was all over and done with by the time he found out about it, he wouldn't bother to make a fuss. Back in New York, Jan-Mark had been legendary for his rages, but that was theater.

At the bottom of the cedar chest there was a stack of leg warmers. Tisha took out the ones that matched the sweater she was wearing, considered exchanging them for a pair in tangerine orange and decided against it. That sort of thing violated her sense of order. She pulled the leg warmers up over her knee socks, anchored her jeans to her ankles with them, and stood up.

"Son of a *bitch,*" Jan-Mark said from his nest of wool and feathers.

"Daughter of one, too," Tisha said equably. Then she turned her back on him and walked away, around the bookcase, across the balcony, to the spiral stairs that led to the balcony above. She could hear him snoring after her as she went.

The balcony above was where their "offices" were—her office, really, and Jan-Mark's studio. They were both simply large open spaces divided by a four-inch construction of good drywall. Tisha had to pass Jan-Mark's studio to get where she wanted to go. She looked in on paints and canvases and easels and palettes and a life-sized poster of Arnold Schwartzenegger from *Terminator II.* Her office was much more organized, much more efficient. The MacIntosh had its own hard-plastic work station in one corner. The corkboards that lined the walls were themselves lined with pictures, portraits of the people in her latest project. Tisha Verek was a "writer," particulars undefined, but she was a "writer" with good connections. She had had four true-crime books published already and was now working on a fifth. This time, instead of writing about a single crime, putting the details together the way she'd put together a novel, she was working on a concept, on a theory. The photographic portraits on her corkboards were all of children between the ages of five and twelve years old. Each and every one of those children had committed at least one murder, and three had committed more than five.

Tisha sat down in the big armchair she kept next to her phone and looked up at her favorite corkboard of all, what she thought of as her gallery of grotesques. On this corkboard she had Mikey Pellman, who had cut the throats of three of his kindergarten classmates during a school picnic in Andorman, Massachusetts, in 1958. When he was asked why he'd done it, Mikey'd said he wanted to know if everyone had the same color of blood. She also had Tommy Hare, who had waited until he was twelve but shown a good deal more imagination. He had killed his ex-girlfriend and the boy she'd dumped him for by electrocuting them in a swimming pool. That wouldn't have gotten Tommy onto this corkboard in and of itself, except for the fact that there had been twenty-two other people in that swimming pool at the time, and Tommy had had to stand at the edge of it with a cattle prod in his hand to get the job done. All in all, this was by far the best of the corkboards, much better than the one she kept near her computer, to give herself inspiration. That one had the pictures of people who fit her theory without stretching, like Stevie Holtzer, who at the age of seven pushed the father who beat him down the cellar stairs and broke his neck, or Amy Jo Bickerel, who put a bullet through the head of the uncle who forced her into finger-probing trysts in the front seat of his car when she was eleven. There was something about *those* people that Tisha didn't like at all—as if it were less attractive to kill for a reason rather than for the sheer ecstasy of doing it.

She got the phone untangled from its cord, checked the number on her phone pad although she knew it by heart and began to punch buttons. The beeps and whirs that sounded in her ear made her think of R2D2 and those silly *Star Wars* movies. Then the phone started to ring, and she sat back to wait. Tisha could be as patient and as understanding as the next woman if she wanted to be, and today she wanted to be. She had been thinking long and hard about what she was going to do and how she was going to do it. She had even consulted a lawyer in New York and paid him eight hundred dollars for his opinion. She was as sure as anyone could be that nothing on earth could stop her.

All she had to do now was set her little time bombs and wait.

3

FRANKLIN MORRISON had been the chief lawman for Bethlehem, Vermont, for far longer than he wanted to remember, and during most of that time he had been desperately dreaming of escape. Exactly what he wanted to escape from, he wasn't sure. Sometimes he thought it was just the job. He kept telling himself he could quit any time he wanted to. He didn't even have to think of anything else to do. He had his Social Security and a little pension the town had helped him set up twenty years ago. He owned his house free and clear, and the taxes on it weren't heavy. He could retreat to his living room and his vast collection of the novels of Mickey Spillane and never have to hear another word about the Bethlehem Nativity Celebration as long as he lived. Sometimes he thought it was all much more complicated than that. What he really wanted to escape from was Vermont, and snow, and winter. His best friend, Charlie Deaver, had gone down to live in Florida a year ago, and in the letters Charlie's wife sent, Florida sounded like a cross between Walt Disney heaven and the Promised Land. Then Franklin would get to thinking about it, and even Florida would not be enough. He'd begin to wonder what was out there. He'd begin to dream about spaceships to Jupiter. He'd find himself standing in the checkout line in the supermarket at the shopping center over in Kitchihee, New Hampshire, staring long and hard at the front page of *The Weekly World News.* "Woman Murdered By Fur Coat." "Psychic Reveals: ELVIS CAPTURED BY ALIENS FOR EXPERIMENTS ON ALPHA CENTAURI." "A Diet That Eats Your Fat Away While You Sleep." He'd begin to think he was going nuts.

On this second day of December, Franklin Morrison didn't have to think he was going nuts. He knew he was going nuts. It was the opening day of the Celebration. Peter Callisher might look out on the town and think that all was quiet, but Franklin knew better. Oh, there was nothing major going on, not yet. Jackie Dunn hadn't had enough liquor to want to bed down in the crèche. Stu Ketchum hadn't staggered in from the hills with an illegal deer over his shoulders and too much ammunition left for that damned automatic rifle he'd bought. Even Sarah Dubay had been reasonably quiet. Now there was a lady who believed in life on Jupiter—and in Elvis being captured by aliens, for all that Franklin knew. The only reason that Sarah wasn't a bag lady was that places like Bethlehem, Vermont, didn't allow old women to wander around the streets with nowhere to go.

So far, Franklin's problems on this cold morning had been mostly procedural. Henry Furnald wanted two dollars for every car parked on his lawn instead of the one the town allowed him to charge while calling himself an official parking area. Henry was therefore threatening to take his lawn out of the car-parking business and had to be cooled down. God only knew what would happen if people started streaming in from Burlington and Keene and there was no place for them to put their cars. Then there were the camels, which had broken free of their tethers and come to rest in the middle of the intersection of Main and Carrow. They had to be moved to allow the truck bringing sausages from Montpelier to get to the food arcade. Then there was the food arcade itself, which seemed to be falling down. The damned thing was put together with plywood and penny nails, and the wind had been strong all week. Franklin kept getting calls from people who had passed by and been convinced it was about to collapse on their heads.

All in all, the Bethlehem Nativity Celebration was just as much of a pain this year as it had ever been. Franklin would have been for abolishing it, except for two things. In the first place, it paid his salary. In the second, it kept him from thinking. Of these two, the keeping-him-from-thinking part was the more important. As long as camels were poking their noses into Beder's Dry Goods Store, Franklin would not be visited by any middle-of-the-day paralyses. As long as the local juvenile delinquents kept trying to paint the Star of Bethlehem green, Franklin would not find himself coming to in the middle of empty rooms while his brain tried furiously to figure out What It All Meant—or if it meant anything at all. Franklin didn't know what It was—maybe, at seventy-two, he was finally getting old—but he was sick and tired of It. It would have made more sense to him if he'd developed a sudden passion for pissing up.

Now he came back to the squad room from the john and looked around, sighing a little. The squad room wasn't really a squad room—the Bethlehem, Vermont, Police Department didn't have a squad—but it was closer to it than anything anywhere in Vermont outside Montpelier. In fact, in spite of the fact that it was just a room in the basement of the town hall with two cells down the corridor next to the boiler room, it was better equipped than any squad room north of Boston. Back in the thirties, the town's proceeds from the Bethlehem Nativity Celebration had gone to pay for necessities, like cleaning the streets and keeping the elementary school in business. Now, after decades of post-War prosperity only intermittently disrupted by recessions—and the steadily rising popularity of the Celebration itself—those proceeds went to pay for the spectacular. The elementary school had a computer room with fifty-four top-of-the-line IBM PCs, a gymnasium with two swimming pools and enough exercise equipment to qualify for a Jack LaLanne franchise and a music program that provided any child who wanted to learn to play an instrument with an instrument to use to learn on, for free. The volunteer fire department had a fully mechanized hook-and-ladder truck with a ladder that could stretch to 120 feet. Since the tallest building in Bethlehem was Jan-Mark Verek's four-story log contemporary, the 120 feet weren't likely to be needed anytime soon. The police department had what police departments get, when money is no object. Franklin had computer hookups, patrol cars, a mobile crime unit out of a Columbo fantasy, a full fingerprint classification and retrieval system with access linkage to the FBI, even a crime lab capable of microscopic blood, earth and fiber analysis. What he didn't have was any crime worth speaking of, which he often thought was too bad.

He let himself through the swinging gate in the low wooden rail and walked up behind his one deputy, Lee Greenwood, who was sitting with his feet on his desk and *The Boston Globe* opened in front of his nose, doing what he was always doing: reading the paper with enough fierce concentration to memorize the punctuation. At the moment, he was reading the latest in the *Globe*'s series of articles on what everybody had been calling The Thanksgiving Murder for a week or so now, in spite of the fact that it hadn't taken place on Thanksgiving at all. Franklin saw fuzzy pictures of "billionaire Jonathan Edgewick Baird" and "mysterious arbitrageur Donald McAdam." He passed over these to the even fuzzier picture of Gregor Demarkian, looking tall and broad and Middle Eastern and nothing at all like an "Armenian-American Hercule Poirot." Going to a law-enforcement convention last year, Franklin had not been surprised to find that every small-town cop in America seemed to know all there was to know about Mr. Gregor Demarkian. In places like this, where nothing much ever happened, it was intriguing to think that you might one day land in the middle of a mess interesting enough to call on the services of "the most skilled expert on the investigation of murder in America."

It was also intriguing to think that you might one day abscond with the town treasury and go to live in Borneo, but it wasn't likely to happen. Franklin brushed it all out of his mind and tugged at the top of the paper to get Lee's attention. Lee was as young and hairy as Franklin was old and bald. When Lee put his paper down, his hair seemed to bristle and crackle with static electricity, and maybe to throw off sparks.

"Listen," Franklin said, when he could finally see Lee's face. "Don't you think you should be out there doing something? Don't you think you should at least be seeing to those camels?"

Lee smoothed the paper out against his desk. "I don't like this one as much as I liked the last one," he said, tapping his finger right on Gregor Demarkian's oversized nose. "This one has too many rich people. The last one, that happened in a town just like this."

"A town full of nuns and Catholics isn't a town just like this,"

Franklin said irritably. "And what about the camels? We can't just leave them sitting in the middle of Main Street, causing a traffic hazard."

"They're not causing a traffic hazard," Lee said reasonably. "Betty Heath called in and said they'd moved on to that open lot at the end of Carrow Street, and the only thing that's causing a hazard now is what they left behind, and I don't do that kind of work. I called Don Francis over to Clean-up and he said he'd send somebody out. You got a call from Benjy Warren."

"Benjy Warren," Franklin repeated. "Benjy" Warren preferred to be known as "Ben" Warren, now that he'd been all the way to Harvard Law School and back again, but he was fighting a losing battle and he knew it. He'd been Benjy in grammar school and Benjy in high school and Benjy when he'd come home for vacations from Bowdoin College, and he would go on being Benjy as long as he stayed in town. It didn't help that he worked for a friend of his father's, who had been calling him Benjy all his life and didn't intend to stop. Franklin sometimes wondered about that. This friend of Benjy's father's was Camber Hartnell, until Benjy's return the town's only attorney and still the town's most prominent son of a bitch. He wouldn't have been Franklin's first choice for a boss if Franklin had been the one with the degree from Harvard Law School.

Franklin leaned over Lee's paper again. There was a second picture of Demarkian there, a smaller one, walking next to a small woman with a face as close to perfect as Elizabeth Taylor's at twenty-five. Franklin knew that face—it popped up in stories about Demarkian all the time, and sometimes even in accounts of Demarkian's cases—but he couldn't remember the name. He wondered if Demarkian was sleeping with her. He supposed Demarkian had to be. All those people from Away hopped in and out of bed with each other all the time.

Franklin backed up a little and cleared his throat. "The thing is," he said, "even if there isn't anything to do, we ought to look like we've got something to do. For the papers."

"Papers?"

"The Away papers," Franklin said patiently. "I told you about this last year. The Away papers always send reporters, so do the television stations in Boston; they get people up here the first day and talk about the gala opening that isn't so gala if you ask me. I was a tourist, I'd come in the second or third week when I could count on people knowing their lines. Never mind. The papers are going to be here, and we ought to look like we've got something to do."

"Like what?"

"How the hell should I know like what? Like anything. Like fighting crime. That's what we're paid for. Fighting crime."

"There isn't any crime to fight," Lee pointed out. "We'll get some pickpockets later tonight when the crowds get thick. We catch a couple every year."

"I know."

"We'll get some fifteen-year-old jerk trying to steal some Boston lady's Ferrari," Lee said, "and then he won't be able to figure out how to get it out of the lots, and we'll haul him in and yell at him for twenty minutes and send him home. If I'm guessing right that ought to be Hal Bonnard this year."

"Hal Bonnard." Franklin nodded. "Him or Joey Fay."

"We'll get six anonymous calls saying people are going at it in the bushes in the park, and the calls will all come from Dodie Fenner, and there won't be a pair of squirrels necking by the time we get there. We'll get Bill Varley calling in to say he's seen a spaceship. We'll get a lot of petty vandalism. This is Vermont, for Christ's sake. You've been here long enough. You ought to know."

And, of course, Franklin did know. He knew better than Lee Greenwood. Lee was only thirty-two and had been on the job only thirty months. Franklin looked down at the newspaper one more time. There was Mr. Gregor Demarkian, looking a little like a diplomat and a little like a czar, looking important and busy and oversupplied with interesting things to think about, walking along beside a beautiful woman who looked like she did aerobics and who had hold of his arm. There was Franklin's own desk, not six steps away on the other side of the room against the wall, piled high with message slips demanding immediate attention to falling Christmas lights, muddied angels' costumes and straying animals that would only stray again as soon as they were brought back to where they were supposed to be. Franklin didn't even have a wife at home to keep him warm or make his life miserable. It hardly seemed fair.

Franklin looked up at the clock, saw it said only 8:15, and frowned.

"Lee," he asked, "when Benjy called, was he calling from the office?"

"He was home," Lee mumbled, deep in his forty-second perusal of this installment of the Adventures of Gregor Demarkian. "It wasn't even eight o'clock, for Christ's sake. He said you should call him right back."

"At home," Franklin insisted.

"That's right, at home."

"Fine," Franklin said.

He walked over to his desk, sat down in his swivel chair and picked up his receiver. Then he punched himself into the first of his six lines and tapped out Benjy's home number on the pad. Benjy's father had been one of Franklin's less-astute drinking buddies before he died, but Franklin would have known the number without looking it up in any case. He knew the numbers of everyone in town who had anything to do with the government, officially or unofficially. In small towns like this, anyone with a law degree automatically becomes part of the unofficial government, and a man whose number it's good to know.

"Going to be nothing," Franklin said to himself, as the phone rang once and started to ring again.

Then the ringing was cut off in mid-squeal, and Benjy Warren's breathless voice said, "Yes? Who is it?"

"It's me," Franklin said, surprised. "Are you all right, Benjy? What's your hurry?"

"Hurry," Benjy Warren said. Then he laughed, long and hard enough to start himself coughing. "Oh, God," he said. "You're the one who better hurry. Guess who I just talked to. Tish."

"Tisha Verek? So what?"

"So you got to know why she called. She wasn't looking for me. She was looking for Cam."

"That makes sense."

"Cam's in New Hampshire, skiing for the day. Left at six this morning. She wanted to get in touch with him."

"You could do that for her," Franklin said.

"I could, but I haven't yet. I wanted to give everybody a little time."

"A little time for what?"

"A little time to head her off at the pass," Benjy said. "God, Franklin, I'm sorry. If I'd known this was brewing, I'd have warned you all long ago. I've been trying to figure out the paperwork ever since I heard."

"Figure out the paperwork for *what*?" Franklin demanded, exasperated. "What could Tisha Verek possibly do that would—"

"I'll tell you what she could possibly do," Benjy said. "She could take the ACLU up on their standing offer and file an injunction."

4

THE FOUR CORE ROOMS of Stuart Ketchum's house had been built in 1687 by the very first Ketchum to come to Vermont—far enough back, in fact, that the flatlanders who ran the Historical Society thought it might be the oldest house in town. Whether it was or not, Stuart Ketchum didn't know and didn't care. The core wasn't much to speak of anyway—just a big room with a fireplace that now served as the kitchen and two smaller rooms upstairs Stu used as spares—and it wasn't really *in town* anyway. Until 1947, it hadn't even been in the town limits, which had caused a few interesting situations with the land-tax people. It had also caused a few interesting situations with the state government in Montpelier. Montpelier always wanted to know what was going on and why it was going on and what they were supposed to do about it. Like governments everywhere—at least in Stu's opinion—Montpelier took to busybodiness as a holy cause. Stu Ketchum didn't have much use for governments, in Montpelier or anywhere else. It was the principal bone of contention he had with his best friend, Peter Callisher, since forever, when they managed to get together to drink a few beers in peace. It was getting harder and harder to drink a few beers in peace, because there were the drunk-driving people and the save-your-heart people and the if-you-really-*need*-that-one-beer-after-dinner-you-must-be-an-alcoholic people. Stu never listened to the alcoholic people, because his father had been an alcoholic and Stu knew one when he saw one. Stu's father had frozen to death one night in 1956, after falling down dead drunk in the back pasture after a six-hour visit with Johnny Walker Black. Stu had been ten years old at the time.

It was now eight-twenty-five on the morning of Monday, December second, and Stu was sitting in his kitchen, nursing a cup of coffee, watching Peter Callisher's car pull up the drive, and thinking that 1687 might have been a very good year, but he was just about ready for a house built the day before yesterday with a whirlpool bathtub and vinyl on the kitchen floor. He'd been thinking this way for six months now, and working it out, and he thought he was set. If he had a good enough take during the Celebration, he could break ground, as soon as the frost began to ease, out on that same back pasture where his father had died.

He sure as hell didn't need the pasture for cows, because he didn't have any cows. He didn't have any sheep anymore, either, and he was just about ready to give up on pigs. The back fifty acres of this farm had returned to forest decades ago. Stu went out there whenever he wanted and bagged whatever deer he needed to keep himself in meat. He couldn't see slaughtering a pig he'd known all its life or a lamb he'd helped deliver. It didn't make any sense, and he knew it didn't make any sense, but he couldn't help himself. Sometimes, when he'd had a few beers or a very long day or a particularly awful run-in with the Environmental Protection Agency, he put his copy of *The Deer Hunter* in the VCR and tried to relate it all to his years in Vietnam. That, Stu had once told Peter Callisher, would be how he finally knew he was losing it. He'd put that damned movie in the VCR and sit down in front of it and, *pow,* life would start to make sense.

Peter Callisher had a Jeep Wagoneer, a little too country for his image, but at least not Japanese. That was one of the things that divided the flatlanders from the natives up here, and Peter was always careful to let the town know which side he was on. So was Stu, who had been Away himself, even if it was only to get shot at. Stu would rather have defected to the Viet Cong than let himself be anything at all like one of *them.*

Peter pulled the Wagoneer to a stop in the middle of the chicken yard—the chickens being safely in the barn for the winter—and Stu stood up to go out to him. Normally it would have been Stu's wife who went out, and Stu's mother who saw to the boiling water and the jar of instant coffee, but Liza (Stu's wife) and Dinah (Stu's mother) were both down in town setting up a stall in the food arcade and were going to be there for all of the rest of the day. Dinah even had a small second stall in the souvenir place where she was offering quilts for sale. There were six quilts priced at nine hundred dollars apiece, each hand sewn, each showing a picture carefully calculated to appeal to a flatlander's idea of the Real Vermont. Flatlanders had very strange ideas about the Real Vermont.

Stu went out the kitchen door, through the gun room and to the back door that led outside. He looked up and down his racks of guns automatically, making sure every one of them was in place. Why they wouldn't be in place, he didn't know. Nobody came out here unless they had a reason to visit. Anybody who came out to visit would know better than to touch anything he didn't have permission to touch. Stu had 122 rifles of every conceivable make, type and era. He had almost as many marksmanship medals, awards, trophies and citations. He had enough ammunition to restart the American Revolutionary War. Except for every once in a while, when those damn fools in Montpelier pulled something he really couldn't make himself believe, Stu never even thought of using his guns for anything but deer or target practice.

Peter got out of the Wagoneer, came stomping across the yard, and climbed the short flight of wooden steps to the gun-room door. He passed between the door and Stu's chest and looked around at the weaponry. Then he shook his head and went on through to the kitchen. Stu shut the outside door and followed him.

"I got that Winchester I was looking for," Stu said. "Found it night before last in an antique shop down in Burlington. Damn idiots thought it was a decoration."

"It ought to be a decoration," Peter said. "I'll never understand what you've got against a lot of poor, defenseless deer."

"It was Bambi that did it to me," Stu said seriously. "All that fire. All those gunshots. Bambi's mother felled with a single shot. It got me hooked. I've never been able to stop. I'm powerless over my addiction. Maybe they've got a twelve-step program for it."

Peter dropped into a kitchen chair and looked around for coffee. "Maybe they've got a shrink who wouldn't go crazy trying to examine your head," he said, "but if they do, he's no one I ever met. Aren't you interested in what got me out here?"

"Mostly I'm interested in why you didn't call first. It's the first day of the Celebration. If I hadn't been up all night refereeing, I'd be down in town already."

"Liza and Dinah not getting along?"

"Liza and Dinah never get along," Stu said. "The real surprise is that they haven't killed each other yet. You notice our beautiful Christmas decorations?"

Peter frowned. "You don't have any Christmas decorations."

"I know. I don't have them because they both made a set and they won't either of them let the other's go up, not even to put the two sets up together. That's what they kept me up about, last night. Dinah says Liza's are too hick, and Liza says Dinah's are too arty. Dinah, by the way, has been having her portrait painted by Jan-Mark Verek. It's got Liza fit to spit."

"Jan-Mark Verek," Peter said musingly. "You got some coffee somewhere, Stu? Even bad coffee?"

"I've always got bad coffee."

"I couldn't call you up because we're putting out the paper today, and besides, you know what it's like, calling from town. Even since the party lines died, you know what it's like. How do you figure they do it without party lines?"

"They listen at doors."

"Yeah, you're probably right. God, that does look like bad coffee. That looks like awful coffee."

"It tastes worse."

Stu put the cup full of black sludge down in front of Peter and stepped back. Peter looked tired and wrung out and just a little bit angry, but the drive up here must have leeched most of the fire out of him. That there had been fire, Stu was in no doubt. Peter wouldn't have bothered to make the trip otherwise. It wasn't as if he could be on his way to anyplace else. This farm wasn't on the way to anyplace else. Even the only other thing out here—the Vereks' brand-new ultra-bizarre log house—could only be reached by picking up the Delaford Road.

Stu got a fresh cup of coffee for himself—if you could call freeze-dried crystals fresh; this stuff really was awful—and sat down at the other end of the table. Years ago, when he and Peter were boys, they had sat for hours just like this. When it got dark, they didn't turn the lights on. They talked instead. They talked about the things they would do when they finally got to Away. They talked about the men they would be once they knew they never had to come back. They never considered the obvious: that the place you were born and raised has a hold on you you might not ever be ready to give up.

Stu reached around to the shelf at the back of his head and found his pack of cigarettes. He got them down and lit up, offering the pack to Peter in the process. Peter shook his head, and Stu wondered if he was having another go at trying to quit.

"So," he said, dragging and blowing smoke at the ceiling. "What's up? What couldn't you talk to me about on the phone?"

"It wasn't that I couldn't talk to you about it," Peter said. "It's just that I didn't want to. I mean, hell, they want to know my opinions, that's what I write editorials for."

"Opinions about what?"

"Tish." Peter jerked his head, more or less in the direction of the log house. "She's finally gone and done it, you know. Or she's on her way to go and do it. That's what I hear from Franklin Morrison."

"Done what?"

"Filed that injunction the ACLU has been blathering about for I don't know how long now. Except she hasn't filed it yet, it's too early. She's leaving for the federal courthouse in Montpelier at nine-thirty. Camber Hartnell's taking her."

"Camber Hartnell would, wouldn't he?" Stu sighed. "You figure we're really violating anybody's constitutional right to freedom of religion, running this Celebration?"

"I figure we're violating the Constitution six ways to Sunday. I've told you that before. With the case law the way it is—"

"The guy who's playing Joseph this year is the biggest atheist in town."

"The guy who's playing Joseph this year is Bobby Beggen and he was born here," Peter said. "Tish wasn't born here, but she's a bona fide resident and she qualifies as a potentially injured party under the law. She is therefore allowed—"

"Yeah, yeah. I know." Stu took another drag on his cigarette. "So what does this mean? Is she going to get the Celebration closed this year? With the tickets already sold and the inns booked?"

"I don't think so. I talked to Benjy and he says he'll file a countermotion for the town, and that ought to hold up any action until after the holidays. It's not this year that's the problem."

"Once we get through this year, we might be able to talk her out of the whole thing," Stu said. "You know. Using persuasion."

"We might," Peter agreed. "The problem is—"

"What?"

"Well, it's like cancer, isn't it? We've been getting away with this for years, basically because no one wanted to be the first to complain. Now Tish is going to be the first to complain, and if we deflect her there's sure to be half a dozen other people who won't mind at all being second. And sooner or later—"

"Ah," Stu said. "Sooner or later."

Peter took a long gulp of his coffee, made a face and put the cup down. "I've worked it all out," he said. "After I talked to Benjy and Franklin, I mean. You have any idea how much of the town budget gets paid for by the Celebration?"

"Nope."

"Almost a third. A third. Can you believe that? And it's not only the fancy stuff, either. I mean, good years, we go fancy. But bad years, we pay for the roads without raising taxes and we pay the heat on a lot of houses with nobody but widows in them and—well, God knows what. We've been doing this since 1934, Stu. I don't know if we can survive without it."

"Everybody else does."

"Yeah," Peter said, "but they don't survive very well. Oh, hell, Stuart. I don't want to see us get to be like one of those places upstate with nobody in them practically and the town hall falling down and everybody sucking up to the flatlanders because they bring in the money. At least here we only have to suck up to the flatlanders once a year."

"And it's once a year too much," Stu said.

Peter shot him a look. "I wish you wouldn't joke about it. I came up here to make you give me some help. We've got an hour. I think this is something we ought to do something about."

"Like what?" Stu was surprised.

"Like go up there," Peter said. "Go up there now. Make her see reason."

"Tish?"

"*Make* her see reason," Peter insisted.

Stu was about to shoot him another flippant comment, and then he saw it. Peter's eyes were straying. Peter's eyes had left the conversation and come to rest on the gun-room door, riveted, as if he were Superman and his X-ray vision had just caught sight of Lois Lane being held captive on the other side. There were faint beads of sweat on his forehead and his upper lip, and an odd flush under his skin—odd because his skin itself seemed too white. Stu didn't think he'd ever seen him look so strange.

"Peter?" he said.

Peter Callisher came to with a shudder. "For Christ's sake," he said. "I think I'm losing my mind."

5

"W H A T I don't understand," Betty Heath was saying, sewing another glass ruby onto the hem of Balthazar's robe, "is what difference it makes if she does file this injunction. I mean, it's just her, isn't it? It's just Tish? Why should she be able to shut everything down when she's the only one who's complaining?"

The glass rubies were in a cardboard box on a long narrow table pushed up against the wall under the window that looked out on Main Street from the basement of the First Congregational Church, and right next to them was another cardboard box full of shiny nylon satin ribbons. Sharon Morrissey pawed through the ribbons and came up with one in green. She turned it over in her hand and put it back again. Out on Main Street, Amanda Ballard was jogging along the sidewalk on her own, her Christmas spirit decorously displayed by a big chunk of red-and-green yarn tied into her hair. Sharon Morrissey hated women who wore big chunks of yarn in their hair. She could never wear anything in her hair herself, because she had a big white streak across the left side of it, and the streak always made her self-conscious. It was worse because she'd had the streak for as long as she could remember. Pictures of her at the age of three showed it clearly, looking out of place and vaguely painful, as if it were the result of a terrible tragedy. Of course, she didn't like Amanda Ballard much in any case. There was that. She would have looked at something else, but everything else she could think of to look at seemed to be a snake pit. She couldn't look at Betty Heath, because Betty would suspect just how stupid Sharon thought she was, which was infinitely so. She couldn't stare at the gold felt Christmas bell she had been painting over with glitter, because the damned thing was insipid and even Betty would realize that. Most of all, she couldn't stare at Susan Everman, who was sitting at her elbow putting glitter on a green felt Christmas tree. Sharon Morrissey and Susan Everman lived together in a small two-bedroom house on the town end of the Delaford Road. They had bought that house three years ago, while on a vacation trip up from New York City. They had moved into it six months later, giving rise to a kind of town talk that was neither gossip nor speculation, but a half-curious statement of fact. Sharon Morrissey wrote children's books that Susan Everman illustrated. They used one of their two bedrooms for the guests who arrived with regularity every weekend of the winter. They had a savings account together at the Vermont Savings and Loan. Everybody in town knew perfectly well what was going on. Most of them, in good New England fashion, didn't care a whit. Unfortunately, one of the few people who did care—or who at least found the whole thing so uncomfortable that she couldn't stop talking about it once it was brought to her attention—was Betty Heath. As Sharon had told Susan more than once, being around Betty was much worse than being around someone who definitely didn't like lesbians, because with somebody who definitely didn't like lesbians, you

25

could just not like her back. Betty was such a mass of confusion, she made Sharon's head ache. She also had a memory like a sieve. Betty would insist on having something explained—wasn't it difficult, for instance, to get the bank to allow you to have an account *together?*— and Sharon would explain it, and ten minutes later Betty would have to have it explained all over again. Talking with Betty, Sharon sometimes felt as if she were teaching a class at the New School, with all the good parts left out. Betty would never ask about sex and never listen to anything she considered pornographic. Sharon never got to say anything that might have caused a serious and fatal shock.

Now Susan put aside the green felt Christmas tree she had been plastering with glitter balls—the felt decorations were for the children's wing of the hospital over in Hanover; the town always used its extra materials to make ornaments for the chronic ward and the ICU—and picked up a spool of bright pink thread. Then she shook her short gold hair, shot Sharon a look it was impossible for Sharon to miss, and said, "It's precisely because she's only one person that she has a case. That's what the Bill of Rights is all about. Protecting the rights of the individual against the will of the majority."

"Rights," Betty Heath said slowly. She put down Balthazar's robe and reached for the next bit of emergency sewing on her table, a sky-blue angel's costume whose hem had begun to drag. "I don't get all that about rights. I have rights, don't I? And so does everybody else in town. I don't see why Tisha's are the only rights anybody has to think about."

"They aren't," Susan said patiently.

"Well, they sound like they are. Peter Callisher coming here all upset like that and saying we're not going to get to put on the Celebration anymore. I've known Peter Callisher all his life. He never behaves like that."

"He was pretty upset," Susan said noncommittally. She shot Sharon another look, and Sharon smiled. Peter Callisher had not been "pretty upset" when he'd blown through on his way out to Stu Ketchum's. He'd been foaming at the mouth when he wasn't breathing fire. He'd been so hot that Sharon imagined she could still feel the heat, twenty minutes later. She looked at the big institutional clock on the back wall and saw that it said quarter to nine. Peter had probably made it out to Stu's by now and been calmed down. Sharon thought that was too bad. Tish Verek could use a good talking-to by somebody who wasn't in control of himself at all, and not just because of this silly injunction.

Sharon didn't really believe that the injunction would shut down the Celebration, now or ever. Too much depended on the Celebration's going on. Too many people counted on the money it brought in. Where Tisha was really a danger was in her penchant for creating discord and the tactics she used to get it moving. Tisha *hinted,* that was the problem. She hinted about Sharon and Susan, knowing just how delicate a balance their lives were. She hinted about other things, too, that could not possibly be true. Lately she'd been picking on poor fat Timmy Hall, saying he reminded her of someone, flashing around that picture she had of the boy who had killed all those people in a swimming pool. It would serve her right if Timmy turned out to be far less placid than he looked.

The gold felt Christmas bell was finished. Sharon tossed it into the box she and Susan were using to transport the things and said, "It won't really matter this year anyway. She didn't start soon enough to shut the Celebration down. And between this year and next, there's an awful lot of time for things to happen."

"An awful lot of time for her to hire more lawyers," Betty Heath said. She adjusted her glasses, poked at her thinning and badly dyed brown hair, and stabbed hard at the hem of the angel's gown. "I never liked either one of them, not since they came here. Building that silly house that looks like it's going to fall down any minute, and then that man talking to the newspapers about all that nasty sex. That's all people think about anymore, you know, sex. It wasn't like that when I was growing up. We had interests. Now all people want to do is go to court and go to bed, and I can't see much difference between the two except you do one of them naked. Oh, I'm sorry, dears, I didn't mean anything. Of course you wouldn't know about any of this. You're both much too nice to know anything at all about that sort of thing."

"Right," Susan said, blanching a little.

Sharon grabbed a piece of red felt cut into the shape of a leaping reindeer and bent her head over it.

Betty Heath leaned forward to look out the window onto Main Street and said, "Oh, there's Dinah Ketchum. She must be on her way over to the barn. I've got to get hold of her."

"Go right ahead," Susan said.

"We'll be fine on our own for a few minutes," Sharon said.

"Take your time."

Betty Heath looked doubtful. "If you're sure," she said slowly. "I really do have to talk to Dinah. It's important. But there's so much work to do here, and there'll be more coming in. . . . You know what it's like on the day the Celebration opens."

"Awful," Susan agreed.

"Horrific," Sharon echoed. "That's why you shouldn't put off anything important. There's nothing to say you won't be even more swamped later than you are now."

"Well," Betty Heath said, "there is that."

Susan took her firmly by the arm and began to guide her to the steps leading up to the foyer and the door to the outside. "Of course there's that," she said. "What do you take us for?"

"Take you for?" Betty looked bewildered.

"Mrs. Ketchum just went into Heckert's Pharmacy. If you hurry you can catch her before she comes out." Susan flung open the door to the stairs, pushed Betty through it and stood back. Betty got up four or five risers and then looked down again, undecided.

"Well," she said.

"Go," Susan said.

"All right," she said. And with that, Betty Heath brightened, turned and began to hurry up the stairs—or came as close to hurrying as legs with veins like that could manage. Susan Everman watched her until she reached the landing and then shut the basement door.

"Well," she said. "That got her out of the way. What do we do now?"

It was exactly what Sharon Morrissey had been wondering herself, all the time that Betty Heath had been hesitating about running out to meet old Dinah Ketchum—and all the time before that, too, ever since Peter Callisher had come bombing in with the news. She watched Susan flit back and forth in front of the narrow table, her fine-boned body moving like a dancer's or a model's, her perfectly chiseled face a vision out of some expensive photographic artist's portfolio of seminal work. Sharon Morrissey was not like that and never would be. She was too thick and athletic and awkward, too much like what a lesbian was *supposed* to be. Susan was the kind of lesbian men were always offering to fix.

"Susan," Sharon said, "I've been thinking about it. About Tish."

"So have I."

"Well," Sharon said. "What do you think? How dangerous do you really suppose she is?"

"More dangerous than she knows she is," Susan said decisively. "*Very* dangerous to us, if that's what you meant."

"That's what I meant."

"It's not as if everybody in town doesn't know," Susan said slowly. "It's not that we've been keeping it a secret. We were smarter than that this time."

"We were bowing to the inevitable," Sharon told her.

"There's nothing wrong with bowing to the inevitable if it gets you where you want to go. And as for the other thing—"

"Right," Sharon said. "The other thing."

Susan came to a halt and put her hands down on the narrow table right next to the nylon ribbons. "As for the other thing," she repeated, "I'm sure Tish couldn't know—well, anything. She really couldn't. But I worry."

"So do I."

"So I think that this might be the perfect time. Don't you agree? We could go up there and—and look around. See what she's got in plain sight. Of course, if the information's on a computer, we couldn't do anything about that, but you know Tish. All those pictures she carries around. And those corkboards it talked about in the paper. There might be something."

"Yes," Sharon said solemnly. "There might be something."

"And if there was something, we'd finally know what we had to do." Susan sounded decisive at last. She bent at the waist to get a better look out the window onto Main Street. "Betty Heath'll be gone for a while," she said, "and we wouldn't be conspicuous. If anybody saw us leaving town, we could just say we were going out to the house. It's on the same road. And with Peter Callisher and Stu all worked up and half the town worked up with them, I'll bet there's going to be a convention up there this morning anyway. Lots of people out to stop Tish. Lots of people milling around that house. Lots of—cover. No one would ever guess."

"Mmm," Sharon said.

"Never mind," Susan said. "Get your coat. If we don't get out of here before Betty gets back, we *will* have a problem."

To Sharon Morrissey's mind, they already had a problem—a problem that might or might not have been discovered by Tisha Verek—but that was almost beside the point. One of the things that had made Sharon Morrissey happy when she first realized she was a lesbian was the possibility that she would never fall in love again in that dizzying, sickening, soul-abandoning way she had when she had fallen in love with men. Then Susan had come along, and Sharon had realized not only that love hadn't changed, but that it had gotten worse. The addition of passion to the rest of the symptoms was enough to make her choke.

Sharon Morrissey had spent a great deal of her life before coming out in therapy, and even after all these years she could hear the sound of her therapist's voice, telling her just what he thought of the way she fell in love.

It didn't matter.

Sharon Morrissey was one of those people for whom the world was either well lost or not lost at all, and she wasn't about to change into a creature of logic and reason at this late date.

6

IT WAS ten minutes to nine by the time Candy George got to rehearsal, and by then she was probably the only person in Bethlehem who hadn't heard that Tisha Verek was on her way to file an injunction in the federal circuit court that would shut the Nativity Celebration down. Candy hadn't heard for the same reason she never heard everything—because in spite of the fact that her house was within walking distance of the town library, her husband Reggie had arranged things so the two of them might as well have been in Kathmandu. Candy wasn't entirely sure where Kathmandu was. She hadn't been too great in geography, or in anything else, either, when she was still in school. She did know that Kathmandu was far away and not on the local telephone exchange. There was something about the name that caught at her. Boston, New York, even Montpelier, all seemed impossibly exotic and far away. When Reggie got like he got and things went really bad, Candy couldn't imagine hitching a ride to the nearest Greyhound station and getting on a bus. She couldn't imagine using her little plastic bank card to take the fare out of the account she shared with Reggie. She couldn't imagine much of anything. When Reggie got really, really bad, Candy got confused, so confused she couldn't remember where she was or who she was with. It all seemed to come together somehow: Reggie and her father; Reggie and her stepfather; Reggie and Reggie; beaten beaten until the blood flowed on the screen porch out at the farm; beaten beaten until the blood flowed in the storeroom at the pharmacy; beaten beaten until the blood flowed on the brand new sheets from

Sears Reggie had bought her to go along with their brand-new bedroom suite. First Candy got confused and then she got depressed, because there didn't seem to be anything else but this. Sometimes she wondered about the women she saw on television. Where did they get hit? How did they keep the bruises from showing? What did they get hit for? Lately Reggie had taken up a new and terrifying hobby. He'd brought home a lot of leather straps from a sex store in Boston and started tying her to the bed. He'd brought home a lot of leather whips, too, and what he did with those Candy wouldn't think about even when it was happening. Her head ached almost all the time now, and she thought her life was over. She had turned seventeen years old exactly two weeks, four days, and twenty-two hours ago.

The rehearsal was being held in the auditorium in the basement of the Episcopal Church. The town had been talking about building an auditorium to hold the Nativity play in for several years, but never got around to it. Candy went down the back steps and through the back basement door and into the locker room. Then she took off her jacket and hung it on one of the hooks that lined the wall. As soon as she was free of the jacket, she felt better. She took in the multicolored tinsel garlands the Episcopal Church ladies had strewn around on everything and the pictures of the Christ Child in the manger done by children in the Sunday School. When the committee had first approached her about taking the part of Mary in this year's Nativity play, Candy had been sure that Reggie would make her refuse. He wouldn't even let her get together for lunch with the girls who'd been bridesmaids at her own wedding. Then there was her mother, whom Reggie hated. If Candy never saw her mother again as long as she lived, Reggie would be only too pleased. That was why it had come as such a shock when he had taken to the idea of her being Mary, wearing a pale blue robe and talking somebody else's words in front of strangers for three weeks straight. It had tickled him in a way Candy couldn't explain. It was as if it was something he had done himself, that he had a right to be proud of. When Candy dared, she resented it. It was something that had come to her and that she wanted to keep for herself alone.

Of course, Reggie wasn't about to let things get out of hand. Since rehearsals for the play had started, he had upped the frequency of his rages, moved their game just a little farther out on the way to out of control, done everything he could to let her know that she would die without him. She was beginning to think she would die with him. This morning she hurt so badly she could barely walk, and it was a condition that was only going to get worse. She could feel the hot on her kneecaps and high up on the insides of her thighs. Reggie was different from Candy's father in many ways, but most of all in this one. Candy's father hadn't cared a damn about who saw Candy's mother black and blue. Reggie was always extra careful to hit Candy where it wouldn't show, and once—when it had been all over for the night and she had been curled up on their new Dupont Stainmaster bright green carpet, trying too hard to breathe—he had told her that he always hit her in ways that would keep anyone she complained to from being able to prove it. That little lecture had been more than confusing. It had been halluci-natory. Who did he think she was going to complain to? And what would she complain about?

If Candy could make life be like anything at all, she would make it be like these rehearsals, where people smiled and nodded at her and talked to her about recipes and nobody was ever angry with her for a minute. She reached into the pocket of her jacket and took out the wadded sheets of paper that were what they were going to rehearse today. She didn't mind rehearsing, but she didn't really need to. Unlike Reggie, she had learned to read and read well. She had read the script four or five times a day since the day she had been given it, seven months before. She had everybody's parts memorized, and the business and the stage directions, too. Other people hadn't, though, so she was careful to bring the script with her. She wanted to look normal.

The basement door opened behind her and Cara Hutchinson came in, the front panels of her good navy wool coat flapping in the breeze she created with the air lock. Candy checked out her hair—silver-blond, blunt cut—and her dress, and sighed a little to herself. Cara Hutchinson played John the Baptist's mother and Mary's cousin Elizabeth, and when they weren't onstage Candy couldn't talk to her at all. Cara Hutchinson was also seventeen years old, but she wasn't married. She was a senior at the regional high school, vice president of her class and a member of the National Honor Society. She got her picture in the paper a lot, getting awards or being sent to national student conferences or giving her opinions on who should be President and what he should do when he got elected.

Cara put her coat on a hook, hanging it carefully from the silky tab at the back of the neck. Then she sat down on the bench and began to kick off her snow boots. She wasn't particularly pretty—that was why, in spite of a long and vigorous campaign, she hadn't got to play the part of Mary—but she had something, and Candy could recognize it. She smells expensive, Candy always said to herself, and left it at that.

Cara shoved her snow boots under the bench and wriggled her toes in her black leather pumps. "My feet feel like hell," she said, "but I had an interview this morning, and I didn't want to look like a hick. I've applied to Smith, did I tell you that? They like you to talk to their alumnae when you're applying, and I had to spend the morning with this perfectly idiotic woman who spends all her time trying to save some kind of owl from development. I mean, I'm all for environmentalism, for God's sake, but you ought to have something else on your mind at least some of the time. I'd have gone home to change except that I didn't have time. I was supposed to have time, but I got caught up. Because of Tisha Verek and closing down the Celebration, you know."

"Mmm," Candy said, looking away. Candy knew what Cara thought—which was that Candy didn't understand half the things that Cara said—but it wasn't true, not exactly. Candy George was not stupid, although most people thought she was. It was just that she felt as if she were holding a large heavy boulder on her shoulders and her head, and the effort took so much energy there wasn't enough left to do anything else. The boulder was always particularly heavy when she was around Cara Hutchinson—almost as heavy as it was when she was around Reggie himself. It would have been even worse around her father or her stepfather, but they were both dead.

The basement door opened again and in came Mrs. Johnson, who was playing the innkeeper's wife. She gave a suspicious middle-aged look at both of them and began to unwrap herself from her shawl.

"Are you two the only ones here yet?" she demanded. "Honestly, I don't know what's gotten into people these days. It used to be an honor and a privilege to have a part in the Celebration."

"We don't know that nobody else is here yet," Cara Hutchinson said. "We haven't looked into the auditorium."

"We don't have to look into the auditorium," Candy said. "There aren't any other coats here."

Cara whipped around, contemptuous. "What does it matter if there aren't any coats here? They could have brought them with them into the auditorium and left them on the seats. They could be wearing them. It's cold in here."

"Oh," Candy said, flushing. "Yeah. Well."

"Don't say 'yeah,'" Mrs. Johnson said automatically. "It makes you sound cheap."

Cara Hutchinson coughed. "Well," she said with false brightness. "I've just been talking to Candy here about Tisha Verek. Have you heard about Tisha Verek, Mrs. Johnson?"

"Everybody in town's heard about Tisha Verek," Mrs. Johnson said. "Benjy Warren called Franklin Morrison and Franklin called Peter Callisher and everybody at the newspaper overheard it. Lord, but isn't this just like that piece of baggage. Doesn't even have the decency to hide behind her man. Just goes right out and does it on her own, and sits back and waits for the rest of us to applaud."

"Does what?" Candy asked, confused.

"It's about Tisha Verek," Cara said slowly, as if she were talking to a mental defective. "You know Mrs. Verek? Who's married to that artist who lives out at the end of the Delaford Road?"

"I know Mrs. Verek," Candy said stiffly.

"Well, Mrs. Verek is going to court to sue the town about the Celebration," Cara said, slowing her voice down, making any word of more than a single syllable take long seconds to get out. "That's because there's this law, called the Bill of Rights—"

"The Bill of Rights isn't a law," Candy said sharply. "It's part of the Constitution. I know what the Constitution is, Cara."

"Oh. Well. I'm sorry. I didn't think that was the kind of thing you were interested in."

"Who cares what she's interested in?" Mrs. Johnson demanded. "I'll tell her what it's all about and I'll do it in less time, too. What you're going on about, Cara, is beyond me. It's all that freedom-of-religion business, like the reason we can't pray anymore in school. Tisha Verek is going to the federal court and saying that our Celebration keeps her from having freedom of religion, and that the court ought to make us stop."

"Going?" Candy shot a quick look at the clock, bewildered.

"She's supposed to leave at nine-thirty," Cara put in. "At least, that's what she seems to have told everybody. Camber Hartnell's going with her. They're going to try to get an injunction to shut the Celebration down. Maybe it won't matter that we've done all this rehearsing. Maybe we'll just have to fold our tents and go home."

"Don't exaggerate," Mrs. Johnson said. "Peter Callisher was absolutely positive that there wouldn't be anything like that, this year at least. He told Betty Heath that Tisha Verek had waited far too long, and now it would be at least a year before she could get the Celebration shut down. If she can get it shut down at all."

Cara Hutchinson shrugged. "Maybe," she said, "but if you ask me, it all depends on the kind of judge they get down there in Montpelier, and with all the flatlanders we've got here now and that woman in the governor's mansion, you can't tell how things are going to turn out. I'm going to be ready no matter what. I think it's the only sensible thing."

"I think getting your name in the paper has gone to your head," Mrs. Johnson said. "Nobody's going to shut down the Celebration. If you're using this as a way to excuse not knowing your lines—"

"I *always* know my lines," Cara said.

"Well," Mrs. Johnson conceded, "you probably do. But I say we get to work and keep working until we hear we shouldn't, because if we don't work, it will surely turn out we should have. Let's go in to the auditorium and wait. Maybe it'll be warmer in there. Candy?"

Candy went "mmm," and then, realizing that both Cara and Mrs. Johnson were looking at her, forced a smile. The boulder felt bigger now, enormous, and Candy was doing as much as she could just to remember how to breathe. Cara and Mrs. Johnson were staring at her as if she were the stupidest person in the world—which, in Candy's opinion, they had every right to do. Candy knew she was stupid in much the same way she knew she was ugly. She could look in the mirror and tell.

Candy backed up a little and made herself take a deep breath. "Excuse me," she said. "I think I have to go to the bathroom."

"Are you feeling ill?" Mrs. Johnson asked her.

"There's that nasty flu going around," Cara said. "It could put you in bed for a week."

"I just have to go to the bathroom," Candy said again. Then she turned her back on them and began to move faster, chugging down the hall, heading for the polished wooden door with "Ladies" printed on it. Behind her, Cara and Mrs. Johnson were muttering to each other. For one awful moment, Cara's voice floated into the dead silence and steam-heated calm.

"God only knows what the committee was thinking of when they picked her," Cara said. "She can't think her way out of a paper bag."

"*Shhh,*" Mrs. Johnson said, sounding frantic.

Candy got through the ladies' room door, across the carpeted expanse in front of the vanities, down the tile corridor in the back room and into a stall. Then she shut the stall door and locked it and laid her forehead against the cold comfort of the gray metal partition wall. She didn't care what Cara said about her mind. Everybody said that kind of thing about her and had been saying it for years. She didn't care what Mrs. Johnson thought ought to be kept a secret, either. She knew enough about secrets to start her own college of witchcraft. What she did care about was—

All of a sudden, it felt very quiet in the ladies' room, quiet and ominous, the way the house got just before Reggie really took off or just before her stepfather used to come into her room. That was another house, of course, but it all ran together, it was all one and the same place except for here. Here was different. Here was air that was full of oxygen and quiet that was comforting instead of dangerous and laughter that never got crazy and out of control, and here would be that way as long as she, Candy George, went on being somebody else in a long robe with an angel to come and visit her. That was the key. That was the small wedge of light in this sea of black ink. When the Celebration was over, she would go back to being what she really was, and that was . . . that was—

Suddenly, Candy George got a very clear picture of a woman she had seen only two or three times in her life. She was Tisha Verek, and in Candy's vision, she was standing next to a small German car at the side of a road, looking like a deer that had frozen at the sound of an approaching hunter.

7

I T   W A S ten minutes after nine when Gemma Bury got her third and last call of the morning about Tisha Verek's lawsuit, and it was nine-twelve when she decided that the situation was likely to drive her straight into a nuthouse before it was resolved. Gemma Bury liked putting it that way to herself—straight into a *nuthouse*—almost as much as she had once liked smoking cigarettes in the boiler room at her very expensive girls' boarding school in Virginia. There was something about indulging in the forbidden that produced a kick nothing else could. Gemma was thirty-eight years old, and she had spent much of her life in search of that kick. At school, it had been easy to find. Gemma's parents had been fond of the kinds of schools whose rule books were thicker than their curricula. At college, it had been harder. Gemma had gone to Sarah Lawrence right in the middle of the sexual revolution. There hadn't seemed to be anything that was really out of bounds. Then she'd decided to enter the seminary. At the time, she had made a point of telling everyone who asked that she had finally gotten in contact with the Force of the Universe. Since she was entering a self-consciously modern, studiously New Age conduit for professional practitioners of Anglican alternative, this was even taken as admirable spirituality. Gemma didn't know if she was spiritual or not. She liked being an Episcopalian because there was so little of it—at least in her branch— that would try to hold her back from experiencing anything in the world at all. She also liked it because it had developed a moral code so involved, so convoluted and so entangling, it was as impossible to escape as the Iron Mask. Of course, she didn't put it that way to herself. To herself, she said she was an Episcopalian because it was the one truly progressive branch of Christianity, the one that recognized the legitimate aspirations of women, the one that had true compassion for homosexuals, the one that had dedicated itself to the full range of psychic actualization and human growth. She also told herself that there must be something wrong with her, something close to pathological, because in the secret recesses of her mind she used words like "nuthouse."

Hanging up on old Mrs. Garrison, who had talked for two straight minutes about the tragedy that would ensue if the Bethlehem Nativity Celebration was shut down, Gemma decided it was about time to go upstairs and talk to Kelley Grey. Kelley Grey was Gemma Bury's assistant, and the one really good idea Gemma had had since coming to Bethlehem, Vermont. Whether coming to Bethlehem, Vermont, had been a good idea itself, Gemma wasn't sure. It certainly wasn't what she'd expected it to be. What she'd expected it to be was a re-creation of her seminary, populated by upper-middle-class escapees from Boston and New York and more progressive than a meeting of the American Sociological Society. She'd got some of that, but she'd also got a sur-prising amount of something else—meaning older people with very reactionary ideas. The amount of sexism, racism and homophobia run-ning rampant in the Vermont hills was truly astounding. It was a blessing most of these people didn't object to having a woman priest. Gemma had no trouble imagining what they might have objected to, if given half a chance. That was why she didn't give them half a chance. She had tried preaching about the Goddess once, about how we had to give

God Her female face, and the fuss had lasted for weeks. Now she only preached about the Goddess to the Women's Awareness Project, where she could be sure of her audience.

The phone Gemma had answered to take Mrs. Garrison's call was in the office off the main vestibule of the church. When Gemma hung up, she went out the office door, across the vestibule and into the church itself. It was a fine old church, over 200 years old, built of stone and mortar. The ceilings were high and the leaded stained-glass windows were full of agony. It was an ecological nightmare, of course. It was impossible to heat and sucked up fossil fuels like a fat baby sucks up formula. It was one of Gemma's secret vices that she really didn't care. She liked this church, its gracefulness, its grandness, its majesty. She swept through it sometimes feeling like Queen Elizabeth the First.

Now she just jogged through, not bothering to imagine queens, and went down the steps to the door to the tunnel that went under the lawn to the rectory. The rectory was only 100 years old, but it was just as magnificent a building as the church was. The ceilings were fourteen feet high. The staircase at the front entrance was a curving sweep worthy of hoop skirts and Scarlett O'Hara. The cubed patterns that surrounded the interior doors had been cut from three-inch pieces of teakwood. It was a house built at a time when Episcopal priests were assumed to be Episcopal gentlemen, with all that that entailed in a nineteenth-century world. Gemma would never have believed it, but she looked perfectly natural in this place. Her genetics were in favor of it. She was, after all, the descendant of the very same aristocratic WASPs who had wanted their rectories to look like this one. Her temperament was in favor of it, too. No one who had known Gemma Bury for ten minutes would have been the least surprised that she imagined herself as Queen Elizabeth the First. They would have suspected her of imagining herself as Catherine the Great. Given the time and place of her birth, she had turned out to be an Episcopal priest—but she had been born to be an empress.

She made her way to the rectory's second floor, down a short corridor and then through a door to a longer and narrower one. In the old days, these had been the servants' quarters. Gemma now used the rooms as offices for the church groups she especially favored. The Women's Awareness Project had an office up here. So did the Social Justice Committee. So did the Ecumenical Society. Gemma had considered turning one of the rooms over to a Sikh who had been expelled from

El Salvador, but the Sikh had found other Sikhs and Gemma was never able to figure out what he had been doing in El Salvador anyway.

Gemma stopped at the third door on the right, listened for a moment to the sound of an IBM electronic typewriter rattling away and knocked. Knowing Kelley, she didn't wait for her knock to be answered. She just opened the door and stuck in her head. Kelley was sitting with her back to the door, hunched over the typewriter, copying something out of a notebook she had to scrunch over to read. Kelley was working on her dissertation for a doctorate in sociology at the University of New Hampshire, and she was always scrunching over something trying to read.

Gemma flicked a glance at Kelley's one sentimental concession to the season—a glass snow ball with a Vermont-like town scene in it—and cleared her throat. Kelley sat up straight and took her glasses off, but didn't turn around. Gemma went over to the side of the desk instead and sat down on the metal folding chair that had been left there, as if Kelley were trying to signal that guests were welcome, but not very. Ordinarily, Gemma would not have put up with this sort of behavior. It was inappropriate, and Gemma hated all things inappropriate. Kelley, however, was Kelley. She was short and squat and very, very neurotic.

Gemma stretched out her legs, looked up at the ceiling and said, "Well. I've interrupted you. You know I had to."

"Did you?"

"Oh, yes," Gemma said. "I've been taking phone calls all morning. From all the old ladies. I'm afraid I was beginning to lose it."

"About Tisha Verek?" Kelley was finally interested. Kelley was always interested in Tisha Verek. Gemma didn't know why.

"The thing is," Gemma said, "on the subject of the lawsuit, we can hardly blame her, can we? Tisha, I mean. You know, I've thought about bringing a lawsuit like that myself."

"It would have caused a terrible mess," Kelley said wrily. "The old ladies would probably have given up writing to the bishop and gone down and picketed instead. Or they would have picketed you."

"I know. I still think I should have done it. It would have been a wonderful opportunity to show the community what real Christianity is all about. It would have been a splendid object lesson in true tolerance."

"It would have been professional suicide." Kelley laughed. She had been threading a pencil through the fingers of her left hand, a nervous habit she fell back on at the start of every conversation. Now she put the pencil down and stretched. "Just be glad Tisha came along and decided to do it herself. I don't care how you feel about tolerance or Christianity or any of the rest of it. This is a small town. I grew up in a town like this."

"And you hated it," Gemma said solemnly. "It stifled you."

"Not really." Kelley shrugged. "I felt a lot more stifled at Swarthmore, if you want to know the truth. Stifling isn't my point. My point is that towns like this tend to get involved in very us and them–oriented wrangles. It's not true they care so much about your not having been around for twenty years. What they really care about is whose side you're on."

"I'm sure I'm on everybody's side," Gemma said disapprovingly. "We're all on the same side, after all. We'd realize that if we only took the time to determine our true interests."

"Right," Kelley said. "You tell that to the Bethlehem school board when it wants to put in a language lab and it doesn't have the money because the Celebration's been shut down."

"I don't want to talk about the Bethlehem school board," Gemma said. "I want to talk about Tisha. She's supposed to be leaving for Montpelier in just about fifteen minutes, and once she does, we're going to have to have a policy. In advance. If we don't have a policy, the old ladies are going to end up running right over us."

"The old ladies are going to run right over us anyway," Kelley said. "They always do."

Gemma wanted to protest that they did nothing of the sort—Gemma wasn't the sort of person who let other people run over her—but Kelley had gotten out of her chair and wandered off to the room's single window, and there was something about the way she was standing at it that made Gemma pause. Head cocked, hands in the back pockets of her jeans, one foot rubbing the calf of the other leg—what could she possibly be looking at? Gemma came up behind her and stared over her shoulder at what seemed to be undifferentiated white. There was nothing to look at out there, not even a bird. Then the scene shifted into sharp focus, and she understood. The rectory property bordered the Verek property on one side. Because the rectory was on a much higher hill than the Verek property was, and because of the way Jan-Mark had had his trees cleared, they could look right down into the Vereks' drive.

Gemma backed away a little, put her own hands in her own pockets, and said, "Oh."

"Oh?" Kelley asked her.

"Well," Gemma said, uncomfortable. "It's not nice, is it? Spying on people, I mean."

"Well, you can't see anything important," Kelley reasoned, "just people getting in and out of cars and driving away or coming home. I was looking out here earlier, while you were on the phone. I was thinking what a perfect spot it would be."

"Perfect spot for what?"

"For a sniper," Kelley said lightly. "There have to be dozens of people in town this morning who would love to see Tisha dead before she got a chance to go to Montpelier. This would be a perfect place to kill her from. You could just stand right here at the window and aim something really accurate, one of those fancy rifles Stu Ketchum is always carrying around. You'd be so far away, the hick cops around here would never be able to figure out where you'd done it from. Or who you were, either."

"The hick cops around here would probably have the sense to call in the state police," Gemma said sharply. "What's all this talk about guns? You know how I feel about violence."

"I know how you feel about everything, practically. That's what you do, isn't it? Feel? You've made a profession of it."

"I don't know what you're talking about."

"No," Kelley said wearily. "You probably don't."

Gemma watched her walk back to her chair and drop down in it, looking tired. "This isn't like you," she said to the back of Kelley's head, when Kelley had turned around again and begun to pretend to be working on her essay. "I don't know what's got into you this morning. You were just the way you usually are at breakfast."

"I'm just the way I usually am now. You aren't used to paying attention. I wish you'd go take the phones off the hook or something and leave me alone. I really do have a lot of work to do."

"I don't believe that's true," Gemma said tightly. "I think you're playing games with my mind. I think you're trying to punish me."

"For what?"

"How should I know? In spite of the way you're behaving, I can't believe it's over Tisha Verek and her silly lawsuit."

"Of course you can't."

"Tisha Verek isn't important. She's just—God's chosen instrument, that's all. She's just a vessel."

"You should know," Kelley said. "You're the one who's sleeping with her husband."

41

And with that, Kelley Grey picked up her much-battered Sony Walkman, jammed the earphones in her ears, shoved the switch to "on" and closed her eyes. She had the music up so loud, Gemma could hear faint strains of "Silent Night." Gemma stared at the back of Kelley's head and then at the window and then at the back of Kelley's head again. She wanted to break some furniture or smash the Walkman into fragments. She did neither.

She sat right back down in Kelley's metal folding chair and gave due consideration to just how many people had known for just how long that she was having an affair with Jan-Mark Verek.

8

EXACTLY TWENTY-ONE minutes later, at nine forty-one, Jan-Mark Verek himself rose from the tangled torture of his bed, walked around his bookcase headboard, and went to stand at the rail that looked out over the living room of his house. His mouth was full of cotton and his head was full of cotton candy. He had aches in places he was sure aches ought to be fatal and that sour taste in his mouth that meant he had drunk just enough to be hung over without ever having had the pleasure of being first-class drunk. He was wearing a pair of Jockey shorts and nothing else. If he had been entirely sober the night before, he wouldn't have been wearing the Jockey shorts. The balcony looked out not only on the living room but on a wall of windows. Through those windows he could see his driveway with its detached garage and circular sweep of gravel. It was definitely the case that he was sick of that circular sweep of gravel, as he was sick of his house and his trees and the deer that came down out of the hills when the mornings were especially cold. He'd started talking to anybody who would listen about how much he appreciated forest fires.

Down in the driveway, a rust-red Cadillac Seville was pulling in, maneuvering gingerly along the curve, trying not to scratch itself on the rocks and trees that jutted out of everywhere in a random hash the landscape designer had assured them was "ecologically aesthetic." Jan-Mark identified the car as the one belonging to Camber Hartnell just seconds before he saw Tish come out on the gravel, dressed in her most constipated New York lunch clothes and actually holding a handbag. Tish never carried handbags unless she was meeting with an editor from

The New York Times. She came hurrying across the gravel, seemed to trip, and stopped to bend over and fuss with her shoes. She was just standing up straight again when it happened.

At first, Jan-Mark wasn't entirely sure what had happened. It was all so fast and so neat. It was all so simple. First there was that odd popping sound, nothing too loud, nothing ominous. Then Tish seemed to rise a little in the air. Then she jerked backward at the neck and spun around. Then she fell. Jan-Mark stood at the balcony railing with his mouth open, staring. Tish was lying on the ground, seeping the smallest threads of blood onto the stones. The blood had to be coming from holes, but they were holes too small for Jan-Mark to see.

They were not holes too small for Camber Hartnell to see. He slammed his Cadillac into gear, revved his engine so abruptly it made the car squeal and took off in a spray of flying gravel.

9

FIFTEEN MINUTES later and six miles farther down the road, in a hollow on the side of the road that had once been the edge of a farm owned by a family that had ceased to exist, old Dinah Ketchum lay in a nest of twigs and snow, listening to her murderer get into a car parked on the shoulder not ten feet away. Her murderer was the murderer of Tisha Verek, too, and Dinah Ketchum knew that. She knew everything there was to know about everything that had happened in the last half hour, and the only thing that really bothered her was knowing she would never get a chance to tell anyone about it.

Old Dinah Ketchum was eighty-two years old, old enough, and as she closed her eyes, she told herself she should have known better. She should have seen. She should have understood. She should have wondered what the gun was doing there in the back of that car instead of up on Stuart's rack at home where it belonged. Dinah Ketchum had never liked Stuart's guns, and she didn't like them now. The blood that was oozing out of her shoulder into the ground was so hot it was making the snow melt.

Go to sleep, she told herself. Go to sleep.

The only thing that matters now is to go to sleep.

PART ONE

*Above thy deep and
dreamless sleep
The silent stars go by*

o n e

1

IT WAS CALLED *J. Edgar Hoover: The Man and His Secrets,* and what Gregor Demarkian told people who asked him what he was doing with it was: Bennis Hannaford gave it to me for an early Christmas present. This, of course, was true. *J. Edgar Hoover* was a book, and Bennis Hannaford had indeed given it to Gregor Demarkian for an early Christmas present. She had even wrapped it up in shiny silver paper. Back on Cavanaugh Street in Philadelphia, where they both lived, Gregor thought Bennis had thought there might actually be sense in the idea. Gregor had spent twenty years of his life in the Federal Bureau of Investigation, the last ten of them either establishing or heading the Department of Behavioral Sciences. He had chased serial killers from Florida to Oregon to Massachusetts and back around again. He had sat kidnapping stake-outs from Palm Beach to Palm Springs. He had known three presidents and more senators, congressmen and departmental functionaries than he cared to remember. He'd been spoken of as a possible candidate for Director of the Bureau itself, although that sort of talk had mercifully died an early death. To Bennis Hannaford, one thing and one thing only would have been important, and that was that Gregor had known J. Edgar Hoover himself.

It was now ten o'clock on the morning of Sunday, December fifteenth, and Gregor was standing in the lobby of the Green Mountain Inn in Bethlehem, Vermont, letting Bennis and Father Tibor Kasparian deal with their bags and the sour-looking woman at the polished mahogany check-in desk. It was the sort of job he usually took on himself, because he was better suited for it. For all her authority of manner—for all her damn plain arrogance—Bennis was not only a woman but a small one. She measured just about five-foot-four and weighed in at less than a hundred pounds. Sometimes, no matter how hard she tried, she got overlooked. Bennis called it "the experience of drowning in tall people." Father Tibor Kasparian had a different set of problems. He was also small—Lida Arkmanian back on Cavanaugh Street said there were two kinds of Armenian men, big and broad and small and wiry; Tibor was the latter—but his difficulties getting service at crowded counters came less from his size than his manner. Tibor was parish priest at Holy Trinity Armenian Christian Church in Philadelphia, and to many people who didn't know him, he seemed as ineffectual as a parish priest could get. He was hunched and tentative. He was quiet and self-effacing. Countermen and bureaucrats took him at face value, and they really shouldn't have. In spite of what he looked like, meaning just plain old, Tibor was actually four years younger than Gregor Demarkian. His grizzledness had been earned the hard way. First, he had preached Christianity underground in Soviet Armenia. Then he had preached it quite publicly in one gulag or another. Then he had found his way to Israel, and Paris, and finally America, and it had almost been too much. Holy Trinity was supposed to be Tibor's reward for all the suffering he had done for the Faith, and it was. Tibor liked being pastor and he liked America the way Garfield the Cat likes lasagna. He liked Cavanaugh Street, too, which was an upper-middle-class Armenian-American enclave in a city that sometimes seemed to be falling apart in every other way. The truth was, he really wasn't fitted to survive in the rough and tumble of an openly aggressive society. He had spent too much of his life making himself invisible. He had spent too much of his time thinking about the true meaning of Christian humility, which he had decided must be absolute. There were people who called Father Tibor Kasparian a saint— and Gregor agreed with them—but what he also was was a mouse, and mice stood in lines forever while the cats got served before them.

Gregor Demarkian was the other kind of Armenian, big (almost six-foot-four) and broad (carrying twenty extra pounds that drove his doctor crazy) and forceful when he wanted to be. He was a modern American man in a camel's-hair topcoat and good cashmere-lined gloves, but he carried the seed of a wild and savage manhood, a masculinity of the steppes. At least, Bennis Hannaford said he did. When she did, Gregor always wondered if she could possibly be on drugs.

Up at the check-in desk, Bennis seemed to have finally gotten someone's attention and held it less than a minute. The words were indistinguishable, but Gregor caught the rhythm and the timbre. There was nothing in the world like Bennis Hannaford's voice. It was Main Line to Farmington to Smith. It was as maddeningly, gratingly elitist as the one Katharine Hepburn had sold to her adoring and oblivious public all through Gregor's childhood. It should have driven Gregor's democratic soul totally insane—but it didn't. It was just Bennis's voice, and Gregor was so used to it, it had begun to sound comforting.

It cut off in the middle of what seemed to be a lecture, and Gregor looked up. Bennis had moved away from the sour-looking woman and gone back to Tibor, who had taken a seat next to a chicly decorated Christmas tree near the fireplace. All the Christmas trees at the Green Mountain Inn were decorated chicly. The one next to Tibor held gold balls and gold satin bows and nothing else. The one near Gregor's elbow had received the same treatment in blue. Gregor preferred the Cavanaugh Street kind of Christmas-tree decorations himself. Lots of tinsel. Lots of blinking colored lights. Lots of candy canes. Lots of kitsch. That was what children liked. To Gregor's mind, there was something inherently wrong with a Christmas tree that had been decorated to satisfy adults.

Bennis finished talking to Tibor, straightened up and came across the lobby to Gregor. Gregor stuck his finger in his book and watched her. For the trip to Vermont, Bennis had added something extra to her everyday uniform of jeans, turtleneck, flannel shirt and down vest. This was an oversized thick-weave cotton sweater in a color she insisted on calling "pumpkin." It reminded Gregor of really good pumpkin pie. It made Bennis look like a street waif with the face of a Botticelli angel.

She came to a stop at Gregor's side, shoved a hand into the great black cloud of her hair and looked down at Gregor's book. It was dog-eared into twice its original thickness and stuffed full of small scraps of paper. Through the space created by Gregor's finger, Gregor knew she could see a fresh infusion of written-in-the-margins comments. Gregor had had this book for less than a week, and it was a total mess.

"For God's sake," Bennis said. "If I'd known the trouble that was going to cause, I'd never have bought it for you."

"I'm *glad* you bought it for me," Gregor told her. "This sort of thing is dangerous. It's crazy. You can't let something like this—"

"It's a book, Gregor. It's not an atom bomb."

49

"I know it's a book. It could have been a medieval book. It's a demonology. It's very dangerous to overestimate the capacities of psychopaths, Bennis; it produces mass paranoia."

"Right," Bennis said.

"If J. Edgar Hoover had the kind of power this man wants us to believe he had, then J. Edgar Hoover would have taken over the country and declared himself king. I knew J. Edgar Hoover."

"Right," Bennis said again.

"Don't patronize me," Gregor told her. "I put up with that fool for ten years and I know what he was like. Tell me what's going on with the room. Tell me what's going on with Tibor. Tell me what I'm supposed to be doing here."

Bennis looked down at the book again, doubtful, but then she turned and looked back at Tibor in his chair. He looked settled and happy enough to Gregor, but Gregor was beginning to wonder if he knew enough about Tibor to make a judgment like that. They weren't in Vermont because Gregor wanted to be there. They weren't there because Bennis wanted to be there, either. They were there because after months of dealing with wandering Armenian refugees from the newly formed Armenian republic and points across the collapsing Soviet Union, Tibor had collapsed himself. What worried Gregor was that he hadn't guessed that anything like that might be close to happening, and that he had been the only person who hadn't guessed. He could still hear the sound of Lida Arkmanian's voice coming over the phone to him at two o'clock in the morning, telling him that she'd called the doctor in and the doctor kept saying that everything was going to be fine, but that Tibor looked dead.

"Do you think he's happy?" Gregor asked, feeling suddenly worried all over again. "Do you think he looks relaxed? This is what he wanted, right?"

"I think he looks happy as a clam," Bennis said. "And this is definitely what he wanted. Five days of a Nativity play in Bethlehem, Vermont. You know what he told me? He told me he'd read about this thing in a newspaper in Bethlehem, Israel, when he was waiting around for his visas to come through so he could come to the United States. Do you suppose that's true?"

"I don't know," Gregor said. "I've never been in Israel. Have you?"

"I've been in the Tel Aviv airport. And in Kabul once."

"I don't think that counts."

"I don't think that counts, either," Bennis said. "I suppose we ought to go upstairs," she said. "I had hell's own time with that woman at the desk. She kept saying we were here early and we couldn't go up until noon, but I finally dragged it out of her that there wasn't anyone actually in those rooms, she just didn't have the cleaning done. I promised her we'd stash our bags and wash up and then go out for breakfast. Or brunch. Or something. I don't know if he looks relaxed, Gregor. Do you think he does?"

"I asked you first."

"God, we're awful. We should have brought Lida or Donna or Hannah or somebody just to make sure we had a grown-up. What are we going to do if he collapses again?"

"He's not going to collapse again," Gregor said stoutly. "You know what Dr. Evanian told Lida. It's all that running around that did it to him, and not eating so he'd have food to feed his refugees."

"I'm still furious about the food for the refugees," Bennis said. "I mean, I'm rich, Gregor. Tibor didn't have to starve himself to feed a lot of refugees."

"I think you got that across to him in the long run, Bennis."

"I should have been able to get it across to him in the short run. Oh, never mind. I'm just as worried as you are, and I don't know what to do about it, either. He looks so pale."

"He looks so excited," Gregor said.

Bennis shot him an exasperated look, then turned thoughtful and spun around, so that she was not only looking at Tibor but facing him directly. Gregor caught her expression at the exact moment when she began to realize it was true. When Tibor had first sat down, he had been shaky and ashen, much as he had been for the past two weeks. Mostly, he had seemed infinitely sad. It was a change in demeanor that had scared Gregor Demarkian to death, because Gregor Demarkian had seen it before, in legions of old people who had given up and decided it wouldn't be such a bad idea to die. It wasn't a decision that automatically accompanied old age. The man who owned the ground-floor apartment in Gregor's four-story, four-apartment brownstone back on Cavanaugh Street was well into his eighties, and if there was one thing old George Tekemanian hadn't done, it was give up. What frightened Gregor was that he'd never known anyone to look like that and stay alive for more than a few months. What frightened him more was that he didn't understand why Tibor should look like that in the first place. Fatigue, the doctor kept telling him. The doctor was a nice Armenian boy from over in Ardmore and the son of a friend of Sheila Kashinian's.

He seemed competent enough, but Gregor didn't trust him. Gregor hadn't trusted doctors since his wife Elizabeth had died of cancer in terrible pain. Gregor had always been convinced that the pain could have been avoided, since the treatments that caused it were worthless anyway. As for Tibor, Gregor just didn't know. Fatigue. Tibor certainly seemed fatigued. He seemed *terminally* fatigued.

All of a sudden, Tibor didn't look fatigued at all. He had a newspaper folded open on his lap. He was jumping up and down in his country print—covered blue wing chair. His face was shiny bright. If Tibor's eyes hadn't been sparkling, Gregor would have thought he'd developed a fever.

Gregor moved up closer to Bennis and said into her ear, "Let's both of us go over there and find out what's going on."

"I think we'd better," Bennis agreed.

"I wonder what the newspaper is. Do you suppose he's got hold of *The Boston Globe*?"

"Not if he's looking that happy."

Gregor decided not to pay attention to Bennis's aspersions on the city of Boston—Bennis used to live there, and the experience did not seem to have left a good impression—and led the advance across the room to Tibor instead. By then, Tibor had gone from shining and sparkling to chuckling. He seemed entirely unaware of their approach. Then, at the last minute, when Gregor was just about to loom up at his side, Tibor looked up at both of them and smiled the widest smile they'd had out of him in two months.

"Krekor," he said enthusiastically. "Bennis. This is wonderful. You must see what I have here."

"We want to see what you have there," Bennis said.

"Yes, yes." Tibor began to unfold his paper, got tangled in it and then forced himself to be patient. Finally he got the paper into the shape he wanted it in and held it up. "It was lying right here on the coffee table, and I picked it up with no idea at all. Isn't it wonderful?"

Bennis Hannaford might have thought it was wonderful. Gregor Demarkian definitely did not. The paper was the *Bethlehem News and Mail*, and the double-page inside spread Tibor had opened it to was headlined:

THE DETECTIVE IN ACTION
HOW THE ARMENIAN-AMERICAN HERCULE POIROT
SOLVED THE CASE OF THE ARTFUL ARBITRAGUER
(Part Two of a Three-Part Series)

Gregor Demarkian had been called "the Armenian-American Hercule Poirot" before. He had been called that by the *Philadelphia Inquirer*, *People* magazine and *The CBS Evening News*. He had even done something recently that might provide an excuse for this article, meaning investigate a murder on the Atlantic ocean that had rich people and expensive eccentricities in it. The problem was, it hadn't been recently enough, and he hated articles like this one. He had expected to suffer through five days of bad playwriting and sentimental Christmas pageantry for the sake of his friend, Father Tibor Kasparian. He had not expected to have to suffer through the local newspaper's latest idea for increasing their circulation.

It didn't help any that Tibor had leaped to his feet and was bouncing up and down saying, "The paper only comes out once a week every Tuesday. This is last Tuesday's paper, Bennis, and if this paper had come out every day like an ordinary paper, then I would have missed it. Wouldn't that have been a shame?"

2

BENNIS HANNAFORD was a woman with resources and connections, and one of the ways she used both was to ensure that she never had any inconveniences with travel or accommodations. The Bethlehem Nativity Celebration had been a harder assignment than most. It wasn't the kind of thing the kind of people Bennis knew usually had a hand in. Neurotic rich girls who had once come out on the Main Line moved to Vermont all the time, but they tended to move to the more New Age, socially aware parts of it. Camels and angels and Magi and the Christ Child in a manger were not what they were used to or wanted to be used to. Then, too, all this had come up at the last minute. Tibor had collapsed three days after Thanksgiving. The doctor's lecture on getting Tibor away from Cavanaugh Street and responsibilities and the persistent temptations to do just one more thing had come two days after that. Bennis hadn't had much time to arrange things. Gregor had wondered if she was going to be able to arrange things at all. The Bethlehem Nativity Celebration might not be his first choice for a winter vacation, but that it was the first choice of a great many people was something he knew well. He'd fully expected every hotel room in town to be booked solid.

Bennis, however, always had more resources than Gregor gave her credit for. In this case, she had a fellow writer of fantasy novels. That was what Bennis Hannaford did for a living. She wrote sword-and-sorcery fantasy novels full of unicorns and damsels in distress and knights in shining armor and evil trolls—and very successful ones, too. She had a wide range of acquaintances in the field and an intelligence network on the activities of other writers that rivaled the CIA's files on known terrorist organizations. Through this network she had come up with a man named Robert Forsman. Robert Forsman was a very minor writer, as far as commercial successes went. He produced a slim book a year that showed up on the shelves at B. Dalton for a week and then disappeared. He would have gone along in much the same way as dozens of other writers who knew better than to quit their day jobs except for one small thing, and that was that in 1981, a Very Famous Movie Producer had decided he wanted to make a picture out of Robert Forsman's latest novel. Hollywood deals are notoriously disadvantageous to book writers. The ordinary scenario is for the book to be bought for the Hollywood equivalent of twenty-five cents and made into a blockbuster that turns everybody but the creator of the original story into a zillionaire. It worked out differently in Robert Forsman's case, because the Very Famous Movie Producer was stark raving nuts. He was stark raving nuts with a lot of money behind him because he had made the top-grossing movie in each of the previous six years.

As far as Gregor could figure out, what Robert Forsman had to do with the fact that Bennis had been able to book them three of the top-floor rooms in the nicest inn in Bethlehem, Vermont, only two weeks in advance of the third week of the Nativity Celebration was that Robert Forsman owned the nicest inn in Bethlehem, Vermont. That was what he had done with the ridiculous amount of money the Very Famous Movie Producer had paid him. Forsman had intended to move in and run the place himself. He had even tried it for a while. It hadn't worked out. He was much too much of a creature of city lights and dark plots to live among the calling moose for long.

"And it's just as well," Bennis had told Gregor, "because he's really the most odious little shit. Don't tell Tibor I used the word 'shit.' But you know what I mean. Odious."

"Right," Gregor had said. It had occurred to him that Tibor had probably heard Bennis use the word "shit" a hundred times, and he hadn't complained yet.

Now Gregor looked around and decided that, odious little shit or not, the man owned a nice hotel. The building was obviously very old, maybe even Revolutionary War old, but it had been more than kept up. Gregor didn't have much patience for antique houses and picturesque inns. They too often meant antique plumbing and picturesque ceiling heights. It always astounded him how short people had been in 1776. This inn had been refitted for twentieth-century people. The hall was made of good hard oak that had been polished into a glowing mirror. The carpet runner down the center of it was green and thick. The ceiling had been raised high enough for even someone as tall as Gregor to find it comfortable. The tall thick doors to the rooms had been decorated with sprigs of evergreen and bright red bows. Bennis had the room on the right side of the hall. Gregor and Tibor were supposed to share a three-room suite that opened on the left. Gregor waited until the bumbling high-school boy who was serving as the bellhop stowed all the wrong bags in all the wrong places, tipped him a dollar, and then looked through into the common room of the suite himself. It was a beautiful room, complete with high ceiling and broad bowed window looking out on what seemed to be a small Palestinian village. These were even better rooms than Bennis had promised. That small Palestinian village had to be the site of the Nativity play itself. It only made sense. If they'd had one of those high-tech listening devices, they'd be able to watch and listen to the whole thing right from here.

Gregor went all the way in, walked to the window and looked out. The Palestinian village looked empty, and so did the rest of the town. Gregor noticed a hardware store, a pharmacy, a real estate agent and a doctor. There was no grocery, and Gregor supposed the people here drove out to a shopping mall to buy their food. He turned slightly and found a two-story wooden building with the words ''Bethlehem News and Mail'' carved into a wooden sign that had been placed on the facade between the two floors. The sign was painted blue and the letters were painted gold. The blue and gold were almost the only extraneous colors Gregor could see. Bethlehem, Vermont, took Christmas seriously. The park where the Palestinian village was had been left more or less bare, home only to what would be needed in the production, but the rest of the town had been conscientiously decorated. Storefronts sported wreaths and bells. Houses had turned their porch rails into candy canes. The public library had a carved-wood crèche on its front lawn. Gregor thought Donna Moradanyan would be pleased. Donna Moradanyan was his upstairs neighbor on Cavan-augh Street and Bennis Hannaford's closest friend in Philadelphia. Donna Moradanyan believed in decorating everything to within an inch of its life, just on principle.

There was a knock on the door and Bennis came in, her down vest open over her sweater and her hair in even more of a mess than usual. Bennis always wore her hair loose on her first visit to a place, until it got so tangled she couldn't deal with it anymore. Then she pinned it up and started a battle with falling hair barrettes.

"Where's Tibor?" she asked Gregor as she came inside. "I thought for sure he'd be running back and forth in front of the window taking in the panorama of the Nativity play. You don't know what Robert had to go through to get us this suite. You don't know what I had to pay for it, either."

"I don't think I want to know what you had to pay for it," Gregor said. "And I don't know where Tibor is. I saw him come in here—"

"I went to use the private room, Krekor, please. You will embarrass me."

"Oh," Gregor said.

Tibor emerged from one of the north-side doors—the one that led to the bathroom, Gregor assumed—still carrying his paper with him. He gave Bennis a shy smile and went to sit down in one of the heavy club chairs by the window.

"I have gone past the article on Krekor and read the rest of the paper," he said, "and do you know what? I think Krekor is famous in this place. He had a part in an entirely different article."

"You mean there were two articles on Gregor?" Bennis asked.

Tibor shook his head. "It was an article on hunting accidents. Two weeks ago—it is Monday the second, it says here—there were two hunting accidents and two people died. I would have thought this was an occupational hazard in a place where there is hunting, but apparently not. According to the paper, the deaths have the town very, very upset. And the town is more upset because no one knows who's responsible."

"Don't they really?" Bennis took the paper from Tibor and turned it over in her hands. "How strange."

"There's nothing strange about it," Gregor said sharply. "It's just the ordnance equivalent of hit-and-run."

"Well, Gregor, I know what it is. I just think it's odd. I don't think

I've ever heard of a case where a hunter gunned someone down and then didn't tell anybody about it. Never mind gunning down two people."

"I don't think it was the same hunter," Tibor said. "Look in the paper there, Bennis. It was two different women in two different places. Miles apart."

"Was it?" Bennis unfolded the paper and searched until she found the front page story. "It doesn't say anything about the bullets. They must have found them. They always do. Maybe the hunter was someone from out of the area."

"They say there they could use Krekor to solve the crime," Tibor said. "I find it very flattering, Bennis. I find it fascinating. This is our Krekor, and they could use him to solve the crime."

"You make me sound like I'm two years old," Gregor said. "And they couldn't use me to solve the crime, because I'd be no good at this kind of thing. It's a kind of hit-and-run, just like I said. They need firearms experts and tech men, the kind of people who can take footprint impressions and identify the treads of tires. That's how you solve something like this. Not with a poisons expert with a sideline in motivational psychology."

"Is that what you are?" Bennis asked him.

"I'm a very hungry man in a hotel room that hasn't been cleaned yet. Let's get our things together and go find some food."

"Just a minute."

Bennis dropped down in the chair across from Tibor's and spread the paper out on her knees, reading with a concentration that dismayed Gregor. Gregor had met Bennis Hannaford in the middle of what he thought of as his first "extracurricular" murder case. They had been friends ever since—although not the kind of friends some people, like Lida Arkmanian and Hannah Krekorian, back on Cavanaugh Street, wanted them to be. The problem with Bennis was that she had developed far too strong a taste for just the kind of situation he had first found her in. She was as passionately interested in esoteric murder investigations as a dedicated Baker Street Irregular was in Sherlock Holmes's blood type. Gregor could just imagine what was going on in her head, as she squinted at the newsprint with the intensity of the farsighted when presented with small type when they didn't have their glasses. She was turning a pair of simple hunting accidents into *Murder on the Orient Express.*

Then Bennis dropped the paper and stretched and nodded. "I've got it," she said. "Patricia Feld Verek."

"What?" Gregor asked her.

Bennis motioned at the paper she had dropped. "Patricia Feld Verek. One of the victims. Of the hunting accidents."

"Bennis," Tibor said. "You aren't making any sense."

"In the paper they called her Tisha Verek," Bennis explained patiently, "not Patricia and without the Feld. So I wasn't sure. But I am sure she was married to Jan-Mark Verek, who's a painter and from what I hear an all-around world-class bastard—"

"Bennis." From Tibor.

"Wait a minute," Gregor said. "Do you mean this what's-her-name Verek was somebody you knew?"

"Not knew," Bennis said. "Just knew of. And of course I knew of Jan-Mark Verek because he used to be this enormous noise in modern art, and you know how my sister Myra got about modern art. Anyway, Patricia Feld Verek was a writer. She did—true crime, that sort of thing. Mid-level sellers, I think, but better than average. Her editor on *Cry of the Wolf* was later my editor on *Zedalian Mirror.*"

"But you never actually met," Gregor said.

"Well, of course not. I can't have actually met every writer with a publisher in New York. There have to be millions of them."

"There are forty-six thousand books published in the United States every year," Tibor said innocently. "I have read this in a copy of *Publishers Weekly.*"

"I don't care where you've read it," Gregor said, "as long as Bennis has never actually met this woman. Which, she has just assured me, she hasn't. So why don't we all get out of here and go to brunch?"

Father Tibor Kasparian was looking more innocent than ever, but Gregor didn't care. He knew what Bennis was up to—or what she could get up to if given half a chance. He knew what Tibor was up to, too, but he didn't mind very much. Mischief, excitement, curiosity, a proprietary interest in Gregor Demarkian's career—all these were good signs, intimations of the return of the old Tibor. Gregor was perfectly willing to put up with them if they would help Tibor recover on all the levels he needed to recover on. That did not mean Gregor had to put up with a Bennis gone wild.

Gregor's coat had come up draped over a brace of suitcases. The brace of suitcases had been placed just inside the suite's door. Gregor marched over to it, picked up his coat, and began to get dressed for the cold.

"Come on," he told them. "There's got to be some place in this town where I can get a corned beef sandwich."

t w o

1

AS A MATTER of fact, there wasn't any place for Gregor Demarkian to get a corned beef sandwich in Bethlehem, Vermont, or a hot pastrami sandwich, either. Gregor did not think of himself as a particularly "ethnic" man, in spite of the fact that his parents had been immigrants from Armenia. He didn't think of himself as particularly "urban," in spite of the fact that he had been born and brought up in the middle of Philadelphia. A medley of factors—college, graduate school, the army, the FBI—had conspired to make him what he thought of as "cosmopolitan," meaning at home in most places in America. His work with the Bureau had taken him from lushly secured compounds in Beverly Hills to back-alley flophouses in Phoenix, Arizona. Surely by now he had a feel for the country and how it worked. Surely by now he understood its parameters. Ten minutes after he, Bennis and Tibor had stepped back out of the Green Mountain Inn and started down Main Street in search of something to eat, he was wondering if he had been transported to another planet. Five minutes after that, when they had come to a stop at one corner of the small park that had been roped off to serve as a stage for the Nativity play, he was sure he had been. It wasn't the fact that the three restaurants they had looked at so far weren't serving lunch yet. Gregor told himself he should have remembered that in smaller towns without delis or Greek coffee shops, nobody started serving lunch until at least eleven. It wasn't the fact that one of those three restaurants was self-consciously "healthy," either. "Healthy" had gotten to be such a fad, Gregor had almost gotten used to it. What really stopped him was

the realization that not one single item on any of the three menus they
had read so far seemed to have a spice in it. Health-food restaurants in
Philadelphia usually offered a set of Mexican dishes that promised to
be liberally laced with chopped jalapeño peppers. Jalapeño peppers were
supposed to be good for your metabolism and contain a lot of vitamin
C. This health-food restaurant stuck to "delicately flavored" vegetable
ragouts and tofu stir-fried with mint. Gregor had often complained about
the way the good ladies of Cavanaugh Street refused to send him off
on any journey without a hamper or two full of food. He'd gotten his
way and taken off foodless this time because of all the fuss with settling
the refugees. Now he was sorry he had. He would have killed for a
suitcase full of *yoprak sarma* and those big meatballs with bulgar crusts.
He would have done more than kill for some of Lida Arkmanian's
marinated shish kabob.

They had come to a stop at this corner because Tibor wanted to
look at the set-up for the Nativity play. There was a lot to look at, too.
A middle-sized octagonal gazebo had been artfully camouflaged with
driftwood and reeds to look like a stable. The manger inside it was rough
and gray and seemed to be a thousand years old. The ground around
it was bare of snow, in spite of the fact that the rest of the town was
buried under at least six inches of white. Gregor decided that that was
because this ground had to be cleaned up regularly when the animals
did what animals will do no matter how strenuously you try to talk
them out of it. Gregor could see some of those animals on the other
side of the park, penned up in a circle behind a makeshift picket fence.
Three sheep, a cow and a camel—according to the brochure they had
gotten from the travel agency, there were supposed to be three camels,
but Gregor didn't want to ask where the other two were. This camel
was munching on something, as were the cow and all three of the sheep.
Since the ground was barren, Gregor assumed someone had put food
in there with the beasts to keep them quiet. Maybe that was what had
happened to the camels. Maybe they had decided the food wasn't good
enough and gone off in search of more interesting stuff. There were two
small stands of tall evergreen bushes in the park, one at Gregor's end
and one at the other side, but camels might not have wanted them.
Camels were Middle Eastern beasts.

The rope fence came up to the middle of Gregor's thighs. It came
close to both Tibor's and Bennis's waists, and they were both leaning
forward over it, balancing on the balls of their feet but looking as if they
were letting the rope support them. Their posture made Gregor uncom-

fortable, and so did the wind. In spite of the incessant whine of com-
plaints he had heard since they first drove across the state line this
morning, the weather in Bethlehem did not seem to him "warm." It
felt downright cold and getting colder. The wind was frigid. The sidewalk
under his feet felt frozen solid. The thin leather soles of his shoes provided
so little protection, his toes felt iced into a block. Gregor leaned forward
and tapped Bennis on the shoulder.

"Let's go and eat something," he told her. "At least let's go somewhere inside. I'm getting frostbite."

"You're wearing silly shoes," Bennis said. "Just a minute, Gregor.
They're having some kind of animal rehearsal or something, can't you
see? Tibor is interested in what they're going to do, and so am I."

Now that Bennis had pointed it out, Gregor could indeed see. The
other two camels hadn't absconded. They had been in another part of
the small park in the charge of a short, muscular man in a bright red
ski parka. He was leading them around in a wide circle, pulling them
along on leashes that ended in three feet of wooden stick that he held
onto. The camels did not look pleased.

Gregor tapped Bennis on the shoulder again. "It's not an animal
rehearsal," he said. "The man's just making sure the camels get some
exercise. You see those sticks? That's so they can't get close enough to
bite him. Camels bite."

"I know camels bite," Bennis said.

"I have read about it in my pamphlet," Tibor put in, waving the
long booklet in the air. "This year they have fourteen different kinds of
animals for the Nativity play and later for the living crèche. Camels.
Cows. Sheep. Horses. Donkeys. Pigs. A black bear. A family of deer. A
moose."

"A moose?"

"They got it from a zoo in Oregon, Krekor. They also have three
lion cubs and a tiger cub and a panther cub that they got from a firm
that supplies animals for television commercials. It is going to be most
symbolic."

"It is going to be an unholy mess," Gregor said. "I wonder how
they get them all here. This isn't a major intersection. Do you figure
they block off Main Street?"

"If you read your brochure you'd know," Bennis said. "Main Street
is closed to all but pedestrian traffic from six o'clock every night until
two o'clock the next morning. So are the two blocks closest to Main
Street on something called Carrow. That's so people can mill around

and not get run over, and there isn't any traffic noise to make it hard to hear the play."

Gregor shook his head. "That doesn't answer my question. That just means Main Street is going to be full of people instead of cars. How are they going to get a moose and a black bear and a family of deer through all that?"

"Maybe they get them here before, Krekor," Tibor said. "Like these sheep and this cow they have here now."

"If they did that, you'd have other reasons besides traffic for not hearing the play. This isn't that big a park."

"Well, they have to get here somehow," Bennis said, "and they obviously do, because they've been having this play for the last two weeks, and nobody's complained that I know of. I don't understand you sometimes, Gregor. You get a perfectly interesting problem like a couple of shootings and you don't think anything of it. And then you take off after some simple piece of nothing like this business of the animals as if it were the most fascinating puzzle since the Gordian knot."

"It's because he's lonely," Tibor said. "You should consider this, Bennis. It is not good for a man of Krekor's age to be without a wife."

"You're my age," Gregor said, "or just about. You don't have a wife."

"I have the grace of God to see me through my difficulties, Krekor. You have only Lida Arkmanian's cooking."

"I wish I had Lida Arkmanian's cooking," Gregor said.

"I wish we had some kind of map," Bennis said. "That's the one thing the people who wrote this brochure didn't think of. I suppose they thought in a town this small there was nothing to draw a map of. Never mind. I'm with Gregor, Tibor, we ought to get in out of the cold and at least get some coffee or something. What time is it?"

"Ten to eleven," Tibor said.

"I don't know what you think you're trying to do," somebody else said, "but I'm not going to let you do it. It's been my part in this play for the last two weeks, and I haven't done a single thing wrong with it."

Gregor turned around. In the beginning, he had thought the voice was coming from somewhere in the middle of the park. Then he'd realized that couldn't be true. The park was what out-of-staters would have called a "common." It was a flat, empty stretch of land with nothing but the gazebo in it and a few benches. The animals were there, and the small man who was walking them. Nobody else was. The voice they had heard was high-pitched, hysterical and definitely a woman's. It had cut through the cold-thickened air as if it had edges made of razor blades.

"There they are," Bennis said. "Up by the *Bethlehem News and Mail.*"

Bennis was right. They *were* up by the *Bethlehem News and Mail*—all the way up. You couldn't really talk about "blocks" in Bethlehem, Vermont, although everybody, including the brochure on the Bethlehem Nativity Celebration, did. Main Street was sort of broken up into them, since it was paved and crossed by smaller streets here and there. The intersection pattern was random, though, and not neatly or precisely laid out. It was as if cows had wandered over this area many years ago, and the paths they made had been paved and christened roads. What Gregor meant when he thought of the offices of the *Bethlehem News and Mail* being "at least two-and-a-half blocks" away from where he was standing was two-and-a-half Philadelphia city blocks. A long way away, in fact. Far enough to make it surprising that they had heard this woman's voice at all.

There were three of them, two women and a man. Gregor knew immediately that the voice he had heard had come from the small blonde woman and not the other one. The other one was blonde, too, but a studied kind of blonde, as if she had her hair dyed strand by strand to produce the proper effect. In spite of that, she was not particularly attractive. There was something leaden about her face, something un-inspired about the way she held her body. That could have been the distance from which he was looking at her, but Gregor didn't think so. The smaller woman looked to him like a Botticelli angel, and the way she held herself was—he couldn't pin that down. There seemed to be a dozen things going on in her at once, but there was fire and passion in all of them.

The other woman was talking now. Gregor could see her lips move, but hear nothing of what she said. Beside her, the man was rocking back and forth on his heels, his hands in the back pockets of his jeans, his denim jacket open to the wind. Gregor had a hard time deciding whose side he was on, or which woman he was with. The smaller blonde one, he finally decided, because the other one looked too expensive. The other one looked as if she'd only be interested in men in suits.

"I'm fine," the smaller blonde woman said now, her voice still hysterical, still carrying, still sharp. "I'm just plain fine. I don't need any help from you. I don't need any help from anybody."

The man leaned over, said something, leaned back. The small blonde woman recoiled instinctively and then seemed to force herself to stand perfectly still. Then she turned her back on both of them and crossed her arms in front of her chest.

"Look," Tibor hissed in Gregor's ear. "Right in the brochure. She's the girl who is Mary."

"What?" Gregor said.

Bennis had her brochure out, too. "Tibor's right. The small blonde one who was getting hysterical is playing Mary. There are pictures of all the people playing the major roles right here in the back. It says she's seventeen."

"That can't be the same person," Gregor said. "She has to be twenty."

Bennis looked amused. "I thought she was *fifteen*. Look. The other one is the one who's playing Elizabeth. She's seventeen, too. Quite a difference, isn't there?"

"I wonder what the fight was about," Gregor said.

Bennis shrugged. "I'd say Elizabeth thinks she'd be a better Mary than Mary. The Elizabeths of this world always do. I met a million and a half of them in boarding school. Mary looks like she's all right. I don't think she's going to give in. With any luck, the people who run the Celebration are too intelligent to let her. There's a place in this brochure called The Magick Endive, spelled with a 'ck.' Let's go there."

"I like The Magick Endive, too," Tibor said. "And it's eleven-oh-two. I don't think it's right, Mary and Elizabeth fighting over their parts in a religious play."

"Of course it isn't right," Bennis said.

"I don't like that man," Gregor told them.

They all turned around in unison, to look again at the little group in front of the *Bethlehem News and Mail*. There was nothing to see. The little group had gone.

That's what happens when you start making mountains out of molehills, Gregor told himself. You make yourself feel silly.

2

SURPRISINGLY, The Magick Endive didn't turn out to be such a bad idea at all. Gregor had been convinced because of the name that the place would be a holding pen for the vegetarian and the leftover hippie.

He expected to find salads made of nettles and tofu and honey-sweetened sassafras tea. He found all those things—although not the nettles, not really; nobody could eat nettles—but he also found a good deal more, and the good deal more made him very cheerful. "We use the Moose-wood cookbooks," the menu said. Gregor had never heard of the Moose-wood cookbooks, but after reading a few of the descriptions under the listed dishes, he decided those books must be absolutely peachy. Meat there was not. Cheese there was, as well as sour cream, real butter and enough different kinds of pasta to make an Italian feel he'd gone to heaven. There were some items on the menu that would actually have been healthy for him to eat—low-fat, low-cholesterol, high-complex carbohydrate—but Gregor didn't pay any attention to them. As far as he was concerned, the entire healthy-foods movement had been in-vented to make comfortable middle-aged men like himself feel bad.

He picked out a bean-and-pasta casserole with a sauce made of sour cream and dill, ignored Bennis's pointed "beans and pasta this early in the day?" and then applied his mind to his surroundings. That scene on Main Street was nagging at him. There was no reason it should. It was none of his business. He just couldn't get it out of his mind. The man especially had made him uncomfortable, and he just wished he knew—

Their waitress was a small girl in jeans and a ponytail. After she'd taken their order, she'd gone through a swinging door at the back, been invisible for a few seconds, and then come out again. She was now sitting at a table carefully placed behind two potted evergreen trees. There was another girl with her, much the same physical type, as if this restaurant chose its help with an eye to physical stature. Gregor won-dered how old they were, and whether he ought to be using the word "girl" to describe them. They looked impossibly young to him, but they also looked hip.

Bennis was sitting next to Tibor on the other side of the table, bending over an open brochure and plotting the day.

"I don't think we ought to go souvenir shopping first thing," she was telling him. "We ought to look around a little first and see how we feel. What about the tableaux for this afternoon? They've got 'Cel-ebrating the Winter Solstice Around the World' in the basement of the Episcopal Church."

"I don't understand this 'Celebrating the Winter Solstice,' Bennis. I am not celebrating the winter solstice. I am celebrating the birth of Our Lord."

"Right. Well. How about Christmas carols? The Baptist children's choir is singing Christmas carols on the steps of the Baptist Church right here on Main Street starting at one-forty-five. That would even give us time to go back to the hotel and change."

Gregor wanted to go back to the hotel and sleep, but he figured he could fight that out with the two of them later. Now he stood up, stretched a little and said, "I'll be right back. You two have a good time."

"Us two can use your input," Bennis said pointedly. "It might be nice if we knew what you wanted to do."

"Surprise me."

"Fine," Bennis said. "I think the Druids used to celebrate the winter solstice by getting dead drunk and dancing naked around a bonfire. Maybe we'll do that."

"We will do no such thing," Tibor said. "Bennis, you must not say such things. Not unless you mean them."

"You mean you wouldn't mind if I meant them?"

"Krekor—"

"I'll be right back," Gregor said again.

Bennis started to say something else, but Gregor slipped past her. With anybody else, he would have been worried that she would sit staring after him, thereby discovering that he was not on his way to the place he had implied he was on his way to. With Bennis, he didn't worry at all. He knew she would throw herself right back into the job of planning every minute of Tibor's day as soon as he was out of voice range.

Gregor rounded the artificial island created by the potted evergreens and came to a stop in front of the small table where his waitress was still sitting with her friend. They both looked up at him at the same time and paused politely in their talking. Gregor hesitated. When he'd been an agent for the Bureau, he'd had a set of credentials that provided him with a reason to question total strangers. Since his retirement, his involvement in various criminal cases had usually been accompanied by authorization of one kind or another from the local authorities. Now he not only didn't have credentials or authorizations, he didn't even have a crime. He had no idea why he wanted to ask the questions he wanted to ask. He simply felt a compelling need to ask them.

His waitress—Faith, if he remembered correctly—started to rise from her seat.

"Could I get you something?" she asked him. "Was there something you forgot to order?"

"No, no," Gregor said. "Sit down. I'm just—ah—yes. So. I'm just being nosy."

"Of course you are," the other waitress said. "I told you, Faith. He looks just like his picture in the paper."

"It was a week ago when I saw his picture in the paper. I didn't really look at it. Crime isn't my thing."

"It isn't my thing either, but I looked at the picture." The other waitress gave Gregor a big smile. "You are Gregor Demarkian, aren't you? The one in the paper?"

"Yes," Gregor said. "Yes, I am."

"Are you investigating a crime?" Faith asked. "That seems like such an odd thing to say about this place. Investigating a crime. There isn't any crime here."

"There were those hunting accidents," the other waitress said.

Faith crinkled her nose. "It's not the same thing. You know what I mean. There isn't any crime."

"I'm not investigating a crime anyway," Gregor told them. "I'm just being impossibly nosy."

"And you came all the way up to Bethlehem, Vermont, to do it?" Faith looked skeptical.

"I came all the way up to Bethlehem, Vermont, to see the Nativity Celebration," Gregor said. "I really am just being nosy. About some people I saw having an argument down on Main Street near the newspaper building. I've got no good reason for wanting the information at all."

"You mean you want to gossip," Faith said, laughing. "Sure. Go ahead. We gossip all the time. Ginny was born here, but I came out just for the year—"

"We're both taking a year off from Middlebury College," Ginny said.

"—and we spend most of our time talking about the people, because I can't stand not being filled in. What do you want to know?"

Gregor glanced back at his own table, but there was nothing to worry about. Bennis and Tibor were still bent over the brochure, and Bennis had started to write on paper napkins. Once Bennis started writing on paper napkins, she was occupied until someone came along to distract her. Gregor turned back to Faith and Ginny and described the scene on Main Street in as much detail as possible, including his impressions of both women and his instinctive distrust of the man.

"Well," Faith said when he had finished. "Your friend was right.

The small blonde woman is Candy George. She is playing Mary this year."

"The taller one is Cara Hutchinson," Ginny said. "She was two years behind me in high school—in fact both of them were—but Cara is a big deal. Vice president of her class. Honor student. On the debate team. Candy is—"

"Married," Faith said.

"To Reggie George. He was in my class in high school, if you could call that being in a high-school class, if you know what I mean. Bikes and black-leather jackets. He's supposed to be a good mechanic, though. My father says Reggie got a job out at Mitchell's Texaco and he's doing really well."

"He hides her," Faith said.

"What?" Gregor asked.

"He hides her," Faith repeated.

Ginny explained. "He won't let Candy leave the house usually," she said. "He won't let her have friends over, and he never lets her have enough money to have lunch in town or keep up with anyone she knows. Of course, everybody just assumes he's beating her up—"

"When I first came here, she'd just been chosen to be Mary and it was a big deal," Faith said, "because everybody was surprised he let her try out, and everybody was even more surprised he let her take the part when she got it."

"And it was all Peter Callisher's fault in the first place," Ginny said. "Peter Callisher owns the paper. He's on the Celebration committee every year, and he saw Reggie and Candy in the pharmacy or someplace one Saturday last July and he just walked right up and told Candy she ought to try out."

"It's supposed to have made Amanda Ballard fit to spit," Faith said.

"Who's Amanda Ballard?" Gregor was confused.

"She's Peter's girlfriend," Ginny told him. "She's supposed to have wanted to play Mary herself, but she didn't try out and that might just be talk—"

"Because nobody likes Amanda Ballard anyway," Faith summed up. "I mean, it's hard to like someone who looks like a miniature version of Michelle Phillips at twenty and is supposed to be a saint at the same time."

"Not that she's twenty," Ginny put in. "She's supposed to be something like thirty-five."

"Why is she a saint?" Gregor asked them.

Faith shrugged eloquently. "It all depends on who you listen to. It's because of this man, Timmy Hall, who is mentally retarded and was in Riverton, which is a place with a lot of different things going on for people who aren't all there. You know, like the mentally retarded and crazy people and—"

"And druggies," Ginny said. "That's why there's so much talk—"

"—because Amanda knew Timmy Hall when Timmy Hall was at Riverton, and then she got him the job here when he was ready to come out and live on his own because they train mentally retarded people to be self-sufficient, that's one of the things they do. And then some people started to say that she knew him because she used to work with retarded children up there, but other people said it wasn't retarded children at all, it was a drug problem, and they met in the patients' lounge or something because all the patients mingle together up there unless they're like in maximum security."

"And she's so cold," Ginny said, "people don't take to her."

"But it's probably all a bunch of junk, because around here people just go on talking." Faith laughed again. "Listen to this," she said. "You get a little gossip going, you get information about people you're not even interested in."

"If you let us go on for a while, we'd probably give you capsule histories of everybody in town," Ginny said. "But if you're worrying that Reggie was going to hurt Candy over some scene with Cara Hutchinson—Cara was probably just trying to get Candy to quit; she's been at that for months—anyway, I wouldn't worry. Reggie really wants Candy to play Mary. It inflates his ego."

"Do wife beaters have egos?" Faith asked.

"Oh, well, they must," Ginny said. "If you don't have an ego, you aren't anybody."

"Is Reggie George anybody?"

"I think I'd better get back to my table," Gregor said. "My friends are going to start wondering where I've been. Thank the both of you very much for the information."

"Thank you for asking for it," Ginny said. "Now, the next time we run into Peter Callisher, we get to tell him we've actually spoken to his hero, the great detective, Gregor Demarkian."

"The Armenian-American Hercule Poirot," Faith said brightly.

"The Armenian-American Hercule Poirot is going back to his table," Gregor said, and he started to do just that. He was so intent in escaping the rash of jokes on Poirot, Christie and Armenian-Americans that he was sure were about to arise from the cauldron of bubbling giggles that was Faith and Ginny talking to each other, that he was halfway there before he realized Bennis and Tibor were not alone. With them was an older man with gray hair and a sagging face, holding his hat in his hands and standing just a little to the side of Bennis's chair. Bennis was looking up into his face and trying to seem interested, when what she really was was amused. Gregor knew the signs.

He walked up to the table, put his hands on the back of the chair that would be his if he sat down and said, "Excuse me? Do we know you from somewhere?"

"We don't know him," Bennis said solemnly, "but he knows us."

"He has read about you in the paper," Tibor said. "You see, it is how I have told you, Krekor. In this place, you are famous."

"It's not just in this place," the older man said fervently. Then he blushed, turned away, looked at the ceiling, looked at his shoes, looked out the window. Then he turned back to Gregor and stuck out his hand. "I'm Franklin Morrison," he said. "Chief of police for Bethlehem, Vermont. And Mr. Demarkian, you have no idea how glad I am to get my hands on *you*."

three

1

FOR AMANDA BALLARD, having sex was like eating vanilla ice cream: a fundamentally unpleasant physical activity that could be endured with patience; an unfortunate social necessity that could be learned well enough to put on automatic pilot. It was now four o'clock on the afternoon of Sunday, December 15th, and Amanda had been on automatic for several hours. That was because Peter had wanted to spend the day in bed. Peter always wanted to spend Sundays in bed. He said it was his new religion, now that he had given up the old one, which had been Presbyterian or something equally Old New England. Amanda hadn't been paying attention when he told her. She had been paying attention when he told her about the sex, because she had had to. His attitude bewildered her completely. Peter was not the first man Amanda had slept with. He was not even the first man she had made the decision to sleep with. He was the first one who had been really involved with sex. In Amanda's experience, what men really wanted in bed was a fast and furious in and out and a ricocheting payoff. If they got that, they really didn't care about anything else. Peter always wanted her to feel things and make little cries in the dark. In the beginning, it had left Amanda feeling frustrated, confused and angry. Then she had done a very sensible thing. She went to Burlington twice a month to buy books. On one of those trips, she stayed a little later than usual and went to the movies. The movie she saw was called *Having Miss Smith*, and it had been a revelation. At times it had made her physically ill. Amanda thought she might have missed half the movie—which was shockingly

72

short, considering what they charged for admission—because of the amount of time she spent with her head between her knees, trying not to vomit. What she had seen had been very useful in the long run, however, and so made all the rest of it worthwhile. On the following Sunday, when Peter had wanted to spend the day in bed, Amanda had come to the project with a whole new set of moves, and Peter had been delighted. He was still delighted. Every once in a while he referred to her "wonderful awakening" and her "exciting responsiveness." Amanda made noises in his ear, closed her eyes and counted backward from one hundred in her head.

Right now, Amanda wasn't counting backward from one hundred in her head, because she didn't need to. The physical part of this session had reached a climax half an hour ago, and was unlikely to recommence until after dinner. She and Peter were sitting up in bed, half-watching *It's a Wonderful Life* and half going through the notes Peter had for the upcoming issue of the paper. They had *It's a Wonderful Life* on videotape, which was a good thing. Peter was always complaining about how, in the old days, the television stations used to show Christmas movies in the Christmas season. Now they showed reruns of *The A-Team* and *Starsky and Hutch*.

"We're going to have to put in more about the shootings," Peter was saying, "even though Franklin doesn't know anything and the staties don't care. It's all people are talking about. I'm going to put it on an inside page, though."

"It's old news," Amanda said judiciously.

"It's bad news for the Celebration," Peter said. He put his hands up and rubbed his face. "God, wouldn't that be awful. All those flatlanders think we're the next thing to hillbillies up here anyway. Hootin' and hollerin' and shootin' up the scenery as soon as we get lickered up. That's all we'd need."

Amanda cocked her head. "Do you think that's what happened? A couple of hunting accidents, I mean. Do you think all that's true?"

"I don't know what you mean by all that. I know what the state police said, and they're supposed to know their job."

"Well, yes," Amanda said doubtfully, "but in this case it's different, isn't it? I mean, they didn't know Tisha the way we knew Tisha."

"They didn't know Dinah the way we know Dinah," Peter pointed out. "You can hardly say somebody murdered her. She was eighty-something, for God's sake. She was harmless."

"Maybe. But I don't think anybody is ever harmless, not really. People—people push. It has nothing to do with age."

"I'd've thought this was one conspiracy theory even too bizarre for you. You can't be serious."

"Well, I'm not, really," Amanda said, but it wasn't true. She was perfectly serious. She had been thinking all this out for weeks. "It's just that you have to admit it's curious. All that with the guns and everything."

"They weren't killed with the same gun."

"I know. But wouldn't you have expected it would have been Dinah who was killed with Stu's gun and not Tisha? And how did Tisha end up getting killed with Stu's gun anyway?"

"Tisha ended up getting killed with Stu's gun because some asshole teenager took it off Stu's wall and went blasting into the distance without paying attention to what he was doing. Amanda, we've been through all this before. Stu couldn't possibly have killed Dinah or Tisha or anybody else. He was with me when both those people got shot and for a good long time before and a good long time after. It just won't add up."

"I know it won't," Amanda said. "I just can't help wondering. I mean, the timing was perfect, wasn't it? Now Tisha can't file for an injunction and the Celebration is safe."

"For the moment."

"What does that mean?"

"It means that in all probability the Celebration is unconstitutional as all hell and not long for this world. Is that the downstairs bell? I think somebody's trying to get in to the office."

Somebody was definitely trying to get in to the office. Amanda could hear not only the bell, but the sound of feet pounding against the mat on the porch, trying to stay warm. She got up, took Peter's terrycloth bathrobe off the chair next to the bed and wrapped herself up. Then she went to the window and looked out. The porch out there had a roof, but only a partial one. If you got the right angle, you could see who was out there calling on you.

"It's Cara Hutchinson," Amanda said. "Should I go down there and see what she wants? We're supposed to be taking ads today. And announcements."

"I've got to start hiring somebody to sit at the desk," Peter said. "This is getting ridiculous."

"Should I go?"

"I'll go if you want. Just call down and tell her I'll be a minute."

"That's all right. It'll take me less time to get dressed than you. I'll do it."

One of the reasons it would take Amanda less time to dress than Peter was that Amanda already had more on than Peter. Peter liked to sit up in bed all day naked, but it made Amanda self-conscious. She got into her underwear as soon as it seemed feasible. She opened the window and stuck her head out into the cold.

"Cara? It's me, Amanda. Give me a second. I'll be right down."

Cara backed up and came down the first of the porch steps to the street. "Amanda? Did I wake you up?"

"No, no. I'm fine. I'll be right there."

"Hurry up. I'm freezing out here."

Amanda knew how freezing it was. The wind was blowing in on her and her bones were chilled. This was what they called a "mild" winter in Vermont, and "warm" weather for December. It made Amanda crazy. She searched around in the wardrobe until she found one of her jersey dresses, dropped Peter's robe to the floor and pulled the dress over her head. It had short sleeves and a wide neckline and was totally inappropriate for the season, but it would have to do. She shoved her bare feet into moccasins and said, "I'll only be a minute. Why don't you think about what you want to do about dinner."

"Mmm," Peter said.

"At least think about thinking about it."

"Mmm."

Amanda bit her lip. It was impossible, really. It was always impossible with men. They didn't listen. It had seemed new and unusual with Peter for a while only because he didn't listen to different things. Amanda let herself out of the bedroom, made her way across the living room and came out on the landing to the stairs. When she got to the next landing, she chose the door into the newspaper offices and made her way around the equipment to let Cara in the front door. She didn't see any reason to get any colder than she absolutely had to.

She reached the front door, pulled it open and practically pulled Cara inside. It was getting dark out there, and Amanda always thought it was colder in Vermont in the dark.

Cara didn't seem to have spent much time noticing the dark. She came stomping into the newspaper office, her cheeks rosy, her eyes bright. She was a plain girl and not one Amanda cared for much—she was too ambitious, for one thing, and too likely to cut corners to get what she wanted—but this time her excitement was attractive. She was waving a piece of paper in one of her gloved hands, so Amanda assumed she wanted to place an announcement or an ad. Amanda went behind the ad counter and waited.

"Oh, Amanda," Cara said, twirling around on the heels of her snow boots. "You just won't believe what happened. You just won't believe what happened to me."

2

SHARON MORRISSEY spent her late Sunday afternoons in the basement of the First Congregational Church, teaching reading to a small collection of old people who came in from the hills and back roads to expose themselves to this humiliation one day of every week. Most of her old people were women, all but two of them were white, and every last one of them was embarrassed. Sharon got past that by pulling the shades tightly down on the half-windows that looked out on the street and keeping the door shut. She got her old people moving by promising them they would be able to read the Bible in church on Christmas Day. There was now exactly one weekly session left before she'd have to make good on her promise, and she thought it was going to work out. Her group wasn't ready to plunge into the more unfamiliar recesses of the King James Version, but they ought to do fine with the familiar Nativity narrative of St. Luke. It made Sharon feel as high as liquor ever had, and without the worry about waking up with a hangover. Everything about her involvement with the First Congregational Church made Sharon high. Sharon didn't know what Congregational churches were like in general, but this one had been wonderful to her without being condescending, and she was grateful. Nobody had made a big fuss about what she was, one way or the other. Nobody had made a point of not making a big fuss about what she was. She and Susan had been accepted without comment or unease. The fact that the literacy project she was working in was sponsored by the First Congregational Church was another reason Sharon liked teaching her old people to read.

The one thing Sharon didn't like about it was the walk home. Sharon walked home because Susan used the car on Sundays to go up and visit her mother in New Hampshire. Sharon and Susan didn't visit together because Susan's mother wouldn't let them. Sharon could have asked Susan to pick her up at the church—Susan never stayed that long in New Hampshire—but it seemed like an unnecessary bother when it was perfectly safe to walk. The problem was, in order to get home, Sharon had to go down Main Street to Carrow and down Carrow to the Delaford Road, and when she did that she passed Candy and Reggie George's house. The problem with passing Candy and Reggie George's house was that the same thing was always going on inside it: Reggie was beating Candy into a pulp. The first time Sharon had heard this, she had done what she knew was the right thing to do. She'd marched straight home and called the cops. She even had to give Franklin Morrison credit. He'd come out. He'd thrown Reggie in jail. He'd taken Candy to the hospital. He'd done everything he could do without some cooperation from Candy herself, and Candy refused to give it. Sharon didn't know if Vermont had a mandatory-charge law for battering or not—she had never been entirely sure what happened after Reggie and Candy had been carted off to their separate public institutions—but she had come to realize this: Without Candy's cooperation, mandatory-charge law or not, it was going to be impossible to convict Reggie. The second time she had called, Franklin Morrison had asked her if she *really* wanted him to come out, and Sharon hadn't blamed him. The time Franklin had come out, Reggie had put a load of buckshot in his knee that had messed him up for weeks, and what had he got to show for it? It was so frustrating, it made Sharon want to scream. *Candy* made Sharon want to scream. How could you go through life with so little self-respect? How could you get out of bed in the morning weighed down by so much fear?

Tonight, things were quieter than usual, but not quiet. Sharon wondered if they had gotten an early start. Candy seemed to be moaning. Reggie seemed to be slapping something, but not human flesh. Sharon thought what she was hearing was the sound of a belt being slapped against a wooden table. She stopped under cover of the Georges' evergreen hedge and listened for a while, but that was all she could hear. She was glad she could hear Candy moaning. If she hadn't been able to hear Candy doing anything, she would have been worried she was dead.

She knocked snow off her boots and got moving again, through the dark, down the road, toward home. It wasn't far. The house she shared with Sharon was on the northeast corner lot at the intersection of Carrow and Delaford, if you could call that an intersection. Sharon supposed that it was, but using that term for it bothered her. Intersections had sidewalks and streetlamps and stoplights.

Half a mile past Candy and Reggie's house, Sharon started to jog, and she jogged the whole last three-quarters of a mile, right down her driveway to her back door. The lights were on all over the house, meaning Susan was home. Sharon hopped up the back porch steps and let herself into the mudroom, humming a little under her breath. The humming was not a good sign. It was "The Wearing of the Green," and the only times Sharon had ever heard "The Wearing of the Green" was at funerals.

She stuck her head into the kitchen and said, "Susan?"

Susan came into the kitchen from the dining room on the other side. She must have been in the living room and heard Sharon coming up. "Get on in," she said. "It's cold out there. How was your class?"

"Class was fine." Sharon had kicked off her snow boots and left them to lie on the drip-dry grate. Now she shoved her parka onto a hanger and came sock-footed into the kitchen. Susan was putting on a kettle of hot water for tea. There was fresh bread in the middle of the kitchen table, on a board with a knife and a tiny crock of butter at its side. It was this sort of thing that made Sharon's commitment to Susan so absolute. This sort of thoughtfulness. This sort of care.

"Class was fine," Sharon said again, sitting down. "It's coming home I don't like."

"I know."

"It wasn't half as bad as usual, believe it or not. Or maybe it was worse. She was moaning in there. I kept standing there in the snow, trying to make sure I could hear her breathing. Which I couldn't do, of course. Just moaning. I suppose that's good enough."

"You did what you could, Sharon. If you want, we can call Franklin Morrison again."

"No, that's all right. What good would it do?"

"Maybe it would do some good for you."

Sharon shook her head. "I'll be fine. What about you? How was New Hampshire?"

"The way New Hampshire always is," Susan said, light and tight. "I had my problem with my mother long before I had you. Or anybody like you. If you know what I mean."

"I know what you mean." Sharon sighed. "Do you ever wonder about it? The way people are, I mean. Candy and Reggie. Your mother."

Susan smiled. "The men I knew in New York before I met you? I don't wonder how jerks get to be jerks, Sharon. They just are."

"Do you think Candy is a jerk?"

"I think anybody who can't take care of herself is a fool. Especially any woman. Come on now. There must be something we can talk about that isn't depressing. What went on in town today?"

Sharon pulled the bread to her and cut a slice. The kettle began to boil and Susan turned to take it off the stove. Susan had a perfect jawline, tight and well-defined, flawless. Susan was flawless all over, in spite of the fact that she was getting on to forty. Sharon ate bread and butter and watched Susan pour them both some tea.

"Well," she said, "Jan-Mark Verek is apparently finished grieving, or he likes to work when he grieves. You remember how he was painting a portrait of Dinah Ketchum?"

"Oh, yes."

"Well, now he's painting one of Cara Hutchinson. At least, according to Cara Hutchinson he is. She was all over town with it this morning. She's supposed to go up there tomorrow for a sitting, and she can hardly contain herself."

Susan looked amused. "He'll make her look like a lot of puke-green blobs on a piece of recycled paper. Do you think she'll mind?"

"I don't even think she'll notice. She's already gotten him to give her the grand tour. She was all over town about that, too. How wonderful the house was. How he keeps Tisha's office practically as a shrine."

"Horse manure," Susan said.

"I'm with you." Sharon put too much sugar in her tea, because she always put too much sugar in her tea. "Still, it had me worried, for a bit. About what Tisha might have left lying around her office that Jan-Mark hasn't bothered to clean up yet."

"I don't think Tisha left things just lying around her office. She was much more organized than that."

"I know," Sharon said. "Maybe there isn't anything we can talk about without getting depressed. Do you want to get thoroughly down?"

"No."

"Well, I'm going to get you thoroughly down anyway. I ran into Franklin on my way to class today. In the pharmacy. I was buying Blistex and wishing we were in Florida."

"Franklin can't get me thoroughly down," Susan said. "For a cop, he's almost a nice man."

"Well, nice or not, he was just beside himself today. And I'll bet you can't guess why."

"You're right. I can't guess why."

Sharon cut another piece of bread and buttered it. "Well," she said, "it seems that his hero is in town. The man he most wants to meet. The absolute paragon of law enforcement. The wet dream of every small-town lawman from here to Arizona—"

"What are you *talking* about?"

"Gregor Demarkian," Sharon said. Then she put her bread down on the bare wood of the table and said, "I don't know if he's here because Franklin asked him here or if it's just a coincidence or what, but we've got those two deaths that were very nicely put down to hunting accidents—especially the one of them—and now we have *People* magazine's favorite expert on murder as well. I've been thinking about it all afternoon, Susan, and I just don't like the way it stacks up."

3

WHAT STU KETCHUM didn't like was the way his rifles looked, stacked up on the floor of the gun room the way they were now. Ever since his mother had been found in the snow at the side of the road and Franklin Marshall had come back here to find Stu's Browning .22-caliber semiautomatic Grade I rifle gone from its place on the wall, Stu had been taking his rifles down and putting them back up again, over and over, as if, if he did it enough times he could make the count finally come out right. Finding out that Dinah had not been killed with one of his guns had not helped. It had made him feel just a little less sick, but it had not really *helped*. Stu didn't know what would help. Sometimes he thought he had invented a new kind of therapy, shot therapy, weapons therapy, whatever you wanted to call it. Sometimes he would take all the rifles down from the wall and go out into the yard and shoot holes in the side of his barn. Fortunately, there wasn't much of anything in his barn.

It was now seven o'clock in the evening, and not only were Stu's guns all on the gun-room floor, but his ammunition was there, too, and his special sights and his tripods and his skeet traps and all the rest of it, all the paraphernalia of using guns for a hobby. Looking at it all piled up like this made him feel dizzy and bewildered. Thinking about himself shooting at things made him feel sick. He kept expecting the missing gun to show up, by magic or by sleight of someone's hand, and not to notice it until it was too late. He kept expecting to find himself standing outside by the barn pumping bullets into wood and suddenly recognizing the gun he was holding as the one that killed Tisha Verek. He tried to count the number of men he had killed in Vietnam and couldn't. It didn't feel like the same thing.

He felt a breeze on his hands and looked up to see that his wife, Liza, had come to stand in the doorway. Behind her, the wood stove in the kitchen seemed hot enough to be glowing. Stu dropped the cartridge he'd been holding and straightened up.

"Yes?"

"What do you mean, yes?" Liza said. "Aren't you going to come inside? Aren't you going to eat anything?"

"I'm not hungry."

"You haven't been hungry for weeks. That's not the point. You have to eat."

"I've been thinking it all through again, the day they died. I've been trying to make it make sense."

"I don't see why you think you can make it make any more sense than the police have. Come inside and eat."

"Why doesn't it bother you?" Stu asked her, but he'd been asking her that for two weeks solid now and getting no good answer. It didn't bother her because it didn't bother her. Dinah had been her mother-in-law. Liza hadn't had much patience for her when she was alive. Tisha Verek had been nothing at all. Stu tried to fathom it and couldn't. His gun. His mother. It all seemed much too connected to him.

"I don't like you out here fooling around with those guns," Liza said. And then she retreated, back into the kitchen, back behind her door. It had been that way between the two of them since Dinah died. Maybe it had been that way between the two of them forever.

Stu got up, picked his stainless-steel Plainfield Model M1 gas-operated semiautomatic out of the pile, found a clip for it and loaded. Then he went out into the yard and positioned the gun on his shoulder. This one was more like a machine gun than a standard semiautomatic. It looked like a machine gun, too. It made a lot of noise when it fired.

Stu sighted along the side of the barn, aiming at nothing in particular, wanting only to hit wood and cause damage. He pressed the trigger
and listened to the splintering of wood in the darkness, the groaning of
old boards, the moaning of the wind.

It had been two weeks now since his mother had died, and he had
finally come to a decision, one of the few real decisions he had ever
had to make in his life. He was going to have to go through with it no
matter how Liza felt and without consulting good old Peter Callisher.
He was going to have to do it on his own and that was all there was
to it.

He pulled the trigger again, listened to the splintering of wood again,
thought of them both out there in the snow with the small holes from
.22-caliber bullets leaking blood into the ground.

He thought about himself out here shooting up the barn.

He thought he was probably going crazy.

f o u r

1

WHEN FRANKLIN MORRISON had first come up to Gregor Demarkian in The Magick Endive, Gregor had been sure that the man was just another avid reader of the local paper, a slightly less sophisticated specimen than either of his two waitresses who wanted to shake the hand of the Armenian-American Hercule Poirot. It wasn't the kind of thing Gregor had ever imagined happening to himself back when he was still with the FBI. While he was there, he'd made the media often enough—if you head task forces chasing serial killers in a country full of crime-story fanatics and horror-movie junkies, that is inevitable—but it had been as an officer of the organization, the designated human face of a faceless institution. What had been happening to him since he first walked into Bennis Hannaford's father's house three years ago and found a dead body lying on the study floor was different. If it had been *just* that body in Bennis Hannaford's father's house, it might not have mattered. Bennis Hannaford's family was rich and well-connected—in Philadelphia. The rest of the country had been interested mostly because the Hannaford house had forty rooms and the Hannaford girls had all "come out" in extravagant style and one of Bennis's brothers was what old George Tekemanian back on Cavanaugh Street called "a corporated raider." It was the second extracurricular murder that really got the ball rolling. Gregor had taken that one on for a friend of Father Tibor's. That friend just happened to be John Cardinal O'Bannion, the most publicly flamboyant and outrageously controversial Catholic prelate in the country. Gregor wouldn't have guessed it beforehand, but Catholics are much better than debutantes at making a man famous. There are fifty-two million of them from one end of the country to the other, and even the ones who haven't been to Mass in twenty years are passionately interested in the Church. A lot of other people are also passionately interested in the Church, either in romantic attachment to their prettified images of pre–Vatican II ritual or from outright hostility. The Hannaford murder had gotten him a two-page spread in *People* magazine. The murder he investigated for John Cardinal O'Bannion got him on the cover, and on the covers of *Time, Life, Newsweek, U.S. News and World Report,* and *The Ladies' Home Journal.* It also got him on all three networks and into two of the three best-selling supermarket tabloids. After that, it really got crazy. More extracurricular murders. More publicity. Gregor thought every once in a while about the original Hercule Poirot, who had wanted so badly to be famous and who wasn't, really. Poirot should have lived in America in the second half of the twentieth century, where the publicity machine is all cranked up and ready to go, where "legends" have become something Directors of Market Research invented three of before breakfast. Gregor seemed to have become one of these "legends." *Esquire* wanted to interview him. So did *Vanity Fair.* He had received three invitations to appear on Ted Koppel's *Nightline.* God only knew what any of these people expected him to talk about. He didn't break confidences, his life wasn't all that interesting and he couldn't talk with any authority about the Catholic Church. He didn't even believe in God. What frightened him was the way it had gotten out on the street, especially in smaller towns. People stopped him. People touched him. Once a man in a plaid sports jacket and high-top Reebok shoes had grabbed him by the lapels and demanded to know his "secret."

Standing in The Magick Endive, watching Franklin Morrison talk to Bennis and Tibor with all the deference of a B-movie butler taking directions from the lady of the manor, Gregor had wondered uneasily if what was about to happen was going to be weird. Nothing very weird had happened to him so far, except for the man in the high-top Reeboks, but he had heard of such things. Actresses gunned down by men they had never met. Talk-show hosts invaded by deranged fans who knew how to use a set of burglar's tools. A television anchorman assaulted in a manner so bizarre it became the stuff of real legend—not hyped—within hours of the anchorman's escape. Fame was not only instantaneous in America, it was dangerous. It was especially dangerous for anyone whose name was connected in any way with violent death. The author of a series of best-selling novels about slash-and-run murders.

The star of an Oscar-nominated movie about covert operations in Vietnam. The cop who had brought in the evidence that finally convicted a famous mob boss in Miami. It was sickening what had happened to some people—and always the wrong people. The last time the violence-sickened public had gone for the throat of a killer was when Ruby killed Oswald. Since then, the killers had been perfectly safe. The television newswoman who produced a ground-breaking report on battering had to have her mailbox checked routinely by the bomb squad. No one was out to assassinate Jeffrey Dahmer.

Actually, Franklin Morrison didn't seem to Gregor to be a prime candidate for the role of nutcase. He was too old—if there was one thing Gregor had learned in twenty years in the FBI, it was that most stranger-to-stranger violence is committed by men between the ages of fifteen and thirty-five. Most acquaintanceship violence is committed by men in that age group, too, but Gregor didn't have to worry about that. Franklin Morrison wasn't an acquaintance. He wasn't in very good shape, either. That was another thing about stranger-to-stranger violence. Acquaintanceship violence usually had a drug or alcohol element to it. Stranger-to-stranger violence, at least of the most serious kind, usually had a workout element to it. When Gregor had first noticed that, he had thought he was losing his mind. Then another agent had made the same observation, and the connection had become impossible to ignore. Charles Manson, Ted Bundy, John Wayne Gacey—fat or thin, in shape or out, it was remarkable how many serial killers and other assorted nasties worked out. The only one Gregor could remember who definitely hadn't had been David Berkowitz. Gregor didn't think that counted. He had always been uncomfortable with the verdict in the Berkowitz case. He was sure enough that Berkowitz had committed the crimes he had been charged with. He was also sure that Berkowitz was no psychopath. Gregor Demarkian knew the difference between a psychopath and a lunatic.

Psychopaths, lunatics—what am I thinking about? Gregor had wondered. Here he was, presented with what he had no sane reason to expect was anything but a harmless old man—and a harmless old man in a police uniform, at that—and he's spinning interior movies in Technicolor about the repressed blood instincts of secret serial murderers. He had been worried about that kind of thing when he was still at the Bureau. Toward the last years of Elizabeth's life, the two of them had talked endlessly about whether Gregor was getting "hard."

Once on his own, away from the Bureau in the everyday world, he hadn't expected to have to fear for his humanity—but here he was. Somehow, here he always was. There had to be a way he could keep his opinions of all that part of the human race that did not live on Cavanaugh Street from sinking to the level of his opinion of Vlad the Impaler.

Franklin Morrison had shifted from one foot to the other and back again, from one foot to the other and back again, as if he were on a boat and correcting for the roll. Bennis had sat with her chin on her hands and her huge blue eyes wide and mischievous. Tibor had sat with his back very straight and his face frozen into gravity, but without being able to hide his excitement. That was when reality had come washing over Gregor like a tidal wave. He might obsess about serial killers and rogue fans. He might prepare himself for fantasized attacks from unexpected quarters. What Gregor was really in danger of was not violence, but imposition. Franklin Morrison had a gleam in his eye that Gregor knew well. It was the gleam of a man with an illness who has finally found a specialist. Franklin Morrison had a problem, and he couldn't think of a single person on earth better qualified to solve it than Gregor Demarkian.

2

"IT'S NOT THAT I mind being consulted," Gregor told Tibor the next morning, leaning over the small basin in the bathroom and trying to see his lathered face in a mirror encrusted with poinsettia leaves, holly sprigs, Santa's elves and leaping reindeer. The Green Mountain Inn may have taken its inspiration for its lobby decorations from the Place de la Concorde, but it had taken its inspiration for its room decorations from Donna Moradanyan. "In fact, I even like being consulted. It's nice to know I haven't lost my touch—"

"Of course you haven't lost your touch," Tibor said soothingly, and absently. He was sitting on a stool just outside the bathroom door, half lost in a book. Tibor was always lost in a book. His apartment behind Holy Trinity Church on Cavanaugh Street was not much more than a repository for books—in English, French, German, Italian, Spanish, Arabic, modern Greek, ancient Greek, Latin and Hebrew. He had furniture no one had ever seen because it was so deeply buried under books. He now had hotel furniture no one could get to because it was so deeply buried under books. It had taken him less than half an hour last night to transform his room into a replica of the ones he remembered so fondly from home. Now he tapped the page of the book he was holding with the tip of a single finger and sighed. He had been reading all morning—it was now ten o'clock on the morning of Monday, December 16th—and getting gloomier by the second.

"Krekor," he said carefully. "I am worried. I am very worried about Bennis."

"I'm always worried about Bennis," Gregor said grimly, "but it doesn't do any good. She won't listen. If she insists on going out with brain-addled rock stars and action-movie actors who identify too strongly with their characters, there's nothing we can do. Do you want to hear about Franklin Morrison or not?"

"Of course I want to hear about Franklin Morrison. It is a difficult problem he had, Krekor. Maybe you can solve it."

"I can't solve it by looking at his evidence files," Gregor said. His razor was full of foam. He turned on the tap and ran the blade under the water. "I'm no good at physical evidence, that's what I kept trying to tell him. Everybody specializes, Tibor. I specialized in analysis. I don't know a rifle bullet from Little Orphan Annie."

"I do not think it is necessary that you know the rifle bullet, Krekor. I think he already knows what he had to know about the rifle bullet. Bullets."

"No, he doesn't. He doesn't know why they were fired."

"Isn't this analysis?"

Gregor raised his razor to his face again. "It's analysis for anybody who knows anything about rifle bullets. Tibor, it's as if you didn't know anything about Western literature and you sat down to read *Finnegan's Wake*. It can't be done. You wouldn't have the context. I don't have the context here. Anyway, I tend to agree with the Vermont State Police."

"You mean you think these two deaths were accidents?"

Gregor peered at his nearly naked face, decided it would have to do and reached for the towel. "I don't see any reason not to think they were accidents—or at least I don't see any reason but one, and that's more than a little weak."

"What is it?"

"Position of the wounds. I'll have to check the papers, of course, but from what Morrison said yesterday, it sounds as if both bodies had two wounds, one of them in the shoulder and one of them in the neck.

I'd like to know if those are common places for hunting-accident wounds. If they're not, the coincidence is interesting."

"There now, Krekor."

"But not interesting enough," Gregor insisted. "Two different guns. Two different places. Two very different people—and what could the motive be? Nobody seems to have liked this Tricia Verek—"

"Tisha, Krekor."

"Whatever. Nobody seems to have liked her, and this legal action she wanted to file had everybody mad as hell—even if we give Franklin Morrison both those things, they don't add up to a motive for murder—"

"Not even the legal action?" Tibor looked surprised. "Mr. Morrison was saying that this Celebration is everything to the town, Krekor. To shut it down would be to make the people here poor."

"To shut it down would be to make the town operate like all the other towns in Vermont and most other states. If it wanted a new pool for the school gymnasium, it would have to collect taxes to get it. Granted, the way they do it now seems to be both less painful and more effective, but putting the town in the position of having to operate more conventionally does not add up to a motive for murder. Only psychopaths kill in cold blood, Tibor. Everybody else—and that includes wives who murder their husbands for the insurance and plan it all out for six months—everybody else kills under extreme emotional stress. That includes soldiers in war. That's what all that training is about; it's like a crash course in autohypnosis to psych the men up for battle. If the men didn't get psyched, there wouldn't be a battle. I can't imagine a situation where somebody would get psyched enough to kill Tisha Verek over something as esoteric as a lawsuit that hadn't been filed yet and wouldn't have any effect until a year after it had been filed. And what about the old lady?"

"Mmm," Tibor said, absent again. "What about the old lady?"

Gregor reached to the hook on the back of the bathroom door, where he had hung his shirt. He pulled the shirt on, buttoned the sleeves, and then went hunting for his belt.

"The old lady," Gregor repeated deliberately, "was someone named Dinah Ketchum, and she wasn't the enemy of anybody as far as Franklin Morrison told us, and she wasn't out to sue the town over anything, either. She was just an old lady. Tibor?"

Tibor was back in the middle of his book again. Because of the way he was holding it, it was impossible for Gregor to see the cover. It was one of those large-format paperbacks, though, which meant it wasn't a novel by Dick Francis or Judith Krantz or Mickey Spillane, which was what Tibor liked to read for relaxation. Gregor put his hand on the top of the book and forced it down into Tibor's lap.

"Tibor?"

"I am very worried about Bennis, Krekor."

Gregor read the book's title upside down on the top of the left-hand page: *Get Thin, Stay Thin, Be Thin Forever!* He blinked.

"Thin?" he asked dubiously.

Tibor flushed. "It is not the first I have read, Krekor. In my room, I have others."

"Diet books?"

"Yes, of course diet books. *The Pritikin Program. Fit for Life. The Woman's Advantage Diet.* I must have two dozen of them, Krekor, and I don't have half of what I found in the bookstore. There are millions of these books."

"You don't need to lose weight."

"I know. Bennis, she also does not need to lose weight."

"Bennis is trying to lose weight?"

"She has bought a diet book, Krekor. *The Raise Your Metabolism Diet.* I have read it."

"Why?" Gregor asked him.

"Because I am worried, Krekor. And I have a right to be worried. This is a book for crazy people."

"What is? The book you're reading or the book Bennis was reading?"

"Both. I am telling you, Krekor, it is a conspiracy."

"What's a conspiracy?"

"Diets," Tibor said seriously. "It is a conspiracy against the women of America."

"By whom?"

"Male chauvinist pigs," Tibor said.

Male chauvinist pigs. Gregor's belt had gotten itself wound around the bamboo pole that held the utility shelves together. Gregor got it unwound and began to thread it through his belt loops. The utility shelves had been pasted over with sprightly red-and-green holiday shelf paper. Gregor's head felt heavy, as if he had smashed it into something harder than itself. His head often felt this way after long-term discussions with Father Tibor Kasparian on any subject that related directly to modern American life. It wasn't that Tibor was unintelligent or unsophisticated in the ordinary sense. Nobody who could read that many languages was unintelligent. Nobody who had spent so much time in the great capitals of Europe—and in the gulags—was unsophisticated. The problem was more like a matter of tone, a shift in emphasis. Tibor didn't think like other people, and he had no sense of time. Did he realize that nobody said "male chauvinist pig" anymore? Did he care?

"Tibor," Gregor said cautiously, "I don't think—"

But Tibor had jumped up from his seat and begun to pace. He was patroling the hall Gregor needed to get through to get back to his room. "I am telling you, Krekor, it is right. Think about it. We have now many women in this country like Bennis, they have very good educations, they have the chance to build empires and write books and make world peace—although the way the world is, I am not sure there is ever going to be peace. Never mind. They have this chance, and what do they do instead? They diet."

"Tibor—"

"It is not right for women to be as thin as they try to be in America, Krekor. The good God did not make women thin. He made them round. When they try to be thin, they do not eat enough, they make themselves starve—and let me tell you Krekor, I know about starving. I have starved. In the last days before I was able to leave the Soviet Union, I had nothing to eat for four days, and then when I got to Israel, I had no money and so not much to eat for the next two weeks, and let me tell you what I thought of, Krekor, I thought of food. All the time food. It was only after I had started to teach at the university and I had money to eat all the time that I could concentrate again. You see."

"Not exactly."

"Bennis will begin with this diet and then she will not write her books, Krekor, instead she will think only about food. Like the other women, they do not build big business empires, they do not get together to elect a woman president, they do not write philosophy as much as they could because so many of them are thinking only about food. It is a plot, Krekor. I know plots. I have spent my life in the midst of plots."

Gregor was beginning to think he was condemned to spend his life in the middle of another one—Tibor's against the male chauvinists, maybe. He caught Tibor at the start of a new lap in pacing and darted through the window of opportunity, relieved once he stopped to find himself in the middle of the hall. Tibor had not quit his pacing. He had simply created a new route, around Gregor, past the bathroom door and around Gregor again. He had his hands clasped behind his back and a frown on his face as furious as any he could ever have directed at the people who had persecuted him.

"I am worried about Bennis," he repeated, "and if you have any sense, Krekor, you will be worried about Bennis, too. You will help me stop this thing."

"I have to go see Franklin Morrison," Gregor said. "I promised."

"You have to take responsibility for the people you love," Tibor said. "She will not listen to me."

"She won't listen to me, either," Gregor told him. "At least, she hasn't until now."

There was no longer any reason why Gregor shouldn't go to his room. His door was standing open on the other side of the hall. Tibor was no longer walking back and forth in front of him. There was no point in continuing this conversation. Tibor's eyes were fierce. He was ready to go into phase two—practical attack plans. Franklin Morrison was waiting.

"I've got to go," Gregor said, and then, at the first sign of a possible response from Father Tibor Kasparian, he went.

From the very beginning of this second career in extracurricular murder, Gregor Demarkian had discussed his involvements with Tibor. That was what he had been trying to do by telling Tibor how he felt about Franklin Morrison's request to "just look over" the evidence file. That was what he'd expected to do when he'd asked Tibor to talk to him while he shaved. That all this had been sidetracked by Tibor's new obsession with diets was more than unsettling. It put Gregor in a distinctly bad mood.

3

HE WAS STILL in a bad mood ten minutes later, when he emerged from his room in his best camel's hair topcoat, carrying his best leather gloves and feeling more than a little ridiculous to be going out in such a formal way. Wanting to look professional, he hadn't had any other choice. He had brought casual clothes and this formal suit, but nothing in between. If Elizabeth had still been alive, she would never have allowed it. She'd have packed his suitcase herself and made sure he had everything he might possibly need.

He stopped at the door to Tibor's bedroom, unable to get over feeling guilty for ducking out on a conversation that had been important to Tibor even if it hadn't been important to him. Tibor was propped up in a green wingbacked chair with his feet on a matching green ottoman, deep in a volume called *The Super Fat Loss Diet and Maintenance Plan: The Revolutionary New Program That Takes the Weight Off and Keeps It Off Forever!* Towers of books rose from the floor around Tibor's feet, including *The Complete Scarsdale Medical Diet, The Beverly Hills Diet, The Mayo Clinic Diet Manual, The Crystal Healing Diet, The Carbohydrate Addict's Diet, The New American Diet,* and *The Last Diet You'll Ever Need.* There was also something called *Fat Is a Feminist Issue,* but it seemed to have been stabbed. Gregor decided not to go in and disturb the man. He not only had diets on the brain, he had them everywhere else, too. Any interruption of the reading process would only bring on another tirade. At least for today.

Just as Gregor was turning toward the stairs, he had a second thought. Maybe Tibor was right. Maybe he ought to be worried about Bennis Hannaford. God knew, Bennis gave every one of her friends cause enough to worry. She had a far too well-developed spirit of adventure and absolutely no sense of self-preservation. She'd never been particularly sensible about food, but her lack of sense hadn't run to diets. It had run to eating like a horse. Maybe Tibor knew something he didn't know, though. It wasn't a subject Gregor had paid much attention to— his rather substantial bulk was evidence of that—but he had heard some things in passing, and those things were very disturbing. Weren't there women out there who thought they were fat when they weren't, and then went on starvation diets until they died? Weren't there others who ate enormous amounts of food and then made themselves throw up? None of that really sounded like Bennis. None of that was really her style. Still, you never knew.

Gregor went across the hall to Bennis's room and knocked. He heard a muffled "come in," turned the doorknob and stuck his head through. Bennis had a single, not a suite, with no living room. She was sitting on her already made-up bed in a pair of jeans and a turtleneck, the phone in one hand and a large jelly doughnut in the other. She certainly didn't seem to be dieting. When she saw him she said "just a second" to whomever was on the phone and took the receiver away from her ear.

"It's Donna Moradanyan," she said. "She thinks she may have found a place for the Kaldikians. Sheila Kashinian's brother's daughter's husband owns a small apartment building in Paoli. You want to talk to Donna?"

"I just came in to see how you were doing."

"I'm doing fine. You going to see Chief Morrison?"

"I am."

"I'll expect a full report when you get back. Just a minute." Bennis put the phone back up to her ear. "Donna? Gregor is here. I was telling him about Sheila's—"

It didn't matter what Bennis had been telling Donna about Sheila Kashinian or anybody else. Gregor backed out of the room and closed the door, feeling a little easier in his mind. Surely nobody who was dieting would have been eating the sort of thing Bennis had been eating. And surely nobody who was making herself vomit after every time she ate could be so concerned with hapless refugees like the Kaldikians, who were now sleeping in Father Tibor's apartment and defying the best efforts of the Support for an Independent Armenia Society to resettle them in America.

Gregor made his way to the stairs, then down to the lobby, then out onto Main Street, feeling better with every step he took. Franklin Morrison might not have a problem worth bothering with, but discussing forensic impossibilities with a small-town policeman had to beat holding Tibor's hand when he was in the grip of one of his fanaticisms.

Gregor thought he'd let Bennis do that this time. After all, she was the one who had started it.

f i v e

1

TO GET TO the police station, Gregor had to go down Main Street to Carrow and then down Carrow to Williams. Williams was easy to miss, because it was just a finger-dart to the left of the road. The major intersection on Carrow was with Delaford. Gregor walked through town slowly, his hands in the pockets of his coat, his scarf pulled up over his skin. It was very cold, but he seemed to be the only one who noticed. Main Street was full of activity. It probably wasn't, usually. Gregor imagined it on an ordinary day as half-deserted, inundated irregularly by children getting out of school or choirs being released from practice at the Congregational Church. Even with the out-of-town tourists clotting up the sidewalks, Bethlehem looked like the inspiration for all the usual subjects: Currier and Ives, Norman Rockwell, Pissaro's painting *Winter*. That was why the usual subjects were usual. It helped that the tourists all seemed to be either wearing a uniform or costumed for the next production of a science fiction circus. Half of them were identically attired in Baxter State parkas, baggy blue jeans and neon orange- and lemon-striped snow boots. The other half were like fruit salad. Gregor saw a woman in leopard-print Lycra stretch pants so tight they looked like skin. She was wearing a bright blue feathered jacket with silver spangles that jingled when she walked. Then there was the woman in the spike-heeled boots and the Victorian riding costume, right down to the little velvet hat. Gregor had a vision of the older women on Cavanaugh Street—Lida and Hannah and Sheila and the rest of them—sitting around an outdoor table the way they would have sat on the church steps in a village in the old country, watching these oddly dressed women go by. Gregor did not speak Armenian, but sometimes he thought he could hear it in his head, and this was one of those times. His mother's voice came to him out of nowhere and he got the word for *menopause,* intact.

He passed the offices of the *Bethlehem News and Mail* and looked through the big plate-glass window on the ground floor to see a dozen people scurrying around, apparently being directed by a young blonde woman with Alice-in-Wonderland hair. A tiny evergreen tree had been set up on a desk near the middle of the room and decorated with twinkly lights and too much tinsel. Gregor had always been partial to too much tinsel. He passed the pharmacy and looked in its window at a display of spray-snow and Santa Claus. He passed the town's only three parking meters—all in front of the Town Hall—and saw that red ribbons had been tied just at the top of the poles holding up each one. The small town park was almost exactly at the intersection of Main and Carrow, so he passed that, too, but he didn't stop to look at it. Nothing was going on there that hadn't been going on yesterday. The first of the week's performances would start tonight at eight. Anything he might be interested in that might be going on in the park would keep till then.

Gregor got to Carrow, turned the only way he could, and went on walking. The townscape changed from blocks of stores to blocks of houses with shingles on their lawns, advertising treasures within. Gregor passed a small Victorian that called itself Ethan Allen's Used Books, a smaller colonial that promised Hand-Sewn Quilts, and a positively minuscule Cape Cod whose sign read "Yankee Fashions—Original Needlework and Crochet." All the houses had wreaths on their doors and some sort of bright abeyance to Christmas in their front windows. The Cape Cod had a hanging row of knitted reindeer with bits of glitter in their fur. Gregor thought Christmas stockings would have been more to the point, but admitted he didn't really know. Who patronized shops like these on out-of-the-way streets? Who turned in at the sign in front of the decaying farmhouse that said "Fish Taxidermy Done Here"? Who bought birdhouses from the stack in the yard of the small brick ranch? The houses were all so small and so close to the road and so close to each other—old for real, then, and not just built recently to look old. Just how old, Gregor couldn't tell. The Cape Cod might go back as far as the Revolutionary War. The small brick ranch probably dated from the end of the Second World War. The people who lived in these houses could be anybody at all, but Gregor was willing to bet they were people who had moved here from other places. In his experience, people who grew up with antique houses didn't appreciate them half as much as people who'd spent their childhoods in splendid suburban comfort, complaining all the time that perfect plumbing and instantaneous heat made their lives "plastic."

Fish taxidermy. Quilts. Used Books. Birdhouses. Gregor couldn't use any of those, but Bennis liked hand-knit cotton sweaters and he hadn't bought her anything for Christmas yet. What he ought to buy her was a critical review of the fantasy genre that rated Stephen Donaldson's books several notches above her own, just to drive her as crazy as she had driven him with Curty Gentry's take on the FBI, but he was better than that. He backed up until he was standing in front of the Cape Cod and looked at its window. The knitted reindeer were lumpy and creased. They didn't give him a great deal of confidence. Still, you could never tell. And if everything was awful, it might not matter. What could something cost, being sold in a place like this?

Less than two minutes later, Gregor was standing in the Cape Cod's front hall, knocking snow off his shoes onto a mat and answering his own question. There was an absolutely beautiful knitted sweater draped over the top of a dressmaker's dummy in the corner of what seemed to be the only room on this floor. The sweater was a bright red with black-and-white reindeer leaping across it in rows. It was exquisitely done, and it had a sign under it that said $360. Next to that sign was another sign that said VISA AND MASTERCARD ACCEPTED. Gregor was relieved.

At the back of the room, a young woman with long brown hair was sitting at a long table, talking to another young woman whose hair was just as brown but very short, and enlivened by a broad streak of white that was startling because it was natural. The short-haired young woman had to be thirty-five at least, but she reminded Gregor so strongly of girls he had known in high school, he had to keep reminding himself of the fact. What the girl who was standing looked like was the captain of a field hockey team, all raw bones and awkwardness and tomboyish delicacy. It was a look Gregor had always found peculiarly attractive. The long-haired young woman was more traditionally feminine, but she seemed to Gregor the clone of hundreds of others, all relentlessly addicted to Indian prints.

The two young women had stopped talking when he came in. Now they stared at him politely, waiting for him to make a move. Gregor looked back at the red sweater, checked his pockets for his wallet and said, "I'd like to buy this."

The short-haired young woman laughed. "My God, Marla. The man must be in love."

Marla stood up and came around the table. "It's not possible," she said. "Gregor Demarkian is a great detective. Great detectives don't fall in love."

"I don't believe it," the short-haired woman said. "It didn't say that in the article."

"It didn't have to."

"I think if it were true, Peter would at least have mentioned it."

"Peter mentioned him having a 'constant companion,'" Marla said, "but I figured that was just his overworked girl Friday. You know what men are like. She probably makes him coffee, carries his books, runs his theories through the computer and gets a reputation as a bubblehead for her trouble."

Gregor Demarkian smiled as best he could. "If you're talking about Bennis Hannaford," he said, "she's never been anyone's girl Friday in her life, she doesn't carry anything and she blows up her own computer at least twice a month. She does make coffee, but I think that's in self-defense."

"You probably think you need some self-defense," Marla said. "Have we been very bad? Have we thoroughly embarrassed you?"

"No, not really," Gregor admitted. "When I saw that newspaper story, I resigned myself to the inevitable. I take it your name is Marla."

"That's right," Marla said. "And this is Sharon. Sharon Morrissey."

"How do you do," Sharon Morrissey said.

"Do the two of you run this shop together?"

Marla was getting the sweater down from the dressmaker's dummy, being careful to remove the pins one by one and straight out, so they wouldn't snag on the cotton yarn.

"I run the store," Marla said. "Sharon lives out on the Delaford Road and writes children's books her housemate illustrates."

"My housemate is named Susan Everman."

"They came out here from New York together and went native."

Marla stopped in her removal of the pins and looked back over her shoulder at Gregor. Sharon crossed her arms over her stomach and looked at Gregor, too. Gregor didn't know whether to feel amused or exasperated. Obviously, this was the test they put people to—these broad hints that Sharon and her housemate were gay, these long seconds waiting for a reaction. What did they expect him to do? He made it a point never to have opinions about the consensual sexual behavior of other people—even Bennis—but even if he had been stuffed full of hostility to homosexuals, what could he possibly have done? Tibor would have sailed blissfully past the question, as if it hadn't existed, and asked Sharon to see one of the books she wrote for children.

Whatever he did do passed muster. Sharon looked at Marla and Marla looked back, and there was a recognizable easing of tension in the room. Marla went back to getting the sweater down from the dummy, and Sharon took the seat behind the table.

"The problem is," Marla said, "everybody already knows you're here, and it's such a surprise. I mean, it would have been less of a big deal if you'd registered at the Inn under your own name."

"I didn't register at the Inn at all," Gregor said. "Bennis registered. Do you want some help getting that over the top?"

"I'm fine." Marla had kicked a stepstool into place and was climbing on it. "It's just that Peter Callisher made such a big deal about that Thanksgiving thing, with your picture all over the paper three weeks running and all these gory details he kept picking up from his friends in Boston and New York."

"And then there were the shootings," Sharon said.

"So when you showed up, it looked like a conspiracy." Marla draped the sweater over her arm and headed back for the table. Gregor got out his wallet and began searching for his Visa card. Marla put the sweater down and got out a sales-slip book. "It really does look like a conspiracy," she continued, "especially since everybody in town knows that Franklin Morrison has always been a big fan of yours—Franklin Morrison is the chief of police."

"I know," Gregor said. "That's what I'm doing here. I'm going down to the police station to visit. Invited."

Sharon cocked her head. "*Are* you here to investigate the shootings?"

"No." Gregor handed over his credit card. "I'm here to give a friend of mine a vacation, and myself a vacation, and Bennis Hannaford a chance to nag. From what I've heard of your shootings, I tend to think the state police were right."

"You mean that they were hunting accidents." Sharon frowned.

Marla spread tissue paper across the top of the table. "The sweater you're buying was made by one of the women who died," she said. "Dinah Ketchum. She was eighty-something. Best handwork artist in all this part of Vermont. She did quilts, too."

"She has some still on sale over at the Celebration," Sharon said.

"Last year she sold an eight-by-seven wedding quilt for fifteen hundred dollars."

"All the people who make this sort of thing and do it right are old ladies," Marla said. "Part of that's the experience—the more of it you do, the better you get at it. Nobody's going to be able to make a sweater like this one at twenty. But part of it's the patience. Women now don't seem to have the patience. I don't have the patience."

"It paid off for Dinah," Sharon pointed out. She looked up at Gregor. "Jan-Mark Verek was absolutely obsessed with her stuff. Usually you only get really big prices during the tourist invasions—Christmas for the Celebration, July and August with people on vacations, sometimes winter if the snow's been good and we have some overflow from the ski places. Dinah could get what she wanted any time at all. If she made it, Jan-Mark would buy it."

"He said he painted them, but you couldn't tell from what came out," Marla said. "I mean, he's very abstract and very postmodernist."

"In fact, he's probably crazy." Sharon nodded. "That's the big theory in town, you know. That Jan-Mark shot Tisha and got rid of the gun."

"Just Tisha?" Gregor asked. "Not Dinah Ketchum?"

"People think the police were right about Dinah Ketchum," Marla said. "She was way far out in the middle of nowhere, and Jan-Mark couldn't have gotten to her. Besides, she wasn't shot with the same gun."

"She wasn't that far out," Sharon insisted. "Everybody here is always talking about how far away things are, but they aren't. This isn't Wyoming."

"Well, Jan-Mark was standing in the living room of his own house not ten minutes after Tisha was shot, looking at her bleeding to death in the driveway and not doing a damned thing when Stu and Peter showed up. I don't care how close Dinah was, Jan-Mark couldn't have gotten to her and back in time."

"You're acting like this is *Mystery Theater*," Sharon said. "Timetables and who could have been where when. Life isn't like that. In life, things just happen. Isn't that right, Mr. Demarkian?"

"Mmm," Gregor Demarkian said.

The sweater was wrapped in tissue paper and deposited in a bag. The bag was blue and gold and had twined gold handles to carry it with. Gregor put his credit card back in his wallet.

"Could I come pick this up on my way back?" he asked. "I can't see myself walking into a police station with it in hand."

"I'll take it over to the Inn and drop it off for you, if you want," Sharon told him. "It's on my way. I'm supposed to read for the kindergarten at the library today."

"I think it's too bad you didn't come to town to investigate the shootings," Marla said. "I don't care what anybody thinks. They were creepy."

Gregor didn't know if they were creepy or not. He did know there was something very odd about that fact that no one at all—not Chief Morrison, not the newspaper article—had mentioned that there was any connection between Dinah Ketchum and Tisha Verek.

In fact, everybody seemed to have been going out of their way to imply that there wasn't one.

2

IF GREGOR DEMARKIAN had been a speculating man, he would have guessed that the Bethlehem Police Department would be a hole-in-the-wall operation—and when he first got there, that was what he thought it was. The hand-lettered sign that marked the turn from Carrow to Williams Street said TO POLICE AND NEW TOWN HALL. Just as Gregor had suspected from that oracle, the police department was in the basement of the New Town Hall. Just why Bethlehem, Vermont, needed a new town hall when the old one was apparently still in operation on Main Street, Gregor couldn't begin to imagine, so he didn't try. Instead, he made his way up the carefully shovelled steps to the New Town Hall's wreath-adorned doors, let himself inside, and followed the meager directions on another hand-lettered sign to the basement. New Town Hall was better than he had expected, because it was very new, very clean and very well built. Most of what you got in very small towns was decaying infrastructure and secondhand accoutrements. There were more hand-lettered signs in the basement, and Gregor followed these, too, looking with interest at one that said *"jail cells"* and pointed to the back of the building. The jail cells in Bethlehem, Vermont, must have all the cheerfulness of the dungeon rooms at Glencannon Castle. Another sign said MCU and had been appended to: ANYONE TAKING OUT THE MCU MUST SIGN FOR THE KEYS IN THE OFFICE. For Gregor, "MCU" would always mean "mobile crime unit," but here he didn't believe it. Mobile crime units were enormously expensive. Towns the size of this one didn't have them.

Gregor finally reached a door that said BETHLEHEM POLICE DEPART-MENT PLEASE COME IN with a sign that wasn't hand-lettered at all. He gave a perfunctory knock and walked in, expecting to find himself in a small room with a few desks scattered around it and an ancient metal filing cabinet full to overflowing. What he got was a very large room and no metal filing cabinet. The desks were new, and each one of them held a computer work station that seemed to be hooked into some larger system. There were a fair number of desks and a fair number of work stations, but not very many people. In fact, there were only two. A young man was sitting at a desk at the front, tapping things into his computer and swearing under his breath. Franklin Morrison was stand-ing at a desk in the back, talking on the phone.

Franklin saw him, nodded and waved. Then the younger man looked up, flushed and stood.

"Oh," he said. "You must be Gregor Demarkian."

"That's right," Gregor told him. "Who are you?"

"Lee Greenwood." Lee Greenwood looked down at his computer terminal, swore again and retook his seat. He tapped a few more things into the machine and sighed. "Excuse me," he said, "but someone stole one of the camels again last night, and we've got to track it down. I mean, it can't have gotten very far."

"Kids," Franklin Morrison said from the back of the room. He had hung up the phone and begun coming forward. "The kids always steal the livestock, meaning our kids, and don't you know it was a mess the year we had the elephants. I don't remember whose idea nat was. Anyway, their kids, meaning the tourist kids, steal cars."

"We've got a couple of those, too," Lee Greenwood said. "The staties will find them."

"Yeah, they will." Franklin nodded. "They drive 'em out to the roadhouses on 91, and then when they can't get served they have a fit. I still say it makes more sense than stealing a camel and sneaking it into Betty Heath's barn. No, it was the elephant that ended up in Betty Heath's barn. Woman damn near had a heart attack. Hello, Mr. Demarkian."

"Hello," Gregor said.

Franklin Morrison shook his head. "I suppose we sound like a pack of hicks to you. I guess we might as well. We are a pack of hicks."

"Oh, I wouldn't exactly say that," Lee Greenwood protested.

"The only reason you wouldn't is because you don't have the sense God gave the rear end of a mule." There was a small gate between the desks and the narrow front of the room. Franklin pushed it open and motioned Gregor inside. "Come take a look at the world's most expensively outfitted hick cop shop. We got computers. We got labs. We got nationwide information hookups. We got anything you care to name, and the day those two women died I was sitting here feeling sorry for myself because we never got to use any of it. I'm seventy-two years old and I still don't know a damn thing about a damn thing."

Gregor looked around at the interior of the office, at the desks and the computer terminals, at the paper scattered around. What this police department needed was people. A dispatcher. A clerk. Somebody to take care of the paperwork housekeeping. He drew out a desk chair and sat down in it.

"Do you have a mobile crime unit?" he asked Franklin Morrison.

Franklin Morrison laughed. "I've got an MCU any station in New York City would die for. I've got a lab—"

"A lab?"

"Set up for fiber analysis, earth analysis, I don't know what. Got this kid, Mary Dempsey's oldest, goes to MIT on scholarship now. When I need something done, I pay him and he comes down and does it."

"Do you need the lab often?" Gregor couldn't imagine Bethlehem as a hotbed of crime. He couldn't imagine Bethlehem as a hotbed of anything, except the terminally colonial.

But Franklin Morrison was nodding. "Traffic accidents," he was saying. "And at least one outbreak of cabin fever every February, some asshole gets snowed in up in the hills and gets tanked up and decides life isn't worth living. We could ask the staties to run the tests for us, but what for?"

"Rather not ask the staties for anything," Lee Greenwood put in.

Franklin Morrison scratched his head. "Of course, sometimes the staties are useful. Like with these shootings here. I think we'd have had no end of trouble with those if we hadn't had the staties standing by, ready to step in. They took the heat, if you get what I mean."

"They did the tests and they made the pronouncements and whatever they said, it wasn't your fault." Gregor nodded. "But I'm surprised. I'd have thought you'd want to use that lab of yours when you had the chance."

"We did," Lee Greenwood said.

Gregor raised an eyebrow at Franklin Morrison and watched the chief blush.

"We didn't tell anybody about it," Franklin Morrison said, "but we ran the same tests here the staties ran downstate. Just to be sure, if you get what I mean."

"Just to be sure of what?" Gregor demanded.

Lee Greenwood jumped in. "Franklin thought the state police were leaping to conclusions before they had any real evidence," he said, "and I know what he meant, because I sort of felt that way, too. They hardly looked at anything at all before they decided we had hunting accidents."

Gregor looked from Lee Greenwood to Franklin Morrison and paused. "Did you find anything different from what they found? Did you find any reason to doubt their conclusions?"

"No," Lee Greenwood said.

Franklin Morrison had been standing near the gate he'd let Gregor in through. Now he pulled out a chair and sat down, moving his bulk carefully, and propped his feet up on an open desk drawer. In some men, that would have constituted attitude. In Franklin Morrison, Gregor thought, it was fatigue. Franklin Morrison was an old man. His feet hurt.

"Tisha Verek," Franklin said, "was shot at nine-forty-one on the morning of Monday, December second, with a Browning .22-caliber semiautomatic Grade I rifle we now know belonged to Stuart Ketchum, son of Dinah Ketchum, who was also shot that morning but with a Marlin Model 7OP Papoose—which also happens to be a semiautomatic and also happens to be a twenty-two, but a twenty-two long. Meaning the ammunition would not have been interchangeable. Anyway, both women were hit twice, once in the shoulder and once in the neck. We have a time for Tisha Verek because her husband says he saw her fall. We don't have one for Dinah Ketchum because she wasn't found until hours later, but we do have her schedule for the day, and the possibility is that she was shot close to the same time Tisha Verek was."

"Are twenty-twos what people use to shoot deer?" Gregor asked.

"They're a little light, but women use them sometimes. And flat-landers will use anything. We had the kid run the tests and the staties ran the tests, but I knew that Browning bullet just by looking at it. Stuart has a whole collection of guns out there. He puts in a lot of target practice and he likes to have company."

"Meaning you've shot the gun yourself," Gregor said.

Franklin nodded. "When we first saw this mess, I thought Stuart had gone round the bend, had some kind of delayed Vietnam syndrome and shot them both, but it couldn't have been Stuart. He was with Peter Callisher all morning and the two of them went up to Tisha's together. If you believe Jan-Mark Verek—and I only sort of half do—they got there within minutes of Tisha's going down. Most people in town think Jan-Mark killed Tisha himself, stole Stu's gun and just did it, but most people in town would do anything they could to get rid of Jan-Mark Verek. As a matter of principle."

"Was he opposed to the Nativity Celebration, too?"

Franklin shook his head. "He's just a general pain in the butt, that's all. Speaks with a phony accent you can hear the Brooklyn under with no trouble at all. Goes berserk if anybody crosses his property, which means he goes berserk on a regular basis, because when it's minus six with the wind chill and hip deep in snow, people take shortcuts. Then there's the money. Jan-Mark isn't so good about money. Remembering to pay people what he owes them, I mean. Most of the people up here who run small businesses or do personal work—chopping cordwood or raking leaves or painting houses—don't have much of a cushion. If they put in the time, they expect to get paid."

"He sounds altogether charming," Gregor said. "Is there anything else wrong with him?"

"Probably. We just don't know about it yet. So, Mr. Demarkian, you want to look at this stuff I've got for you."

Gregor stood up. "I will if you want me to. You still have to understand that this isn't the kind of evidence I'm used to dealing with. I mean, I've dealt with it, of course, but I've always relied on other people's reports."

"Yeah, yeah," Franklin Morrison said. "So have I. But it isn't the physical stuff I want you to see right this minute. I've got the Dempsey kid coming in; when he gets here he can walk you through that. It's something else. I want your opinion about a probability."

"A probability?"

Franklin Morrison took his feet off the open desk drawer, got up and went to the wall at the back of the room. The wall was blank, and along the top of it was a shade roll of the kind Gregor remembered from elementary school, the kind that pulled down to reveal a map of the United States. This one pulled down to reveal a map, too, but it was an extremely detailed map of the village and township of Bethlehem, Vermont, complete with roads, hills, woods and houses, with property lines clearly marked. It was in color, too. Franklin Morrison was very proud of it.

"Come here," he told Gregor Demarkian. "I want to show you something very odd."

s i x

1

GEMMA BURY believed unreservedly in the primacy of experience—believed, to be precise, that the emotional response of a person experiencing something was infinitely more important than any matter of fact related to that something in life. Putting it into words was damn near impossible, but acting on it was not. Acting on it made Gemma Bury's life a hundred times easier than it might have been. It saved her a lot of work, too. She believed the conspiracy theories in Oliver Stone's *JFK*—in spite of the distortions everybody else seemed to find in it—because Oliver Stone's *JFK* expressed the way the Kennedy assassination *felt* to her better than the Warren Report. She believed in astrology, too, at least in the sense of thinking that her destiny was at least partially controlled by the stars (and her menstrual cycle by the moon). It didn't matter to her that the stars were not actually in the places that astrologers said they were. Gemma didn't know where astrologers said they were. She didn't know where astronomy said they were, either. It just *felt* right, this connection to the universe, this vast undifferentiated primal muck of space and time. Fortunately, Gemma never seemed to feel anything flagrantly opposed to common sense, such as that gravity wasn't operating one day. She never went tripping out a tenth-story window, trusting the emotions that told her she could float. What she did do was write a lot of theology, both in the seminary and after she came to take up her position as pastor of the Episcopal Church in Bethlehem, Vermont. This theology had a great deal to do with Love, in the twentieth-century use of the term. It also had a great deal to do with sex, but Gemma never put it that way. Gemma thought of herself as a very natural personality. She enjoyed sex the way the ancient Greeks had—as an activity, not an identity—and liked to believe she had a lot in common with the Wife of Bath. What bothered her was that, since the deaths of Tisha Verek and Dinah Ketchum, she was becoming more and more convinced that her parishioners saw her the same way, and that wouldn't do at all. What was really frightening was that they seemed to have known about her affair with Jan-Mark Verek all along. The phone in the rectory had started ringing only minutes after the news of Tisha Verek's death had reached the village, and gone on ringing almost every hour of every day of the two weeks since. It was now two o'clock on the afternoon of Monday, December 16th, and Gemma's head was aching. The little old ladies were driving her crazy, that was the truth. They were also having the time of their lives. Nothing this exciting had happened in Bethlehem since the Great Depression had given the Celebration its start.

There was a big evergreen wreath in the window of Abigail's Fine Cheeses, and Gemma sat behind the wheel of her little Volvo, staring at it and wondering how long she could go on sitting in her car on Main Street before somebody stopped to ask her what was wrong. She'd left the rectory half an hour ago because she hadn't been able to stand the idea of staying in it one more minute. Every time the phone rang, she wanted to scream. Every time Kelley asked her a question, she wanted to scream, too. She hated being around Kelley these days. She had hated it since the conversation they had had just before Tisha's death, but she had begun to hate it more and more afterward. It was all mixed up. What did a philosophy of experience mean if you didn't know what you were experiencing? She didn't want to be near her phone. She didn't want to be near Kelley Grey. She didn't want to be near Jan-Mark, never mind in bed with him, where all she could remember was a hairy, boozed-out torso with sagging skin and too much flesh around the middle. She had driven out there today, before she'd come into town, and ended up parked by the side of the road, nauseated.

Abigail's Fine Cheeses was right across the street from the *Bethlehem News and Mail*. The *Bethlehem News and Mail* was lit up more brightly than the town park and on fire with activity. The *Bethlehem News and Mail* was always like that, even on the day after they put out an issue. Peter Callisher was some kind of throwback to the nineteenth century, a capitalist baron with a stable of wage slaves. Either that, or they were having orgies in there. Gemma Bury thought of Tisha hinting and hinting about the points of resemblance between Tommy Hare and Timmy Hall, and found herself getting nauseated all over again.

If I go on like this I'll never get anything done, Gemma told herself. Then she popped the door to her car and swung her legs out into the road. Main Street had been closed off to traffic at one, as it was on every day when an actual performance of the Nativity play was scheduled. Gemma didn't have to look out for cars or worry about being crushed by a farm vehicle on its way to the Grange. She stretched a little in the cold air and shut the car door behind her. She didn't bother to lock it because nobody but tourists ever locked anything in Bethlehem, Vermont. There were people on the street, but nobody around she knew, which was a blessing.

She crossed the street, walked down the sidewalk on that side very carefully so she wouldn't slip on the patch of black ice that had begun to form on the surface, and then crossed the intersection that brought her to the front door of the *Bethlehem News and Mail.* Main Street was not quite straight. Gemma had to make a little arc to get where she was going, and when she got there and stood on the highest of the concrete steps, she could look back over her shoulder and see the park and the settings for the play as if they were on a distant stage, presented for her amusement. She knew the other place you could do that—the top floor of the Green Mountain Inn. If she'd been interested in the Nativity story, she would have rented one of those rooms and watched the spectacle from above. It was one of the worst drawbacks of living in the rectory that she had no view of the town at all.

She stamped her feet on Peter Callisher's L. L. Bean flying-duck welcome mat, gave herself one more chance to change her mind, and then tried the door. It opened easily, in spite of the magnetic seal Peter had installed to save on heating bills and turn himself at least a light environmental Green. Gemma stepped through into the big room and looked around. Not many people were there. The paper would have been sent to the printers at noon, for distribution tomorrow. Timmy Hall was sweeping up. Amanda Ballard—whom Gemma had cordially hated from the moment they met—was filling out a form at the front desk. Cara Hutchinson was leaning against the counter and babbling. Peter was nowhere to be seen. Gemma shut the door behind her. Cold air had been pouring in around her calves.

"It was just absolutely the most wonderful thing," Cara Hutchinson was saying, presumably to Amanda Ballard, although it was hard to tell. Amanda didn't seem to be paying much attention. She must have been paying some, however, because Gemma could see she was agitated. Amanda was usually very careful to keep the hair over her right ear, so that the lack of earlobe and the stunted little end didn't show, but when she got excited she forgot. She had forgotten now, and had her hair firmly behind both ears.

"You know," Cara told her, "when I went up there today, I was half-convinced he was going to have me pose nude. I mean, he hadn't said anything like that yesterday, but what did that mean? He might have assumed I'd understand. After all, everybody knows about artists. So I went up there and I'd absolutely made up my mind, I really had, that I was going to do it if that was what I was supposed to do. I am going away to college next year. I don't intend to spend all of my life in some backwoods town that doesn't understand Art. Never mind Literature. I was reading *The New York Review of Books* in the library the other day, and you wouldn't believe the stares I got from practically everybody."

"Mmm," Amanda Ballard said.

"Well," Cara took a deep breath, prepared to go on.

Amanda looked up, saw Gemma at the door and put down her pen. Gemma smiled. She did not say what she wanted to say, which was that if "practically everybody" had been staring at Cara Hutchinson in the library the other day, it wasn't because Cara had been reading *The New York Review of Books*. It might have been because Cara was muttering to herself, which Gemma had seen her do when she read, but that was something else again. Amanda was rubbing the side of her neck with the flat of her hand and looking quizzical.

"Gemma," she said. "Cara is Jan-Mark's latest local model."

"So I've gathered," Gemma said.

"It's really been the most wonderful experience," Cara repeated, with a trace of a smirk in her voice that could have been detected by a deaf woman. "He showed me his wife's office. His *late* wife's office. He keeps it like a shrine."

"She was a bad woman," Timmy Hall said suddenly. "She was Evil."

Amanda picked up her pen again. "All right," she said. "I think we all have that established. I'm sorry, Gemma. All anybody ever talks about around here is Tisha and the shootings. And now that Gregor Demarkian is in town—"

"My old ladies keep talking about Gregor Demarkian," Gemma said. "You'd think Peter Falk had arrived to shoot an episode of *Columbo*. Did Franklin Morrison really hire him to look into Tisha Verek's death?"

"You can't hire him," Cara Hutchinson said. "He doesn't take money, except sometimes he asks for donations to some Armenian refugee relief society or this homeless shelter in Philadelphia. The Archdiocese of Colchester gave twenty-five thousand dollars to the homeless shelter last year after all that mess with the nuns being killed around St. Patrick's Day. Or maybe it was one nun. I don't remember. But I'll tell you—"

"He's here to attend the Celebration, just like everybody else," Amanda said, cutting Cara off. "You can read all about it in the paper tomorrow, Gemma. When Peter found out he was here, he put a story right on page one. About his being here, I mean, and with a picture. We tried to get an interview, but it didn't work out."

"He doesn't give interviews," Cara Hutchinson said.

"Did you want to see Peter?" Amanda asked. "He went upstairs to lie down, but he wouldn't mind coming back again. He only lies down when he's bored, anyway. I could call upstairs and get him."

"I wish he'd let me write something for the paper," Cara said. "It wouldn't have to be about Art exactly. I mean, I know that won't sell papers in Bethlehem, Vermont. It could be about Tisha's office and be all hooked in with the shootings. She has the most interesting office, really, with all these pictures in it of children who killed people when they were children and then some pictures of the children grown up. It's very interesting, really."

"Gemma?"

Gemma had been staring at a little collection of Santa's elves on the counter near Amanda's elbow. Cara Hutchinson had always made her eyes glaze over, and this new obsession with Art, Artists and the Artist's Wife just made the situation worse. Gemma straightened up. Since Cara obviously knew that Gemma and Jan-Mark had been having a relationship—since the whole town obviously knew—it ought to have occurred to her that Gemma had been in Jan-Mark's house, and seen Tisha's office, more times than Cara herself ever would, unless Jan-Mark decided to go all French and take up with his own underaged model. Cara was horse-faced and grating and less than half Jan-Mark's age, but Gemma wouldn't put anything at all past the stupid rutting fool. Whether that negated all the hours of deeply spiritual communion she and Jan-Mark had shared together, Gemma didn't know.

"Gemma?" Amanda said again.

"Yes," Gemma answered. "Yes. I'm sorry. I'm very tired. I do want to see Peter. I have something I need to talk over with him."

"I'll call him right down."

"Thank you."

Over on the other side of the office, Timmy Hall was leaning against a broom, contemplating the women set out before him. Gemma watched his gaze move from Amanda to herself to Cara and then pause, frowning furiously, as if what he saw angered him. Gemma sometimes argued in favor of women's intuition—which she translated as "a natural biological affinity for extrasensory perception"—but she didn't need women's intuition or ESP or anything else to tell her what she was seeing now. The way Timmy Hall was looking at Cara Hutchinson made Gemma Bury's blood run cold.

2

CANDY GEORGE didn't know exactly what change had come over her relationship with her husband Reggie, but she did know when the change had started to happen, and it intrigued her. Candy had rehearsed for the part of Mary in the Bethlehem Nativity Celebration play for months. Aside from giving her something else to think about besides her own misery—which was a relief—it hadn't changed anything at all. What had was the experience of her first performance in public before real people. She had expected to be frightened, and she was. She had expected to be paralyzed, but she wasn't. Candy George had indulged in a drug or two over the years, marijuana and beer, cocaine and animal tranquilizers. Sometimes the relentless pressing weight of her life got so bad, drugs were a form of medication, a temporary relief, like the morphine fed in small doses to men whose limbs had to be amputated on battlefields. Sometimes the night terrors got so bad she needed drugs simply to sleep. Night terrors were what she called the half-waking dreams she had, lying at Reggie's side in the dark, neither in this place nor in any other, when her stepfather's hand would come up out of the blackness and reach for the cleft between her legs, the tips of his fingers as rough as sandpaper, the warts on his knuckles hardened into razor-edged marbles made of pumice and steel. She would try to sit up and not be able to. She would try to call out and not be able to. She would tell herself it was a dream and find it made no difference. When it was over, she would get up and go into the kitchen and smoke a couple of joints. If Reggie caught her at it, he would beat her up. Like everything else in the house, the marijuana was supposed to belong to Reggie alone. He was allowed to dole it out but she was not allowed to take it without permission. That was true even of her own clothes. He told her what she could wear in the morning. He told her what to put on before she went to bed. He put his belt across her back if she tried to argue with him.

What had changed on that stage that first night of the Celebration was Candy George's assessment of her possibilities in life, and she didn't think she would ever be the same again. She had heard of heroin highs and cocaine highs and crack euphoria. She had tried heroin and cocaine and crack without ever being able to figure out what everybody else was talking about. Either her body put up too much resistance, or her mind did. That was why she had never become addicted, although a couple of her friends had. That was why she had never become an alcoholic, either, although from everything she'd heard she ought to be one. Her mother was one and her father was one and her stepfather was one and Reggie was definitely on the way. She could easily become addicted to the way she felt on stage. It was like stepping out of her life and into another one, Mary's life. It was like going from being one of those girls who was so little use to anyone she had no right to anything at all, to being the most important woman in the history of creation. That was what her Sunday School teachers had taught her. Candy hadn't paid much attention at the time. Now she thought they must have been right. *From this day all generations shall call me blessed, for God has done great things for me.* Candy had to say that every night right after the angel came to announce the birth of Christ, and from the first night of the first performance she had believed it absolutely. It swelled up in her like a molten silver champagne. It changed the shape of her body and the contents of her mind. It rearranged the bones of her face, so that instead of the ugliness she saw every morning in her mirror, she looked like what Peter Callisher said she looked like. She wasn't particularly religious and didn't want to be. She didn't know if the world was controlled by a benevolent Father, a swirling mass of auras or nothing at all. She didn't much care. All she knew was that somebody somewhere was about to do great things for her, that she was no longer the person she used to be, and that it was only a matter of time. A matter of time for what, she hadn't figured out yet.

Neither had Reggie, but he had figured out that something was different, and therefore wrong, and he had been worrying at it for the whole of the last two weeks. Today he had stayed home sick from work, which he never did, and Candy suspected the reason was the argument she had had yesterday with Cara Hutchinson. In the old days, Candy would never have had an argument of any kind with Cara Hutchinson. She would have let Cara push and push, and if Cara had pushed hard enough and long enough, Candy would have given her what she wanted. Then if Reggie hadn't liked it, *he* would have had the argument with Cara. That was how it was all supposed to happen, but yesterday it hadn't. Yesterday she had told Cara Hutchinson no—in a voice that wasn't too strong and wasn't too firm and wasn't too sane, either, now that she thought about it—and in spite of everything, she felt good about it. The everything she had to feel good about it in spite of included the position she was in now, at three o'clock in the afternoon on Monday, December 16th, and had been in since eight o'clock this morning. Eight o'clock was when Reggie decided she had ruined his breakfast, over-cooked his eggs, undercooked his sausage, turned his coffee into goat's piss. That was when he had leaped up from the table and grabbed the front of the dress he had told her to wear and ripped it right off. His nails had cut into the skin between her breasts and his fingers had caught on the underwire of her bra. Her bra had come off with the front of her dress. The snaps in the back had popped—which had made Reggie even more furious; he hated bras that snapped in back; he preferred the ones that fastened in the front, even though it was hard to get them in Candy's size—and then the metal underwire had come loose and whipped across her nipples like an electric prod. By the time Candy had gotten her breath back, Reggie had gotten his belt off. He was standing over her like a robot sentinel, the belt pulsing through the air like a rattlesnake defying gravity. Reggie grabbed the collar tab on the back of the dress and ripped at that too, tearing what was left of blue cotton and elastic into shreds, bringing the belt down first on Candy's back and then on the back of her legs. Candy knew what it was about. Even in her dizziness she couldn't forget, and usually when she got dizzy enough she forgot everything. Reggie had come to hate having her in that damned Nativity play, but he was stuck. He cared so much about his public image. The police had been called to this house once because of their fighting. He didn't dare do anything to make it obvious they might have been right to come. He was stuck with her in this play and with what being in this play was doing to her, and he hated it.

When it was over, he had made his usual request, demanded the thing he liked to demand above all else. Candy had welts on her back and calves and across her breasts. The dark areas around her nipples felt bitten and swollen and set on fire. Reggie had her put on a small white frilly apron that started at her waist and didn't quite cover her abdomen. Then he had her put on the garter belt he had bought her and the silk stockings and the four-inch spike-heeled shoes. That was the way he had dressed her last year when he had taken the picture he had sent to the "Beaver Hunt" section of *Hustler* magazine. Before he'd set up the camera, he'd made her sit on the table and spread her legs. Candy had always thought of that picture as the very last word on her life, the thing that named her. *You are not a woman,* that picture said. *You are a hole.*

Reggie was lying on the couch in the living room, watching Oprah Winfrey and pretending to have a fever. He wanted a bottle of Molson's Golden Ale and a bowl of potato chips. Candy put them both on a tray and brought them out from the kitchen, moving carefully so she didn't spill anything. Spilling something could get Reggie started all over again, and spilling something would be easy. She had never really learned to walk in these shoes.

Candy put the tray down on the coffee table at Reggie's side. Usually, by this point in one of their bad days, she would be feeling totally washed out, nonexistent, invisible. She would at least be giving herself a mental lecture, telling herself she had to stop being so stupid, had to learn not to provoke him, had to get her act together so she wouldn't do the things that made sessions like this necessary. Today, she wasn't. Today, she was gliding along in total numbness, her body still, her mind silent.

"Do you want anything else I can get you?" she asked Reggie. "We've got sour cream. I could make onion dip."

"Onion dip will give me gas," Reggie said. "I told you I was sick, for Christ's sake. What are you trying to do to me?"

"If you don't need anything else, I'd like permission to go back to the kitchen. The stove needs cleaning."

"*You* need cleaning," Reggie said. "To hell with the stove."

"Do you want me to take a bath?"

"You're going to have to take a bath before you go pretend to be a movie star tonight. If you go looking like you are, they'll probably fire you and find somebody else."

Candy shifted a little on her feet, redistributing the pain. These shoes always hurt. Listening to Reggie talk about the Nativity committee getting someone else for her part panicked her. Candy kept expecting it to happen. She was astounded that it hadn't happened yet.

Reggie stuffed a handful of potato chips in his mouth. "What's that book you left out there in the kitchen? Since when do we have money for you to throw away on trashy paperbacks?"

"We don't," Candy said virtuously. She was lying. She had seen the book in the window of the used-book place on Carrow for days, and finally she'd stolen enough change from Reggie's pockets to buy it. "I borrowed it from the reading room over at the Congregational Church the time we went there to rehearse because they were putting on some children's thing in the auditorium. It's something to do when I'm waiting around backstage."

"Why do you need something to do?"

"Because it's boring. Just sitting there, I mean."

"Why don't you talk to people? It's just too damn bad this happened to you instead of me. You're too stupid to make anything out of it. Practically everybody important in town is in that play or has something to do with it. If it was me, I'd get to know them. I'd get myself a few opportunities."

"You're not supposed to talk backstage when the play is going on," Candy said, "and all they ever talk about between acts is the shootings. I don't have anything to say about the shootings."

"You don't have anything to say about anything. It's too damn bad. It really is. It's just too damn bad. I wish I was the one who'd shot 'em, though. I wouldn't have bothered old Dinah Ketchum. I'd have gone straight for those two dykes down the road."

"Everybody in the play says it was Jan-Mark Verek getting rid of his wife so he could marry that Gemma Bury who's the priest now at the Episcopal Church. They're supposed to be very much in love."

Reggie stuffed more potato chips into his mouth and followed them with a swig of beer. "Love crap. She's an old bag. His wife was an old bag, too, but why kill one old bag for another?"

"I don't know."

"I know something," Reggie said. He sat up and reached for his belt. He had left it draped over the back of the couch, in case he needed it, in case he could think of some other use for it. Candy felt her stomach turn over and her mind go blank.

"You know what I know?" Reggie said. "I know how I like to see you best when you're wearing that stuff."

"Yes," Candy said.

"Hands and knees," Reggie said. "On the floor."

"Yes."

"When I get done with this, I'm going to take you just like a dog," Reggie said. "Just like a dog. That's all you are anyway, you stupid bitch. Just a dog."

"Yes," Candy said again, and thought: *The carpet needs cleaning. It's supposed to be green and now it looks like swamp.*

In the air above the back of her the belt was whistling and screaming, really screaming, as if it were alive. It was talking to her and she could hear every word it said. *You asked for it. You always ask for it. You're so stupid and so bad, if you didn't have somebody like Reggie to do this for you you'd go straight to hell, just straight to hell, because you're bad, you're evil, you're rotted right to the core and if a doctor had to cut you open all he'd find was pus and stink.*

That was what the belt was saying, but oddly enough, for once it wasn't what Candy's conscious mind was saying as well. Candy's conscious mind was on a tangent of its own, and what it was telling her was this:

It was a damned good thing that Reggie couldn't read too well, because if he could, and if he read the back of that paperback book she had left sitting on the kitchen table, he would probably kill her, in self-defense.

The name of that book was *The Burning Bed,* and it was all about a woman whose husband had beat her up and beat her up and beat her up day after day and year after year until one night when he'd passed out dead drunk on the bed, she doused him with gasoline and lit a match.

s e v e n

1

YEARS AGO, just after the Second World War, when the money had first started really rolling in, the citizens of Bethlehem, Vermont, had had an argument about the seating for the Nativity play. From the beginning, the Nativity play had been staged in the town park with the gazebo as the stable. From the beginning, people coming to watch had stood along the park's edges in the cold, their heads covered with thick woolen hats and their ears straining to hear whatever they could. It was a kind of theater in the round *gigantus*. Some of the people in Bethlehem wanted to leave this as it was. People had been coming and standing for over a dozen years and would probably come and stand for over a dozen more. One citizens' committee had insisted on the construction of a bandshell with poured-concrete audience tiers. They envisioned busloads of tourists from Delaware and Ohio, all in search of the post-War definition of reasonable American comfort. They envisioned Bethlehem ringed by discreetly placed motels, Howard Johnsons taking up the slack when the inns in town couldn't provide the New American with the New American idea of plumbing. A third group wanted to do something sensible, but not drastic. Obviously, the crowds were getting out of hand. They couldn't just go on letting people crowd along the edges of the park. There were too many of them, and too many of them were from Away. People pushed. People shouted and got angry. People drank. The Nativity play needed an organizing principle, and what that organizing principle was was this: a set of collapsible bleachers with a canvas tent shield and portable space heaters, combined with a very sophisticated sound system that included spot mikes and strategically placed speakers. It was elaborate, unwieldy, ridiculous and expensive as all hell, but it worked, and the town stuck with it. By the time Gregor Demarkian was making his way from the Green Mountain Inn to the center of town in the company of Bennis Hannaford and Father Tibor Kasparian, on his way to the first night of his first performance of the Bethlehem nativity play, it had become a town tradition. The original collapsible bleachers had been replaced with new ones that included cushioned benches. The original canvas tent shield had been replaced with one especially designed for the Celebration and including air vents and low-noise fans to blow the heat from the space heaters upward at the people who needed to be warmed. The new sound system had benefited from decades of experimentation by rock musicians and the CIA. That was frosting. The Bethlehem Nativity Celebration had always been the transformation of the center of a small New England town into the center of a small Palestinian one. It always would be.

The collapsible bleachers were divided into six sections with natural aisles in between. Each section was split in the middle by a makeshift stair, so that older patrons didn't have to climb the bleachers like monkeys or junior high school students. The natural aisle at the very northernmost part of the park, the one nearest Carrow Street, was triple the width of all the others. Coming into his own set of bleachers, just to the left, Gregor could see the dark shapes of animals shifting and shuddering at the far end of it. Tibor, who had been so interested in how and where the animals would come, now seemed not interested at all. He plodded along behind Bennis with an air of leaden pessimism, the black skirt of his cassock brushing against the snow. Leading them, Bennis kept referring to their tickets and muttering to herself. Gregor thought it was a good thing. He had gotten back to the Inn just after lunch, his pockets stuffed with notes and a crudely reproduced map of what he and Franklin Morrison had begun to call "the problem." He had been trying ever since to talk it over with somebody. At first, he had been alone, deserted by Bennis and Tibor, who had gone off to listen to Christmas carols or check out the souvenir stores or something. Then he had been in the midst of too much activity, with Bennis and Tibor getting back late and scurrying to get ready to leave in time, with Tibor mumbling about everything Bennis had and hadn't eaten, with Bennis panicking because she couldn't remember where she'd put the tickets or the program or her reading glasses or her cigarettes or anything else. Now, of course, they were filing in to see the Nativity play, which would effectively cut off conversation for the next two hours. Gregor thought it was typical. When he didn't want to talk about crime or cases or bloody murder, Tibor and Bennis were all over him like feathers, probing and prodding, driving him crazy. When he did want to talk about them, they had something else to do.

Up at the front of their single-file line, Bennis had stopped, checked their tickets again and started to turn. "This is it," she said. "Second row up. No problem at all. I'm going to have to do something really spectacular for Robert Forsman to pay him back for this."

"Please," Tibor said, "Bennis, listen to me. Nothing too spectacular."

"I was thinking of sending him a nice inscribed Rolex watch." Bennis gestured at the bleachers. "Twenty-one, twenty-two and twenty-three. Next row up. You want to climb or use the stairs?"

"I will use the stairs."

The "stairs" were slightly modified, closed-fronted bleacher slats in the center of the stand. Gregor watched Bennis watch Tibor walk over to them, step up one step, and start coming down the bleacher back to them. Then she climbed to the second row herself and shook her head.

"It's been crazy all day," she told Gregor. "He keeps trying to make me eat. I mean, he's always trying to make me eat, they all do, that's half of what Cavanaugh Street is all about, but not like this. We went to this little performance the grade school was giving and I ate six of these enormous chocolate chip cookies—the size of dinner plates, Gregor, I'm not kidding—and he kept trying to make me eat two more. And then when I wouldn't, he got *mad* at me."

"Mmm," Gregor said.

"I think it's the stress," Bennis told him. "I always did think he was under too much pressure. I just hadn't realized how far it had gone."

"I have seen the camels," Tibor said, seating himself between Bennis standing on their own bleacher and Gregor standing on the ground. "We are right where the animals come, it is very good. I still cannot see where they come from in town."

"There's a field back there somewhere," Bennis said brightly.

Tibor ignored her.

Gregor climbed up, sat down, and decided to remove his coat. In spite of the fact that it was more than fairly cold outside—the forecast was for snow and more snow over the next three days—in the bleachers it was actually warm. The space heaters and the fans and the specially made tent with its air flaps worked. Gregor looked across the park and saw that now that he was sitting down, one of the two stands of tall evergreen bushes effectively cut off most of his view of the animal passage. Since he didn't want to see the animals coming in and out anyway, he didn't worry about it.

Gregor got his little map out of his pocket, unfolded it on his knees and waited. Bennis sat down, looked at Tibor and finally turned to Gregor. She had to talk over Tibor's head, but there was nothing for it. Tibor was staring glumly in the direction of the gazebo, ignoring them both. The gazebo was lit up with colored spotlights and dressed in distressed wood and evergreens. Gregor didn't think it looked much like Palestine, but he did think it looked nicer than it had the day before, when it had apparently been in some kind of rest state. The whole town had apparently been in some kind of rest state. Now it looked energized.

Gregor held his map up, looked around to see that they were still more or less alone, and decided that Tibor and Bennis had once again made him much too early for something he had only wanted to be on time for. Tibor was bad, but Bennis was the worst Gregor had ever known. She had once gotten him to the dentist forty-five minutes before his appointment. He waved the map in the air and acquiesced when Bennis reached out to take it.

"It's very nice," she said politely. "You're learning to draw better. Donna would be proud of you."

"Yesterday you were chomping at the bit for some sort of mystery," Gregor told her. "Today, all you can do is insult my drawing."

Bennis handed the map back. "I don't understand why it's such a mystery. Now all that about the guns. What were you saying back at the Inn? Both of them took two hits, in the shoulder and the neck. That seems like a mystery to me. Do you suppose it was some kind of gangland hit?"

"In Bethlehem, Vermont?"

Bennis shrugged. "It sounds like that sort of thing. With the two guns, I mean. I suppose I don't understand why any ordinary person would have two guns."

"To make the deaths look unrelated?" Gregor suggested.

"Well, yes, Gregor, I understand that. But you wouldn't think of it, would you? I mean, if you were a normal person."

Gregor was about to say that if you were a normal person, you wouldn't kill two people in cold blood on a bright shiny morning at the beginning of December, but that wasn't fair, and he knew it. What

Franklin Morrison had told him had made him a little uneasy, but it had fallen far short of convincing him that Bethlehem had a pair of premeditated murders on its hands. The similarity of the wounds was bad, but there was still no motive to be found, or at least no motive that he liked. Franklin liked defense of the Nativity Celebration. The townspeople he talked to liked Jan-Mark Verek at the end of his rope. Nobody had the faintest idea why anybody would want to kill Dinah Ketchum—and yet, if there was going to be grounds for a murder investigation here, that was precisely the person who had to have been murdered. Without that, Bethlehem might have had a murder—the murder of Tisha Verek—but unless something more definite showed up than what they already had, they wouldn't have a murder investigation. Gregor had read dozens of novels in which the fictional detective had had a lot less to go on than Franklin Morrison had here, and yet had gone on to bring a murderer to justice, but life wasn't like that. You had to have someplace to start. Gregor handed the map back to Bennis, insisting.

"Look at this," he said. "Look at it carefully. Those little bubble things on the lines are stone walls."

Bennis held the map in her hands and stared at it dutifully.

"Well," she said. "So what?"

Gregor reached over Tibor and tapped the map at the place it said "Episcopal Church property." Tibor didn't appear to notice.

"The state police," Gregor said, "argued for two different gunmen causing two different hunting accidents for a number of reasons, but one of them was time. They said that there was no time for one person to have stolen a gun from Stuart Ketchum's house, shot Tisha Verek, and then gotten to Dinah Ketchum and shot her, too—"

"I thought they didn't know what time this Dinah Ketchum was shot," Bennis said. "That was in the paper."

"I know, but all that means is that they're not sure in which order and all the rest of it. The two women were shot close enough together to present no differences in forensic examination even after having been discovered very close to the times of their deaths. Therefore the time differential can't be huge."

"Yes, but Gregor, you're still talking about—"

"Bennis, I know. My feeling is that the state police were looking for any excuse they could find not to call these two deaths murders— at least, that's my feeling now that I've seen what Franklin Morrison had to show me—but there's nothing to say I'm right. It's not like this

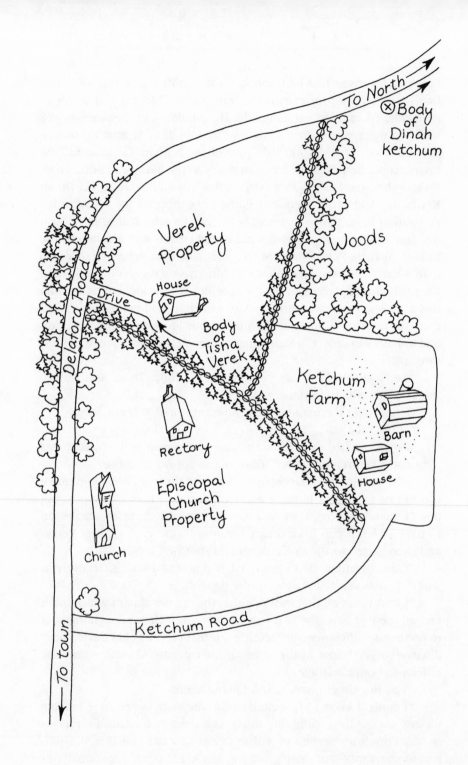

To North

⊗ Body of Dinah Ketchum

Verek Property

Woods

House

Drive

Delaford Road

Body of Tisha Verek

Ketchum Farm

Barn

Rectory

House

Episcopal Church Property

Church

To town

Ketchum Road

was a poisoning, where I would have some specialized knowledge. Franklin Morrison doesn't have any specialized knowledge at all. So we went looking for an explanation even a idiot couldn't shake and we found one. Look at the walls."

"I'm looking."

"According to Franklin, the stone walls are lined on both sides by tall evergreen trees, but the walls themselves are the broad flat kind, not the pudding-stone bumpy sort that tend to be narrow. Delaford Road is lined with trees on both sides, too, and very wooded for several feet in off the shoulder anyplace past the Ketchum Road turnoff and for maybe half a mile or so before. All anybody would have had to have done was to park out of sight in the trees across the road from where the stone wall and the Verek driveway meet the Delaford Road close together, walk up the wall to the Ketchum house, steal a gun, and walk back again along the wall. Whoever it was could have been fairly sure of not being seen, at least according to Franklin. The trees would have provided good cover and the time of day would have ensured there wasn't much to need cover from. There was no snow on the ground. The barnyard around the Ketchum house is dirt, and the ground had been more or less stiff with frost for weeks. When it's all over, he gets back in his car—"

"But Gregor, it's crazy. Why go to all that trouble? And where did he find Dinah Ketchum? He couldn't have left her in his car and then toted her out another—how far along the Delaford Road?"

"Six miles. Don't trust my scale."

"I wouldn't," Bennis said. "If you really want to know the truth, I think this sounds nutsier than what I was telling you yesterday. And you accuse me of having a whodunit mentality."

"I know," Gregor said, "but there's a problem."

"What's that?"

"If one person was responsible for both those shootings—and I know why Franklin Morrison wants that to be true; the hits are mind-numbing any other way—then whoever did it had to go through the process I've just described to you at some point."

"You mean it could have been two separate hunting accidents, or one double murder, but it couldn't have been two hunting accidents caused by the same person."

"There's always the town's favorite explanation," Gregor said. "It could have been one hunting accident and one murder."

"But you don't like that."

"Do you?"

"Since when have you ever considered my opinions on law enforcement to have any more validity than a rogue troll's?"

"I'm talking about common sense here, Bennis. When you put your mind to it, you have a great deal of common sense. Apply that common sense to this. One hit to the shoulder. One hit to the neck—to the throat, to be precise."

"Gregor—"

On the seat between them, Tibor stirred. While Bennis and Gregor had been talking, and not noticing, Tibor had been shedding layers of clothes, all from beneath his cassock. His sweater had come off first, then his flannel shirt, then a pair of thick cashmere mufflers. He now looked twenty pounds lighter than he had when they had arrived, and strangely depleted. His chest had gone from convex to concave.

Down in the park there was a great deal of movement, a shifting of lights, a flurry of men and women in thick woolen robes and rope cinctures getting in place. Gregor looked up to see two women taking their places to Bennis's right. One of them was relatively young but not very attractive. Her hair was dark and her look was sullen. The other had to be in her late thirties or early forties, with salt-and-pepper hair and tiny crease lines at the corners of her eyes. She was not sullen at all, and the thick, brightly colored wool of her coat—tangerine orange, for God's sake—spoke of serious money. The unattractive sullen one sat down, shucked her parka and stared resolutely out into the park. The one in the tangerine orange coat looked the three of them over and smiled. Gregor knew that smile. It was the smile of a woman who had read last week's paper.

"How wonderful," the woman in the tangerine coat said. "A seat so close to Peter Callisher's favorite person, Gregor Demarkian."

"Say it louder, why don't you?" the sullen one said. "Maybe you can talk the crowd into making life perfectly miserable for him."

"I hope I'm not trying to make life perfectly miserable for anyone," the one in the tangerine coat said. Then she held out her hand to Bennis Hannaford. "I'm Gemma Bury. I'm the priest at the Episcopal Church here. This is my assistant, Kelley Grey."

"Bennis Hannaford," Bennis said.

"It says here they take down the bleachers every night and put them up again every evening," Tibor said, biting his lip as he stared at his brochure. "If you're the Episcopal priest here, you must live in town. You must know."

"Know what?" Gemma Bury was puzzled.

"Why they take the bleachers down and put them up again all the time."

"Oh. Well, that's because if they don't, there are people in town who complain that they can't use the park, and tourists who complain that the bleachers make the place look less like New England, and all kinds of things. It makes things a lot simpler just to take them down and put them up."

"I do not think simpler is the word for it," Tibor said. "I do not think it is simple at all. It shows a lack of cooperation that is not a good sign for the enterprise."

Gemma Bury raised an eyebrow. "Is that what this is, an enterprise?"

"To Father Tibor, almost everything is an enterprise." Gregor Demarkian nodded politely at Gemma Bury and waited, but nothing happened. Gemma did not seem inclined to pursue this or any other conversation. She took a brochure of her own out of one of her voluminous pockets and flipped it open. "This is going to be very interesting," she said. "I've never actually seen the Nativity play before. I've always meant to go, but I've just never had the chance. I've always thought the Christian Nativity myth was one of the more beautiful stories to come down to us from the ancient world."

"Winter solstice," Tibor muttered under his breath.

After that, it might have gotten sticky, but fortunately there wasn't enough time. The bustle around them had grown louder as people arrived from the inns and motels and buses, all looking frantically for their seats. The noise from the center of the park grew louder, too. A huge cluster of children ranging in age from about three to about ten— as far as Gregor could tell—had gathered to the side of the gazebo and begun to sing. The words floated in the air above them all like a benediction.

"O little town of Bethlehem, how still we see thee lie."

Tibor pulled a brown paper bag out of his cassock pocket and handed it to Bennis.

"Here," he said. "This is chocolate cake, Bennis, very good. I had it sent up with room service. Eat it and it will make up for you because you have not had any dinner."

Gregor folded his arms across his chest and let himself drift into the sound of children's voices, Christmas music, thoughts of Gemma Bury and her odes to the winter solstice, anything at all—as long as he didn't have to let himself think about Tibor thinking about Bennis's diet. Assuming that Bennis was on a diet.

It was impossible.

2

GREGOR DEMARKIAN had heard a great deal about the Bethlehem Nativity play over the years, and a great deal more over the last few weeks, and he knew that it was supposed to be much like the Passion play staged every ten years at Oberammergau, only more frequent. The point of such a comparison was to indicate that the production was professionally done, of a quality more likely to be found on Broadway or in London's West End than in a small hamlet in Vermont. Reflection would have made it clear that that was necessary. No rankly amateur production could have attracted the crowds this one consistently did, not even with the rest of the town thrown in for atmosphere. According to the brochure, the play had had the same director for the last ten years, who had apprenticed with the previous director for ten years before that. It was all very well put together and carefully planned, with spontanaeity limited to the fringe operations and the naturally effervescent enthusiasms of local craftspeople presented with a captive buying public. For some reason, none of this seemed to have sunk into Gregor Demarkian's brain. The play ended up shocking him—with its power, with its elegance, with its flawlessness. It helped that most of the words had come from the King James Version instead of some earnest playwright's pen, and that the young girl playing Mary was so luminous. At one point during the Annunciation, Gregor thought Mary was actually going to float. She seemed naturally farther above the ground than the young man playing the angel. She moved with a slightly stiff, slightly awkward grace that gave her infinite dignity. Gregor almost found himself falling in love with her the way he had once fallen in love with the women in the movies he had seen as a child, sitting in a darkened place far from home and spiritually transported to another dimension. The livestock and histrionics came and went without affecting him. He found it hard to pay attention to anything else when Mary was in sight, whether she was speaking at the moment or not.

Standing up at the intermission—there was only one, fifty minutes after the play's start, lasting twenty minutes, giving anyone who wanted to a chance to use the portable bathrooms that had been set up in a vacant lot on a side street near the Carrow Street intersection—Gregor found Tibor just as enthralled as he was, so that it hardly mattered that Bennis was not.

"She is just the way I would have expected the Holy Virgin to be," Tibor said, nodding solemnly, "except that she is blonde and a girl of that place and time would not have been. But that is all right. It is the way she moves. It is a combination of vulnerability and invincibility. It is a miracle."

"It is an injury," Bennis said cynically. "She's hurt."

"What are you talking about?" Gregor demanded.

"She's hurt," Bennis repeated. "It's her back. Don't look at me like that. I've thrown my back out often enough. I ski. That's how you move when your back hurts when you walk. Assuming you can move at all."

"People in town say her husband beats her," Gemma Bury broke in pleasantly. "It's terrible what goes on in places like this. It's the ultimate American disease."

Tibor glared at her and began to tromp off across the bleachers in search of a bathroom or some peace and quiet. Losing him in the crowd, Gregor followed Bennis onto Main Street and picked up a sausage-and-cheese calzone from a truck that said "Gus Petrakis's Mother's Greek-Italian Cooking." There was another truck across the street that said "Eat the Healthful Chinese Way." Both trucks had plastic Christmas bells and drummer boys and colored packages strung up around their open serving windows. Gregor wondered where they came from. Biting into the calzone, Gregor sent up a prayer that Gus Petrakis's mother delivered to the Green Mountain Inn, or was at least close enough to walk to from there. It was the first decent food he'd had since getting to Vermont.

Back at their seats, Gregor rearranged things so that Tibor was farther away from Gemma Bury than he had been, mixing things up so that Gregor ended up next to Gemma himself. Gemma smiled at him and gestured toward the park, where a thin blonde woman was walking away, tugging at her hair as she went. Gregor thought she would have looked like Alice in Wonderland if it hadn't been for the odd stunting of her right ear.

"Amanda Ballard," Gemma said pleasantly. "Peter Callisher's lady friend. Do you know Peter Callisher?"

Gregor only knew of Peter Callisher, so he made a strangled noise and looked apprehensively at Tibor, who was glaring at them. Tibor had come back to the bleachers with a hand full of knishes, and as the lights began to dim again, he shoved them into Bennis's lap.

"These are kosher, Bennis, you should try them. When He was alive in Palestine, in Israel, I don't know what to call it, when He was alive the Christ Himself would have eaten food that was kosher."

"The Christ Himself would have been hungry," Bennis told him.

"Shh," Gregor said.

And, remarkably, they did shush, both of them, for the time being, so that Gregor was able to lose himself once again in Mary and the story of her pregnancy. Before this, he wouldn't have said a pregnancy could have been so interesting, unless it was being undergone by his own wife carrying his own child, and Elizabeth had been dead now for over four years. Even if she had been alive, she would have been in her fifties. Did they have the technology to produce pregnancies in fifty-year-old women these days? Did fifty-year-old women want to have pregnancies produced in themselves? Sometimes Gregor got thoroughly tired of the twentieth century. It was so damned confusing.

He did not get thoroughly tired of the play, which took the story only to the wedding of Mary and Joseph, long before they knew they would have to go to Bethlehem for the census. It ought to have been interminable, but it was not, because whoever had written the script had turned the story into one about the hiding of an untimely pregnancy in a harsh and unforgiving world. The wedding came as a relief in the way that the cavalry came as a relief at the end of John Wayne movies. For a while, you almost thought it wasn't going to work out.

When the lights went up again, Gregor stood and stretched and grinned and decided this had not been such a bad idea after all. Then, thinking that he could have been more gracious, and besides it was Christmas, he turned to say something nice to Gemma Bury, in spite of how Tibor was inevitably going to feel about it. He leaned over, tapped her on the shoulder of her tangerine orange coat and said, "It's a magnificent production, isn't it? Entirely remarkable."

That was when Gemma Bury slid sideways, into Kelley Grey's uninviting lap, and her head fell back across Kelley's knees and onto the bench on the other side. At that moment it was all clearly visible.

The wound in the shoulder, half-hidden by the thickness and the color of the coat.

The wound in the throat.

Gemma Bury was dead.

PART twO

But in the dark night
shineth
The everlasting light ...

1

LATER, THEY WORKED out how it could have happened—how she could have sat there for nearly an hour, with nobody knowing she was dead. That it had been almost an hour was something Gregor was sure of from the moment he had discovered the death. Each act of the Bethlehem Nativity play took exactly fifty minutes, with that long twenty-minute break in between. Gregor knew Gemma Bury had been alive for at least part of the intermission. He had spoken to her and she had spoken back when he and Bennis returned to their seats after he'd bought his calzone. Gregor also knew Gemma could not have been killed during the second act of the play. The play had been absorbing, but nothing could be that absorbing, not to him, not after twenty years with the Federal Bureau of Investigation. If he had been sitting in his bleacher seat, staring straight ahead at the performance going on in the gazebo, in relative quiet, with nothing going on to distract him, he would at least have felt the impact. Bodies hit by bullets shudder and jump, even if death is so close to instantaneous that the dying makes no noise. Gregor had felt that shudder and jump three times in his life—once when he was in the army, twice when he was on kidnapping detail for the Bureau. There was nothing on earth like it. He would have recognized the feeling in his sleep.

As for the sound of the gun, that was an easier thing. Gregor suspected they would find the remains of a homemade silencer somewhere, meaning a raw potato that had been stuck at the open end of the barrel of the gun—or maybe rifle, in this case. A raw potato was a dangerous silencer to use, because guns as often blew up as had their noise muffled by the method, but if you were in a hurry or didn't want to call attention to yourself, it was the kind of thing you might decide was worth the making do. If the killing had occurred when Gregor thought it had, that would have made it easier, too. The park was anything but quiet during intermissions. Even a minute or two after the lights were dimmed, there was noise: talking, giggling, rustling, shushing. Before the lights were dimmed, Christmas carols played loudly and enthusiastically from the loudspeakers. The sound made by a small-caliber gun—or a small-caliber rifle—would have been negligible. Gregor gave a long thoughtful look to the tall stand of evergreen bushes near the animal corridor and then returned his attention to Gemma Bury.

The reason Gemma hadn't fallen over was that she had been propped up by her large canvas tote bag, occupying the stretch of bench directly between Gregor and herself. Her back had been resting against the edge of the bleacher behind her, forcing the two women back there to do their best not to smash their knees into her head. At least, that was what the two women said when Franklin Morrison questioned them, as he questioned everybody in the immediate vicinity, as soon as he arrived at the scene. Gregor was impressed. The Bethlehem Nativity Celebration was important to the town. Everybody had been telling him that since he got here, and before. Gregor thought any other small-town cop would have done his best to cover up and tone down—to hustle the tourists out, to hide the fact that a murder had been committed, to do everything possible not to upset the paying customers. Instead, Franklin had gotten his Mobile Crime Unit and his regular deputy and his three special deputies and the Dempsey boy from MIT and had gone to work.

The Dempsey boy from MIT was, in fact, Asian. His name had originally been something Franklin couldn't remember, but his parents had changed it as soon as they'd come to the United States from Cambodia. The Dempsey boy was sixteen years old, more American than Mickey Mouse, and the single most intelligent human being Gregor had ever met. Gregor Demarkian was not subject to many cultural stereotypes, except about Armenians, which, because he was an Armenian-American, didn't count. He had known dozens of Asian men and women in his career, and he knew they were not all cookie-cutter academic achievement clones. Quite a few of them had been gangsters in the old-fashioned use of the term. Quite a few others had been drug lords. A fair number of prostitutes. This one might have been the prototype from which the myth of Asian intelligence had been manufactured. He liked to be called Demp. That was because his real name was Jack.

"My father did it on purpose," he had told Gregor this afternoon, soon after they had been introduced. "My father said Jack Dempsey was a great fighter and if I had his name I would be a great fighter, too. He said I was going to need it. I love the old man, but if you want to know the truth, I think all that refugeeing made him cracked."

Now he moved carefully through the snow-encrusted grass under the bleachers, looking for spent bullets and calling up to Gregor as he went. Franklin was in the middle of the park, talking to more people. Bennis and Tibor were sitting with Kelley Grey only a few feet away. In the sky, the stars looked bright and hard and hostile. Eternity looked black.

"I'm looking for twenty-twos," Demp called up, "because anything much bigger than that would have caused a lot of damage to the body and probably done some damage to the bleachers or the ground or the tent as well. That's the thing about bullets. You don't need a big caliber to kill a man—or woman either, of course—but it's a lot harder to do any kind of serious physical damage. I mean—"

"I know what you mean," Gregor said. "Tell me about trajectory. Can you figure out where the bullets came from, once you find them?"

"I can try. Wait. No. That's a marble. There must have been some kid in about the fifth row spilling marbles out of his pocket. Anyway, yeah, I can probably work that out for you if I get a little help—and when the staties get here, they'll try it, too—but I think what you were saying before was right. I think it had to be sometime in the intermission before the seats were all filled up again. Either that, or whoever's doing the shooting is really nuts."

"Of course whoever's doing the shooting is really nuts," Franklin Morrison said, coming up out of nowhere. "What the hell else could he be?"

"Nuts and lucky," Gregor told him, moving aside to give the chief room to sit down. "Whoever it was could have fired into the crowd meaning to get Gemma Bury or somebody else and gotten only Gemma Bury—could have just by accident not managed to hit any innocent bystanders."

"Nobody is that lucky," Franklin Morrison objected. "And nobody is that good, either. You never know what a bullet is going to do once it gets inside a body. I don't care what kind of killing-machine dream hit men show up in the latest spy-for-hire movies. There isn't a man on earth who could put a bullet into someone and know for a certainty it wasn't going to hit a stray bone or not hit anything and come out the other end and kill a passing dog."

"Have you talked to everybody?" Gregor asked him.

Franklin nodded glumly and looked back out into the middle of the park, still surrounded by tented bleachers. Out on Main Street, the church clocks were ticking toward midnight. Gregor didn't think there was far to go.

"Nobody heard anything," Franklin told him, "and nobody saw anything, either, and nobody is going to, if you ask me. I suppose they're all telling the truth to an extent. I can't believe anybody would have seen somebody aiming a firearm across the park and not done anything about it or said anything about it or anything else. I can't believe she sat there dead for so long and you didn't notice, but there it is. You're sure that's how it happened?"

"It has to be how it happened," Gregor repeated, "both because of what I told you before—I really would have noticed, during the play—and because of what we've just been talking about. Nobody is that good or that lucky. If the bullet didn't exit from the body and hit something or somebody else, especially somebody else, the chances are there wasn't anybody to hit. Bennis and Tibor and I were talking about knishes just before the lights went down. It had to have happened then."

"There weren't people on the bleachers behind you then?"

"Not many," Gregor said, "and not those two women. People wander back late. You know how it is."

"I know how it is. The actors hate it."

"I can just imagine."

"Got one," Demp said from underneath them. His hand snaked up through the slats and he felt around for his black leather instrument case. It looked like a doctor's bag, but not quite, so that it gave Gregor the uneasy feeling that it had been designed for a quack. He picked it up and put it in Demp's hand.

"Thanks," Demp said.

Franklin Morrison looked glum. "Whoever it was took an awful chance, even so. It's like he didn't care. You know it's got to be somebody in town. You know it does—"

Gregor frowned. "The first two happened on the first day of the Celebration. I don't know if you can rule out a stranger yet."

"I can rule out a stranger," Franklin said grimly. "This is the third one looks just the same and everybody dead has been somebody in town—"

"Tisha Verek wasn't from town," Gregor said.

"No," Franklin admitted, "and Gemma wasn't, either, but she was an Episcopal priest. I mean, no matter how nuts the Episcopalians have gotten lately, a priest is still a priest. Although I got to say, I like your priest a lot better than I liked Gemma. Anyway. Dinah Ketchum was from town. Never in her life been out of it except to go shopping down-state or to have her gallbladder removed over to Mary Hitchcock in New Hampshire. Nobody would have wanted Dinah Ketchum dead if they weren't from town."

"Maybe nobody did," Gregor said. "Maybe that much of the local speculation is right. Maybe Tisha Verek was deliberately killed—and now Gemma Bury, too—but Dinah Ketchum's death was the result of an accident."

"Tisha Verek was killed with Stuart Ketchum's gun," Franklin said.

"Stuart Ketchum's guns are in the back of his farmhouse in a room open to anyone who wants to walk in," Gregor told him.

Franklin gave Gregor a fishy look. "Do you really believe all this horse manure?"

Gregor sighed. "No, of course I don't," he said. "And I'm talking through my hat, anyway, because all I know is what you've told me and what I read in the paper, which isn't much. I haven't really seen anything for myself except for what Demp showed me this afternoon, and I've already told you how bad I am with forensic evidence. I'm just trying to work it out logically. You're going to have to call the state police in eventually—"

"Maybe I'll skip it."

"—and I want you to have your arguments ready. Actually, what I really want to do is go over and talk to Kelley Grey. Tibor's been trying to stuff her full of food for more than an hour now and she's probably ready to scream. Besides, there are a few things I'd like to talk to her about."

"I've already talked to her," Franklin said.

"I know. Now I want to talk to her myself."

Franklin gave Gregor a long and suspicious look—unjustifiably, Gregor thought, since it had been Franklin's idea to bring Gregor into this mess to begin with—but when Gregor stood up Franklin didn't try to stop him. Gregor had lost his gloves, he didn't know where. He was always losing his gloves. He shoved his hands in his pockets and looked down the bleachers at Bennis and Tibor and Kelley Grey.

"I think," he said, very slowly and very calmly, because he didn't want to drop a bomb on Franklin Morrison's head just moments before he walked away, "that what we'd better do right now is concentrate on motive. I mean, we had better hope there is a motive. Because if there isn't a motive, by which I mean a motive in the ordinary sense—"

"Oh, hell," Franklin Morrison said.

"I'm bringing it up," Demp said. "Hey, Franklin. Guess what. It's a .22-caliber bullet for a Browning."

"A Browning," Franklin marvelled. "Oh, double *shit*."

2

FROM THE MOMENT they had first met, Gregor Demarkian had had trouble focusing on Kelley Grey. There was something about the young woman that slipped away from him, something inside her that seemed to will itself into invisibility. It wasn't her plainness. One of the most arresting women Gregor had ever met had cheerfully called herself "plain as sin" and been accurate in her assessment, but she'd been one of those women you couldn't take your eyes off nevertheless, and she had never walked into a room and sunk into the woodwork. Kelley Grey was a woodwork inhabitant, an occupant of the fringes, and with the attitude she seemed to be taking to everything, Gregor thought she'd be living on the outside for a long time. He reminded himself that he knew nothing about her attitude in general, on a day-to-day basis. This might have been a night when she was angry at Gemma Bury or upset about something personal he couldn't begin to guess. He watched her with Bennis and Tibor as he came down the bleachers and couldn't make up his mind. Kelley Grey wasn't behaving like one thing or another. She wasn't behaving at all. She was just sitting there, watching, while Bennis and Tibor talked to each other.

Out across the park at the gazebo, the movements had changed, the flow of traffic had switched directions. Franklin Morrison's deputies were bringing their investigations to a close, at least temporarily. Someone—Gregor hoped it was Franklin—had given the stage hands permission to strike the set. The three donkeys that had served for verisimilitude were already gone. Gregor supposed permission for them to leave had been given early, on the assumption that there was no point in subjecting a lot of innocent animals to cold and wind to no good purpose.

Gregor picked up the brown paper bag Tibor had brought back to the second act full of knishes and carried it down the bleachers to where the three of them were sitting, not far away but huddled together, in spite of the fact that the bleachers were still more than warm. Nobody had turned off the space heaters in this section. Nobody looked likely to any time soon. Gregor didn't even know where his coat was.

Gregor reached Bennis and Tibor and Kelley Grey by coming up behind Tibor's back. He could see the side of Bennis's face but not the look in her eyes. He could hear Tibor talking in that low, oddly cadenced voice of his, so altered by so many different accents it now sounded all-purpose "foreign," rather than of any particular ethnic variation.

"I have only your very best interests at heart," he was saying. "I have only the thinking about you which is what matters. I do not fuss. I am not Hannah Krekorian. I am very scientific."

In Gregor Demarkian's opinon, Father Tibor Kasparian was about as scientific as a novel by Robert Heinlein, but that was neither here nor there. Gregor knew what had been going on in this group while he'd been talking to Demp and Franklin Morrison. He caught Kelley Grey's eye and watched her raise a single eyebrow into her hairline. He knew only one other person on earth who could do that, and that was Bennis Hannaford. He thought that by this time in this night's series of Father Tibor lectures, Bennis had to be mentally asleep.

Gregor tapped Tibor on the shoulder. "Excuse me," he said. "I want to talk to Miss Grey for a while. If the two of you wouldn't mind?"

"I wouldn't mind," Kelley Grey said promptly.

"I have been neglecting Miss Grey, Krekor," Tibor said, without a trace of remorse. "I have been trying to talk some sense into this other young woman's head."

Bennis Hannaford rolled her eyes. "He's been giving me a lecture about vitamins. I told him we had all that in biology when I was at boarding school, but he just won't listen to me."

"We could go higher up the bleachers," Kelley Grey said. "That way we could talk without interrupting them. It's all been very interesting, really."

"It's all been boring me to tears," Bennis said.

Gregor held out a hand to Kelley Grey and Kelley took it. He helped her out of her seat while her arm was stretched over Tibor's head and then led her up the bleachers a little way, but not too far, because he had never really liked bleachers. In high school, he had always been convinced that he was about to fall through the cracks. He went up to the fourth tier and sat down again. He was far enough from Bennis and Tibor so that he couldn't hear what they were saying, although he could see Tibor's hands working, rising up and down, one hand smashing into the other for emphasis. He was far enough away from Franklin and Demp so that they couldn't hear what he said to Kelley Grey, although he wouldn't have minded if they had. He thought Kelley might have minded. She had to know she was going to have to talk to them at length, over and over again, and probably to the state police, too. A couple of hours after a dead woman's head had fallen into her lap might not be the time to press that matter home.

Gregor waited until Kelley had sat down herself and then asked, "How are you? Holding up?"

"I'm all right," Kelley said. "Sort of on automatic pilot."

"That goes away."

"I was afraid it did."

"It doesn't have to go away now," Gregor told her. "I'm not interested in your emotions at the moment. Just in a few procedural and background things. Then I'm going to tell Franklin you ought to go home."

Kelley looked across at Franklin Morrison. Franklin was bending over something Demp had handed him. His shoulders were slumped. He looked depressed enough to die.

"Is it true he's hired you to investigate what happened to Tisha Verek and Dinah? That he's brought you in as some kind of super private dectective?"

"No one can bring me in as a private detective because I'm not a private detective. You need a license for that, and I don't have one. I do consult on occasion, with police departments and private individuals, if the case falls within my area of expertise and there is a problem that interests me."

"Is this a problem that interests you?"

"I think so," Gregor said. "Yes."

"Is it all the same problem? Were they all killed by the same person? Is it some kind of plot?"

"I don't believe in plots," Gregor said. "As for the rest of it, I don't know."

Kelley Grey grimaced. It was an ugly expression and it made her plain face plainer. "What do you think the odds are, that it's not?" she asked him. "I read the papers. Shoulder and throat, shoulder and throat, shoulder and throat."

"There is that, yes."

"So what do you want to know?"

Gregor settled his hands on his knees. Kelley had a tiny pair of smiling Santa faces in her pierced ears that he had just noticed. They looked ludicrous.

"When we sat down this evening," he said, "Gemma told me that she had never seen this play before, even though she had been here a while. Do you know how long a while?"

"It was three or four years, I think. I've only been here eighteen months, myself."

"Do you know why she hadn't seen the play?"

"I know she didn't approve of it," Kelley said. Then she shook her head, dissatisfied. "It wasn't like that. It wasn't an emotional thing. Gemma had a set of principles, you see, and she didn't approve of whatever was opposed to those principles, but there was nothing— worked up about it. It wasn't like Jesse Helms or anything. She didn't get all passionate about things like that."

"What did she get all passionate about?"

"Nothing, really," Kelley said. "Gemma was strange that way, Mr. Demarkian, if you ask me. Emotions were something she talked about all the time, but she didn't really have any, not the way other people do. She was always in control. She'd say, 'I'm very angry with you, Kelley.' But she wouldn't sound angry. She'd sound . . . reasonable."

"Did you like that?"

"I hated it."

"Was she often angry at you?"

"I was more often angry at her." Kelley smiled slightly. "I've got my principles, too, but I'm not like Gemma was about them. I yell and scream and pound tables."

Gregor smiled back. "I think I prefer it that way," he said. He stretched his legs and considered what she'd told him. "I would have thought, that as a priest, Gemma Bury would have been overjoyed with a production like the Bethlehem Nativity play. I would have thought she would at least have been interested in seeing how it was done."

"Gemma wasn't that kind of priest," Kelley said. "She wasn't that kind of Episcopalian. I don't think she believed that there was any truth to the story. And then there was the constitutional thing. She was very firm about the constitutional thing."

"Firm how?"

"In thinking that having the play and making money for the town was illegal because of the separation of church and state and the town shouldn't do it. She was really happy when we heard Tisha Verek was going to file that lawsuit. She said she'd been thinking about doing it since she got here but then she hadn't because she was worried about the effect it would have. Her parishioners would probably have killed her— Oh."

"Do you think one of her parishioners would have killed her just for believing what she believed?" Gregor asked gently.

Kelley was shaky. "I don't know."

"Do you think Tisha Verek was shot because she was going to file a lawsuit against the Celebration?"

Kelley just shrugged. "I don't know why Tisha Verek was shot, or Dinah Ketchum either. I barely knew either of them. Tisha used to come to the rectory sometimes to visit Gemma, but she didn't have time for me. And as for Dinah Ketchum, she might as well have been on another planet. We had virtually no contact at all. Except for the inevitable, of course. Everybody runs into everybody else in a town this size at least once in a while."

"Mmm," Gregor said. He decided that was likely to be true. It was difficult for him to work in small towns because he had never lived in one. He had been born in Philadelphia and stationed in New York and San Francisco and Los Angeles and Washington, D.C. Like the Armenian traders who were his ancestors, he was a man of the cities. It was hard for him to believe that there were places anywhere where everybody ran into everybody else at least once in a while.

That, however, was not his problem. The shooting death of Gemma Bury was, in no matter how unofficial a capacity. Franklin Morrison had every intention of sticking him with it. Gregor knew himself too well to believe he had any intention to refuse.

"Let's talk about tonight," he told Kelley Grey. "Why did the two of you decide to come tonight?"

"It was because of Peter Callisher," Kelley said. "Gemma went to talk to Peter Callisher this afternoon, and he had a pair of tickets he didn't need, and he gave them to Gemma."

"Surely, she could have gotten tickets before this?"

"Of course she could have, and free, too, just like the ones Peter gave her. But the impression I got was that they were just there and she just sort of said what the hell."

"What did she go to see Peter Callisher about?"

Kelley shrugged again. "I don't know. Peter runs the paper. Gemma goes—went—over there a lot, or sent me, you know, to put notices in and things like that, for when the church groups were going to meet or when the jumble sales were going to be or whatever. And the church ran a regular ad every week that gave our times for services and counseling hours and that sort of thing. All the churches do."

Gregor hated explanations that amounted to "it happened for no good reason at all" and he hated them twice as fiercely as he might have because they were so often true.

"Did Gemma tell anyone she was going to attend this performance?"

"Tell anyone?"

"Was there anyone who knew?" Gregor insisted.

"I suppose a lot of people knew she had the tickets," Kelley said, "but I don't see why they would know she was going to be at the performance. I mean, she'd never been to one before. And I don't think she made up her mind until she came home and talked to me."

"You don't think but you can't be sure."

"No, I can't be sure. But Mr. Demarkian, I've got to say it doesn't make much sense."

Gregor was afraid it made entirely too much sense. If everyone in town knew Gemma Bury was going to be at the Nativity play tonight, then everyone in town had a chance to premeditate a shooting that Gregor was convinced had to be premeditated. If it hadn't been—if it had been brought off on the spur of the moment by someone who just happened to have a rifle handy for use in auspicious circumstances—they were dealing with something worse than a nut and worse than a psychopath.

"What about once you got here?" Gregor asked. "You came in together at the beginning. Bennis and Tibor and I saw you."

"We saw you, too," Kelley said. "Gemma was amused. We'd been reading about you for weeks. Because of Peter liking to put your cases in the paper."

"What about at the intermission? Did you come back first or did Gemma?"

"I never went away," Kelley said. "Gemma got up and walked around. There were a couple of parishioners in the section just to the other side of the animal aisle from this one. She went over to talk to them, and she was gone almost the entire intermission, but I never left."

"And she came back when? Before I did, I remember."

"She wasn't gone long," Kelley agreed.

"What about the people immediately behind you and immediately in front of you?"

"The people immediately behind us didn't come in until after the play had already started. They were a pain in the butt, let me tell you. The people immediately in front of us were back, but they weren't sitting still. That's the ground-level bleacher, you know. The people down there had this small child, and it kept wandering up and wandering away, and they'd go chase it. I saw one of those men questioning the parents, I think. Didn't you?"

"No," Gregor said, "I didn't. Did you talk to anyone tonight? You didn't go anywhere, you say. Did anyone come to you?"

"Amanda Ballard came up to talk before she left. She and Peter had tickets for the section directly opposite this one on the other side of the park. Peter gets tickets every year. Anyway, Amanda was feeling sick and was on her way out, and she saw me and came up to say hello."

"She left and Peter Callisher didn't."

"That's right."

"And Peter Callisher had tickets over here to give to Gemma and tickets over there to use himself, all on the same night."

"Oh, that. Peter had friends who were supposed to come up from Boston to see the play, and they only made up their minds about a month ago, so when he got them the tickets he couldn't get them to go with the ones he already had. Then the friends couldn't come up after all, so there he was."

"Anybody else?"

Kelley thought about it, long and hard, but it only made her face go as grey as her name. She didn't come up with much.

"I saw Candy George's husband Reggie," she said. "Candy's the girl who plays Mary. And I saw Stu Ketchum wandering around. He operates a food stall during the intermissions. Oh, and I saw Timmy Hall. He works over at the paper. He's here every year, too. Peter gets tickets for his whole staff, but not all on the same night. Timmy must have been with Peter."

Gregor prodded one more time. "You didn't have a chance to talk to any of them?" he asked.

Kelley shook her head.

"And you didn't see anyone else? Were any of the people you did see on bad terms with Gemma Bury?"

"Nobody was on really bad terms with Gemma," Kelley said, "because she was like I told you. Always reasonable. Of course, that meant that nobody was very close. At least—"

"What?"

"Nothing," Kelley said.

Obviously, there was something. Gregor could tell. If he'd had the least suspicion that Kelley Grey could have been materially involved in Gemma Bury's death, he would have pushed for it. However, he was sure she did not. She had been telling the truth about her activities during the intermission. He had seen her sitting in her seat when he'd come back with his calzone, and Franklin had reported at least one witness who'd come back early and seen her sitting there, too. After that, she'd been caught up in the returning crowds and the performance. If she'd gone clattering around then, somebody would have mentioned it.

Kelley's face had gone from grey to green, from firmly young to sagging, in a blink. It was time to let her go home and get some rest. Gregor got to his feet and held out a hand to help Kelley to hers.

"Get out of here," he said. "Go get some sleep. If we need to talk to you some more, we can do it in the morning."

t w o

1

TIMMY HALL was one of those fat men who seemed to be fat mostly through inertia. Peter Callisher couldn't remember ever seeing him eat much, but he waddled and rocked and jiggled all the same. It was now eight o'clock on the morning of December 17th, and Peter was bleary-eyed and tired. It had been bad enough last night just after the body had been found, when Gregor Demarkian had been keeping everyone he could penned up in the park and Franklin Morrison had arrived with his notebook out, trying to look professional. Amanda had gone home by then, of course, but Peter had felt an obligation to stay once he realized what happened, and he'd felt an obligation to keep Timmy with him. Timmy was not only fat but stupid, and like all stupid people he panicked. Being part of a police investigation made him paranoid and petrified and threatened to send him out of control. Peter had been thinking about the paper, of course. The *Bethlehem News and Mail* couldn't let a shooting death at the Nativity play go by without comment. It couldn't even leave such a thing safely to next week's issue. Peter didn't believe in extras or special editions or sixty-four point type. He'd left all that behind him in the city—and the *Times* had never gone in for that kind of sensationalism anyway. This was not the city, and for just that reason Peter found he was going to have to take it much more solemnly than he wanted to. His first line of offense had run into snags. Timmy had been so agitated, Peter had had a hard time paying attention to what was going on around him. If he had had to write an eyewitness

144

account of what had gone on during the first hours of the investigation himself, it would have been a flop. Fortunately, he had snagged old Mrs. Johnson, the English teacher at the high school, just as she was getting ready to leave. She was in the cast as he couldn't remember who. The bright look in her eyes told Peter that she had seen and heard everything there was to see and hear. Memory told Peter she would be able to write it accurately, succinctly and with a certain amount of verve. It hadn't even surprised him when she had agreed to come back to the newspaper offices with him, or that she'd been so matter-of-factly efficient writing it all down at a typewriter in the middle of the big ground-floor room. Competent. That's what she had always been. Competent. After a couple of hours dealing with Timmy in crisis, she was a relief.

Actually, old Mrs. Johnson had been a relief from what Peter had had to deal with in Amanda, too, although he had had to admit that that might have been partially his fault. He had come storming across from the park, determined to get his first—and, he hoped, only—extra edition ever mocked up and ready for the printers before dawn, and come pounding into the building like a crew of firemen looking for the source of the blaze. He had forgotten that Amanda had not simply gone home early, but gone home sick. He had forgotten that she was very likely to be asleep. He had forgotten how crazy she got when she was abruptly woken by loud noises or a hand on her shoulder. Peter thought of Amanda as one of the better things to have happened to him since he got back to Bethlehem. She was the lover he could never have found in the city, because the women he knew in the city were all too tense. Amanda was tense, too, but not in the same way. Maybe that was because she really wasn't all that interested in working on a newspaper. Back in the city, all the women Peter knew were reporters. In the Middle East, they had been reporters or whores. It was enough to drive any sane man to a hermitage. Then there was Amanda, who would have been perfect, except that she had one or two quirks. One of those quirks was that she jumped out of bed and screamed when she was awakened abruptly. One of the others was that she nagged him about it for hours afterward. Peter had put up with that last night because it was all so damned important. Right after he'd found Mrs. Johnson, he'd dumped Timmy on her and gotten as close to the scene as possible. He'd seen them wrapping Gemma Bury up on a stretcher and covering the place in her bright orange coat where the blood showed. That was at least one thing Peter could attest to for himself. Gemma Bury had been

wearing her much-too-expensive, Boston-bought, high-fashion tangerine orange coat, and it had hidden her death for at least an hour. Peter
liked the sound of that. It had overtones of divine retribution.

Divine retribution. Peter rubbed his eyes, then put his hands back
down on the desk he was sitting at and looked out over the newsroom.
The fluorescent lights were on above his head. Ouside, the sun was
straining its way through the clouds and not having much success. It
looked like it was going to snow. Peter didn't think he'd stayed up all
night without sleep for years.

Peter didn't know if Amanda ever had. She was sitting at the desk
she had staked out as "hers," playing with a pencil and looking about
ready to fall over, her blonde hair pinned to the top of her head. Timmy
kept moving back and forth across the room, always coming back into
her orbit, never letting himself get too far out of it. Timmy had always
trusted Amanda.

"The printer isn't open until nine o'clock," Peter called across to
Amanda. "That's what comes of taking the low bid instead of using
someone used to newspapers."

"Most of the time," Amanda said reasonably, "we don't need somebody used to newspapers."

"I have to go lie down now," Timmy said. "I'm very tired."

Peter was sure Timmy was very tired. He was sure they all were
very tired. He almost wished he'd listened to old Mrs. Johnson's advice,
delivered when she was shrugging herself into her coat to make her
own way home.

"This isn't Boston," she'd told them. "You won't do anybody any
good staying up all night and making yourselves sick. You should all
go get your rest and start again in the morning."

Right. Timmy was waiting by Amanda's desk, hesitating, looking
miserable and a little frightened. Amanda gave him a tired smile and
said, "You go and lie down any time you want to. You don't need
permission."

"Maybe I'm supposed to work," Timmy said.

"You're supposed to work during normal working hours. This was
special. It was a favor you did the newspaper. You get paid extra. You
don't have to do it until you die."

"Did we call Mrs. Jeanings? Did we tell her I was here?"

"I told her," Peter said. "I told her about Gemma Bury, too."

"I shouldn't make her worry," Timmy said. Then he looked around
helplessly, and Amanda got up to find him his coat. When she did,

Timmy brightened, and Peter felt himself go queasy. There really was something about watching the two of them together that was unsettling. Amanda found the coat under Peter's and her own on the rack and handed it over. Timmy touched the place where her hand had been with a thoughtful expression on his face.

"Mrs. Jeanings will keep me up," he said with a sigh. "Mrs. Jeanings will want to know all about it."

"Tell her we're putting out a special edition of the paper," Amanda told him.

"Mrs. Jeanings won't care. Mrs. Jeanings will want to know how I feel about it. She always wants to know how I feel about everything."

"She means well."

"I know. She makes good eggs, too. And she gives me Marshmallow Fluff."

Timmy went plodding to the side door, his coat open, his hands hanging motionless at his sides. Peter didn't think he'd ever seen a fully normal person walk with his hands like that. When he got the door open, Timmy turned and looked at the two of them, grinning, and said good night. Then he plodded out and closed the door behind himself. Peter heard him go through the vestibule and out the door.

"I wish you hadn't talked me into hiring him," he told Amanda. "He gives me the creeps."

"He's just a little retarded," Amanda said. "He does a very good job. He's very conscientious. And he's more responsible than half the back-to-the-land refugees we hire. Can we go back to sleep now?"

"We've got to make arrangements for the printing."

"We can leave a note for Sally or Jonathan. One of them can drive the mechanicals over."

"I don't want to leave a note for Sally or Jonathan. I want to—I don't know what I want to do. I don't think I've had this much fun in ages."

Amanda cocked her head, giving him the strangest look. "Is that what this is to you? Fun?"

Peter was astonished. "Why not?"

"Well," Amanda said, "for one thing, the poor woman is dead. I didn't like her much, but she is dead. For another thing, she probably wouldn't have been dead if you hadn't given her those tickets. In fact, if Franklin Morrison is right instead of the state police and Tisha Verek's death wasn't a hunting accident, then just maybe Gemma Bury is dead *because* she came to talk to you. If you see what I mean."

147

"No."

Amanda rearranged a few things on her desk. She had gone back to it after she'd found Timmy's coat. She look slumped, sitting in the chair. There was nothing on her desk to rearrange.

"I know what you were talking about when she was here," she said. "You were talking about lawsuits. Like Tisha Verek's lawsuit. And about how Gemma was going to file one."

"So?"

"So that was what started all the trouble the last time, wasn't it? I mean, with Dinah dead and all the rest of it, people seem to have forgotten all about it. And they gossip. They really love to gossip. So they keep talking about who was sleeping with Jan-Mark and who wasn't—"

"Maybe that's the connection," Peter said. "Maybe they're both dead because they were sleeping with Jan-Mark Verek."

Amanda shot him another strange look and then got up again. With one thing and another she had been bopping up and down like one of those flamingo water dolls. She shoved the papers on her desk into the long center drawer and said, "I think I'm going to go back to sleep now. For at least a couple of hours. Are you going to tell Gregor Demarkian what she came here for?"

"Yes."

"Are you going to tell him she was sleeping with Jan-Mark Verek?"

"Yes again."

"That's good," Amanda said.

She went to the side door without bothering to pick up her coat—she was going upstairs, not outside—and stepped just into the vestibule, where a small manila envelope lay, the one with the single copy of the paper the printer always sent over before delivering the bales. It must have been there last night when Peter came in, but he hadn't noticed it.

"Throw that to me," he told her, and she did. Then she gave him another of her odd looks and said, "I think you ought to tell Gregor Demarkian everything. I really think you should."

Peter didn't know what exactly that was supposed to mean, but he was much too tired to care.

2

WHEN JAN-MARK VEREK first started his affair with Reggie George, he thought no more of it than he would have thought of deciding to have a banana for breakfast instead of an apple. In the New York City art world scheme of things, where Jan-Mark had spent almost all of his adult life, that was about the level on which such a decision would have to be considered. Jan-Mark had had affairs with a lot of people, male and female, over the years. It had annoyed him no end that Tisha had refused to do the same. To Jan-Mark, sex was a wonderful game with lots of variations to keep it from getting boring. It wasn't so much natural—the natural was always boring, like tofu and alfalfa sprouts— as naturally available. To be attractive and refuse what attractiveness offered you was like winning the lottery and refusing to pick up the money. It didn't make any sense. It didn't even make any sense when picking up the money was dangerous, as it was with Reggie. Jan-Mark was beginning to think Reggie was very, very dangerous. He hadn't thought so in the beginning. There was nothing about Reggie to remind him of the few examples of rough trade he'd picked up in the Port Authority back in the days when he hadn't been so all-fired paranoid about AIDS. At the start, Reggie had seemed to Jan-Mark like just another rustic country boy who swung both ways, not so unusual this close to the third millennium. After a while, Jan-Mark had begun to pick up little things. An attitude here. A comment there. A sudden swift kick to the side of a table that resulted in a broken table leg. They had been going at it for six months now and Jan-Mark Verek had to admit it. Reggie George was a certifiable mess.

Lately, Jan-Mark had begun to wonder if Reggie might be dangerous in a way more subtle than the obvious one, if what he had to fear from this yokel was less an outburst of rage—although that was coming; that was surely coming—than an indiscretion. Bisexuality might be par for the course in SoHo, but Jan-Mark was not stupid enough to believe it would be accepted with equanimity in Bethlehem, Vermont. It would be a wonderful excuse for an orgy of released repressed hostility, if that was the way to put it. Everybody up here hated him anyway. They'd just love to find a way to make his life a living hell. They'd made it hard enough over his affair with Gemma, which he had always known was an open secret, even if she had not. They probably hated art. Jan-Mark thought it might be about time to go back to the city, where homosexuals were of the out-of-the-closet, unconflicted, normal variety and bisexuals were as common as fast-food joints on an urban strip. He wished Tisha were still alive, so that he could tell her all about all of it and be comforted by the familiarity of one of her patented tantrums.

Last night, Jan-Mark had seen Reggie for an hour starting at seven-thirty, a quick roll and knock around while Reggie's wife was off being in that idiotic play. Much later, he had seen Reggie again, unexpectedly, well after midnight, when Reggie came to tell him about Gemma Bury being dead. Reggie should have called, but he hadn't wanted to, maybe because it was a kind of victory. Jan-Mark had three lovers and now two of them were dead, leaving Reggie to rule the roost alone. Or something. Jan-Mark hated psychoanalyzing people. He was bad at it and it only made a mess anyway. There were a thousand clinical explanations for why Reggie George was coming up his driveway again at eight-forty-five on this Tuesday morning, coming for the third time in under twenty hours, but Jan-Mark wanted to ignore them all. He preferred to think Reggie was just being a pain in the ass.

Reggie had come in his pickup truck, which he almost never did. That pickup truck was a signature, identifiable as Reggie's from here to Montpelier. He had to be on his way to work. Jan-Mark watched as he stomped through the new snow to the basement door and punched at the bell. He waited a few moments before flipping on the intercom switch next to the kitchen table where he was sitting and calling down to his guest.

"I'm awake and watching you march through the nice clean precipitation," he said to Reggie. "Come on up if you have to."

"I have to."

"I'm out of liquor."

"It's important."

Jan-Mark was not out of liquor. He had three untouched bottles of Glenlivet sitting in his trunk upstairs, but he had no intention of bringing them out at this hour of the morning, and no intention of bringing them out for Reggie George at any time. Reggie was impressed when Jan-Mark got him a six-pack of Heineken beer. There was the sound of heavy boots coming up the open, polished cedar staircase. The staircase was spiral and Reggie always slipped on it once or twice when

he came up. When he did he swore in the most direct and least im-
aginative way. He got to the kitchen level and worked his way out of
the curving trap, shaking his right foot side to side in the air as if he'd
minorly damaged his ankle.

"Shit," he said. "I hate those stairs."

"I know you hate those stairs," Jan-Mark said patiently. "What *do*
you like? Can I pour you some coffee?"

"I've got some coffee in the truck. And I'm in a hurry. I'm supposed
to be on my way to work."

"Maybe you talked to your wife about what we talked about last
night. About making things a little more interesting."

"No, I haven't talked to my wife. I haven't hardly seen my wife.
She was asleep when I got back from here last night. It's what I heard.
That's what I wanted to tell you. What I heard at breakfast this morning."

"What did you hear?"

"That they found the gun, that's what I heard," Reggie said. "That
foreign guy did it. Or he told Franklin's people where to look, I guess.
Right there in the park where it happened. It's all over the CB."

"You mean on the police band?"

"I mean people talking about it." Reggie was impatient. "The news
is all over town, JM. The only reason you don't know about it is that
you're stuck all the way out here. And you don't talk to anybody."

"I talk to lots of people."

"You don't talk to anybody in town."

All this time, Reggie had been bouncing around on the balls of his
feet, rocking back and forth, taking his hands out of the pockets of his
jacket and putting them back in again. He had said he was in a hurry
and he was damn well going to look like he was in a hurry. That was
how Jan-Mark saw it. Now Reggie seemed to decide that this was stupid,
or to change his mind, or something. He pulled out one of the bentwood
kitchen chairs and sat down.

"They found the gun," he repeated.

"You said that." Jan-Mark nodded.

"It was up in a tree. There aren't a lot of trees in the park. Just a
couple. It was in one of those, near that place where the animals go in
and out. Maybe it was in a bush."

"Maybe?"

"Well, I'm trying to remember what the park looks like, JM. I don't
go traipsing around in parks on a regular basis. Only time I've been

through in years except to take a shortcut from Main Street to Carrow is going to see Candy in this play. And I guess it's a bush, not really a tree. Big round pine bush, like the kind they use for hedges.''

"Clipped?''

"I don't know,'' Reggie said. "How should I know? Why the hell would anybody want to know?''

"Just asking,'' Jan-Mark said.

"The point isn't the bush,'' Reggie said, "it's the gun. That's what I had to tell you. And about the silencer. Did I mention the silencer?''

"No,'' Jan-Mark said.

"Whoever it was stuck a potato in the barrel for a silencer. Can you beat that? It must have been a woman. I mean it. Who'd do something that stupid? The damned rifle could go off right in your face.''

"But it didn't,'' Jan-Mark pointed out.

"No,'' Reggie said, "no, it didn't. But that's the way it always is with bitches, isn't it? All the dumb luck in the world.''

"Right,'' Jan-Mark said.

Reggie George sniffed. "I mean, for Chrissake, JM, I wouldn't have driven all the way out here in my own goddamn truck just because of a goddamn bush and a goddamn gun and a goddamn potato if it didn't mean something.''

"So what does it mean?''

"It means it was the same gun,'' Reggie said. "Stuart Ketchum's gun. The Browning .22-caliber semiautomatic Grade I rifle. It had his name scratched right there in the base.''

"That's the same gun as what?''

"What do you mean, the same gun as what? The same gun that blew away your goddamn wife, that's as what. I mean, Christ, JM, where have you been? Don't you even read the papers?''

"If you mean the local paper, not exactly. I do read the ads.'' Jan-Mark sighed. "How could they possibly know it's the same gun? Don't they have to test the bullets? First test the bullets that hit Tisha and then test the ones from the gun and then test the ones that hit Gemma? Don't they have to do all that before they know it's the same gun?''

"They already did that with Tisha,'' Reggie said. "They tested the bullets she was hit with, and then when Stuart found the gun missing, he got some spent shells from all that target practice he does and they tested those and the bullets that hit his tin cans and I don't know what else, so they definitely know that's the gun that killed your goddamn wife.''

"Right," Jan-Mark said. Of course, none of that proved that this gun was the gun that had been shot at Gemma Bury. They'd have to test the bullets in Gemma's body for that. None of it said that the gun was what it appeared to be, either. They'd have to test for that, too. He could have explained all this to Reggie, but he didn't want to. It would have been too tiring. Explaining things to Reggie was about as easy as teaching a chicken to talk.

Jan-Mark looked into his coffee cup, reached for the Pyrex coffee pot on its warmer and considered lighting his sixteenth cigarette of the day. He even considered getting himself some booze.

Somehow, with Reggie George and phantom guns that mysteriously appeared in town park bushes, the day seemed to demand it.

3

UP THE ROAD toward town, on the other side of the stone wall, Kelley Grey sat in the kitchen of the Episcopal rectory, drinking her third cup of black coffee since six o'clock and wondering if she was ever going to get to sleep again. If she stayed at the rectory, she thought the answer would be no—which made it not so bad that the parish council was going to want the rectory back, and her out of it, in no time at all. How long no time at all was, Kelley didn't know, but it presented problems. She might not be able to sleep in this place, but she didn't have anyplace else to sleep. It was strange, the things she did even when she knew better. Gemma Bury hadn't been her lover, but in some ways Gemma Bury might as well have been. They had been on those kinds of terms with each other in every way but the sexual. They had shared the house. They had shared the things they owned. They had shopped for food together and gone to the movies together and treated the car as if it was jointly owned between them. The difficulty was that nothing had been owned between them. Gemma was gone and with her everything that had served as a material foundation for Kelley Grey's life.

As for the emotional foundation of Kelley Grey's life, that was something else again, something that didn't concern her for the moment. For the moment, she had no emotional life. It had been driven out of her like those small pieces of blood and skin and bone had been driven out of Gemma's throat, through the back of Gemma's neck, when the bullet had passed from her windpipe to her neck muscles to the empty air beneath the bleachers. Kelley wondered if that Gregor Demarkian person would call Gemma's death an easy one, quick and painless, over before she knew it. It must have happened so fast and it seemed to Kelley to have been so terrible. Ugly, that was the word for it. Ugly. Kelley had been called ugly most of her life, behind her back, in whispers in the corners of girls' rooms in high schools and colleges and scout camps and Sunday schools. She knew what the word meant. To her, Gemma's death was about as ugly as it got. She just couldn't feel it.

She just couldn't feel anything—and that, she thought, was an advantage. At some point her armor of ice was going to melt, and from then on in she was going to be of no use to anyone. She was going to really believe that Gemma had been killed stone dead by a bullet aimed at her while Kelley herself was sitting right next to her and then it was all going to come apart. In the meantime, she had this small space in which to decide what to do and how to do it.

She got up, walked away from the kitchen table, walked down the hall to the foyer and the stairs. She looked up the stairs but didn't climb them. That numb she was not. She couldn't bear the idea of going up to her room or out of easy access to the door. The rectory was too big and it echoed. In the dark, in the halls of the second and third floor, out of sight of any human person, it whispered. Kelley had spent the night curled up on the couch in Gemma's office, and she was going to spend every night curled up there until she found an apartment and could move out to be on her own. Now she moved around behind the staircase and let herself in to Gemma's office. It was nine o'clock and the bells in the church were ringing. They were heavy cast-iron things and they tolled heavily, the way the bells had in a movie Kelley had once seen, about Marie Antoinette and the guillotine.

Kelley walked over to Gemma's desk, pulled out the long center drawer and felt beneath it. The key to Gemma's wall safe was there, fastened with tape. Kelley unhooked it without being careful. She had been careful all the times before, but there was no point to it now. She walked over to the large portrait of some fat dead divine that took up most of the north wall and pulled it aside. It swung on hinges like the safe-hiding portraits in English detective movies. It was odd to think that there had been an era when people really indulged in things like this.

The safe was high on the wall. It had been built by men and for men. Gemma had been tall. Kelley ignored the swivel chair behind the desk and got one of the wingbacks from near the couch instead. In the days when she used to be careful, she'd brought a straightback from the kitchen so she wouldn't leave shoe prints in the wingback's yellow upholstery. The wingback was a soft chair with a springy seat and hard to stand on. Kelley had to concentrate on her balance to keep herself from falling over. She pulled the chair as close to the wall as she could and got to work.

The safe was a simple one and there wasn't much in it. Gemma's birth certificate. Gemma's bank books for the four investment accounts in Boston. Gemma's packet of sentimental photographs, showing her arm in arm with all the wrong people in Boston. Gemma had never trusted the safe to hold anything anyone might want to steal. She'd kept her mother's jewelry in the drawer of her night table next to her bed. The safe was for documents, and it was documents she kept in it, including the thick one in the stiff brown envelope in the back.

Kelley got that out, shut the safe and got back down off the chair. She pushed the portrait back against the wall and congratulated herself on not breaking her neck. Then she looked down at the envelope and frowned. It was a perfectly blank envelope except for a notation in the corner, in Gemma's handwriting, in pencil, that said: "*TV/MS/SKC.*" Just to be sure, Kelley opened it up and pulled out the inch-thick sheaf of papers inside. The top one said: "*BORN IN BLOOD. A Book About Children Who Kill.* By Patricia Feld Verek." Kelley could see Gemma sitting in this room, playing with the manuscript pages and saying, "When this thing is published, it's going to tear this town into tiny little shreds and throw them down over the Connecticut River like confetti. Always remember something, Kelley. It's not how many people you offend that matters. It's who."

Well, Gemma had certainly offended somebody, and maybe so had Tisha Verek. Kelley just wished she understood who.

She hadn't told Gregor Demarkian about the affair Gemma was having with Jan-Mark Verek, but maybe she ought to tell him now. And while she was at it, maybe she ought to give him this manuscript.

At least it would get it out of the house.

t h r e e

1

GREGOR DEMARKIAN was fifty-six years old, the product of a generation that believed in reason, frugality and hard work, not magic and intuition. He had had a good career and a celebrated one, entirely—he believed—because of the time and effort he had put in. If he had had brilliant moments of insight, they had arisen from his years of patient, plodding study. If he had appeared to be possessed of mythic wisdom in his field, it was because he had applied himself so thoroughly to understanding his field. That was why this business with the rifle made him so nervous. Gregor Demarkian didn't know anything about rifles. He had never bothered to learn. He didn't like guns, although he could shoot as well as anybody else who had been a field agent for the Federal Bureau of Investigation a dozen years ago. All Bureau agents had to learn how to shoot, of course, and administrators were supposed to go out to the range and keep up their skills, but Gregor had learned quickly that that was a rule easily avoided and happily unenforced. He hated firing ranges at least as much as he hated guns. Heat and noise, anger and hostility: At the Bureau, there had always been somebody around who did like guns, and who studied them, and who could tell Gregor what Gregor needed to know. Gregor didn't understand the first thing about impacts and trajectories.

He had figured out where the rifle would be because of something Demp had said about impacts and trajectories, and also because it was the only solution that made sense. A rifle isn't a handgun. A handgun can be stored in a pocket and walked around in public with impunity. Since no one can see and no one can know, no one will suspect. Gregor couldn't imagine anyone tromping around the park last night with a Browning .22-caliber semiautomatic Grade I rifle. Dozens of people would have seen him and commented on him, even if there had never been a shooting. Someone would have called a cop. The only explanation that made sense was that the rifle was never out in the open at all, and that meant looking for places it could be hidden. Gregor's first impulse had been to look in the bleachers, under the benches, in the stands. Then he had realized that that explanation was almost as bad as the first one. What was the killer going to do, whip this big heavy rifle out from under his seat, stand up in full view of everybody and aim? Gregor thought he hated guns with good reason, one having nothing to do with the noise they made and the harm they caused. They were so damn complicated. When a killer used poison, it was easy. Drop the poison in a glass in full sight of thirty people in the lobby of an opera hall during intermission, and nobody noticed a thing.

"I kept going around and around the park in my mind," Gregor told Bennis the next morning, going around and around her room while she sat on the antique wedding quilt that covered her bed, pinning her hair to the top of her head, "and the more I did the more I realized the whole thing would have been impossible if the rifle wasn't already on the premises before the Nativity play ever started. For a while I thought it would have had to have been there before any of the performances started, back a couple of weeks ago, but it was definitely a bullet from Stuart Ketchum's gun they found—"

"How could you know already it was a bullet from Stuart Ketchum's gun?" Bennis asked, stuffing her mouth with rippled hairpins. Gregor had never been able to understand how she could speak so clearly with her mouth full of pins like that. "Don't you have to run tests before you know what gun that bullet belonged to?"

"To be absolutely sure, of course we do," Gregor nodded, "but I'm relying on local expertise, as the old Behavioral Sciences field book used to put it. Stuart Ketchum marks his ammunition. The spent shells had his mark."

"Why does he do that?"

"It's got something to do with target competitions. Don't ask me. At any rate, there that was, so I was left with the strong possibility that the rifle had to have been put there later than I wanted it to have been, since Tisha Verek was killed with Stuart Ketchum's rifle and that was the morning of the first day of the first week of performances of the play—"

"Well, that was before the play started," Bennis said.

"It wasn't enough before," Gregor told her. "By that Monday, the park had to have had at least periodic intrusions of people, wandering around getting one thing or another done. That was certainly true yesterday afternoon, when I've decided the rifle must actually have been put there, assuming, as I still insist on assuming, that our killer was looking to shoot Gemma Bury in particular, and not just any stray townsperson attending the Nativity play."

Bennis's hair was now securely on top of her head and her mouth was still full of pins. She took the pins out and began putting them back in a small metal box that had once contained Sucrets.

"That's a really terrible thought," she said. "I mean that somebody could be wandering around just offing people for the hell of it. Do you think that could be true?"

"No."

"Why not?"

"He's going to too much trouble," Gregor explained. "I don't mean with things like hiding the rifle in those bushes. That's premeditation, that's all right. You get it with serial killers and you get it with the more normal kind. I mean with Tisha Verek. All the way out there on the Delaford Road. What for? If his only concern is to kill somebody in town, why not pick an old lady off on Main Street?"

"Less chance of getting caught?" Bennis supplied helpfully.

"More. Harder to get away. If you shoot at somebody on Main Street, you can ditch the rifle and hop into the nearest store, and if you've picked your spot and your time, nobody's seen you and nobody's going to suspect."

"Because he stole Stuart Ketchum's rifle," Bennis said. "That was out there and then he killed the first person he came across after he got hold of it."

"Why?"

"I thought we weren't asking why, Gregor. I thought this was an argument in favor of a crazy."

"I wish you'd disabuse yourself of the notion that crazies are people who leap and whirl in supermarket aisles and can't remember their names from one minute to the next. There are people like that, Bennis, but they don't become serial murderers. They get institutionalized."

"That's wonderful to know."

"Serial murderers—and we would have to be talking about a serial murderer here, even if Dinah Ketchum's death wasn't connected to the other two, as long as the motive for the other two was some kind of psychological kick—serial murderers are very organized people. The psychopaths are by definition, of course, but even the other ones, the ones who think the moon is delivering messages from aliens on Saturn or whatever, even those are extraordinarily coherent. That's why they don't get caught."

"But they do get caught, don't they?"

"Some of them do and some of them don't. Most of them take a damned long time." Gregor got up out of the chair he had been sitting in and paced moodily to Bennis's window, looking out on the snow-covered tips of buildings occasionally decked with plastic Santas and reindeer. Bennis was winding ribbons into her hair, green and red, traditional Christmas colors.

"Anyway," Gregor said, "it had to be somewhere there already before the performance started, because he couldn't have gotten it there during, so where could it have been? And that's when this boy Demp said something about the trajectory—about how there had practically been no trajectory, the bullet almost seemed to have gone straight through. And then he laughed and said he realized that couldn't have been possible. For that to have happened the killer would have had to crouch, because sitting on our level of the bleacher, Gemma was actually lower than most standing people would be—"

"Not so much lower than me," Bennis pointed out. "I'm only five-foot-four."

"All right. Somebody five-foot-four could have been standing up. Anybody taller would have to be crouching over. Whatever. I looked around and there were the bushes, one of only two sets of bushes in the whole park. They don't let the bushes grow over there because they don't want vegetation getting in the way of the viewing, but they let these two sets because they help with the play. They're kind of living props. And that's when it hit me. All somebody had to do was leave the rifle in the bushes beforehand—maybe even set it up for aim beforehand—and then wait until the moment was right."

"Whoever it was would have had to know where Gemma was going to be sitting beforehand," Bennis cautioned.

"Exactly," Gregor said. "That gives us, who? Peter Callisher. Peter's girlfriend, Amanda Ballard. That semiretarded man who works for them,

Timmy Hall. Kelley Grey. Anybody who might have been in the newspaper office when Peter Callisher gave Gemma Bury the tickets. Anybody any such person might have told—"

"Oh," Bennis said.

"Exactly. You see where we are. Leave the rifle in the bushes. Wait until Gemma is alone, the stands are mostly clear and you aren't being watched—which wouldn't be that hard. Those bushes are right near where the animals come through into the park. There's a board holdback near there that would effectively screen most of you from the people behind you, and what would they see if they saw you anyway? Someone standing pressed against a bush? Would they even notice?"

"It was still quite a chance."

"It was definitely quite a chance, but it wasn't the miracle Franklin Morrison and the state police want to make it out to be. Did I tell you Franklin called in the state police last night after everybody else had gone?"

"I was part of the everybody else who had gone."

"Of course. Well. They were called. They came. They made utter nuisances of themselves. Give me local cops over state police all the time."

"I know how you feel about the state police," Bennis said. She wound herself off the bed and went searching under it with her feet. A couple of seconds later, Gregor watched her come up with a pair of leather-topped clogs. She slipped her feet into them and went rooting around in the mess on her night table. Her cigarettes were there. So was her copy of something called *The Hilton Head Metabolism Diet*. The copy was dog-eared and destroyed. It even looked like it had been written in. Gregor frowned.

"I'm going down to breakfast," he said. "You could come with me."

"No thanks." Bennis found her lighter, stuck a cigarette in her mouth and lit up. "Tibor was pushing chocolate cake and knishes on me all night. I'm not going to be able to eat for a week. You wouldn't believe what he had when we got back here. Pizza."

"Where did he get pizza?"

"I don't know, but it was hot. Trust Tibor."

"Maybe you ought to sit down this afternoon and let him see you eating a great big lunch. Maybe that will stop him from worrying about you."

"Maybe it would," Bennis said, "but it's not going to happen this afternoon. I'm on my own. Tibor made the acquaintance of the local Catholic priest, and they're going off together to look at facsimile Latin manuscripts or something the man brought back from Rome. I think they're both slightly obsessional on St. Augustine."

"Mmm," Gregor said, and then made up his mind. No matter how much he disliked letting Bennis into the thick of real cases, he had a responsibility. It wasn't that he thought Tibor was entirely right. Tibor had panics. He was having one now. On the other hand, it was also true that he never saw Bennis eating anymore, and that was disturbing. Bennis usually ate like a horse.

"Why don't you come with me?" he asked her. "I'm only going to grab a sandwich on the run, but after that Franklin Morrison and I are going out to Stuart Ketchum's farm. You might come in handy."

"On a case?"

"For target practice."

There was a knock on Bennis's door—hardly necessary, since the door was open; the single and the suite at this end of the corridor constituted a little section of their own that could be closed off by a door in the hall, and Bennis had started to behave as if they were in fact living in a self-contained private suite—and Father Tibor Kasparian stuck his small neat head through. Gregor was intrigued to notice that he was in a much better mood than he had been in the night before, in spite of the fact that he couldn't have gotten much sleep. He had a spring in his step and a large brown paper grocery bag in his arms. Bennis regarded the grocery bag warily, giving off an aura that looked to Gregor very much like despair.

"What have you got?" she demanded, through the smoke curling up from her cigarette and making a cloud above her hair.

"Cookies!" Tibor said triumphantly.

Gregor Demarkian decided it was time he got out of there.

2

WHEN GREGOR DEMARKIAN had made up his mind that there wasn't a single place to get decent food in Bethlehem, Vermont, he had reckoned without breakfast. Breakfast, after all, was the high point of White Anglo-Saxon Protestant cooking, the one thing even the English made better than anybody else. In France you got a sticky bun and overcaffeinated coffee. In Greece and Italy you got rolls so stale you could have used them for roofing tiles and a little weak tea. Only with the English and the descendants of the English could you be sure of being fed and satisfied at nine o'clock in the morning. Gregor had entered the Green Mountain Inn's breakfast room with trepidation the morning before. He liked the suite he shared with Tibor well enough, but the Inn made him a little antsy. It was too studied, too discreet. The Christmas decorations erred on the side of chic. After The Magick Endive, he didn't want to guess what the food would be like. Then he had entered the breakfast room itself and looked around and been instantly, pleasantly surprised. The tables were sturdy and functional without being self-consciously rustic. The tablecloths were good needlepoint covers with sprightly secular Christmas scenes across them. The chairs were solid looking. Gregor Demarkian was a big man, and not just because of the extra twenty or twenty-five pounds he carried. He was inches over six feet tall and thick-boned. He had broad, muscular shoulders and the powerful thighs that ought to have belonged to a former athlete. Gregor had never competed in athletics if he could help it, except in stickball and prisoner's base when he was a boy. The unusual development of his shoulders and legs was entirely inherited. Gregor had had a much older brother once, who had died in France at the very end of the Second World War, and although Gregor remembered him only dimly, one thing that had stuck with him was his brother's size and shape. God only knew what Gregor's father had been like. He'd died when Gregor was so young, Gregor didn't remember him at all.

This morning, Gregor stopped at the desk to buy a copy of the new *Bethlehem News and Mail*, unfolded it to find his face splashed across the front page under the headline, THE GREAT DETECTIVE COMES TO TOWN, and gave serious consideration to going right back to bed. Then he looked at the subhead—*Reports On The Sighting of Gregor Demarkian in Bethlehem*—and decided that what he should have done was strangle Peter Callisher in the park last night, when he'd had the chance. With Peter Callisher's attitude and this new shooting, Gregor knew there was going to be no way to avoid being turned into a local wonder. He folded the paper up and put it under his arm. The young girl at the checkout desk was staring at him. When he looked straight at her she snapped her spine rigid and gave him a great big smile. He sighed and headed for the breakfast room. If this was the way things had started, it was going to be a very long day.

Actually, things were even worse than he'd feared. Gregor had eaten breakfast early on Monday morning, well before seven. Then the breakfast room had been deserted, and he had taken his seat without the help of a hostess or the need to consider how full the waitresses' stations were. This morning, he couldn't do that. There were a lot more people around at nine. The tables were full and the waitresses looked harried. He stood patiently in the doorway and mentally hoped to be led to the table near the window, where he could look out on Main Street. At least that would give him something to do besides reading about himself in the local paper.

As it turned out, he could have been led anywhere he wanted to go, to the Pitti Palace, even, or to a moon made out of green cheese, because the hostess seemed to have decided he was at least as much of a celebrity as the Pope. She rushed up at him, gushing, the oversized menus clutched in her arms like two-dimensional children.

"Oh, Mr. Demarkian," she said. "It's just so wonderful to see you here. I'm sure we're going to try to give you a wonderful breakfast!"

"You gave me a wonderful breakfast yesterday," Gregor said, "and you weren't trying. Can I have that table by the window?"

"Of course you can have the table by the window. You can have any table you want."

"Fine," Gregor said.

"Just follow me," the girl said.

Gregor did just that, reminding himself as he went that the child couldn't be more than fifteen or sixteen years old. It did some good but not as much as it might have, because Gregor didn't like girls who gushed. He didn't like boys who were too aggressive, either, and for the same reason. There was something about people who were too much of what they were stereotypically supposed to be that made him suspicious. The girl put a menu down in front of the chair Gregor didn't want. Gregor sat down in the other one. The girl blushed and moved the menu. Gregor made an heroic effort not to sigh.

"Could I get you some coffee?"

"Please."

"Oh, it will be a pleasure, Mr. Demarkian, it really will be. Will you be joined by anybody this morning?"

"No."

"Yes, he will," a woman's voice said. "I'm going to sit right down."

Gregor looked up and caught his breath. In front of him stood one of the most beautiful women he had ever seen, and beautiful in that impossible way, small, delicate, fine-boned to the point of looking as if she were made out of spun glass. Her blonde hair was tied loosely at the back of her head with a scarf. The fingers on her hands were so long they looked surreal. Her eyes were a deep blue, wide-set and large, under eyebrows that arched perfectly but didn't look as if they'd been made to. Gregor didn't know what the woman was wearing. It wasn't anything special. The effect was breathtaking nonetheless.

The effect was breathtaking on the hostess, too. She had gone from gushing to mute. She was standing at the side of the table in paralyzed awe. The blonde woman looked up at her and said, "It's all right, Melissa. Mr. Demarkian and I are old friends from Away. Why don't you find Shirley and have her get the man his coffee and me another pot of tea."

"Oh!" Melissa said. "Oh! Miss Everman! Of course I will!"

"Miss Everman?" Gregor said.

"Tell Shirley the man eats big breakfasts," Miss Everman said. Then, as Melissa scurried away, she turned back to Gregor. "Susan Everman," she told him. "And we have met. About nineteen years ago. In New York."

"Why don't I remember this?"

"Maybe because I looked very different at the time." Susan Everman smiled. "I've given up make-up in my old age. And dyeing my hair. And getting my eyebrows plucked. I like this effect much better."

"I like this effect period," Gregor told her sincerely. "But you can't be that old."

"I'm thirty-nine," Susan Everman said. "I was twenty when we met. It was about four days after my twentieth birthday. You were questioning my—business partner. Charlie Giambelli."

Gregor choked. He choked just as a middle-aged woman in a standard waitress's uniform came gliding up with a tray of coffee and tea, and immediately began to look alarmed. She looked about ready to drop the tray and Susan Everman caught it and put it gently down on the table. Gregor stopped choking. The waitress looked at them both and then said, "Well. If you're all right, Mr. Demarkian. Miss Everman. Can I get you two anything?"

"You can get me two scrambled eggs with toast, sausage and hash browns."

"Fine. Miss Everman?"

"No thank you, Shirley."

"Fine." Shirley put the coffee in front of Gregor and the teacup and pot of water in front of Susan Everman and picked up the tray. She seemed to want to say something but not to know what. Finally she just backed away and disappeared.

"I've been waiting for you for hours," Susan Everman said. "I came here yesterday, but you'd already gone. So I came here today early."

"You must have been very conspicuous."

"I don't mind being conspicuous. I'm conspicuous in any event, aren't I?"

"You do have a point."

"Well, then. I just didn't want to call up to your room or do something else where I might get stuck talking with Franklin Morrison in attendance. I definitely did not want to explain all this to Franklin Morrison."

"What makes you think I won't explain it to him myself?" Gregor asked her.

Susan Everman poured hot water over her tea bag. "I think," she said, "that I can trust you to keep what I am going to tell you in confidence unless you need it, and I think I can trust you not to need it. I suppose what I mean by that is that I can trust you to find the person who actually murdered Gemma Bury and Tisha Verek, without needing to involve me. That's what you're good at, right? Finding murderers?"

"Sometimes," Gregor said.

"Well, I hope you're good at it this time," Susan Everman said, "because I'm beginning to get a little nervous. You wouldn't think there would be anything in a place like this that could get me nervous, would you? Not after Charlie. Not after what Charlie pulled me out of, for God's sake."

"Pulled you out of?"

"Let me be blunt, Mr. Demarkian. You were investigating some serial murder case when you ran into Charlie, so you probably don't know much about me because you probably didn't bother to find out, but before I met Charlie Giambelli, I was a whore. I wasn't a high-class whore, either. I was a straightforward piece of street trash and I was addicted to more shit than I could name. About a year after you came sniffing around Charlie, the other Feds got on to him and he went to jail and so did I, because I wouldn't tell them anything.

They sent me to this women's place upstate and this smarmy little woman social worker kept trying to convince me I had a self-esteem problem because I was protecting this pig. Well, Charlie is a pig all right. Most of them are. But he was never a pig to me. My mother was a junkie from way back. She put my ass out on the street when I was eleven years old—and she sold it in her bedroom when I was younger than that. Charlie got me up, and off drugs, and into art school. When I came out of jail, one of his people picked me up at the door, found me a room, got me started and kept me supplied with money until I started getting jobs for myself. Then Sharon came along and Charlie was a prince—"

"Sharon?"

"Sharon Morrissey," Susan said. "You've met her. In Marla's place yesterday."

"Oh, yes," Gregor said. "The one who made me think she might have played field hockey."

Susan Everman grinned. "She quite definitely played field hockey. She went to the Olympics with the American women's team when she was twenty-two. She's what I think of as a natural lesbian. She came by it honestly, instead of the way I did."

"Meaning by being battered out of any possible attraction you could have had to men."

"Well, maybe not," Susan said. "I don't know how these things come about. Most of the girls I knew in the life were gay in their spare time, but that might just have been an unwillingness to take busmen's holidays. Sharon thinks about this stuff, you know, and gets into the politics and all that. I'm just glad to have her."

"Does she know about you?"

"Oh, yes," Susan said. "In fact, she's met Charlie. We went up to Attica to visit him before we moved up here. He gave her a lecture on how she had to be very careful to make me eat because otherwise I'd let myself starve."

"Is that true?"

"Not anymore. I was anorexic as hell for years. Here's your breakfast. Don't you even pretend to worry about your cholesterol?"

"I worry that I'm not getting enough of it," Gregor said.

He moved back a little from the table and Shirley put down plates, one after the other, separate ones for each of the item he had ordered. His breakfast had come that way yesterday, too, so he wasn't surprised. Shirley bustled away and then bustled back again, immediately, to refill his coffee cup. He let her do it and waited until she had gone again before resuming his conversation.

"If you don't mind my saying so," he told her, "I'm surprised at how completely you've changed."

"You mean because people aren't supposed to be able to?" Susan sighed. "Well, I'm out of temptation's way up here, of course. I really couldn't get very far out of line without getting clobbered. And I suppose you can buy drugs up here the same as you can anywhere, but the logistics would be more complicated. I was in therapy for a good long time in New York, individual and group, at the same time. Screaming at people. Driving Sharon out of her mind. Maybe I haven't changed much at all."

"But you don't sell yourself."

"No."

"And you don't do dope."

"Definitely not."

"What do you do?"

"I illustrate children's books," Susan said. "It's not very lucrative, but it's all right for what we need to live on up here. And I have some money in the bank. From before."

"From Charlie?"

"Of course."

Gregor cut his sausage patty into quarters and speared a piece. "So what's the problem?" he asked her. "It sounds to me like the perfect bedtime story. You have Sharon. You have work you like to do. You have a life that has to be better than what you had before. You're even on good terms with Charlie. What could you possibly want with me?"

Susan Everman cocked her head. "Is it true Gemma Bury and Tisha Verek were shot with the same gun?"

"I'm never going to get over the way news travels in small towns," Gregor said. "The answer is yes, as far as we know. The lab tests may turn up something different."

"Did you know that Tisha Verek and Gemma Bury were friends? That Gemma was the closest friend—really the only friend of any kind— Tisha had in this town?"

"No," Gregor said, "but it's useful information. I take it you don't believe the theory that Tisha Verek was killed because she wanted to file a lawsuit against the Celebration."

"No," Susan Everman said, "and I don't believe Jan-Mark killed

167

her, either, although Jan-Mark was having an affair with Gemma, if you didn't know that already. God, this sounds awful. What a mess they were running up there. Anyway, Mr. Demarkian, I don't buy either of those theories because I've got a better one. Tisha Verek was trying to blackmail me. And I'll bet if she was trying to blackmail me, she was trying to blackmail someone else."

f o u r

1

LATER, WAITING for it to be time for Franklin Morrison to take him out to Stuart Ketchum's farm, Gregor Demarkian sat in the lounge at the Green Mountain Inn with a yellow legal pad on his lap, making notes about how strange it all was. It was worse than strange. It was absurd. The yellow legal pad came from the stationery store down the block. It was narrow-ruled, which made that stationery store one of only two places Gregor knew of in the Northeast where he could get narrow-ruled legal pads. For some reason, the distinction seemed to make sense. Everything else about Bethlehem, Vermont, was patently bizarre. Why shouldn't it be a material depot for rare, unpopular and nonstandard office supplies? Why shouldn't it be anything? The pen he was using was a standard Bic, which should have ruined his theory, but didn't, because it was the kind of theory nothing ruined. Gregor had no trouble recognizing in himself what he'd often criticized in his subordinates. He had had one surprise too many. Now he was starting to run with them. The list on his legal pad was instructive. Were these things really that odd? Were their convergence here, in a small Vermont town, any odder? Susan Everman had been first a street whore and then the call-girl centerpiece of a small-time hoodlum's stable. She had given it up and decided she was lesbian and moved to Vermont with her woman friend. Gregor had known a lot of whores and ex-whores and junkies and reformed junkies and small-time hoodlums with the bad luck to land in Attica, too. Jan-Mark Verek was a man who had brought all his lack of discipline from New York City. The man would apparently go to bed with anything that moved, including his wife's best friend, assuming Gemma Bury had been Tisha Verek's best friend. Since he had only Susan's word for it, Gregor drew a circle around that line and a star next to it. What looked like "best friends" to outsiders may have been mutual emotional distaste overcome for reasons of emotional isolation. Neither Tisha Verek nor Gemma Bury could have found many other women like themselves in this place. Or could they have? That was what was so maddening. Gregor was not an unsophisticated man. He had spent a good part of his adult life processing the debris left behind by some of the worst people on earth. He had looked into shallow graves in the countryside as often as he had walked through the rooms where bodies had been left in the cities. He knew there was no such thing anymore as a Norman Rockwell town in a Norman Rockwell America, if there had ever been either one. It bothered him that he seemed to have internalized a Norman Rockwell vision of New England nonetheless. It bothered him that it bothered him that there was so much sexual corruption going on in Bethlehem, Vermont.

Tibor would have said that there was so much sexual corruption going on everywhere, that that was one of the things Christianity had been trying for two thousand years to mitigate and explain. Then he would have gone on to show why explanations would be thick on the ground but mitigation nearly nonexistent, and then he would have started down a path that would have led him inevitably to the Greek Schism, which was where all philosophical discussion led Tibor sooner or later. For Tibor, the split between the Eastern and Western churches in the twelfth century—or whenever; Tibor would know, Gregor didn't—was the determinative factor in every disastrous thing that had happened since, from the decline of Latin as a universal language to the Holocaust, from the corruptions of Baroque architecture to Sid Vicious and the Sex Pistols. Tibor had a surprisingly wide range of general knowledge.

Gregor pulled his legal pad close to him and wrote

What Tisha Verek and Gemma Bury had in common

at the top of a page. Underneath it he wrote

Jan-Mark Verek

and then blew a raspberry. Certainly they had other things in common. He tried

not from town
contemplated First Amendment suit against Celebration
lived next-door to each other on the Delaford Road

and considered it. That third one had possibilities. In all the fuss about
Tisha Verek and Gemma Bury and who Jan-Mark Verek was sleeping
with now, Dinah Ketchum got lost. Dinah Ketchum was part of the
equation, even if only as a curiosity. She had either to be incorporated
in any theory that attempted to unravel the intricacies involved in the
other two deaths, or explained away. Dinah Ketchum had also lived
next door to Gemma Bury, although not on the Delaford Road. From
what Gregor remembered of the map he had made with Franklin Morrison yesterday, the Ketchum property also bordered the Vereks', back
to back. He tried

Tisha Verek was blackmailing Gemma Bury

and didn't like it. Gregor had no doubt that Susan Everman had been
telling the truth. He had no doubt that Tisha Verek had tried to take
advantage of what she knew in just the way Susan had said she had.
The more Gregor learned about Tisha, the less he liked her. The problem
with blackmail, though, was that it took not only two people, but two
distinct prerequisites. It made sense for Tisha Verek to try to blackmail
Susan Everman. Susan had had mob connections—otherwise known
as a guilty secret—and it was possible that those connections had made
her flush with money. That was what was needed. A guilty secret. And
the possession of money by the man or woman who harbored the secret.
Gemma Bury may very well have been spending her overnight excur-
sions to Boston worshiping Satan in the back room of a homophobic
gin mill. Tisha Verek may very well have found out about it. That didn't
give Gemma Bury the kind of money she would need to make it worth
Tisha's while not to tell. As for the rest of the actors in this drama—
Gregor was ready to throw up his hands. Nuts they all most definitely
were. Impecunious they also all most definitely were. Something might
come up to change the situation later—something often did—but from
the way it looked at the moment, he thought he could rule the blackmail
out. He tried

Tisha Verek <u>threatened</u> to blackmail people

171

and liked that better. The threat of blackmail, especially to someone who could not pay, might have caused Tisha Verek's murder. The problem with that as a solution, though, was that it did nothing to explain the motive for Gemma Bury's death, never mind for Dinah Ketchum's. Gregor was almost beginning to believe in Bennis's atypical psychopath, the homicidal maniac.

Out on the other side of town, the church clocks began to chime the noon hour, beginning with the traditional bongs and segueing into carillon carols without a hitch. The production must have been coordinated. There were no clashes between songs and no false notes. Gregor hummed "The First Noel" to himself and packed the legal pad away inside the folds of his newspaper. He didn't want Bennis to see it and get silly ideas. Bennis was always getting silly ideas. Her silliest and most persistent one was that his life was just like the lives of her favorite fictional detectives—Hercule Poirot, Nero Wolfe—and if she could just catch him living in it she could share the excitement of it. Gregor didn't think his life was exciting at all. His feet hurt.

He had put the legal pad away just in time. He had been sitting with his back to the lounge's door, which had kept him from seeing into the lobby without keeping the people in the lobby from seeing him. Bennis must have seen him on her way out to the sidewalk with Father Tibor and his friend. Now she came striding back in, dodging the trailing stems of holly leaves that hung from the curved frame of the doorway, and tapped him on the shoulder with an air of pure relief.

"He's gone," she told him, with a kind of wonder. "Off with Father Cooney and happy as a clam. I can't believe it."

"Is that Tibor's friend?" Gregor asked. "Father Cooney?"

"Father Martin Cooney," Bennis told him, "and don't ask me how they met because I don't know. Maybe they were both buying food. It's been the most extraordinary morning. Do you know what's gotten into him?"

"Mmm," Gregor said.

Bennis shook her head. "I was sitting in my room, minding my own business, reading a book and he comes jumping in on me with—this is after the cookies, Gregor, this is impossible—anyway, he comes jumping in on me with Slim Jims. I haven't eaten Slim Jims since I was ten years old. And he's got this whole pile of them, dozens and dozens, and he throws them on my lap, and then when I wouldn't eat them he gave me a lecture about how I seem to have forgotten that my body is the temple of the Holy Ghost. I didn't know what to do."

172

"What were you reading?"

"What? Oh. *The Chocolate Addict's Never Say Never Diet.* Donna Moradanyan gave it to me. Isn't that Franklin Morrison?"

It was indeed Franklin Morrison, unwinding himself from the front seat of a bright yellow Ford Taurus right in front of the Green Mountain Inn's front doors. Gregor thought about telling Bennis how much easier a time she would have with Tibor if she just stopped reading diet books, but he couldn't figure out how to put it. He'd probably have to ask a lot of questions he didn't want to hear the answers to. He'd probably have to have a discussion about emotions, maybe even his own. He couldn't think about a less-appetizing prospect. He got out of his seat and motioned Bennis toward the doorway, keeping a firm grip on his newspaper-covered legal pad all the while. His grip must have been very firm. Bennis didn't notice that he had anything inside the paper. She only noticed the paper. She tapped the oversized picture of him right on the nose and said, "Tibor brought me a copy of that with the Slim Jims. Your life's going to be a living hell around here from now on, if you ask me."

Gregor had not asked her. He pointed firmly at the arched doorway with its drooping leaves, and Bennis went.

2

FRANKLIN MORRISON had fought in the Second World War, and because of that—as he told Gregor and Bennis half a dozen times before he even got the car away from the curb—he didn't like foreign cars and he didn't like automatic transmissions. Gregor understood the part about the foreign cars. Franklin didn't want to hand his money to the same people who had blown up his brother at Pearl Harbor. That was fine. Gregor did not understand the part about the automatic transmission, which he was sure had not been invented by the Japanese. Franklin Morrison could have used an automatic transmission. He didn't seem to know how to drive a standard one. The car bucked and shook and shuddered. The car made strange noises and seemed to sway from side to side. For reasons of space and size, Bennis was in the back while Gregor was in the front next to Franklin. Gregor could just feel Bennis back there, itching to get her hands on the wheel. Bennis was like that.

She preferred to drive and hated being driven. Gregor was usually willing to do almost anything to keep Bennis from getting in control of a car, except drive himself. She was a maniac. In this case, he sympathized. Franklin's incompetence was making him grind his teeth.

They finally got out on the road, and past Bethlehem's three in-town intersections, and out on the Delaford Road. The car was moving more smoothly simply because there was less for Franklin to do. Gregor's nerves were working more smoothly because the landscape was such a natural tranquilizer. They were still more or less in town—the turnoff to the Ketchum place was technically within the town limits—but it was a part of town without the hyperactive peppiness of the Celebration-soaked center. Gregor watched as they passed small white houses with front doors strung around with Christmas lights and snow-laden ever-greens decked out in satin balls and sparkly ribbons. Smoke rose from chimneys. Front walks were shoveled clear and driveways neatly plowed. It was as if they had stepped off the set of some Swedish director's absurdist movie and into the real Vermont. Gregor came out and said so, as soon as he thought Franklin Morrison could be safely distracted from the death-grip of concentration he was directing at the cleared but winding road.

He heard what Gregor had to say and shook his head.

"You can't do it like that anymore," Franklin told them. "It's not the same. Vermont isn't about Vermont these days."

"Which is supposed to mean what?" Bennis asked from the back seat.

"Which is supposed to mean the flatlanders have moved in." Franklin sounded grim. "It's like Colorado up here now, that's what it's like. We've got all these people from Boston and New York. We've got movie stars. We've got guys went to jail for financial hanky-panky and came out with a couple of million bucks. And we've got what follows them, of course. We've got all these people who aren't anybody yet but they want to be hip."

"Sounds wonderful," Bennis said, in a way that made it impossible for Gregor to decide if she was being sarcastic or not.

"It's a pain in the ass," Franklin told her. He was doing about twenty miles an hour, but even at twenty miles an hour a car will get where it's going eventually, and apparently they had. Franklin turned on his right-turn signal and began to buck off the comfortable blacktop of the Delaford Road onto what Gregor thought must have been dirt down there underneath all the packed snow and ice. It was a road whose name might or might not have been "Ketchum." It was impossible to tell. There was a sign that said KETCHUM at the place where the dirt road met the asphalted one, but that could have been a way to indicate that to get to the Ketchum farm you had to go this way. Gregor looked around and realized that Franklin Morrison had been right. The distances weren't what you would expect them to be, if you were a man from the city, like Gregor, and thrown off-kilter by the trees and isolation. Just ahead along the Delaford Road, Gregor could see the tall stone spire of what had to be the Episcopal Church. Almost every one of the Episcopal churches in New England had been built from that kind of stone. A little beyond the church there was a house, built high on a hill. Its position made it look even bigger than it was, and it was very big. Gregor decided that must be the rectory. Where was the Verek house? Franklin Morrison had stalled out. Gregor leaned toward him, straining against his seat belt, and asked. "Go over the distances with me again," he said. "How far is the Verek house from here?"

"How do you want to get there?"

"By the road."

Franklin Morrison did some quick calculations in his head. "The Episcopal Church has got fifteen hundred feet of frontage on the road, and most of that's down this end. Then the Vereks have about twelve hundred feet on the road, but that's mostly down the other end. They built the house right down here near the stone wall, only place they could fit it without having to blast through granite. I don't know. Lot less than a mile."

"Less than a mile," Gregor repeated.

"Maybe I could drive," Bennis suggested. "I'm really very good with standard transmissions."

"It's less than a mile to Stu's place, too," Franklin put in. "It's maybe, I don't know, four, five thousand feet on this road. Less than that if you go behind on the walls."

"I want to get out and walk it," Gregor said.

"Whatever the hell for?" Franklin Morrison demanded.

"You never want to go out and walk anywhere," Bennis said. "You take to exercise the way dogs take to cats. What's got into you?"

"Give the woman your keys," Gregor said to Franklin. "We'll walk and you'll show me the way, and she can take the car down to Stuart Ketchum's farm."

"How are we going to get to Stuart Ketchum's farm?" Franklin demanded.

"You're the one who said it was no big deal to walk on the walls," Gregor told him. Gregor was already out of the car and onto the hard-packed snow. He had the seat pushed forward to let Bennis out. Bennis climbed out obediently and looked at the sky, which was dark. Franklin climbed out disgruntled and tossed over his keys.

"I'm an old man," he said, "and you're not much better. This is nuts."

"Maybe. But I like to see for myself." Gregor turned to Bennis. "Tell Mr. Ketchum we're on our way. Try not to flirt too much. And don't touch any guns."

"It's touching, the sort of faith you have in my common sense." Bennis stomped around the car, climbed into the driver's seat under Franklin Morrison's arm and had the engine roaring in no time at all. Franklin Morrison looked startled.

They had not gone very far on the dirt road before Franklin stalled. It was only a few steps back to the asphalt. Gregor took them immediately, to keep his city shoes from sinking into snow. If he was going to go tramping around the countryside, he ought to have the proper attire to do it in, but he never believed he was going to go tramping around the countryside. It wasn't the sort of thing he used to do much of when he was head of the Behavioral Sciences department for the FBI. It wasn't the sort of thing he'd ever imagined himself doing much of. If he had to pick one of Bennis's fictional detectives to be, it would definitely come down to Nero Wolfe, who sat in a chair all day and ate.

Franklin reached the Delaford Road himself. He was wearing thick-soled hob boots, and he stamped them on the asphalt as soon as he was able.

"You want to walk," he said. "You're absolutely sure."

"I'm absolutely sure."

"Fine."

Franklin started walking up the road in the direction of the Episcopal Church spire and the big white house, and Gregor followed behind. It was cold and windy and miserable, with only sporadic bursts of sunlight to alleviate the gloom, but although it was farther than Gregor might otherwise have chosen to walk in this weather, it was not actually far. In no time at all they were in front of the church itself, rising stone-built and majestic from a bed of untrammeled snow. Less than a minute later, they had reached a place from which they could see the front door of the rectory in the distance. Gregor nodded to himself, checking his watch and counting in his head. They were two older men—older was as far as he would go; he wasn't ready for Franklin Morrison's "old." A younger man or woman would have been much quicker, and it wouldn't have taken him very long at all. Franklin flapped his arms in the air to get warm.

"We could go up there and pay a call on Ms. Kelley Grey," he said, gesturing toward the rectory. "I'd like to talk to her again anyway. I'd like to talk to her for a good long time."

"I'd like to talk to her, too," Gregor said, "but not right now. Does she live up there all the time?"

"Far as I know. She's in some kind of graduate program or something downstate, I think."

"Were she and Gemma Bury close?"

Franklin Morrison shrugged. "Hard to tell with flatlanders. They go on at each other so much. They spent a lot of time together."

"What about Gemma Bury and Tisha Verek?"

Franklin Morrison snorted. "Aside from the fact that Gemma was getting it on with Tisha's husband, I don't know what you could possibly be talking about. I got to tell you, Mr. Demarkian, I do not spend a lot of time worrying how the people out here are behaving themselves, except for Stu and his wife, of course, because they're friends. As for these other people," his sweeping arm took in the Vereks and the Episcopal rectory both, "who can tell?"

"Try to guess," Gregor suggested. "Tisha Verek and Gemma Bury."

"They talked," Franklin said. "They knew each other better than they knew any of us, and that includes better than Gemma knew her parishioners, who would really appreciate it if she'd go off and worship the goddess in Boston. Except now she can't. If you see what I mean."

"I see what you mean. This is a stone wall."

This was most certainly a stone wall. It was nearly covered over by towering evergreen trees, but it was more than broad enough to walk on, assuming the trees did not impede your progress. Gregor hesitated and looked up the road.

"What's just beyond here?" he asked. "The Verek place?"

"That's right. You can't see much with all the trees, but you're only a few hundred steps from the Verek driveway."

"How long to walk?"

"For us?" Franklin grinned. "Forever. For a good healthy young person, less than two minutes. If that."

"All right," Gregor said. He turned back to the stone wall and began to climb slowly onto it, being careful not to slip. Frozen rock is slick. It would be all too easy to fall and break his head. The day Tisha Verek and Dinah Ketchum had been killed, there had been little or no snow on the ground, and the temperature had been warm for the season. Gregor remembered that from the report Franklin had shown him. That was good. If the temperature hadn't been warm, anybody who'd tried to do this would have killed himself long before he managed to kill anybody else.

Actually, it wasn't that bad. Once away from the road and into the trees, the branches were not so encroaching and the surface of the stones did not feel so treacherous. Gregor was able to stand up tall and walk normally, with Franklin panting and swearing behind him. Gregor kept his memory of the map Franklin had drawn him as clear as possible in his mind and plunged ahead, looking to the right and to the left, into the trees on each side.

"All this land used to belong to Stuart's people," Franklin said. "The first they sold off was to the Episcopal Church back in the 1800s, and then just a few years ago they sold the lot to the Vereks. Stashing cash. All the farmers are stashing cash these days. There's not enough money to be made from farming."

"What's that I see through the trees?" Gregor asked. "Looks like glass."

"That's the Verek house," Franklin said. "Look the other way and you can see the hill the rectory's built on, but not the rectory, because it's too high up. The Verek place is bolted into the side of the hill and down in a valley. Don't ask me why they did it like that. Don't ask me why they built all that glass. At my house, glass like that would make my heating bills impossible."

"Do they have a view? Is there something they can see through the glass?"

"Nothing but more trees and the sides of more hills," Franklin said, "which is mostly what flatlanders are looking for, I guess. You want a real good look at some people, you ought to go up to the third floor of the rectory. That's the highest point anywhere for miles."

"Mmm," Gregor said. He ran it through his mind and came up blank. He couldn't see a single reason why the rectory's view of the town of Bethlehem ought to get anyone murdered.

He went plowing on ahead, stone after stone. After a while, he couldn't see much of anything. It felt entirely natural. Walking in trees. Not being able to see the sky.

"Someone," he told Franklin Morrison cautiously, "told me today that Tisha Verek might have been trying to blackmail some people here in town. What do you think of that?"

"I think Tisha Verek had more money than most of the people here in town could even imagine," Franklin Morrison said. "What kind of a damn fool idea is that?"

"It was just a suggestion."

"What would they get blackmailed about? If you're talking about new people moving in, it could be anything, but people in town? I know the people in town."

"What about Peter Callisher? Hasn't he been away?"

"Yeah, but he doesn't have any money. Not real money. He's got what he makes from the newspaper and what comes in from some rental units he owns over at Green Mountain Condominiums."

"Mmm," Gregor said. "That was how I figured it. Just checking. What's that up ahead?"

Franklin looked over Gregor's shoulder. "That's the fork," he said. "At that point you're at the junction of the Verek place, the Episcopal Church property, and the Ketchum farm."

"Fine," Gregor said. He moved a little more rapidly and came to the "fork," which was really more like an almost-open place in the trees, allowing another stone wall to branch off and go up to their left. It would have been an exposed place, except that there was nothing here to expose anything to. They were out of the sight of human beings or any human construction. Gregor Demarkian turned slowly at the center of this wide space and looked into the branches of the evergreen trees around him. Nothing. Then he looked at the base of the stone wall. Nothing. Then he looked into the bushes and the brush just into the trees. That was when he saw it, lying there just where he had expected it to be.

"Just a second," he told Franklin Morrison, as he climbed off the stone wall. It was a problem for him to wade through all that snow and to fight the roots of God only knew what, but he did it. Then he got down on his knees, not caring what was happening to the trousers of his suit, and pulled it out where Franklin could see it.

"Here we go," he said. "Rifle number two."

five

1

A M A N D A   B A L L A R D would not have voluntarily spoken to Gregor
Demarkian for anything in the world. Gregor Demarkian made her
nervous, and his presence in Bethlehem seemed wrong to her, odd and
out of whack, as if the Pope had suddenly decided to put up overnight
at the Waco, Texas, Holiday Inn. Amanda Ballard didn't think of Demarkian as the Pope, of course. She was saner than that. She just found
him intimidating. That was not a surprise. Amanda found a lot of people
intimidating, and a lot of others downright terrifying. It was a form of
shyness she had cured by an effort of will. When she had to talk to
people, she made herself talk to them. She kept her chin up and her
eyes straight ahead. Very few people noticed how tense she was, although Gregor Demarkian might turn out to be one of the few people
who would. It was all very confusing. She was jumpy and nervous and
tired. She really had been sick the night before and she was sick still,
queasy and dry-mouthed and getting worse. She was turning Gregor
Demarkian into the bogeyman and that was dangerous. That was more
dangerous than she wanted to contemplate.

What was most dangerous was the situation with Peter Callisher
and Timmy Hall, which wasn't exactly a situation at all, but an atmosphere. It was twelve-thirty on the afternoon of Tuesday, December
17th, a little more than fourteen hours since Gemma Bury's body had
been discovered sitting on a bleacher in the town park, dead as a nail
and in full view of several hundred tourists. The extra edition of the
Bethlehem News and Mail Peter had worked all night to put together had

arrived from the printer. It was sitting in boxes that had been lined against the wall under the front windows in the newsroom. The boxes seemed to be everywhere and to obscure everything. BODY FOUND IN PARK, the headline read, and then: *Third Death Sheds New Light On First Two.* Amanda kept seeing the headlines when she should have been seeing the new evergreen wreath Betty Heath had brought in while Amanda had still been asleep upstairs. The wreath was covered with gold-painted plastic everythings, from angels to French horns to partridges that would have looked more suitable in pear trees. It was silly and extravagant and wonderful. So was the gift from Sharon Morrissey, left specifically for Peter, which would have made Amanda angry if she hadn't known Sharon was gay. It was a hand-sized angel made of accordion-pleated red-and-white ribbons with a face made from painted straw. Sharon had been making them with a group of children from the Congregational Church last Sunday and come by today to drop one off. We should be thinking about Christmas, Amanda told herself, not all these other things. Then she rubbed the palms of her hands against her face and rubbed as hard as she could. Bad, bad, bad, she thought. It was as bad as it had ever been, and it was going to get worse.

Peter Callisher was certainly going to get worse. Amanda knew that because he had been getting worse, ever since they came downstairs just after noon. Timmy had come in soon afterward, and now he was getting worse, too, picking up the tension, sending back little signals of panic and distress. Amanda saw Timmy as her project, a kind of penance for not really being the kind of caring, socially concerned person she told everybody else they ought to be. She also liked him, because he meant well and had none of the complexities of more intelligent people, and none of the subterfuges, either. Timmy either liked you or hated you, pronounced you good or pronounced you evil. He liked Amanda and had hated both Tisha Verek and Gemma Bury without reservation. Nor did this hatred seem to have engendered in him the kind of telescoped guilt it might have in anybody else. If Timmy thought that by hating these women he had secretly done something that led to their deaths, he must also have thought this was perfectly all right. Nor would he understand the injunction to speak no ill of the dead. You spoke ill of someone because there was ill to be spoken of them. It didn't matter if they were living or dead.

Amanda watched him on the other side of the room, stacking boxes to take out to the truck at the back. He was immensely tall and immensely fat, but he was also immensely strong. He could get two of those boxes into his arms and up on the counter without sweating. He could get the front of the truck up off the ground in one hand, too.

There really wasn't anything to do in the newsroom today. There never was on the day an issue came out, although Peter always insisted they be there, taking in whatever might come in, listening to the music of town gossip that might someday yield some news. This afternoon there was just this electric-wire snappishness that had begun to spill over to the occasional help. Shelley Dee had been cutting off a phone caller when Amanda first came down. Right this minute, Tara Dessaver was in the middle of a tirade on the environmental disasters caused by the tapping of maple trees. The tourists probably hadn't noticed it, but the deaths had had an effect. The whole town was strung tight, natives and flatlanders both. Amanda wanted to get into her car and go to Montpelier.

Instead, she got up off her seat and crossed the room to where Peter was standing, leaning over a drawing board and checking the graphics on the ad for the Penderman Funeral Home as if they really mattered. The Penderman Funeral Home had an ad in every edition of the *Bethlehem News and Mail,* and no matter how often or how forcefully Peter argued with Penderman *pére* and Penderman *fils,* it was always the same ad.

"Peter," she said, "you ought to tell everybody to go home."

"I'm not going to tell everybody to go home." His voice was deadly with patience, as if they had had this discussion several times already today, which they hadn't. "This day is no different from any other day, except that we have the extra to distribute, and that takes more work around here, not less."

"Then I'm going to take a walk," Amanda said. "I'm getting so nervous, I'm getting sick all over again. I want some fresh air."

"I've been arguing with myself for the last half hour whether we ought to put out another extra tomorrow," Peter said. "All the things that keep happening. Finding the rifle."

"They found the rifle last night."

"We didn't hear about it until this morning."

"All that stuff is going to be on the television news."

Peter shrugged that off. "Not everybody watches the television news. Not everybody wants to watch it. I've got to think, Amanda."

Amanda supposed he did, but she didn't see why he had to think about this stuff. This was nothing. Whether Peter liked to admit it or not, everybody watched the television news. They only read the paper

if they had nothing else to do. She opened her mouth to tell him something else and then decided not to. It was like playing pick-up sticks:
Pull the wrong one and the whole house comes down. Peter was definitely a house ready to come down.

Amanda crossed the room to where Timmy was working, tapped
him on the shoulder and had to jump back when he leaped up and
swung around, his fists up, too loosely balled, too tightly cocked. He
saw her and flushed. Then he seemed to deflate, his body going from
taut to flab exactly as if the air had been let out of him. Good grief,
Amanda thought.

"It's just me," she told him.

"I see you," Timmy said. "I didn't mean anything."

"I'm sure you didn't. You have to relax."

"He thinks I did it," Timmy said. "He thinks I killed those two
ladies."

"Who does?"

"The man we talked to last night. The man Mr. Morrison likes."

"Gregor Demarkian?"

"That's him."

"I'm sure he doesn't think that," Amanda said firmly. "He's supposed to be a very famous detective. He works with facts. You haven't
given him any facts to make him think you killed them."

"I told him I was glad they were dead," Timmy said. "I told them
it was right they were dead."

"I think it's right they're dead, too," Amanda said, "but half the
town probably thinks that, and they couldn't all have killed them. And
what about Dinah Ketchum? You aren't glad that she's dead. You didn't
even know her."

"They think I'm crazy," Timmy said. "Because I'm not so bright.
They think I'm so crazy I'd do things with no reason at all."

"Gregor Demarkian does not think you are crazy," Amanda said,
and then sighed inwardly, because she hated telling Timmy things were
certain when she wasn't certain about them at all. Bethlehem had been
pretty good to Timmy. It was a town that believed in live and let live,
and it had left Timmy alone. A few people had even tried to help.
Amanda knew small towns, though. She had been born in one much
smaller than this. Small towns could turn on you if things got bad
enough.

Timmy was tossing another pair of boxes onto the carton, going
on with his work in spite of the fact that she was there, because that

was what she had taught him to do. When she had first taken him under her wing, she had promised to let him know everything he needed to know to survive. "It's just a few simple rules," she had said, and that had been the truth, as far as it went. She had hurt for him in the beginning and she hurt for him now. With things getting this crazy, she was even afraid for him. Part of her wanted to stay and protect him, although she couldn't have said from what, right at the moment. The rest of her wanted to get out where she could breathe, and the rest of her was winning. She patted him on the back.

"I'm going to go for a drive," she told him. "Do you want me to bring you something?"

"You could bring me a Hostess cupcake," Timmy said. "For later. After I get these boxes out to the truck, I'm supposed to drive them around town. I've got to deliver them just like they were the real newspaper."

"I'll get you a Hostess cupcake. You sure you don't want anything else?"

"A soda?"

"All right."

"If they try to hurt me, I'll hit them," Timmy said. "That's all right. I can do that. If someone tries to hurt you, it's all right to make them hurt instead."

"I suppose it is," Amanda told him, "but let them hit first. All right?"

"If you let them hit first, sometimes you're already dead before you can get a chance to hit back."

And to that, Amanda thought, there was no answer whatsoever. She knew entirely too well just how true it was.

She stood up, looked across the room at Peter at the drawing board, knew that he had noticed her and was not going to look up, and went to the coatrack for her jacket. Shrugging it on, she went through the vestibule and then to the door to the outside. The sky had clouded up again in the last few hours. It was going to snow again. The town park looked barren and embittered. The bleachers had been taken down, but the ground under them hadn't been tidied up as it usually was. The earth looked damaged.

Amanda turned up the street and began walking toward the pharmacy, uptown in the direction of Carrow. There were red and green ribbons on the storefronts and the mailboxes all along her path, but they looked wilted. She passed Stella Marvin and said hello. Stella looked straight through her. She passed Liz Beck and said hello, and Liz stopped, said hello back, and looked her up and down as if she were a piece of rotten meat the butcher had tried to sneak into the good stuff in the supermarket. Amanda took a deep breath and let it out again, feeling the cold in her lungs as pain. She had known things were going to get bad. She hadn't expected them to get this bad this quickly.

Her car was parked in front of the pharmacy. She untangled her keys from the gloves in her pocket and opened the driver's side door. Nobody locked their cars in Bethlehem any more than they locked their houses, but Amanda was not so trusting. She never had been.

She slipped behind the wheel and got the engine started, forcing herself to sit still while the motor warmed up, so she wouldn't stall out six times on her way out of town. Frank Vatrie was coming down the street at her, looking straight through her windshield and making no acknowledgment at all. He made no acknowledgment to Betty Heath, either, when Betty came down the street in the other direction. They might have been two strangers passing each other in New York City.

This is a mess, Amanda told herself. Then she swung the car out onto Main Street and repeated what had become her mantra.

Things were going to have to get worse before they got better.

2

C A N D Y   G E O R G E knew that what she had just done was only a temporary solution, but she didn't have time for a permanent solution at the moment, and she had to have something. It had been one of the strangest days of the last three weeks, and the last three weeks had been the strangest of her life. It wasn't that Reggie was getting particularly violent and particularly nasty. Reggie was always violent and nasty. Reggie was terrible, if the truth was to be known, and Candy was beginning to think the truth wasn't as hidden as she'd originally thought. Of course, she knew that at least some people in town had to know that Reggie had hit her at least once. There was that time Sharon Morrissey had called in Franklin, and Franklin had come to the door and tried to talk to her. Candy wished he'd do that again, now, because now she would understand it better than she had. Back then, it had been like he'd been talking Latin. *You can put him in jail. It's against the law for him to do this to you. If you need help getting on your feet, I know some places you can go in Burlington.* The man had looked to her like some kind of Martian. Put him in jail for what? Get on her feet how? And who cared what kind of laws they passed over in Montpelier? Candy really did wish Franklin would show up on her doorstep right this minute. She could use the help.

One of the reasons it had been such a strange three weeks was that Candy had not been able to sleep, in the usual sense, since it had started. For a while she had put this down to excitement. She was so happy to be in the play she just couldn't calm down enough to drift off. This was a prime example of mental con job, and she knew it. She was excited to be in the play, all right, but that wasn't why she couldn't sleep. She couldn't sleep because she was afraid to close her eyes. She was afraid to close her eyes because of how bad her dreams had gotten, and because she knew there were going to be worse ones to come. This was because her dreams were not dreams the way dreams were supposed to be anymore, meaning scenes her mind made up. There was nothing fictional about what she saw when she closed her eyes these days. There was the bedroom she had in the house she shared with her mother and stepfather. There was the set of curtains with the bluebird border swaying in the summer breeze. There were his hands getting bigger and bigger in the moonlight and the pain that never seemed to stop, never never, and only got worse if she cried or asked him to go away. She was eleven or twelve years old, she couldn't remember which. He was huge and the black pupils seemed to take up all of his eyes. When he came near her, she found it impossible to breathe. That was when she got dizzy and started to looked at the stains on the sheets, to contemplate them, to turn them into artwork. She lay flat on her stomach and made artwork out of the trailing blotches he had left the night before and willed the pain out, out of her body, out of her life, out of her mind, into the air.

When Reggie came home from lunch this afternoon, she was lying on the couch on her back, looking up at the ceiling and thinking. She was thinking the oddest thing, a thing that had never occurred to her before. She couldn't figure out why it hadn't occurred to her before. It seemed so obvious. She couldn't figure out what she was supposed to do with it now that she knew. All her life, she had secretly harbored the conviction that there was a secret out there, a special secret some people knew and once you knew it you were free, you could do anything you wanted to do, you did not have to be the person you were born to be. Now she had it, and it had stopped her cold. This was it, this was the secret of the universe, this was what she should have known all along.

What he did to me was wrong.

A few minutes after she had reached this revelation, she had had another one, coming down on her like a light, and the voice it spoke to her in was Franklin Morrison's.

What Reggie is doing to me is wrong.

That was when Reggie had come in, home from work for lunch the way he never was, glaring and prancing and all wound up. She had known what he was after as soon as she set eyes on him.

He threw himself down in the big lounge chair and kicked himself back, so that he had his feet up and his head halfway to the floor. He'd glared at the sight of her on the couch as he walked in, but he hadn't done anything about it. Maybe he was tired. Instead, he'd put his hands behind his head and closed his eyes and said, "Get me a beer, all right? I want a beer."

A beer. Candy got up off the couch and looked down at him. Reggie never had a beer for lunch on a day when he was working. In that way he was better than both her father and her stepfather had been. He had that much control of his addictions. Maybe he was losing it now. She looked at his chin and the way the stubble along the underside of it was flaked with the soap he hadn't rinsed off well enough this morning. She looked at his throat, which was young but damaged, creased already with too much getting high and too many Camels.

"Do you want a beer beer," she asked him, "or do you want some of that stuff you brought home? That Molson's Ale."

"Molson's Ale."

"All right," Candy said.

She walked past him and out into the kitchen, breathing carefully, telling herself to slow down. If all he'd wanted was one of his ordinary Budweiser's, she wouldn't have been able to bring it off. The Budweisers were in the refrigerator. The six-pack of Molson's Ale was on the back porch, just off the landing that led to the cellar, two steps down from the kitchen through a narrow door. There was a lightbulb screwed into a socket on the ceiling of that landing, and they had a ritual about it. Since Candy was short and small, she wasn't supposed to be able to reach the bulb to change it. Since Reggie was tall and big, he was supposed to do it for her. This was one of the many ways in which he brought home his point, which was that men and women were very different, and that men were stronger and taller and better than women, and that all the problems in the world would be solved if women just learned to accept the fact. There had been times when Candy thought the entire Women's Liberation Movement had been invented to give Reggie something to argue about. Reggie and her stepfather.

Candy went down the two steps to the landing and pulled the knob on the outside door. It held, meaning the door was really shut, not half-open the way Reggie sometimes left it. She reached up and turned the switch lock to locked, then threw the bolt. Then she got the old-fashioned key and worked the center lock from its place on the ledge and locked that lock, too, putting the key in her pocket. Out in the living room, Reggie was getting restless.

"What the hell are you doing out there?" he bellowed at her.

Candy came up the two steps into the kitchen again and called back. "There's a ton of crap on the landing. I'm just getting out the door."

There was not, as a matter of fact, a ton of crap on the landing. There was not much of anything at all. Candy waited, but there were no further sounds from Reggie, and she assumed her explanation had held water for the moment. The moment was all she really needed. She went back down to the landing and reached into the stairwell for the broom. When she got it out, she held its handle in the air and aimed for the bulb. The first time, shockingly enough, she missed. She almost panicked. It was such an easy target, such a close thing to hit. If she couldn't do that much, what could she do? Then she tried it again and it worked. The glass shattered. The shards fell onto her hands and her blouse and glittered even in this place where there was almost no light.

Candy took a deep breath and made herself as loud as she could. "Damn," she said. "Damn, damn, damn."

"Candy?"

Candy dropped the broom and came up into the kitchen again. It was very important that she not be on the landing. It was very important that she not be anywhere near the cellar door. She stepped into the middle of the kitchen and called, "Reggie?"

"What is it?"

"I need some help. I was moving some things around on the landing, trying to get to the back porch, where your Molson's is. I picked up the broom and the handle broke the bulb."

"*Broke* the bulb?"

"It's just a lightbulb, Reggie."

"Nothing's just a lightbulb," Reggie said. "It all costs money. It all costs a lot of money."

They kept the spare lightbulbs in the cabinet next to the kitchen sink. Candy got one out—careful to make sure it was a sixty-watt bulb; she didn't want to set him off with the wrong kind of bulb—and stood back a little farther with the bulb held in her hand, held out, like an offering. Reggie came lumbering in from the kitchen with a scowl on his face, and Candy saw it. Always before, she had thought of their fights as inevitable, as stimulus-response, as her fault. She said something or did something to set him off, and then he was out of control. Now she realized there was nothing she could have done or failed to do, because he looked for excuses to start his fights, he began wanting to hit her and then he found a reason he could pin it on. That was what he was doing now. He didn't care about the bulb. He didn't care all that much about the Molson's Ale, either. He just wanted to punch her into a mass of pulp and blood.

"Broke the bulb," he muttered, taking the new one she was offering him. "Stupid bitch. Stupid goddamned bitch."

"It was just an accident, Reggie. I picked up the broom and the top of the handle hit the light. I didn't do it on purpose."

"I don't know what you do on purpose," Reggie said. "You have so many goddamned accidents."

"I didn't think it would be a good idea to leave it there like that," she told him. "That's why I called you."

"You called me because you'd be shit without me. Always remember that."

Candy promised to always remember something, anyway, and held her breath. Reggie went through the door and down the two steps to the landing. She heard him beginning to unscrew the light and swearing under his breath. She counted to five to keep herself steady and then stepped forward and slammed the door shut.

"What the *hell*—"

There were three bolt locks on this door, one at the top, one in the middle and one at the bottom. They were left over from the previous resident of this house, who had raised Dobermans and kept them in the basement. Candy had always thought those Dobermans must have been mean. She got the middle bolt thrown first and then went to work on the others. She worked patiently and without fumbling, without panic, as if all her emotions had gone underground and frozen solid until she had the job done. Reggie was down there bellowing now, screaming and pounding, and Candy thanked God that the outer door had no window in it. That had been because of the Dobermans, too.

"Candy!" Reggie screamed at her. "Candy, you open up! You let me out of here! You goddamned stinking bitch—"

"Right," Candy said, not so much to Reggie as to the air or the world in general or to herself. Then she walked out of the kitchen and back into the living room. She got her coat out of the hall closet and swung it over her shoulders. She stepped out the front door. It was cold as hell outside, but she didn't mind.

"My name is not Candy George," she said to no one and everyone and most of all to herself. "My name is Candace Elizabeth Spear and I can act rings around that horse-face snot Cara Hutchinson."

It was hardly a statement of broad-minded generosity or Christian tolerance or grace under pressure, but Candy didn't figure she was ready for all that yet, because she was barely ready for what she was doing. She went down the front steps to the driveway and got into Reggie's green Chevy station wagon. The keys were just where she'd expected them to be—meaning in the ignition, where Reggie kept all his keys for all his cars—and she was ready to go.

Driving off, she was happy to realize she couldn't hear Reggie bellowing back there at all.

s i x

1

TO GREGOR DEMARKIAN, New England farmhouses were all the same: white clapboard constructions with black roofs and mullioned windows and covered porches, long flat buildings with woodsheds built onto their backs and clotheslines anchored in the wood just outside the kitchen door. Stuart Ketchum's farmhouse had a woodshed, but beyond that it was unrecognizable. Gregor didn't think he'd ever seen anything so obviously old. It bothered him that he didn't know what made him think that. The house was not disintegrating. It had been recently painted a pearl grey with black shutters, and its corners were true enough. The house was not cloyingly precious, either, the way so many houses were when they had been reclaimed and restored by people with money. Stuart Ketchum had had neither the time nor the inclination to indulge himself in replica lintels or decorative wheelbarrows. There were a pair of flowerboxes fixed under the windows on either side of the front door, but Gregor thought those belonged to Stuart Ketchum's wife, or possibly to his late mother. They were a female touch. This was a no-nonsense working farm, as dedicated to its vocation as a cloistered nun.

Stuart Ketchum himself was more on the order of a backwoods philosopher, although Gregor thought the "backwoods" part might be overdone a little for the benefit of visitors. He was tall and thin and straight, in whole and in part. Each one of his individual bones seemed to be elongated, and his hair hung straight and brown and limp from the top of his head to a point midway down the back of his neck. Gregor spent a lot of time watching the back of Stuart Ketchum's neck, with concentration, as Stuart led them into the house and to the kitchen in the back, dodging ceiling beams with every step. Gregor dodged them, too. It reminded him of the *Pilgrimage Green,* the boat—supposedly a replica of the *Mayflower*—he had just spent a couple of weeks chasing a murderer on. That had been a place of low ceilings and imminent danger to the top of his head, too, and he wondered how Stuart Ketchum stood it, day after day, having to duck every time he wanted to come through the front hall and answer the door. Then they came through a door to the kitchen and the ceilings were instantly taller. Stuart Ketchum stood up and Gregor stood up, too. Franklin Morrison heaved the kind of sigh the fat boy does when the running is finally over in gym. At the long, unvarnished, uncovered kitchen table, Bennis Hannaford sat holding a white ceramic coffee mug full of coffee, looking curious and interested and mischievous at once. She looked like she belonged right where she was sitting, just like she always looked like she belonged wherever she was sitting, and she also looked impossibly good. Gregor thought it was a good thing Stuart Ketchum had a wife, because without her he might be subject to one of Bennis's enthusiasms. Not that he would necessarily mind.

There was a small glass bowl full of pine needles and tiny silver balls in the middle of the table, but no other decoration—maybe because Stuart's mother had died so recently—and Stuart took this bowl off and put it out of the way on a wall shelf. Franklin Morrison had given Stuart the gun to carry as soon as he and Gregor arrived at the farm. It made sense, according to Franklin, because even if Stuart was a suspect, he was also the best man in this part of Vermont when it came to the care, feeding and identification of firearms. Besides, as Franklin said, they were chasing a sane person here. Any sane person would have had the sense to wipe the rifle clear of prints.

This was not a line of reasoning Gregor Demarkian relished, or even approved of, but he was on Franklin Morrison's territory. He let Stuart Ketchum take the gun and watched the man for signs of strangeness or evasion. He might not have recognized either, because Stuart Ketchum was not a personality type he had had a great deal to do with. Stuart put the rifle down on the kitchen table, lying diagonally across the surface with its nose pointed into an empty corner. Then he stood back and contemplated it, as if it were a problem in mathematics.

"Mr. Ketchum is very Zen," Bennis Hannaford said after a while. "Hello, Gregor. Hello, Mr. Morrison. We've been having a very nice time here being Zen while you've been gone. I see you've found something."

"You don't have to be some kind of Buddhist not to want to talk so much your tongue falls off," Stuart Ketchum said. "Excuse me a minute." He went back to the shelf where he'd put the glass bowl and came back with a pair of wire-rimmed glasses.

Bennis drew her legs up under her and hunched over her coffee. "You did find something," she said. "Where did you find it?"

"In an evergreen bush," Gregor said, "or maybe it was a low tree. I don't know the difference."

"It was a low tree," Franklin Morrison said.

"It was out near those stone walls," Gregor went on. "We were walking around on them. There's a place where three of them come together—"

"It's just two," Stuart Ketchum said. "Three properties but two walls. It looks like three walls because the line of the Episcopal Church wall is crooked. Never did get things very accurate, those Episcopalians."

"Now, Stuart," Franklin Morrison said mildly.

"Just tell me one thing," Stuart asked. "Is this the way you found it? Exactly the way you found it? You didn't do anything to it?"

"Like what?" Gregor asked.

"Like disassemble it," Stuart Ketchum said.

Gregor was relieved to see that Franklin Morrison was looking just as bewildered as he was. It was embarrassing, after all the movies and television shows, to be an ex-FBI agent who didn't know anything about rifles. The FBI agents in *Bonnie and Clyde* had stood in a field and chewed up the landscape with machine guns. Gregor caught Bennis Hannaford's eye and blushed a little. She knew exactly what was making him so uncomfortable.

Stuart Ketchum hadn't noticed that anyone was uncomfortable in the first place. He leaned toward the rifle, fussed with something Gregor didn't catch and came up with a limp hand-sized object. "There's the clip," he said calmly, "with three bullets gone. That makes it much safer. This is a Marlin Model 70P Papoose, it's a .22 long-rifle caliber semi-automatic with side ejection, but that's not the point of it. It's what's called a quick takedown."

"Meaning what?" Gregor asked.

"Meaning you can do this." Stuart Ketchum picked up the gun and seemed to break it in half, except that there weren't any sounds of breaking and nothing small and vulnerable fell on the floor. Then he jerked his arms and the rifle seemed to snap back together again, as if it were made out of Lego blocks. "The point of something like this," he said, "is to make storage easier and to make the hunter feel like he's still in the army, which is how a lot of these guys want to feel. This is not a military rifle. It's a sports model, not a bad one, I've got a couple in the gun room. Introduced in 1986. Sixteen-and-a-quarter-inch barrel. Hundred fifty, hundred seventy-five dollars, in there. No big deal."

"No big deal," Gregor repeated. "But it could kill somebody."

"Oh, yes." Stuart Ketchum nodded. "I wouldn't shoot it at anything serious, like a bear. Not if I had a choice. But it could kill a person without much trouble. I take it this is what you think killed my mother."

"We don't know," Franklin Morrison said quickly. "We just found it."

"Considering how we found it," Gregor said, "I'd be extremely surprised if it wasn't the rifle that killed your mother. I believe in coincidences, Mr. Ketchum, but not in too many of them in the same place."

"Amateur," Stuart Ketchum said.

"What?" That was Gregor and Franklin both.

"Amateur," Stuart Ketchum repeated. "Nobody who knew what he was doing around guns would have stored this rifle without the barrel cocked, not even in a tree. Never mind stored it with the ammunition clip inside it—the only point to that I can see is that whoever had this thing didn't know how to get the clip out and didn't want to figure it out. It isn't hard to know what you have to do if you look carefully enough. And leaving it out there, all ready to fire with the clip still in. You sure you didn't do anything to it? Take the safety off?"

"I wouldn't know where to find a safety on a rifle if my life depended on it," Gregor Demarkian said.

"Franklin would," Stuart said. "It doesn't matter. Whoever put it out there was stupid beyond belief. Some animal could have come along and set it off. It wouldn't have been easy, but it's been known to happen. Then the bullet flies and who knows what it hits? Or who?"

"Maybe that's what happened to your mother," Bennis said cautiously.

"Once is one thing," Stuart said, "twice is another. I wish I could tell you I don't know a single person who would have put that gun out there that way, but it isn't true. It's incredible what people don't know about guns. I've got a lot of them. I believe people ought to have the right to have them. But dear sweet Jesus, it ought to be like driving a car. They ought to make sure you can operate one before they let you have a license."

"That's the kind of thing Stuart doesn't say in town," Franklin Morrison said drily, "because otherwise people would say he's gone over to the enemy."

"The enemy?" Gregor asked.

"Flatlanders," Bennis Hannaford said. "I have heard a fair amount about flatlanders since I got here. The man does talk, just not a lot, and not about any subject I bring up."

"I couldn't talk to you about the punk aesthetic in science fiction," Stuart said, "because I don't read science fiction."

"He reads histories of the Vietnam War." Bennis stared at the ceiling. "And he knows who Bernard Hare is."

Stuart went back to fussing with the gun. Gregor watched him move the barrel up and down, back and forth, and then pick up the clip and examine it. Every once in a while he shook his head. The lack of emotion was disturbing, but not as disturbing as it might have been. Gregor thought it was Stuart Ketchum's form of self-control. Either show no emotion or go publicly nuts. A lot of men were like that. Gregor leaned over and touched the rifle's barrel gently, to get Stuart's attention.

"Let me ask you a few questions," he said. "Is this a rare gun or a popular one? Would you know who else besides you in town would have one? Are you sure you've got all the ones you own here?"

"I was in the gun room when she drove up," Stuart said, jerking his head in Bennis's direction. "My guns are all in racks. I could tell in a second if any of them were missing. None of them were missing, except the one you and Franklin have already got."

"All right," Gregor said.

"As for anybody else in town who might have one—" Stuart Ketchum shrugged. "It's a decent rifle for target practice and it's relatively cheap. And it's glamorous, if you know what I mean. It makes you look good when you hold it. I know half a dozen people in town who've got them. Maybe more."

"Like who?" Franklin Morrison asked.

"Reggie George," Stuart said promptly, "although why any society in its right mind would let Reggie George have a firearm is beyond me. Someday he's going to push that little girl he's married to just far enough, and she's going to use it to take off his head. At least, I hope she will."

"Yeah," Franklin said. "I hope she will, too. I offered to do it for her once, but she wasn't interested."

"Umn." Stuart ran his hands through his hair. "Let's see. Carl Herman's got one. Keeps it behind the counter of the store—he runs a feed-and-grain store, Mr. Demarkian, out on the Montpelier Road—anyway, he keeps it back there just in case somebody wants to steal a sack of chicken meal. And Henry Dearmott's got one he keeps on his back porch out on the other end of Carrow from Main Street. And there's Eddie Folier, of course, but I don't think it could belong to him."

"Why not?" Gregor asked.

"Because *he* knows what he's doing," Stuart said. "He was in Nam, too, about two years before I was. Came back with an itch for target practice but not as bad as mine. He's got the Marlin and about six other rifles including a thirty-ought-six he takes up to Canada hunting. He'd never have left the rifle out there like that. He'd have known better."

"Where does he keep it?" Gregor asked.

Franklin Morrison answered. "He's got a rack over his fireplace, just like the ones you see in house magazines. Got a nice house, too, just off Main Street, around the corner from the *News and Mail.* Local stone."

"Does he lock the guns in the rack?"

"No," Franklin said. "Nobody does that kind of thing around here. Nobody gets their things stolen around here as a general rule. Or they didn't used to."

"Old Linda Holt has one, too," Stuart said. "She's our resident grand old countrywoman. Came up from Boston about twenty years ago and got more native than the natives. She's seventy-nine. She used to use a Remington Model 7 but it got too much for her."

"Mmm," Gregor said.

"I keep trying to match rifles to the people I saw last night," Stuart said, "and I just can't do it. I run one of the food stalls. I was standing right outside the bleachers when the play was over last night, and I must have seen a dozen people I knew. Sharon Morrissey. Amanda Ballard. Betty Heath. Amanda's shot a rifle or two in her life. She's come out here with Peter for rifle practice. And I know Sharon Morrissey can shoot because she's always winning things at the county-fair booths in the summer. As for Betty Heath—I think if you showed her a gun, she'd probably scream."

"Mmm," Gregor Demarkian said again.

They were all looking at him. Even Bennis, who should have known better, had her head cocked as if she expected him to produce a pearl of wisdom or the perfect solution to the entire mess, wrapped up in ribbons and tied up in bows. Instead, his mind was caught on a couple of snags.

He stirred in his chair, did his best to sound like a Great Detective with the solution already in hand and a secret agenda to his questions and said, "Are the two things contradictory? The rifle is stashed in a way that no one who knew anything about rifles would stash it—which, for your information, is the same way we found the other rifle stashed last night—anyway, there it is, stashed by an amateur, and there the— the bodies are—hit by someone who must have been familiar with firearms."

Stuart Ketchum looked startled. "Why?" he demanded.

"Why what?" Gregor asked him.

"Why did he have to be familiar with firearms?"

Now it was Gregor's turn to be confused. Since it was such a familiar feeling in this case, he didn't mind. "Because he's so consistently accurate," he said. "Always, every time, he hits his victims in exactly the same places."

"How do you know he's aiming at those places?" Stuart asked.

Gregor countered. "How do you know he's not?"

Stuart Ketchum threw up his hands. "Well, hell," he said. "If he's so good he can aim and hit the shoulder and the throat every last blasted time, why hit the shoulder and the throat at all? Why not hit the heart? Why not hit the head? The way he's been going about it, he's been damned lucky one of his victims hasn't shown up alive."

"Now, Stuart," Franklin Morrison said.

But Stuart Ketchum wasn't listening. His winter jacket hung from a peg hammered into the wall near the wood stove. He grabbed it, stuffed it under his arm and started out a door at the back.

"Where are you going?" Gregor asked him.

"Show you something," Stuart Ketchum said. Then he turned back to the room, looked at Bennis and said, "You'll be perfect. Come on out to the yard."

"Come on out to the yard and do what?" Bennis asked.

Stuart wasn't waiting for her, either. He was standing in the back doorway, holding the door open and motioning them all through.

2

THEY HAD TO go through the gun room to get to the backyard. Gregor looked it over and decided that Stuart Ketchum had been telling the literal truth. If a gun had been missing from this collection, Stuart would have known about it. The guns were not only all in racks, but labeled and sorted according to type and caliber. The military collection took up one wall and each of the guns in it had been secured to the rack with a frame lock. Gregor saw a pair of Mausers that looked old enough, and in good-enough condition, to be worth serious money. He decided that Stuart locked them up less because they were dangerous than because they would be tempting to steal for sale. The other rifles were not locked up, not even now, after one of them had gone missing and been involved in the shooting deaths of two people.

Out in the yard, a string of cans was set up on a disintegrating wooden fence for target practice, but Stuart ignored them. He went into the barn and came out again with what Gregor recognized as a folded-up police practice target, the kind that works on a modified tripod. Stuart unfolded it, reached into its back and came out with a sheet of paper drawn to look like the head and torso of a man. He tacked this securely to the target and stepped back.

"There," he said. "Now let me show you something." He hurried back through the door they had all come out of and reappeared a few moments later with a rifle Gregor thought was close to identical to the Browning that had been used in the killings of Tisha Verek and Gemma Bury. He walked to a place about forty feet in front of the target, loaded the rifle and aimed. "Watch me," he said.

They watched him. He hit the target square in the heart.

"There," he told them. "I can aim. And this isn't a bad test, either. I don't know where my mother was or what she was doing when she was hit, but Gemma Bury was sitting close to stock still on a bleacher and Tisha Verek was standing in her own driveway. These shootings have been a lot like target practice from the beginning. Now I need Ms. Hannaford."

"For what?" Bennis Hannaford asked suspiciously.

"This is what we brought you out here for," Gregor said soothingly.

"It's what I meant back at the Inn when I said we needed you for target practice."

"You knew he was going to pull this?" Bennis didn't believe it.

"They knew I wanted a small-sized person to fire a gun," Stuart said. "This is something else. We'll get back to the other thing later if we have to, which maybe we won't. Come up here and hold this thing."

Stuart had the barrel cocked. Bennis took the rifle out of his hands and held it away from her body, at arm's length, as if it were contagious. Gregor had to bite his lip to keep from laughing.

Stuart walked up behind Bennis, put his arms around her shoulders and gripped the gun. Then he brought it closer to both of them and put the barrel back in place. Bennis definitely didn't look happy with the situation.

"I'm going to kill somebody," she warned. "I've never had one of these things in my hands before in my life."

"You're not going to kill anyone," Stuart said. "You're going to shoot at the target. Let me show you how to aim."

Stuart showed Bennis how to aim. Then he stood back and nodded encouragingly. Bennis had let the barrel's nose drop toward the ground. Now she pulled it up again and sighted along the barrel. Gregor thought she looked like she felt ridiculous.

"Now," Stuart told her, "aim for the heart, and pull on the trigger."

"I don't want to aim for the heart," Bennis said.

"It's just a piece of paper," Stuart said patiently. "Just aim for the middle there. I want to show your friends an important point."

Bennis sighted again, and then closed her eyes. She fired in the direction the gun was pointing in without looking at what she was firing at. Then she opened her eyes again and said, "Nothing happened."

"Something did happen," Stuart said drily. "You hit the side of my barn. Couldn't you feel the recoil?"

"My shoulder still hurts."

"Exactly my point."

"I don't get it," Franklin Morrison said.

"It would be easier if Ms. Hannaford here would keep her eyes open long enough to hit something," Stuart Ketchum said, "but in theory it's very easy. Maybe Ms. Hannaford could try again and keep her eyes open this time."

"I don't want to try again," Bennis said. "I'm a nonviolent person."

"Aim."

Bennis looked appealingly at Gregor Demarkian and then at Franklin Morrison, got no help—Gregor wasn't going to give her any; he wanted to see what this was all about—and raised the rifle again. This time, she didn't look so afraid of it. She positioned the stock against her shoulder and sighted down the barrel again. She bit her lip and tensed her finger on the trigger. Gregor thought she was deliberately holding her eyes open, the way people will when they're talking to a very important bore. She pushed her feet a little wider apart, braced herself and fired. Then she pointed the barrel's nose at the ground once again and looked confused.

"Something happened," she said.

"You hit the target," Stuart told her. "A little to the side. You got the appendix instead of the heart. Still, it wasn't my barn."

"But it wasn't that I didn't aim right," Bennis said. "The rifle moved."

"Exactly," Stuart Ketchum said.

"Why did it do that?"

"Because you aren't used to firing rifles and because you have the upper-body strength of a gnat."

"Thanks a lot," Bennis said.

Franklin Morrison was beginning to get restless. Gregor didn't blame him.

"Now see here," Franklin said. "What is it you're getting at, Stuart? So Ms. Hannaford's never fired a gun before. So she's not good at it. So what and who cares?"

"You should," Stuart Ketchum said. "Look, it only makes sense. I've thought it from the beginning. That's why I've never believed all those rumors that Jan-Mark Verek killed Tisha."

"Do you know Jan-Mark Verek?" Gregor asked. "Do you know he knows how to fire a rifle?"

"I don't have the faintest idea if Jan-Mark Verek has ever seen a rifle," Stuart said, "but I do know that if he had some kind of characteristic trouble firing one, this isn't the kind it would be. The man is built like a bull. You do realize it, don't you? All this business with throats and shoulders. It's not what our man is aiming for. It's what the rifle is making him hit."

"Stuart—" Franklin was sounding a warning.

Stuart Ketchum turned back to Bennis Hannaford. "Do it again," he commanded. "Only this time, aim for the head."

Bennis hesitated only a moment. Then she raised the rifle's barrel, aimed at the head and pulled the trigger. When she put the gun's nose down, she was looking confused again.

"It happened just the same way," she said.

"Yes, it did," Stuart told her, "and it will go on happening the same way unless you get enough experience to correct for the rifle's action or you start lifting weights. You got him right in the shoulder."

"I think I'm beginning to understand," Gregor said slowly. "Our man, or woman, is really aiming at the head and the heart, say, but because he isn't used to handling a rifle, he doesn't know how to correct for the weapon's kick. Therefore, every time he aims at the head, say, he hits the throat, and every time he aims at the heart—"

"—he hits the shoulder," Stuart said. "Our guy goes to the right just like Bennis here goes to the left. He also jumps around more than Ms. Hannaford does, but that doesn't matter. It can't be Verek because Verek has too much strength in his shoulders and his arms. He wouldn't need to correct for the rifle's action the way Ms. Hannaford has to because he'd be strong enough to hold the gun steady under any conditions. Unless, of course, the two of you are right and he actually wants to be hitting people in the shoulder and the neck, which I think is rank impossible."

"Mmm," Gregor said.

"I'm getting a headache," Franklin said.

Stuart Ketchum stood with his arms folded over his chest, looking triumphant. He had never put his jacket on. He had it tied around his waist where it couldn't do him any good. He didn't look cold.

"The other thing this proves," he said, "is that all three of the shootings had to be done by the same person. I'm not saying there couldn't be two people in the world with the same reaction to a rifle kick. I'm just saying that as coincidences go, it's—"

"What's that?" Gregor asked.

That was a loud echoing noise, like a Brahma bull bellowing into a bullhorn, and it seemed to fill the air like a sudden hard rain. Stuart Ketchum was looking disgusted. Franklin Morrison was looking resigned.

"That," he said, "is Jan-Mark Verek himself, calling for help. He's probably dead drunk and can't find his way to the bathroom."

PART THREE

The hopes and fears of
all the years
Are met in thee tonight

PART THREE

1

I N   O N E   W A Y , Jan-Mark Verek was more of a traditional artist than a contemporary one. He believed in doing the meet and seemly thing, and it was with an eye to doing the meet and seemly thing that he had built his house. Gregor Demarkian saw it right away, as soon as Franklin Morrison's car pulled into the Vereks' driveway. There was that great expanse of redwood and glass, staring out across the snowed-over front lawn to the line of tall trees that shielded the property from the road. There was the purity of line, the integrity of form, the perfection of detail that spoke of a project pursued for its beauty at completion. There was the expense, too, that spoke of a project pursued by a man who did not have to wonder how his children would get through college. Gregor found something particularly satisfying about the expense. It wasn't a large house—not so large as a four-bedroom colonial in a decent Boston suburb—but Gregor was willing to bet that every square foot of it had cost triple what would have been spent on a more conventional place. Redwood had been chosen over clapboard. Glass had been custom designed and special ordered. Cabinets had been individually and locally made. Gregor knew about the cabinets because he could see them. He could see everything there was to see, through those windows, except the bed, which he guessed was up on the second level behind the partial wall on which hung a red-and-grey Navajo blanket. It was an exposed and vulnerable house, except that, hidden behind the trees like this, there was nothing for it to be exposed and vulnerable to. Still, Gregor didn't like it. He always thought first of security, just in case. There was never any way to tell if your next-door neighbor was a saint or David Berkowitz. Not even if you'd known that neighbor for the past forty years.

Maybe it was fear of vulnerability and exposure that had made Jan-Mark Verek install his alarm. Whatever it had been must have been a powerful emotion. The alarm had been awful enough heard from the safety of Stuart Ketchum's barnyard. Right here at the source, it was devastating. The warning of a nuclear attack would sound like this, Gregor told himself, if you weren't listening to it on television. Gregor promised himself to watch more television in the future, just in case there was a nuclear attack. After hearing this thing, he much preferred spending his last moments with the Emergency Broadcast System.

Behind the wheel, Bennis Hannaford braked, put the car into park and then sat back, looking at the wall of glass and wincing.

"How long does that thing go on?" she demanded. "I mean, what's he calling, the National Guard?"

"That isn't his alarm," Franklin Morrison explained. "He's got one of those goes off automatically if somebody tries to break in, and he's got another one that rings a fire alarm in the volunteer fire department building in town. This is his panic-button alarm."

"That means he has to stand there and pull the damn thing himself," Stuart Ketchum said.

"Does he do this often?" Bennis climbed out from behind the wheel and stood in the driveway, still looking up at the house.

Stuart Ketchum sighed into the back of Gregor Demarkian's head and said, "Once every two or three months. That's all. Just once every two or three months."

"Once there was even an emergency," Franklin Morrison said. "Bear sat down outside the door and wouldn't move. Poor man didn't have any way to get out of his house."

"Man built a sensible house, he'd have a back door to get out of," Stuart Ketchum said.

Gregor Demarkian got his door open and climbed out onto the gravel driveway. As he did, the noise suddenly and abruptly stopped, mid-bellow, and Bennis Hannaford raised her eyes to heaven.

"Hallelujah," she cried. "I have been saved. Why did it go off?"

"Because Jan-Mark turned it off, of course," Franklin Morrison said. He'd gotten out of the car, too, with Stuart Ketchum just behind him. He looked resigned and as tired as Gregor Demarkian ever wanted to see any man. "If Stuart here and Peter Callisher hadn't been coming up the drive just after Tisha Verek got killed, Jan-Mark would probably have set that thing off then, but there you were, the cavalry had already arrived—"

"—like we were the cavalry, for God's sake—"

"—and Jan-Mark doesn't like to waste electricity. The only thing Jan-Mark likes to waste is breath, which he wastes a lot of, especially if he's drinking. Maybe we ought to go up and knock on the door. Although what we'd knock on it for is beyond me. He's got to know we're here. All he's got is windows."

He also had to have a reason to shut off the alarm, but Gregor didn't want to bring that up. Franklin had just said it and forgotten he'd said it, but everybody else had forgotten it, too, and maybe it didn't matter. They were all tired. Gregor moved to the front of the house and the only thing that might conceivably be a door and looked around for a bell. There wasn't one. He tried for an intercom. There wasn't one of those, either. Finally, he knocked.

Gregor had expected a wait, some frustration, a few more futile volleys against the door: That's what door systems like this one were designed to induce. Instead, he got an instantaneous creak and rattle, and the door pulled back in front of his face in no time at all.

On the other side of the door was a man who looked more like Stuart Ketchum's description of him than seemed fair. Jan-Mark Verek was indeed a bull, complete with overdeveloped shoulders and short, thickly muscled legs. Jan-Mark Verek looked like Franklin Morrison's description of him, too—meaning like Brooklyn. Gregor thought the man was more than a little crazy, possibly a borderline sociopath. He had that kind of light in his eyes, that kind of intensity in his every small movement. Jan-Mark Verek was an arresting presence no matter what he was doing, and what he was doing right this moment was just standing there.

A moment later he had backed up and bent over, bowing comically, to let them all in. "It's you," he said, sounding pleased. "The Great Detective. And all I was expecting was Stuart in a pissed-off mood."

"You got Stuart in a pissed-off mood," Stuart Ketchum said. "Why don't you just pick up the phone and call me?"

"You're always out in the yard shooting at cans. You'd never hear me."

"You could call *me*," Franklin Morrison said.

Jan-Mark Verek ignored him, choosing to concentrate on Bennis instead. Bennis had come in last, behind the rest of them, and in the beginning Jan-Mark had not noticed her. Now he had, and his scrutiny was detailed and unmistakable. Gregor was used to men being attracted to Bennis. Men were constantly attracted to Bennis. They weren't usually as nasty about it as Jan-Mark Verek. Gregor started to growl. Bennis shot him a look that said she knew perfectly well how to take care of herself. Which was probably true.

"Oh, you're nice," Jan-Mark told her.

"Only when I want to be," Bennis said. Then she brushed past him and headed for the stairs, as quickly and unselfconsciously as if she'd been invited. The stairs were open-risered and open-railed and open to the windows. Gregor thought climbing them was going to make him dizzy.

"Come in," Jan-Mark said, watching Bennis's retreating back. "Come in, come in. We might as well all go upstairs and review the damage."

"Damage?" Franklin Morrison asked.

"I've been robbed."

Jan-Mark turned his back on them all and went off in the direction Bennis had taken. After a moment, Gregor and Franklin and Stuart followed. Everything was so open, it would have been impossible to get lost. Jan-Mark went up a single set of risers and then waited, near the kitchen, where Bennis had installed herself on a delicate chair. All the furniture Gregor could see was delicate and quasi-abstract. The art was big and bold and brightly colored and not of Jan-Mark's making. Jan-Mark went in for trash collages and found objects. The paintings were all standard abstracts of the kind popular in the twenties. They suited the house.

Jan-Mark waited until they were all assembled just outside the tiled floor that marked off the kitchen and said again, "I've been robbed. It was the most amazing thing. I must have been robbed in my sleep."

"You mean you think you were robbed while you were here?" Franklin Morrison sounded incredulous.

Jan-Mark didn't take offense. "I was taking a nap. I'd had a long night and a long morning, and I was exhausted."

"You must have been wired," Stuart Ketchum said.

Jan-Mark threw him a look of contempt. "When I'm wired, I can't sleep at all. No, that wasn't it. I was just totally done in. I lay down just around eleven o'clock, and somewhere between then and when I set the alarm off, I was robbed."

Gregor Demarkian checked his watch. "It's about half past one," he said. "Let's say we first heard your alarm ten minutes ago. That gives your thief about an hour and twenty minutes to get in and out, assuming you fell asleep immediately and went straight past REM time into a coma—"

"Are you trying to tell me I couldn't have been robbed?"

"I'm trying to tell you your story has some problems in it." Gregor looked around the kitchen again. Everything was clean. Everything was white. Jan-Mark must pay a cleaning lady. "How did you find out you were robbed?"

"I went up to my studio. And there it all was. A mess and a half."

"Your studio?"

"My late wife's office. The studio and the office are two three-sided rooms in the loft."

"This is above your bedroom," Gregor said.

"Exactly."

"And if I wanted to get there, I'd go how?"

"Up these stairs." Jan-Mark patted the rail of the staircase they had all so recently ascended. "It goes all up and down the four levels, or maybe it's five, I don't remember. It's like a dollhouse, here. All the rooms are open to the window wall. All of them are reached by one staircase."

"Well," Gregor said, "that means that this thief of yours not only robbed you while you were sleeping, but robbed you while you were sleeping in a room open to the room he was stealing from, and then he had to go tromping up and down a lot of wooden stairs to get there and get out—I take it there isn't an alternative route?"

"None."

"That must have made the fire marshal have orgasms," Franklin Morrison said.

"The fire marshal notwithstanding," Gregor said, "Mr. Verek may have been robbed, but he wasn't robbed the way he said he was. Which leaves us with three possible alternatives."

"Tell me." Jan-Mark was looking more amused by the second.

"The first one is that you weren't robbed at all," Gregor said.

"But I was." Jan-Mark nodded vigorously. "At least, I ought to say that my late wife was. It's her things that were taken."

"All right. The second possibility is that you were out when it happened, but for some reason you don't want us to know you were out. That would be particularly good if you were trying to establish an alibi for something that has recently happened back in town, while Mr.

Morrison and Ms. Hannaford and I have been at Mr. Ketchum's farm. That's what I will go on to assume if there turns out to be another dead body there when we go back."

"If there was a dead body back there, we would have heard about it," Franklin Morrison said. "That's my personal car we're using, but it's got a two-way radio in it. And I carry a beeper."

"The body might not have been discovered yet," Bennis said blandly.

"There isn't any body." Jan-Mark Verek was impatient. "At least, there isn't one I put there. I will admit I might have taken a tranquilizer or two before I went to sleep."

"Right," Franklin Morrison said.

"Phenobarbital," Stuart Ketchum said. "Without a prescription. And no brand-name packaging, either."

"I keep telling him I won't arrest him unless I catch him selling it to the local population, but he doesn't believe me," Franklin Morrison said.

Gregor paid no attention. He knew Jan-Mark Verek had been on some kind of drug and that that drug had probably been a depressant. He knew that that would account for Jan-Mark's not having heard an intruder, if there had been an intruder to hear. With anybody else, he wouldn't have bothered to go through this song and dance. He hadn't been that kind of agent in the Bureau, either. His attitude had always been that people ought to be allowed to keep their shameful but not case-related secrets to themselves. He just didn't like Jan-Mark Verek.

Still, there was a robbery to be investigated, or something to be investigated. That was why Jan-Mark Verek had set off his alarm. Gregor put his hand on the stair rail and gestured up the stairs with his head.

"That way?"

"That way." Jan-Mark sprang into action. "All the way up. In the loft, like I said. And I'm going to tell you right now that I think my wife was right."

"About what?" Gregor asked him.

"About a certain person who happens to work for Peter Callisher named Timmy Hall. Come on. Let's go up. I've got a lot to show you."

2

THERE WAS a reason for Franklin Morrison to investigate Tisha Verek's office. He was the local lawman and Tisha Verek's husband had
just claimed that the office had been robbed. There was a reason for
Gregor Demarkian to investigate Tisha Verek's office, too. Jan-Mark
Verek wanted him to. There was no reason at all for Stuart Ketchum
or Bennis Hannaford to be investigating Tisha Verek's office, or wandering around in it, or observing the actions of the three people who
belonged in it, but they came all the same. It was part and parcel of the
fact that nothing in this case had been very "official," just as nothing
in Bethlehem, Vermont, was very "official." It all seemed to get done
somehow here. Gregor didn't mind. Since he was going to talk it all
over with Bennis later, he thought it would save time if she saw it for
herself.

Tisha Verek's office was indeed in a loft, a very high loft, higher
even than the one that served as the bedroom. The house was a series
of lofts. They made Gregor, who had never been easy with heights, feel
unsteady. He climbed the stairs doggedly, behind Jan-Mark but ahead
of all the others. Bennis came up right behind him, muttering all the
way. He didn't like Jan-Mark Verek. Bennis didn't like Jan-Mark or his
house, either, on general principles, and now she seemed to be taking
against his carpets. Gregor reached the loft, turned his back on the open
rail and looked around.

What the loft reminded Gregor Demarkian of was not so much a
dollhouse as a stage set, the kind of stage set where two rooms can be
seen at once and two scenes go on almost simultaneously. On one side
there was the bare, unadorned studio space that belonged to Jan-Mark
himself. Because of the way the staircase was placed, they had to cross
in front of it to get to Tisha's office. Gregor saw canvases stacked against
the walls and paints in tubes and jars and bottles on every available
surface. There weren't many available surfaces. To Gregor's eyes, it was
not a happy jumble, but an angry one. Things seemed to have been
flung about in continually erupting fits of pique, and left to lie out of
spite. Maybe that was a form of projection on his part, because of the
way he read Jan-Mark Verek's character. Gregor had never had a chance

to read Tisha Verek's character, and seeing her office he decided he was glad he hadn't. This room was neat, but it was no more a cheerful neatness than Jan-Mark's studio was a cheerful clutter. Gregor's first thought on seeing the precise stacks of paper and the even-rowed photographs on the corkboard was: what a constipated, nasty woman she must have been.

Constipated or not, nasty or not, those weren't his problems. He looked around the office one more time and said, "How do you know anything was stolen? Are you trying to tell me the room was usually neater than this?"

Jan-Mark Verek made a face. "Awful, isn't it? She was the most anal woman. It's neat enough, even now, I'll give it to you, but you've got to see things are missing."

"He's right," Bennis Hannaford said.

She was standing at the back, near one of the corkboards, looking up at it and squinting. Gregor walked to where she was and tried to see what she saw. He saw row after row of small, blurry, black-and-white pictures, each one labeled with a name. In the bottom row, there were two missing—or at least two empty spaces.

"All of these spaces were filled?" Gregor asked Jan-Mark. "Every last one of them?"

"Every last one of them," Jan-Mark said. "Of course, I can't tell you with what, exactly. She used to change them fairly frequently. Especially on that board. But they were filled and they were up there in alphabetical order."

"They're not in alphabetical order now," Bennis said. "Look, Gregor. There's Monica Hammond and then John Ziebert and then Billy Welsh and then Elsie Hastings. Two of the HAs were removed."

"Tommy Hare," Jan-Mark said. "That's one of the ones that were removed."

"Who's Tommy Hare?" Bennis asked.

Stuart Ketchum and Franklin Morrison looked uncomfortable. Gregor said, "Tommy Hare was a teen-aged boy in Devon, Massachusetts, about twenty-five years ago. Not teen-aged. Twelve, I think he was. Anyway, he got a girlfriend and eventually the girlfriend got another boy. He waited until she was giving a party and sneaked into her patio that night and used a cattle prod to electrocute everybody who happened to be in her pool. A lot of people, from what I remember. He ended up at a place called Checkered Tree. It's a facility for what we used to call the criminally insane."

"Oh, yuck," Bennis said.

"Tisha always said she thought Tommy Hare and Timmy Hall were one and the same person," Jan-Mark said.

Bennis thought this over. "That won't work," she said finally. "Timmy Hall is that man we met with Peter Callisher yesterday, isn't he, Gregor?"

"That's right," Gregor said.

"Well, he couldn't have been twelve twenty-five years ago. He's not that old."

"You just think he's not that old because he's retarded," Jan-Mark Verek said. "There's no telling how old he is. There's no way to know."

"I could know if I wanted to," Franklin Morrison said, "except there's no point to it, because I already know he wasn't in anyplace called Checkered Tree. He was at the Riverton Training Facility right here in Vermont. Teacher of his called me up to tell me about him when he first came down here. Woman I went to high school with."

Stuart Ketchum turned politely to Gregor and Bennis. "Riverton is a big complex of mental-health facilities in the Green Mountains. They've got everything up there. This training school for the mentally retarded. A psychiatric hospital. A sort of summer camp, out-patient, group-therapy arrangement for people with chronic conditions. Oh, and an addiction-treatment specialty facility that does everything from cocaine to overeating."

"Sounds wonderful," Bennis said, unenthusiastically. She had wandered across the room and stood now next to Tisha's computer station, looking at the corkboard there. "There's been a bunch of pictures removed from here, too," she said. "I wonder why anyone would take them. There must be a manuscript around somewhere if she was writing a book."

"There are a couple," Jan-Mark said. "She made copies of her proposal and gave them to people."

"A lot of people?" Gregor asked.

Jan-Mark shrugged. "She gave one to Gemma Bury, if you're looking to construct a conspiracy theory. I think she gave one to one of the ladies at the library, too."

"You mean it was general knowledge," Gregor persisted. "It wasn't a case of someone thinking there would only be one copy and trying to get a hold of it."

"They might have thought that if they were mentally retarded,"

Jan-Mark said. "That's the point of being mentally retarded. You're not too bright."

"Someone as stupid as you're making Timmy Hall out to be wouldn't have removed all these pictures so neatly," Gregor said. "He'd have trashed the place and destroyed the computer and had done with it."

"Let's look at what's missing from here," Bennis said.

Bennis had sat down at the computer station. She ran her finger across the corkboard and said, "Bateman, Beddish, Yale, Carter—there's something. Who belongs there?"

"How should I know?" Jan-Mark demanded.

"There's another one further down," Bennis said. "Holby, Warren, Hurt. Who would that be?"

"Maybe you have some way of calling up the information on the computer," Gregor suggested. "Or maybe your wife left notes. Or a manuscript."

"No notes," Jan-Mark said. "And as for the computer—"

He looked dubiously at the blank screen and then sighed, almost resignedly, as if necessity were forcing him into the worst of all possible positions, the need to act like an ordinary man. He tapped Bennis on the shoulder, waited until she stood up and then sat down himself. He reached into a side drawer, looked through the diskettes there, and chose one. Then he loaded up.

"This was her index," he said. "If you want to know the truth, it was the only part of the book I liked. You wouldn't believe how many innocent-seeming little children have been positively homicidal."

Bennis Hannaford frowned. "Isn't that usually because they've been abused?" she asked him. "It's not as if they were born evil or something like *The Bad Seed*."

Jan-Mark was rolling information across the screen. "A lot of them have been abused, I'll grant you that," he said. "Tisha had more stories about child rape than I've got canvases. She used to read them to me at night. It made for no end of wonderfulness in our times of marital companionship. However, some of these kids are absolutely out of it. Just plain bad."

"I don't believe in just plain bad," Bennis said.

"You wouldn't." Jan-Mark tapped a key and the information stopped rolling. "Here's the first one. Actually, the first two. Bickerel, Amy Jo. And Kathleen Butterworth."

Franklin Morrison stirred. "I remember Amy Jo Bickerel," he said.

"Oh, God, but that was a mess. About—what? Twenty, twenty-five years ago—"

"Twenty-three," Jan-Mark said, peering at the computer screen.

"Yeah. Well. Happened right here in Vermont. Girl was eleven, twelve years old. Had an uncle who would take her out for rides and every time he got her alone, wham. One day she got her father's rifle and whammed right back. Waited for him to come up the walk and fired—"

"Wait," Gregor said. "I remember that one. It was ten o'clock on a Monday morning or something like that and the street was full of people—"

"Right," Franklin Morrison said. "It was. And the bullet that hit the uncle first passed right through him and got a car, but it just missed this woman coming home with her groceries, and the second bullet broke the window of a store across the street that was thankfully shut for repairs. It was nuts. Caused a fuss in this state, you wouldn't believe it, especially since it turned out she could prove all that stuff he'd done to her. He'd taken pictures and she knew where they were. He really was a first-class asshole."

"He sounds like it," Bennis said. She was leaning over Jan-Mark's shoulder. "It says here she was—no, it says she *is* at Riverton. Does Riverton have a place for the criminally insane? Did they really send her away for life?"

"Oh, no," Franklin Morrison said. "She wasn't convicted of anything. Even though by the laws of the time she was guilty, and the judge tried to instruct the jury and get them to do what they were legally supposed to do, the jury just wouldn't do it. I didn't blame them. I don't blame them now. I wouldn't have done it, either. Uncle of hers was a first-class son of a bitch and a first-class loser on top of it. Anyway, it was her parents who had her committed, if I remember correctly. She was pretty messed up by the time it was all over."

"Who was Kathleen Butterworth?" Stuart asked.

"Kathleen Butterworth is one of the ones I like," Jan-Mark said. "She offed her baby sister in her sister's crib, and then she got a taste for it and offed a couple of other babies in the neighborhood. She had about ten scalps under her belt before they caught on to her."

"Arizona," Bennis Hannaford said. "Who's the third?"

Jan-Mark tapped a few keys and the information began rolling again. He stopped and said, "Hudder. Cynthia Hudder. This one's recent. She wouldn't be more than maybe twenty-eight, thirty years old."

"Like Kelley Grey," Bennis said immediately.

"Or Sharon Morrissey," Franklin Morrison put in. "Kelley's too young. You can't do that, Ms. Hannaford. There have to be half a dozen young women of about the right age in town right now, all of them from Away and so nobody knows who they are or where they've been."

"What did Cynthia Hudder do?" Bennis asked.

Jan-Mark shrugged. "No big deal. Killed her stepmother. Stepmother was to all intents and purposes a first-class pain and fond of using a belt. Kid was about ten. Happened out in Shaker Heights."

"Did she go to jail?" Stuart Ketchum asked.

"She wouldn't have gone to jail," Gregor said. "A child that young would have been put into a psychiatric hospital and then possibly into a juvenile detention center. If they couldn't place her in a foster home."

"If you were a foster parent, would you take a kid who'd killed her own stepmother?" Bennis asked.

"I think a psychiatric hospital I didn't want to be in and a juvenile detention center would feel like jail to me," Stuart said. "When would she have gotten out?"

"It says right here when she got out," Jan-Mark told them. "It was—twelve years ago. When she was eighteen."

"Most states require the system to release juvenile offenders at age eighteen, no matter what they've done," Gregor pointed out. "Juvenile law is not the same as adult law."

"What about the rest of them?" Bennis asked.

Jan-Mark tapped his computer keys again, rolling the information back. "Amy Jo Bickerel, released from care about three years ago. Going on four. Kathleen Butterworth, released from care about twenty years ago, when she was eighteen. I don't think I'd want Kathleen Butterworth wandering around my neighborhood."

"I don't think I'd want any of these people wandering around my neighborhood," Gregor Demarkian said. He had been standing a little behind the others, not looking at the computer screen, but thinking. Now he was all thought out. He had never taken off his coat. He reached into his pockets, got the gloves he had borrowed from Tibor and began to pull them on.

"I don't think we have anything more to do here," he said. "We've done as much as we're going to do."

"What about my safety?" Jan-Mark demanded.

"Your safety is secure," Gregor told him. "This was a very careful, very gentle theft, if it can technically be called a theft at all. The picture or pictures in question were removed, and the thief went away. That is all."

"If the thief also happens to be the murderer of my wife, he might come back," Jan-Mark said.

"True," Gregor Demarkian told him, and then brightened, as if that was the cheeriest news he had had in ages. Maybe it was. Gregor found that Jan-Mark Verek did not improve with acquaintance.

That made it all the more necessary, to Gregor's mind, that he get out of this redwood-and-glass monstrosity and back to normal life.

t w o

1

SOMETIMES, SHARON MORRISSEY thought that people who lived in Bethlehem had less Christmasy Christmases than people who didn't, because the middle of Bethlehem was so chock full of Christmas spirit they couldn't bear to bring any of it home. That was slightly incoherent, but she knew what she meant. After a day sitting in the Congregational Church, looking out the basement windows at the ribbons and the bows and the ornaments and the statuettes that had been springing up all over town, day after day, since the Celebration began, all Sharon wanted to do was go home and pretend to be Scrooge. Since she and Susan had already decorated their house, she couldn't. As soon as she walked through her front door, she would be confronted with a "stained glass" mobile made from colored plastic wrapping paper, and as soon as she walked into her living room she would be confronted by a crèche. The Congregational Church had a crèche, too, in the lobby on the first floor just outside the room Sharon thought of as "the room with the pews in it." She didn't know what else to call it. She couldn't called it the church proper, or refer to an altar or a sanctuary. Congregational churches didn't have those. Sharon found it all very frustrating. She had been born and brought up Catholic. Everything had been much simpler there.

Sharon had been in the basement of the church holding story hours for the children of tourists—and, of course, for any local children who had the time and inclination to attend. Sharon was considered to be far and away the best reader in Bethlehem. She was in demand at the library not only for children's readings, but for readings to the elderly and public presentations as well. The library always held a read-aloud in the spring to raise extra money for its bookmobile program. Today, Sharon had read six different stories at six different sessions. Now it was five o'clock in the afternoon and her throat hurt. The last of the children had gone. She had been a tiny girl in pink tights and a bright fuschia snow parka, too shy to smile, and she had left clutching a gingerbread cookie iced to look like a snow-covered candy house. Wasn't it the witch whose house had been made of gingerbread and candy? Sharon had wondered at the time. Then she had pushed the thought away from her. It was just one more example of the way her mind had been working lately. Susan kept saying it was silly to go on this way. Susan ought to know. Still, Sharon couldn't stop from being depressed, and she couldn't stop from being worried, either. When she had first heard Tisha Verek had been found dead, she had been relieved. Tisha Verek was the danger. Tisha Verek was gone. There was no more danger. It turned out to have been far more complicated than that. Even Susan thought so. Sharon wondered what she had said when she had gone to Gregor Demarkian this morning.

Sharon had left her parka in the cloak room at the back of the basement. She got it off its hanger and put it on, starting up the steps to the first floor as she pulled her arms into the sleeves. Coming out into the foyer, she looked at the crèche—with the baby Jesus conspicuously in His manger, to show that this was a Protestant, not a Catholic, production—and then went for the side stairs, as if she were going to climb to the second floor. The second floor was new, part of a wing that had been added to the church in the 1950s. The church itself had been built in 1721. Sharon went a quarter of the way up the steps, saw that the door to Toby Brookfield's office was open and the light inside was on and called up. Toby Brookfield was the minister.

"Toby?" Sharon said. "I'm going home."

There was the sound of a chair scraping against hardwood and Toby's face appeared in his office door. "Be careful driving," he told her. "It's supposed to be icing up. Are you sure you're all right?"

"I'm fine."

"You've been depressed all day."

Sharon shrugged. "It's Gemma Bury and all the rest of it, I guess," she said. "It doesn't exactly put me in the holiday spirit."

"Oh, I know what you mean." Toby Brookfield sounded eager and solicitous at once. "It's been terrible. It's been terrible everywhere. I don't know what's gotten into people."

Sharon knew what had gotten into people. She used to live in New York City. "Something terrible is going to happen if something good doesn't happen soon," she said, and then, because she really didn't want to discuss this—and especially not with Toby Brookfield, who was very nice and meant exceedingly well but wasn't very bright—she began to back down the stairs. "Well," she said. "I guess I'd better go. I just wanted to tell you I was leaving."

"Be careful," Toby Brookfield said again.

Sharon muttered something incomprehensible, even to herself, and backed down into the foyer again. She gave the crèche one last glance and then let herself out onto the church's front steps. Five o'clock was late this time of year in Vermont. The sky was already dark. The street lamps were already beginning to look ineffective against the night. Sharon zipped her parka to her chin, wrapped her scarf around the high collar that jutted up around her neck and started down the steps to the street.

On most days, when Sharon came into town to work at the Congregational Church, she parked her car in the church parking lot, just as, when she was working at the library, she parked her car there. During the Celebration, she always used Jim MacAfee's front lawn instead. It cost a quarter, but it guaranteed she was never stuck, because Jim made a point of keeping the cars of people from town in the barn, where they could be easily and quickly moved, in spite of a sea of tourists' vehicles blocking every available patch of grass around them. Sharon had been stuck once too often behind the church or the library or even the *News and Mail,* rendered immobile by escapees from Boston who'd decided that their cars could sit any old place they chose.

To get to Jim MacAfee's front lawn, Sharon had to go up Main Street in the direction of Carrow and turn down Carrow for a few hundred feet until she came to a dirt extension. If it hadn't been for a sign at the start of it that said PARKING 25¢ THIS WAY, only the natives would have known the extension wasn't a dead-end rut. Sharon started up Main Street in the right direction, passing no one from town and glad she was passing no one from town. Usually, the number of people she knew and the extent of her friendly relations with them were a large part of what Sharon liked about Bethlehem. It was like she'd told Toby Brookfield, though. The death of Gemma Bury had broken something, some thread, that Sharon had once thought to be strong but now saw to be fragile. The atmosphere in town was slipping past tension into a kind of hysteria. Sharon had seen it all day in the people who had come to the church to hear her read. The tourists had been fine. The people from town had all been stiff as boards and twice as rough. It was as if they'd all gotten up this morning and taken a pill that made them think: *Shut down. Lock up. Close ranks.*

Up the street and across it in the park, the crews were beginning to put up the bleachers. They were working slowly and it looked like they were starting late. Sharon walked up Main until she was across from them and stopped. The park looked so ordinary. It didn't look like the kind of place a murder would happen at all. At least there was that much. There was no room for mistake. Tisha Verek's death might have been an accident. Dinah Ketchum's death might have been an accident. Gemma Bury's death was the result of deliberate malice, no two ways about it.

Sharon wrapped her arms around her waist, rocked back and forth on her feet and stopped. In there among the carpenters and the teen-aged boys who were their helpers was another figure, small and still and seeming to flaunt her Alice-in-Wonderland hair. She was standing right next to that clump of bushes some people were saying had hidden the gun that killed Gemma Bury, and the gun that had killed Dinah Ketchum, too. Sharon didn't know if she believed this. They had to run tests on guns before they knew for certain that the guns had killed anybody. She didn't think there had been time to run tests like that. On the other hand, town gossip was remarkably accurate. It always startled her. She'd been brought up to believe that gossip was always lies. Sharon stared across the street a little longer and then made up her mind. It was different during the Celebration than it was at other times. You did have to look both ways when you wanted to cross Main Street. Beyond that, it wasn't too bad, because the tourists tended to park their cars as soon as they crossed the town line and go from one place to another on foot. It was a little worse right before the performances started, but that was several hours away. Sharon waited for an Isuzu Trooper that belonged to the commune out in Lebanon to pass and then crossed to the park, half running as she went, to keep herself warm.

On the other side of Main Street, Sharon had to dodge two high-school boys carrying a long ladder between them and a cluster of blue and silver Christmas balls that had suddenly appeared in a bouquet tied to a bench at the street's edge. Christmas decorations often appeared suddenly in the middle of town during the Celebration. It was a measure of how tense things had been under the surface, even before Gemma Bury was dead, that there had been so many fewer of them in the last two weeks than there had been in other years.

Sharon slipped through the line of carpenters and went to the small stand of bushes. Amanda Ballard was standing behind them, toward the middle of the park. Sharon had almost missed seeing her from Main Street. After Sharon had seen her, there had been a moment or two when Amanda seemed to disappear. Now Amanda was back, standing a little away from the bush's stiff needles, frowning as if the evergreens had been schoolchildren refusing to obey their mother.

"Amanda?" Sharon asked.

Amanda turned her head slowly, not startled, not surprised. Then her eyes swept the broad streak of white on the left side of Sharon's head and she blinked. "Sharon," she said. "I saw you across the street."

"I was across the street," Sharon said, feeling like an idiot. Amanda always made her feel like an idiot. Amanda always made her feel conspicuous, too, as if that streak of white was made of neon and glowing and pulsing in the dark. Sharon Morrissey couldn't begin to count the times that that streak had made her feel like a marked woman. She turned away from Amanda and said, "What are you doing here?"

"Trying to check it out," Amanda said simply. Then, seeming to think she might have been unclear, she elaborated. "It's something I heard Peter talking about on the phone. To Stuart Ketchum. That Gregor Demarkian person has a theory about how Gemma Bury was killed."

"Really? How?"

"He says the killer put the rifle right here in these bushes—put it here early, aimed ahead of time at the two seats Gemma and Kelley were going to be sitting in—"

"You mean the killer knew where Gemma and Kelley were going to be sitting?"

"Well, it's assigned seating," Amanda said, "and Peter gave Gemma the tickets right there in the *News and Mail* office, right in front of I don't know how many people. I don't think it was any surprise to anyone, where she was sitting."

"Oh," Sharon said.

"Anyway," Amanda said, "the killer is supposed to have stood right up to these bushes when the time came and squeezed the trigger, with the gun in here at shoulder height so all he had to do was lean forward and aim. But I don't see how that can be true, can you? And if it is true, I don't see that Timmy could have done it."

Sharon stepped forward and examined the bushes. "I could have done it that way," she said finally. "I could have put the rifle right there," she pointed to a cleft in the branches, "and then when I wanted to shoot, it probably wouldn't have been much of a problem."

"Well, you, yes," Amanda agreed. "And me, too. And Susan Everman and Candy George and Betty Heath and I can think of a dozen people. But Timmy couldn't have done it."

"Why not?"

"Because he's too tall," Amanda said patiently. "I'm five-four. You're—what? Not much taller than that."

"Five-five," Sharon said. "Susan's five-three."

"Candy George is five-three, too, and Betty Heath is the same height I am. But Timmy's nearly six-three. His head would have come right up over the top of this thing. He'd have had to bend over to aim, unless he fired without aiming, and I don't believe that. I don't believe Timmy would fire a rifle without looking at what he was aiming at. I don't think Timmy would have fired a rifle."

"Who says he did?"

Amanda looked back over her shoulder, up Main Street to the *News and Mail* office. "Lots of people," she said. "You wouldn't believe the phone calls we've gotten today. They think that just because he's retarded, he's crazy."

"Well, I don't."

"Good," Amanda said. "He's sweet as pie, really, and not violent at all. He was the nicest boy at Riverton. Peter checked out all his records when we first decided to hire him. There wasn't a single thing wrong."

"I'm sure there wasn't."

"They just hate him because he's different," Amanda said. "Even Peter does. I thought when I heard about this that it would clear him, because it is so obviously means he couldn't have done any of it, but instead they've all got their theories. They've all got their fantasies about how he bent over to shoot and nobody saw him. It's sick."

"Yes," Sharon said carefully. "Amanda? Are you all right?"

"I'm fine." Amanda had been standing with her arms wrapped around her body. She'd barely moved from the moment Sharon had first come up to her. Now she shoved her hands in her pockets and turned her back on the stand of evergreen bushes.

"I've got to go back," she said. "Timmy's nervous and Peter's really been crazy all day. I don't think he's been completely all right since Tisha Verek died."

"What?"

But Amanda was already moving away, across the park to Main Street, down Main Street to the *News and Mail* in the direction opposite the one Sharon wanted to take. Sharon stood looking after her, feeling agitated and not knowing why.

Timmy Hall. Peter Callisher. God only knew there had been enough rumors about Timmy Hall. And Tisha Verek had started every one of them.

Sharon went back to Main Street herself and began to make her way toward Jim MacAfee's front lawn. It felt horrible in this place now, sticky and vile, and she just wanted to get out.

It made her wonder why she and Susan had come here to begin with.

2

KELLEY GREY was sitting in the rectory kitchen when the doorbell rang, sitting at the table and looking over the manuscript Tisha Verek had left with Gemma Bury. She was also conducting a running argument in her head about what she ought to do about this manuscript. She had already decided to bring it to Gregor Demarkian or Franklin Morrison or the state police or whoever was really investigating Gemma's death. She may not have liked Gemma much at the end, but she owed the woman at least the courtesy of providing a clue to her murder to the authorities assigned to avenge it. Beyond the mere fact of handing the manuscript over, though, Kelley found it hard to think. Should she discuss Gemma with Gregor Demarkian? Yesterday, Kelley had been sure she ought to tell Demarkian about Gemma's affair with Jan-Mark Verek, but today it had begun to seem less and less important as the hours went by. Maybe if she had been able to get in touch with Demarkian himself—instead of being forced to leave messages at the desk at the Inn—it would have been easier to make up her mind. It hadn't been an important affair. Gemma Bury didn't have important affairs. She didn't want to get tied down. That, Kelley understood now, was why she herself had been so angry with Gemma at the end. Gemma hadn't liked to get tied down to anybody, for any reason. Her idea of the ideal friendship was one whose emotional commitment never surpassed that of a lunch date. God only knew what her idea of the ideal sexual relationship had been. Kelley's idea of the ideal friendship had always had something in common with the ideal of the indissoluble marriage, but maybe thinking like that was out of date.

When the doorbell rang, Kelley had decided to get up, make herself a cup of tea and do something serious about the part of the rectory she was now occupying. This part was shrinking by the minute—she got more and more afraid of the size and the emptiness of the place by the minute, too—but it could do with a few more Christmas decorations than it had been subjected to so far. Gemma had been fairly contemptuous about people who were "sentimental" about Christmas, the way she got fairly contemptuous of those of her parishioners she described as "wedded to the more ludicrous details of the Christian myth." Gemma had preached diversity and nonjudgmental acceptance with the best of them, but she had had no tolerance for either in her own life.

The doorbell was a chime that echoed and gonged for long seconds after the button was pushed. Kelley got up, looked around the kitchen and decided to put the manuscript in the refrigerator. She had a friend in Boston who was an aspiring novelist, and he always put his manuscripts in the refrigerator when he went out. Refrigerators survived fires, that was the point. The house could burn to the ground while he was away, but the manuscript would remain intact, protected along with the leftover scrambled eggs. Kelley put this manuscript next to a half-full bottle of Perrier water—Gemma hadn't been big on abandoning herself to the pleasures of the flesh no matter what they were—and went out into the foyer to answer the door. With her growing nervousness in the house, Kelley had had a growing need to keep the lights on, even in the daytime. Now half the bulbs in the foyer chandelier were dead and she had no way to change them. She didn't know where to find a ladder tall enough to reach and she didn't know who to call for help. She brushed aside the feeling that the foyer was too dark to allow her to admit a stranger safely, stepped up to the right hand door of the front double doors and looked through the viewer. On the doorstep was a small blonde girl in an oversized jacket, looking tired.

Kelley stepped away from the door, thought for a moment and then opened up. If she'd been living in town instead of all the way out here— or if she'd been more in contact with the people who were living in town—she might have caught the paranoia everybody else had caught like the latest round of flu. She hadn't. When she had the door open, she stepped aside and let her visitor in. Then she smiled and said, "Yes? Can I help you? Is there something I can do for you?"

The small blonde girl looked around the foyer, including up at the chandelier. "My name is Candy—Candace. Candace. Never mind. You'd know me as Candy George. If you know me. Do you know me?"

"I know who you are," Kelley said, thinking that Candy George was disoriented, like someone in shock.

"My name isn't really Candy George, though," Candy said. "George is my husband's name. Reggie George. Reginald. You may not know who he is. Not being from town. You, I mean. You not being from town."

Kelley closed the door against the wind. "I've seen him around," she said. "Would you like to come into the kitchen? I've got the tea kettle on the stove, all ready to go. You look all done in."

"My real name is Candace Elizabeth Spear," Candy said. "That's the name I had when I was born. I can't do anything about it now. It says Candy George on all the programs for the play and this is the last week. But after it's over, I can change. And I can change in every other way right away. So I don't want you to call me Candy George."

"All right."

"Call me Candace instead."

"All right."

"And I will have tea."

"Wonderful."

Kelley turned around and walked rapidly back in the direction of the kitchen, assuming Candy—or Candace, or whoever she was—would follow. She was right. Candy did follow. Kelley put out a chair for her and she even sat down, automatically, as if she had been computer-programmed to respond to certain signals in certain ways. Shock, Kelley decided, was exactly what was going on here. The symptoms were so classic, they could have been a paragraph in the training manual of the women's center Kelley used to volunteer in down in Burlington. Kelley got out a clean cup and put it on the table. Then she got the sugar bowl out of the cupboard and put that on the table, too. With any luck, she would be able to convince Candy to have her tea with lots of sugar in it, because that was one of the ways you were supposed to be able to treat shock.

The tea kettle began to whistle. The water had been warm before

Kelley had put the kettle on the burner, because she'd been warming it up and pouring herself cup after cup of tea all day. Just in case Candy liked liquor better than she liked sugar, Kelley took Gemma's only bottle—Johnnie Walker Red—and put it on the table. It didn't go over well. Candy made a face at it and pushed it aside.

"I don't drink liquor," she said. "I don't even drink beer. Alcohol makes people crazy."

"It certainly makes some people crazy," Kelley said.

"Let me show you something," Candy said. She stood up and pulled her sweater up off her head. She undid her blouse and turned around. For one short second, Kelley thought this was the beginning of some weird sexual come-on, but she'd barely had the thought when she saw the reality, and the reality made it very hard to breathe. Then a wave of nausea washed over her and she had to put her head between her knees to keep from throwing up.

"Good God. Good Christ in heaven. What happened to you?"

"What do you think happened to me?" Candy said. "Reggie happened to me."

Kelley looked up. Candy had already pulled her shirt back on and got it buttoned up. She was reaching for her sweater. Kelley could tell now that she was finding it hard to move. The miracle was that Candy could move at all. She had heard the rumors, of course—in a town like this, you always heard the rumors if they didn't have anything to do with you; there'd been whispering for months at least that Reggie George beat his wife—but she'd had no idea of what the reality would be like. Even after all that volunteering at the women's center, she'd had no idea what the reality would be like. She'd never faced the reality before. She'd always been involved in the talk counseling afterward.

Candy settled her sweater around her waist and sat down. Kelley asked her, "Did that just happen today? Just now? Did you escape from him and come running here?"

"That happened yesterday." Candy took the tea bag out of her cup. She reached for the sugar, and Kelley was relieved to see she used a lot of it. "If it had happened today," she said matter-of-factly, "it would still be bleeding. I always bleed for hours afterward. Sometimes for days. He doesn't like me to put bandages on it. He says they make my clothes look funny."

"Right," Kelley said. Matter-of-fact or not, Candy was still disoriented. "Where is your husband?" she asked. "What are you doing here? Is he chasing you?"

"Reggie can't chase me because I locked him in the basement. I tried to call Franklin Morrison to come and take him away, but every time I got the police station, they said Franklin was out. Franklin came once when it was bad and tried to do something, but I wouldn't let him and nothing came of it. He said he'd come back and help any time I wanted him."

"Wouldn't any of them have helped? Couldn't you have told one of the other policemen and had him come and take Reggie away?"

"I don't know," Candy said. "I didn't trust it. I wanted Franklin. I still want Franklin. Reggie will be safe enough in the basement. I threw all the bolts."

"Right," Kelley said again. It didn't seem to be the time to suggest that basements have windows that can be broken, or that the George house was close enough to civilization so that someone might hear Reggie hollering and let him out, or that Reggie was a large and strong man who might break a door or two if he got angry enough. "Well," Kelley said, "you're here now. I've just got to figure out what we can do for you."

Candy looked up from her tea, skeptical. "You're a feminist, aren't you?"

"A feminist? Well, yes. Yes, of course I am." Kelley didn't think it sounded like an accusation, although it would have with some people. It sounded more like Candy was making sure she had her facts straight.

"I've got to go be in the play tonight," Candy said. "And for the rest of this week. You see what I mean?"

"Not exactly."

"Well, I can't do anything about anything now," Candy said, "except get Franklin Morrison to lock Reggie up, and I can do that as soon as I find Franklin, because he once said—well, he said. And then I have to be in the play for the rest of the week, and I won't give that up for anything. But then there's after that."

"After that what?"

"You're a feminist," Candy said, "so you'll know."

"Know *what?*" Kelley was getting desperate.

"Know where to go," Candy said. "I saw it on television, on *60 Minutes*. I know everybody thinks I'm stupid, but I'm not. I watch *60 Minutes* when Reggie's gone out to a bar or someplace, which he does practically every Sunday night. And there it was. All these women who were feminists and the feminists got women whose husbands beat them up the way Reggie beats me up and the feminists helped these women find new places to stay and how to get a job and what to do about school and they give advice, you see what I mean? They give advice, which is all I need, because I sure as hell don't need any guts, I must have been born with those or I'd have been dead by now, but I do need some information and you're always saying you're a feminist and Gemma Bury was, too. I used to think feminists were just women who didn't like men, but on *60 Minutes* it said feminists were women who did this instead. So are you real? Are you a feminist?"

Are you a feminist? Kelley Grey asked herself, marveling. She knew the tone in Candy's voice all too well. She'd heard it from dozens of other people over the course of her life. That tone said: Put up or shut up. And faced with that alternative, Kelley Grey had always failed.

Well, she decided, she wasn't going to fail this time. She wasn't going to have to.

She got up out of her seat and headed for the phone on the wall next to the refrigerator.

"I am definitely a feminist," she said, "and I definitely know what you can do. Let me make a few phone calls. Drink more tea."

"I've had enough tea, thank you."

"Then eat the cookies in the tin on the counter. You need to gain about thirty pounds. When I'm finished here, I'll drive you in to the Celebration."

Candy George—or Candace Elizabeth Spear—went to the counter and got the cookies. Kelley heard the phone being picked up down in Burlington and a familiar voice saying, "Eve's Apple. Can I help you?"

Kelley blew a stream of hair into her bangs and smiled. "Stacey?" she said. "This is Kelley Grey. Listen, I've got a problem I think you could help me with."

t h r e e

1

BY THE TIME they all got back to the center of town—meaning Bennis, Franklin and Gregor himself; Jan-Mark stayed at home and Stuart Ketchum went back to his farm—Gregor was worried, and the closer they got to the Inn, the more worried he got. Even Bennis's driving did nothing to distract him. She had taken over the wheel from Franklin Morrison only yards from Stuart Ketchum's front door and put her foot on the floor as soon as she reached the Delaford Road. Her driving had scared Franklin Morrison to death. Gregor had hardly noticed it. He kept going over and over the whole situation in his mind, and every time he did he came to the same conclusion. He knew who. He knew how. He even knew why. He just didn't know what he could do about it.

Bennis had had to slow down when she turned onto Main Street proper. It was five-thirty, close enough to the start of the performance for activity in town to be heating up a little. The town's one stoplight was operating, instead of hanging from its wire and blinking yellow. Families who had driven up from downstate or over from New Hampshire were strolling along the sidewalk, looking at the Christmas decorations in the shop windows and discussing where to go for dinner. Most of them, Gregor assumed, would end up at The Magick Endive. It was the kind of place the mothers of small children liked to go when they wanted to eat out "nice."

Bennis had to stop at the traffic light. When she did, Gregor looked into the town park at the bleachers that were now almost all the way up and the two small clumps of evergreen bush he could see. If there had been any defections from the population expected to view the performance this evening, the news hadn't got back to the ground crew. Gregor didn't know what kind of publicity there had been about the death of Gemma Bury. The only newspaper he had seen was the *Bethlehem News and Mail*. He hadn't watched television in days. The story might be a total washout. If it was, he didn't think it would be one for long, but that was another matter. It always surprised him, how conscientious murderers were, to do things in the most spectacular possible way. Maybe he ought to say unsuccessful murderers. The ones with sense—the ones who did what they wanted to do quickly and without fanfare; who were interested in seeing someone dead and not in showing the world how absolutely brilliant they were—probably never got caught. In Gregor's experience, the ones who never got caught were all professionals, and sense wasn't exactly what they had.

Bennis was tapping impatiently on the steering wheel. The light was staying at red forever. In the back seat, Franklin Morrison was wheezing away on a cigar. Gregor went on staring into the park and then he made up his mind.

"Pull over," he said.

"Again?" Bennis asked him. "You don't have any stone walls to climb around on here."

"That's the green light," Franklin Morrison said.

"Pull over," Gregor insisted.

Bennis let out a long-suffering sigh and eased the car forward, reaching for her cigarettes as she went. "I can't just pull over," she told him, "I have to go around the corner and then hope I see someplace to park, which I probably won't because the performance is in less than three hours. Are you sure you know what you're doing?"

"Bennis—"

"Never mind."

It turned out not to be impossible after all. The corner wasn't a corner, but a bend in the park. On the far side of it there was a little indentation in the underbrush at the edge of a wooded area that looked like it had been hollowed out for a police car to sit in. Gregor couldn't imagine why a police car would want to sit in it. There wouldn't be anything for a policeman to see. Bennis pulled into this space and put the car in park. Franklin Morrison leaned into the front seat and blew hot thick smoke in Gregor's face.

"What are we stopping here for?" he asked.

"I want to get out and check something one more time."

Bennis shut off the ignition. "We might as well go," she said. "As you should know by now, Mr. Morrison, when the man's decided he wants to haul ass all over the landscape, there isn't any stopping him."

Gregor almost told her to watch her language. Then he remembered that he was trying not to put her under any kind of stress, just in case it was stress that had caused the reading of all those diet books, and maybe even the diet. Gregor certainly hadn't seen her eating anything today. He climbed out of the car and across to the park proper, between two sections of bleachers that would have to be the ones almost directly across from where he, Bennis, Tibor, Gemma and Kelley had been sitting the night before. He got to the center of the park and decided he was just about right. He was directly across, but a little to the west. He started across the park to the bushes, confident that Bennis and Franklin would follow him.

They did follow him, but when they got to the bushes, neither one of them was in a good mood.

"You've been all over this thing a dozen times already," Bennis complained. "That's how you found the gun last night, don't you remember? And that boy from MIT was all over it, too. He took samples. He's running tests."

"I know he's running tests," Gregor said.

"Well, the lady has a point," Franklin said. "I don't think you're going to find anything here. Not anything that we missed. It was real instructive, watching you and Demp working last night. I don't think I've ever seen a scene gone over in quite that way."

Gregor almost said "standard Bureau procedure," but didn't. That was the kind of remark that made local police departments hate the FBI. He stepped farther into the bushes and picked through the branches, thinking.

"Bennis," he said after a while, "I want you to come over here. Come over here and stand in the trees."

"In the trees," Bennis repeated.

"Put out that cigarette."

Bennis dropped her cigarette in the snow, made sure it was out, then picked it up and put it in her pocket. Bennis didn't litter. She walked up to the trees and stood next to them.

"Like this?" she asked.

Gregor shook his head. "Stand in the trees, not next to them."

"Gregor, they're not trees. They're bushes. And they sting."

"That's just pine needles," Franklin Morrison said helpfully. "They won't hurt you."

"They are hurting me. And this isn't a pine tree. These aren't. I don't care. Gregor—"

"Farther in," Gregor said.

Bennis moved farther in, but she looked mutinous. When Gregor insisted she go farther in yet, she started to swear. She also disappeared. Franklin Morrison said, "Hey."

"You can come out now," Gregor said.

Bennis reappeared. "I wasn't in. I couldn't get any farther in. I went to the side—"

"Yes, I know."

"Well, if you know, what did you put me through it for, Gregor? I mean, honestly—"

"Relax," Gregor said imperturbably. "Tell me how tall you are."

"How tall? Five-four."

"What do you weigh?"

Bennis looked exasperated. "How am I supposed to know what I weigh? I mean, I haven't been on a scale in years except at the doctor's, and he's always telling me I'm healthy as a horse."

"Guess."

"Okay, I'll guess. Maybe one hundred. Maybe one-ten."

"Maybe one hundred," Franklin Morrison put in. "She's too thin. Looks just like my niece in Portland got that anorexia nervosa a few years ago."

"No one has ever accused me of not being willing to eat," Bennis said, "except maybe for Tibor who's been going crazy lately. Gregor, what is this all about?"

"Mostly it was just wishful thinking." Gregor sighed. "You know why I'm not really the Armenian-American Hercule Poirot? Because faced with a situation like this, Hercule Poirot would have done something. He would at least have had an idea of something to do."

"About what?"

"About the fact that I know who did it, and why she did it, and how she did it, and I haven't got a shred of proof of any of it, or a chance in hell of being able to get any, either."

"She?" Bennis Hannaford asked.

Gregor Demarkian nodded. Franklin Morrison had a look very much like rapture on his face, but Gregor didn't want to pay attention to that. Apparently, Franklin had just been catapulted into that most exciting of all imaginary detective scenes, the Great Detective's Perfect Solution.

Gregor turned back to the evergreen bushes. "It has to have been a woman," he said, "because any man we've heard about in this case so far has been too big, at least as far as I know. I'd guess five-six or so would be the limit in height to fit into this stand of bushes without being noticed. Also, we have measurements from the ground to the branches where the gun was fired, and assuming the gun was fired by being placed in the bushes beforehand—"

"You said all that last night," Franklin Morrison said. "You didn't say anything about it being a woman."

"Well," Gregor said reasonably, "there are always other possibilities. And last night I wasn't sure of the motive. When you first told me about this case, you spoke of two men I haven't met yet. Either one of them could be small. There was the lawyer who was going to drive Tisha Verek to the courthouse in Montpelier—"

"Camber Hartnell," Franklin Morrison said. "He's six-two and boozed out."

"That takes care of him then." Gregor nodded. "Then there was another lawyer, Benjamin something."

"Benjy Warren," Franklin said. "Yeah, well, he's small enough, but he's not here. He's in Germany visiting his wife's brother who's in the army or something. I mean they all are. The whole family."

"Is he local?" Gregor asked. "Someone who has been around all his life?"

"About as local as it gets," Franklin said.

"That takes care of him then. He wouldn't fit the motive. But forget about the motive for a minute. You must realize that the actual execution was very simple. All she did was pick what was closest to hand and use it."

"Semiautomatic rifles?" Bennis protested.

"We just heard Stuart Ketchum tell us that there are several all over town. Several of them seem to be left lying around where anybody could pick them up. I like that man he was talking about, Reggie George—"

"I don't like him," Franklin said. "First-class son of a bitch and stupid besides."

"Yes," Gregor said, "and for losing a gun and not realizing it's missing, he's a good candidate. The other good candidate is the man who'd been in the army, the one who goes hunting in Canada—"

"Eddie Folier is very careful about his guns," Franklin Morrison said, "and they wouldn't be easy to lose. He's got them right over his fireplace. And—oh."

"What is it?" Gregor asked.

Franklin shrugged. "He's not home. Hasn't been home for over six weeks. He's got some kind of condition left over from the service, something to do with his intestines, every two-three years he ends up at Mary Hitchcock over in Hanover. He's been there since just after Thanksgiving."

"House locked?" Gregor asked.

"If it is, it won't make much difference," Franklin said. "We don't lock houses out here the way you lock up city apartments. We don't go in big time for security."

"Well, we'll have to check it out," Gregor told him, "but the particulars here are not the point. And that was the second gun. The first gun was easy. The first gun was part of her original plan. She heard about Tisha Verek's decision to file the lawsuit. She heard the time the lawyer was supposed to pick Tisha up. Why shouldn't she have? Everybody else in town did. My guess is that she'd been thinking about killing Tisha Verek for a while. So she drove her car out to the Delaford Road, and she parked it in the trees across from the Verek house. But she couldn't kill Tisha from there. By the time Tisha reached the Delaford Road, she'd be in a moving car. She'd be a difficult target and at least partially protected by the glass in the car's windows. That was why the plan for the first gun was so perfect. She had to go walking along those stone walls anyway, just to get to Tisha Verek. She walked a little farther and picked up a gun—"

"That might have been impossible," Bennis protested. "Stuart Ketchum might have been there."

"But he wouldn't have been and she'd have known it," Gregor said. "Peter Callisher was on his way out to pick up Stuart Ketchum and the two of them were going over to talk some sense into Tisha Verek's head. Everybody in town knew that, too. If she got to the Ketchum farm too early, all she had to do was wait in the trees."

"So she got Stuart Ketchum's gun and went back to a place on the wall where she would be in place to kill Tisha Verek and then she did," Bennis said, "and then what?"

"Then," Gregor said, "I think she went back through the trees along the stone wall and stashed the gun. She had to do that just to get away from whatever investigation started happening when the shooting occurred. Then she got to her car—"

"Wouldn't it have been seen?" Franklin asked.

"It depends where she parked it." Gregor spread out his hands. "I said she was across the road, but I didn't necessarily mean directly across the road. If she parked another half mile out of town, she could have gotten back into her car and driven off in the other direction—"

"And circled around when she got to Beaverton and nobody would have been the wiser," Franklin said. "Whoosh."

"Now I've got to indulge in a little speculation," Gregor said. "I think she came back to town not expecting to do anything else for the day, but when she did she was presented with an opportunity. Dinah Ketchum was doing errands that day. She was walking around Main Street. She was an old woman. I haven't heard anything said about the way she got around—"

"Stuart drove her," Franklin said.

"That's what I would have guessed. Even if it hadn't been the case, however, there would have been a way. Let me give you a ride. Come with me to the shopping mall and help me pick up decorations. Anything. It would have been easy. But once she saw her opportunity, she had a problem, because she had already gotten rid of the first gun. She couldn't go back out to the Ketchum farm for another one, so she stole the first one she could think of to get her hands on."

"But how could she have known what to steal?" Bennis asked. "How would she have known who had guns?"

"Well, if it was this Reggie George person, I think anybody would have known. At least, that's the impression Stuart Ketchum gave—"

"Anybody would have known," Franklin Morrison said. "Reggie's infamous."

"This Eddie Folier would have been another matter," Gregor said. "I don't know anything about him, who he sees, who he knows—"

"He's Stuart's friend," Franklin said, "and that means he's Peter Callisher's friend, too, because Stuart and Franklin have been together forever, and you don't get close to one these days without getting close to the other. Oh, and he did a lot of work for those two girls, you know who I mean, Sharon Morrissey and Susan Everman."

"What about Kelley Grey?" Gregor asked.

Franklin shrugged.

"Whichever," Gregor said. "My point here is that she got the second gun, drove Dinah Ketchum out to a remote area on the Delaford Road, and essentially performed an execution. Then she stashed the second gun where she stashed the first one."

"Oh, I see," Bennis said. "In those bushes where you found the gun today. And when she decided to kill Gemma Bury she just went out there and picked one up. Did she go out there today?"

"I don't know," Gregor said. "I don't believe Jan-Mark Verek very much. I suppose he *discovered* the changes in his wife's office today."

"But they could have happened any time in the last two weeks," Franklin Morrison said. "Yeah, I see how that works. It does sound simple when you explain it."

"It's straightforward, rather than simple," Gregor said. "She's a very straightforward killer. She always has been. But she's not very organized and she's not a master planner. If she had been, she would have varied her style from time to time, just to keep us from getting on to her."

"She sounds absolutely cold-blooded," Bennis said. She looked the stand of evergreen bushes up and down one last time and made a face at it. Then she stepped away and began to beat the palms of her hands against her thighs. "It's cold as hell out here. Couldn't we all go inside someplace and talk this out there?"

"Just one more thing," Gregor said, "about how you disappeared to Franklin and me but you didn't really disappear into the bushes. I think that if Gemma Bury hadn't been given these two particular seats, our murderer would have found another time and place to get her killing done. On the other hand, these were the best two seats for our murderer's purpose, because not only was that stand of bushes available to conceal the rifle, but that stand backs up on the passageway for the animals. If you stand where our murderer would have had to stand to fire that rifle and hit Gemma Bury, the only people who could see you would be the people in the passage with the animals. But there wouldn't have been any people in that passage during the second half of the play last night, because aside from two cows that were wandering around the park for atmosphere, there weren't any animals in the play last night. It was intermission. People were strolling around. All she had to do was step up to the bushes, fire and walk out by going down the passage. It was only by bad luck that she was seen."

"Seen?" Bennis said.

"That's proof," Franklin Morrison said.

"She wasn't seen shooting," Gregor said. "She wasn't even seen in the bushes, as far as I can tell. She was seen leaving. And that isn't enough to put her in jail with."

"I don't suppose you're willing to tell us who she is," Bennis said.

"Mmm," Gregor answered.

Bennis gave Franklin Morrison a long-suffering look. "He's always like this. He says he doesn't like to be compared to Hercule Poirot, but he's just as vain as Poirot ever was. He likes revelation scenes with all the suspects assembled."

"I do not," Gregor said.

"I've got to get back to the Inn," Bennis told him. "I'm freezing my patooties off and I want a sandwich. Tibor's been making me so crazy, I haven't eaten since late last night."

She stalked off across the park, leaving them to follow in her wake, and after a while, they did. Franklin Morrison was exhilarated. Gregor Demarkian was anything but. This was not a case he would like to leave lying for lack of usable proof. She was just what he'd said she was—a very straightforward murderer—and that straightforwardness was dangerous in and of itself. It was as if she had tunnel vision. She saw what she had to see and no further. It hadn't worried her that in shooting at Gemma Bury while Gemma sat in the park on the bleachers she might have shot someone else as well, Gregor thought, because it hadn't *occurred* to her that she might have shot someone else as well. She saw the job at hand and nothing else. What that meant for the future, if she was left to wander around loose, wasn't very pleasant to contemplate.

Bennis was sitting behind the wheel when Gregor and Franklin came up, the engine running, the heating on full blast, the doors open so the heater did no good at all. Gregor let Franklin climb into the back seat and then took the seat next to Bennis himself. Bennis had lit another cigarette and was blowing smoke on her hands.

"Let's go," she said. "I want to get my hands on my food before Tibor starts obsessing and spoils it for me."

2

LESS THAN FIVE minutes later, Bennis Hannaford handed the keys to the Ford Taurus to Franklin Morrison and got out on the walk in front of the Green Mountain Inn. Gregor got out after her, holding the seat to help Franklin climb out himself. They all shook hands—why, since they were all going to be at the performance and likely to see each other in under three hours, Gregor didn't know—and then Franklin got back into the car and Gregor and Bennis started on inside the Inn. The Inn's windows had been spruced up a little while they were out. The three gold Christmas balls that had been there since their arrival had increased to eight and had been joined by a gold-painted wicker basket. It reminded Gregor more of Easter than of Christmas. Bennis went through the Inn's front doors, unzipping her parka as she walked. Gregor went in behind her and looked around the lobby. He was glad to see that there didn't seem to be anyone lying in wait for him. He'd half-expected a visit from Sharon Morrissey. Ever since he'd talked to Susan Everman, he'd been sure a visit from Sharon was on the horizon. Maybe Susan hadn't told Sharon she'd spoken to Gregor, or even that she'd intended to. That would explain it.

Bennis had stopped short in the middle of the lobby. Gregor came up next to her and asked, "What's wrong?"

Bennis pointed across the room to the fireplace. "Right there," she said. "Right where he was sitting yesterday."

"Who?"

"Tibor."

"I see Tibor," Gregor said.

Tibor was sitting in a wingback chair, his legs planted firmly apart, his nose stuck in a magazine. Gregor thought it was *Soldier of Fortune*, but he couldn't be sure.

Bennis tugged at Gregor's sleeve. "Look at the floor," she hissed. "Bags. Big brown paper bags. He's got food with him again."

"I thought you were hungry."

"I am hungry. I can't stand this, Gregor. I can't go through this one more minute."

"You can't go through Father Tibor thinking you ought to have something to eat? You're going to have to move off Cavanaugh Street. You're going to have to move to Mars."

"Never mind," Bennis told him. "I'm getting out of here. And if he asks, you haven't seen me."

"We are all attending the performance of the play tonight."

"I'll cross that bridge when I come to it."

She whirled away and started hurrying in the direction of the back stairs, a very inefficient way to go, but the only one that did not require her to pass so close to the fireplace that she might be seen. Gregor watched her retreat with a certain amount of resignation. Relationships among the people who lived on Cavanaugh Street got so damned complicated. Gregor crossed the rest of the lobby and went up to Tibor's chair.

"I'm back," he said. "Are you sitting there waiting for me?"

Tibor looked up from his reading. It was most certainly *Soldier of Fortune.* Tibor was reading an article on mercenary operations in Central America. He closed the magazine and put it down on his lap.

"Hello, Krekor," he said. "If I was waiting for you only, I would have waited in the room. I am here now keeping this young lady company while we both wait for you."

"Which young lady?" Gregor asked.

"Me."

The voice came from the other side of the fireplace, from what was Gregor's back. He turned and saw a young woman putting down a magazine of her own, and not one he would have guessed she'd have much interest in.

The magazine was *Good Housekeeping,* and the young woman was Kelley Grey.

f o u r

1

LATE LAST NIGHT, when they had all come in half frozen from the park and been wandering back and forth across the corridor that divided Gregor and Tibor's suite from Bennis's room, Bennis had said a very odd thing. "Kelley Grey," she had said, "is the kind of woman some other women want to mother." It had been a throwaway line, nothing to do with the case, and Gregor hadn't pursued the topic. Bennis had had a copy of something called *The Medical Miracle Metabolism Diet* in the pocket of her robe. Tibor had been staring at it. It was all Gregor had been able to do to get Tibor to bed and Bennis safely behind her own door before Tibor had an outburst. Or a lecture. Or whatever it was, Tibor was eager to have at Bennis and get it over with. Bennis could have said anything she wanted to about anybody at all. She could have claimed that Queen Elizabeth I was a Rastafarian. Gregor wouldn't have listened to her. Now he was sorry he hadn't paid at least a little attention. Bennis often made him exasperated—and she could be a royal pain in the rear in more ways than one—but she was an intelligent judge of the characters of women. What she said usually had some truth in it. Meeting Kelley Grey in the park, Gregor wouldn't have said she was capable of eliciting maternal feelings from anyone. She seemed to be a thoroughly cold, sullen and hostile person. Now ... now ...

Gregor didn't know what it was about now. Kelley Grey was changed. He just couldn't explain it. For one thing, she didn't look sullen, but determined, if a little nervous. For another, she had a bright red silk scarf draped around her neck. She was still plain—she would always be plain—but at least she didn't look dull at the same time. To be honest, though, he had to go back to attitude. Kelley Grey seemed to have undergone a sea change in the hours since he had last seen her. Underneath the nervousness and the diffidence and the trace of fear, Gregor thought he could smell exhilaration.

Tibor had come up behind him and interposed himself in the open space right in front of the fireplace. He looked small and determined and out-of-time in his plain black cassock, but also very benevolent. He nodded at Kelley Grey and said, "I had come downstairs to wait, Krekor, and they were turning her away at the desk. I couldn't let them turn her away at the desk."

"Of course not," Gregor said.

"I couldn't have stayed much longer," Kelley said. "I've got to be over at the play before it starts. I'm riding shotgun."

"What?" Gregor said.

"I'm going upstairs," Tibor said. "I have been in Bennis's room, Krekor, to leave her a box of cupcakes I bought at the bakery, chocolate with chocolate icing, her favorite. And I have found another one, Krekor."

"Found another one what?" Kelley Grey asked.

"Diet book," Tibor said ominously. "This is *The Sugar Addict's No Willpower Weight Loss Plan*. It will ruin her teeth on top of everything else, Krekor."

"I've tried that one," Kelley Grey said. "It's a good one. You don't lose much weight, but you get to eat buttercream frosting three times a day."

"Buttercream frosting?" Gregor was bewildered.

Tibor backed away. "I am going up now, Krekor," he said. "I am bringing her a ham sandwich from the Village Restaurant and a bag of potato chips. I am going to put a stop to this."

"He's been talking about putting a stop to it the whole time I've been here," Kelley said, watching Tibor as he hurried away. "I wonder why."

"Our friend doesn't need to lose any weight," Gregor explained.

Kelley looked blank. "What does that have to do with it? I mean, everybody's on a diet all the time now, aren't they? It's a kind of entertainment. Like miniature golf or something."

"Right," Gregor said.

Kelley turned around, looked back at her chair, frowned and then brightened. "I thought I'd lost it," she said, leaning over and extracting something from the space between the cushions and the chair's arm, "but I didn't. Here it is. I came to bring you this."

She handed over a manila envelope and stepped back, waiting politely. Gregor opened the envelope and pulled out a thick sheaf of manuscript. It had the impeccable printed look of something typed by a first-class computer printer. *"BORN IN BLOOD,"* the title page said. *"A Book About Children Who Kill.* By Patricia Feld Verek." Gregor said "mmm," softly to himself, and pushed the manuscript back into the envelope.

Kelley was looking at him anxiously. "It isn't one of a kind," she explained. "I wasn't paying much attention at the time, you know, but from what I understood, there were several of these things wandering around. And Tisha had a contract, so there's an editor in New York with a copy of this, and Tisha's agent had a copy of it, too."

Gregor considered this. "Tisha Verek gave this to you?"

"Oh, no," Kelley said. "Of course not. She gave it to Gemma."

"And Gemma kept it," Gregor said.

Kelley Grey shrugged. "She kept it in the wall safe in her office at the rectory. It was silly to do it, you know, because like I said, it's not the only copy. Although it may be the only copy in town. I'm not sure. Anyway, Gemma said keeping it in the safe was symbolic. That the material in it was so explosive, it had to be locked up."

"Mmm," Gregor said again. "Did she tell you what was in it that would be so explosive?"

"No." Kelley hesitated. "The thing is, I don't think whatever it was had something directly to do with anybody in town. I'm putting that badly. It might have had something to do with somebody in town, but that wasn't the point of it, that wasn't what would cause the trouble. Gemma said that the people people are connected to are just as important as the people themselves and that this would really blow the town apart, considering who it would upset. I'm really not doing this very well at all."

Gregor was about to say "mmm" for the third time and decided against it. Instead, he motioned Kelley to sit down again and waited politely until she was seated, then drew up the chair Tibor had been sitting in until he could sit close enough to Kelley so they wouldn't have to raise their voices to talk. "Do you have any idea what's in this thing?" he asked. "Have you read it?"

"Oh, yes, I've read it," Kelley told him. "I made a point of it this morning. It's awful stuff, really."

"Do you mean the contents are awful or that it's badly written?"

"I mean the contents are awful," Kelley said. "All these children and not many of them really sane. I mean, every once in a while there would be one of them who killed in simple self-defense, but mostly they were so calculating. And so deliberate."

"Did you read anything you thought might refer to anyone you know in town?"

"Well," Kelley said, "I did pay attention to all that stuff about Tommy Hare. There's been a rumor around—a rumor Tisha started, by the way—that Timmy Hall who works at the *News and Mail* is really Tommy Hare who killed all those people in the swimming pool. But I don't think it's true. I don't think the dates are right, for one thing. And Timmy—"

"Yes?"

"Well, for one thing, it just doesn't seem like his kind of thing. He wouldn't go sneaking around with a cattle prod or whatever. He'd just pull back his fist and punch. He's not a planner, if you see what I mean."

"Yes," Gregor said. "I see what you mean. I've met him. And I agree with you."

"The other thing is that I don't think it would matter if it was true," Kelley said. "To the town, I mean. Gemma kept saying there was something in here that would 'blow the lid off everything,' by which she explained that she meant that someone important in town would be so upset by the revelation that he or she would do something drastic if it ever came out. Well, nobody would do anything drastic if something damaging came out about Timmy Hall. At least, nobody important would. Amanda Ballard treats him like he's her own child—and no, I don't think he is; he's too old and she's too young—but she isn't anybody important. She's just Peter Callisher's mistress."

"Is Peter Callisher important?"

"Yes," Kelley said slowly. "But if something happened to Timmy, he'd be sorry to see Amanda hurt but he wouldn't be sorry for Timmy. I don't think he likes Timmy."

"Not much of anybody seems to like Timmy," Gregor said.

Kelley Grey sighed. "We can't all be saints like Amanda. I mean, not that I know her that well, but she must have something I don't, to be able to deal with retarded people the way she does. She used to work with them, you know."

"Did she?"

"That's what I've heard. Before she came here and got involved with Peter Callisher. She used to know Timmy before."

"Then I take it you wouldn't consider Amanda herself a candidate for being one of Tisha Verek's child murderers?"

"Oh, no." Kelley was shocked. "She's so gentle and—and calm. If I had to pick someone in town to have been a killer as a child, it would definitely be someone like Sharon Morrissey. She's gentle and calm on the outside, but she has a temper on her, I've seen it."

"Often?"

"No, no. Not often."

"Do you really think Sharon Morrissey is—who? Kathleen Butterworth?"

"The baby killer?" Kelley made a face. "I'm being ridiculous, aren't I? It was just talk. Gemma and Tisha, making themselves important."

"Mmm," Gregor said, caught himself and then cursed himself for it. If he kept this up, he was going to sound like one of Bennis's favorite fictional detectives. "Let me ask you a few more questions," he said. "I would like to untangle a few relationships that seem very strange to me. Like the relationship between Gemma Bury and Tisha Verek."

"Well, that one's tangled enough, all right."

"They were friends?"

"Not really friends. In fact, I think they mutually despised each other. But they spent a certain amount of time together."

"Why? If they mutually despised each other?"

"Because neither one of them had anybody else to talk to. I mean, they couldn't talk to the locals, could they? Not sophisticated enough for them. And most of the other flatlanders in town are like me, college or graduate school age. We all go back to the land until someone offers us a decent position, then we heave a sigh of relief and go off to Boston or New York and tell all the people we leave behind that we just have to, in this economic climate there's nothing to do but sell out."

"So there was Gemma Bury and Tisha Verek, thrown together out of necessity when they would have preferred to have been apart."

"Right," Kelly said. "Sharon Morrissey and Susan Everman were more or less of the same generation, but they kept to themselves and for all Gemma's talk about goddesses and feminism and I don't know what else, she was very uncomfortable around lesbians. Which was maybe just as well, if you know what I mean, because Sharon and Susan are very nice and I don't think they had much use for Gemma. Anyway, then there's Amanda, who's thirty-six, but she's like a nun or something. I don't mean physically. I mean she's sort of ethereal. And who else was there? Nobody, I think."

"I can see that," Gregor said. "Now, I have heard a rumor, a rumor you might possibly find embarrassing—"

"You mean that Gemma and Jan-Mark Verek were having an affair."

"I'm beginning to think that people of your age find nothing at all embarrassing," Gregor said.

Kelley gave him a wry look. "I find it funny, if you want to know the truth. Not funny that Gemma and Jan-Mark were having the affair, that was pathetic. I mean funny that it was a rumor. I thought I was the only one who knew."

"You're just not on the town grapevine," Gregor said.

"Obviously not. Well, they were definitely having one, and if you ask me, Gemma wasn't the only extracurricular project in Jan-Mark's life. Don't ask me who the other one was, because I'm not sure. But you can see, you know."

"See what?"

"Into the Vereks' driveway from the third floor of the rectory," Kelley said. "It's the highest place in at least a six-mile radius. You can see all kinds of things. Especially from the offices on that floor."

"Is Gemma Bury's office on that floor?"

"No, it's downstairs. My office is on that floor."

"Did you see anything on the day Tisha Verek was killed?"

"I didn't, no," Kelley said, "but Gemma saw Tisha Verek die. I went to the bathroom for a minute, and when I came back she was leaning against the office windows, looking positively green."

"You went to the bathroom for a minute," Gregor said slowly.

Kelley looked at him curiously. "It was the middle of the morning," she said. "There wasn't any reason not to go. You make it sound as if I did a terrible thing."

"No," Gregor said. "I don't think you did a terrible thing."

The fire in the fireplace was burning down, retreating from flames into embers. He stared at it a minute, thinking, and then pushed his chair back. He was still holding the manila envelope Kelley had given him, with its thick weight of manuscript inside. He stuck it absent-mindedly under his arm.

"Well," he said. "I have to thank you. For the package and the information."

"And I have to go across to the park." Kelley stood up. "Do you think any of this will be of any use to you?"

"I think it will be of a great deal of use."

"I'm glad. I didn't like Gemma very much. Gemma was a hard woman to like. But I didn't want her dead."

Gregor was going to make all the right soothing noises, to tell Kelley that she was brave and fine and wonderful, to cluck and mutter the way Tibor did when he got worried about one of the refugee children who had come to live on Cavanaugh Street. He never got a chance.

He had just opened his mouth to say the first words when a clatter and crash came from the street outside, and a woman started screaming.

2

GREGOR DEMARKIAN did not like cases with a lot of alarms in them. He didn't like having to jump and twist and chase. He didn't like having to march into the middle of dangerous and unstable situations. He had done all those things in his first years with the Bureau, but the timing in that fact was important. There were Bureau agents who spent their entire careers playing cops and robbers. In the old days, they had chased bank robbers and kidnappers. In the more recent ones, they had chased drug lords. On the day after tomorrow, they would probably be chasing aliens from outer space. Gregor didn't care. He had found his niche behind a desk. He had loved the sheer mental work required to run an investigation on a series of related murders—the sheer mental work that did not require following serial killers down dark alleys with a gun in his hand. Since taking up the investigation of murder as a hobby rather than as a profession, Gregor seemed to have lost his protection from violence. It was infuriating. In all those books Bennis was forever giving him, the police did the chasing and the fighting and the getting shot at, and the Great Detective got to sit home in a chair and cogitate. Definitely cogitate. Not think. That was the way things were.

If Gregor had been a different man from a different generation, he might have insisted on this perogative. He might have refused to go chasing screams when he heard them or murderers when he found them and there didn't seem to be any other way to bring them down. He was of a generation that had been brought up to take responsibility—any responsibility, all responsibility, even when taking that responsibility made no sense of any kind whatsoever. In fact, that was what he had been given to understand was the real difference between men and women, back there in the days when people thought there were real differences between men and women. Women, Gregor Demarkian had been brought up to believe, could take responsibility or give it to their men as they chose, with no loss in status or respect. Men never could.

Exactly how all this archaic thinking might have been applied to the situation as it existed on Main Street when he got there that night, he had no way of knowing, because as it turned out he had no time to do anything but observe. He spilled out onto the street with a clutch of people, all eager to see what the fuss was about. He found himself looking at a long dark expanse of asphalt that seemed to have been cleared of everything but one big man. The man was Timmy Hall, and as he stood there at the center of a circle made by a rim of faceless bodies in ski parkas, Gregor found himself being reminded eerily of Shirley Jackson's "The Lottery." He wouldn't have been surprised if someone in the crowd had started throwing stones. What they all thought they were doing there in that circle, Gregor didn't know.

The woman who was screaming was standing in that circle, at the part of it closest to the Green Mountain Inn and to Gregor himself. She was hopping around and flapping her arms across her body. Gregor couldn't see at what. Her voice was high and thin and hysterical. Gregor thought it was also faintly familiar. "HE GRABBED ME HE GRABBED ME HE GRABBED MY SHOULDER HE GRABBED ME." She kept saying it over and over again. Gregor thought she was one of the people they had talked to the night before, and probably someone from town. He hadn't paid much attention to the tourists while the questioning had been going on.

"It's Betty Heath," Kelley Grey said suddenly in his ear. "I wonder what's going on. I wonder what she's so upset about."

"He grabbed her shoulder," someone in the crowd said.

Timmy Hall was bellowing and scratching like an animal. "LIAR LIAR LIAR LIAR LIAR LIAR LIAR," he roared, and it was an awful sound, a sound that seemed to contain an echo of itself. That was when Gregor noticed the mood of the people around him, the same mood he'd picked up the one or two times he'd stumbled onto cockfights, the will to see blood. He saw Franklin Morrison at the edge of the crowd and started toward him.

"Good," Franklin said when Gregor turned up. "I've got Lee out there but I could use some help. Go get Stuart Ketchum for me."

"Stuart Ketchum? You mean you want me to drive out to the farm?"

"Over there." Franklin pointed. Gregor saw Stuart Ketchum, looking as tensely alert as if he'd still been on sentry duty in the Mekong Delta, standing next to a small, furious woman with a look on her face as wild as the ones in drawings from the French Revolution. Madame Guillotine.

"Dear Jesus Christ," Gregor said. "What's going on around here?"

"Gossip," Franklin Morrison said grimly. "Gossip all over town for weeks now that Timmy Hall is Tommy Hare and guilty of God knows what, and now they're scared and they're not thinking, they're just looking for a blood sacrifice. I'm going to get Peter Callisher. Between the five of us—you and me and Lee and Stuart and Peter—we ought to be able to get Timmy out of here."

"Right," Gregor said.

"All they need is torches," Franklin said.

A big old man came up between them and grabbed Franklin by the shoulders, hard. "Lock the bastard up!" he screamed into Franklin's face, and Gregor could smell the beer. "Lock the bastard up. What are you anyway, Morrison, some kind of jellyfish queer? What are you anyway—"

"*That's* enough," Peter Callisher said, coming up behind the big man and grabbing him even harder than he was grabbing Franklin Morrison. Peter had an advantage, because Peter wasn't drunk. Peter got the man off-balance and pitched him back into the crowd.

"You all right?" he asked Franklin.

Franklin was shaking. "I'm fine," he said. "I was just going to find you. Mr. Demarkian here is going around the circle to get Stuart."

"Good idea."

"What happened out here?" Gregor asked them. "How did this get started?"

Peter Callisher exploded. "It was that damned fool woman, Betty Heath. Timmy came up behind her just wanting to know if she wanted help carrying this bag she had—I don't know what happened to the bag, she doesn't have it now—and when she didn't hear him ask, he tapped her on the shoulder and all hell broke loose. God, people have been crazy all day. You'd better get Stu, Mr. Demarkian. We're going to have to get them both out of here and it isn't going to be easy."

"Both?" Franklin Morrison asked.

"Amanda's over on that side against the wall ready to tear to shreds anybody who tries to lay a finger on him. And she's small. You know how that will end."

"Go get Stuart," Franklin Morrison said.

Gregor went to get Stuart. It helped that Stuart hadn't moved since Gregor had first seen him, even though many of the people in the crowd had. In fact, there was suddenly a lot of movement all around him, and not only of the physical kind. "Riots," his old instructor at Quantico had told him, all those many years ago, "are a matter of emotion." He knew what the old man had meant. The emotions here were shifting. They were not shifting in the right direction. The crowd had been in an ugly humor when Gregor first came out of the Inn. It was now turning vicious.

He came up to Stuart Ketchum and tapped him on the shoulder, very gently, not wanting to set one more person off. Stuart was in far too rigid a state of control to be set off.

"Mr. Demarkian," he said.

"I've come as an emissary from Franklin Morrison," Gregor told him. "Mr. Morrison wants your help."

"I'll bet he does."

"You mean you won't give it?"

Stuart Ketchum brushed this off, as if it were a stupid suggestion, which Gregor admitted it probably was. Then Stuart began to ease out toward the center of the circle, very carefully, trying not to be too obvious. Gregor thought he knew what Stuart was going to do. He was going to enter the circle's almost empty center, and he didn't want to do it in such a way as to start a surge. It would be far too easy to start a surge. Gregor caught sight of Franklin Morrison and Peter Callisher and Lee Greenwood. They had maneuvered their way around the edges of the circle until they were standing nearly opposite the Green Mountain Inn, in that place where they had the least room to move and the least chance of escape. The problem was, if they were going to get Timmy out, that was the only way they were going to do it. To pull him in any other direction would require bringing him past too many irrational people, with no place to stash him once he was through. Where Franklin and the rest were now standing there was a building, and a building meant rooms with doors that could be locked and windows that could be shortcutted through.

Stuart looked back over his shoulder. "Tell Franklin when I start talking, he should start bringing Timmy out of there. To the back. Where it isn't conspicuous."

"I think he already intends to bring Timmy out through the back."

"Yeah," Stuart said. "I do, too. Be careful. Don't give them an excuse."

In the crowd around him, people had started swaying, rhythmically and hypnotically. "Lock him up lock him up lock him up," people were saying, but it was like a murmur, half indistinct, the mantra of hostility and the secret password of fear. Gregor edged through the thinning ranks of people inch by inch, second by second, barely breathing. Not many in the crowd had been willing to stand so close to the buildings that might catch them in an outbreak. That was fortunate. Stuart had gotten about a tenth of the way into the empty center of the circle without anybody following him.

Gregor got to Franklin Morrison and the others and told them what Stuart had in mind. Franklin Morrison said "damn fool idiot," but didn't go any farther, because Stuart was now at least two-tenths of the way into the center and there was no way any of them could stop him. Peter Callisher was sweating, in spite of the fact that it was below freezing. He had a hand around Amanda Ballard's upper arm. Amanda Ballard was crying.

"Go," Peter Callisher told her, nudging her in the direction of the building behind them. Gregor saw that there was an open window very close, probably opened by Lee or Peter or Franklin precisely for the purposes of escape. Amanda didn't care.

"I'm not going to leave him out there," she kept saying, over and over again. "I'm not just going to walk away and let them beat him up. He didn't do anything wrong."

"We're not going to let anyone beat him up," Franklin Morrison said.

"Lock him up lock him up lock him up," the crowd chanted, and then someone in the back screamed, "Stupid retard stupid retard stupid RE-TARD."

Gregor broke away from the others and moved into the middle of the circle, much more quickly than Stuart was doing, because he was at the back and there weren't many people who could follow him. He didn't think there were many people who could see him. He got halfway to Timmy before Franklin even noticed he was gone. When Franklin called out for him to come back, Gregor ignored him.

Stuart had begun to move more quickly. He was now nearly half the way to the center of the circle, and Timmy had noticed him. Stuart motioned with his head for Timmy to look behind him and Timmy did, but his reaction wasn't all that Gregor might have hoped. "Lock him up lock him up lock him up," the crowd was saying. Timmy set his jaw and shouted back. "I DIDN'T DO ANYTHING I DIDN'T DO ANYTHING I DIDN'T DO ANYTHING SHE'S A LIAR."

Gregor reached him, grabbed him by the coat and said, "I know you didn't do anything, Timmy. You have to come with me. You have to get out of here."

"You're going to lock me up," Timmy said stubbornly. "I'm not going to let you lock me up. I didn't do anything wrong."

"Lock him up lock him up lock him up," the crowd said, and then that other voice, vile and high-pitched and not really human, cawing, "Stupid RETARD RETARD RETARD RETARD *RETARD.*"

Gregor got both hands around Timmy's arms and tugged. "Come on," he said. "Your friend Amanda is over there waiting, and she won't leave without you. We've got to move."

Timmy was now out of the center of the circle, not very far out but out. Gregor had managed to move him a little. Stuart Ketchum was occupying the center of the circle himself. Gregor saw him unzipping his jacket. He pulled on Timmy one more time. Then he saw Stuart's hand rise in the air and said, "Oh, Jesus Christ."

Rifles, apparently, weren't the only kind of guns Stuart Ketchum had an interest in. What he had in his hand now was a small pistol. He was pointing it straight up into the air. Enough of the people in the crowd had seen it to cause another sea change in the mood. A lot of people were suddenly very, very uneasy. A lot of people were suddenly even more angry. "Don't let him go," they started to shout. "Don't let him go. Don't let him get away!"

Stuart Ketchum pulled the trigger. The sound that followed was quick and sharp and unmistakable. Gregor got a good grip on Timmy's arm and pulled him the rest of the way to Amanda Ballard.

"Through the window," Peter Callisher said, grabbing on to Timmy's other arm and taking over. "Through the window right now. Let's get out of here."

In the center of the circle, Stuart Ketchum was still standing stock still with his pistol in the air, waiting. At the edges, everybody was quiet. Gregor held his breath. The trouble with firing a shot in the air is that it sometimes provided the occasion for someone to fire a shot at you.

This time, it seemed to be doing what it was supposed to do. Everybody was quiet. Everybody was breathless. Everybody was waiting for something definitive to happen, nobody knew what.

Franklin Morrison seemed to think it was up to him to provide it. He strode into the center to stand beside Stuart and then called out, in a voice that needed no help from electronics:

"All right, everybody, let's go on home, because if you're anywhere near this place five minutes from now, I'm gonna throw you in jail and I'm not gonna give a shit who you think you are."

f i v e

1

SHARON MORRISSEY and Susan Everman were sitting in the Village
Restaurant when it started, and they were still sitting there twenty minutes later, when it finished, as abruptly and nonsensically as it had
begun. Susan was drinking a cup of coffee. Sharon was trying to finish
a hamburger that just wouldn't go down. The shouting was far enough
away so that the words were indecipherable, but clear enough in intent,
to make Sharon think of blood. After a while, everything began to make
her think of blood, even the bright plastic poinsettias on the middle of
the table and the fuzzy red suit of the Santa Claus doll that had been
placed in the window so that it faced the street. It shocked her a little,
to think that Susan could sit there so calmly, drinking her coffee, watching the progress of the riot, watching the death of it—and not twitch at
all. Sharon Morrissey definitely felt like twitching. She even felt like
screaming. Ever since the circle had formed and it had become obvious
what was going on, she had wanted to jump in her car and head for
Boston.

"What are we going to do?" she asked, when the crowd started to
disperse and the thick film of tension in the air began to disperse with
it. "What are we going to do?"

Susan reached into her handbag and came up with a pack of the
cigarettes she so rarely smoked. Susan Everman was the only person
Sharon Morrissey had ever known who was able to smoke cigarettes
only for mental-health purposes, and then only once or twice a year.

Susan lit up with a gold Dunhill lighter and said, "Tomorrow morning we're going to go apartment hunting in Boston."

"But that means we'll have to sell the house."

"We'll buy another house someday," Susan said. She blew a stream of smoke into the air and thought about it. "Maybe we should travel a little," she suggested. "I've never done any serious traveling in my life. And we have the money for it. We could go to Paris and Rome and to Holland. If we have the time."

"If we did something like that, we wouldn't have to sell the house," Sharon said. "We could leave everything where it is and just take off."

"That's true."

"Why do you want to leave this place? Is it just over that or is it something about us?"

"What went on over there isn't 'just' anything," Susan said grimly. "Small towns can turn, Sharon, and I think this one just did. There are already three people dead, and for all we know it's some crazy who doesn't like deviance of one sort or another. I think it's time we got out of here."

And, Sharon thought, Susan was right, just as Susan was always right and Susan was always beautiful, but it *felt* wrong, that was the problem. It felt like running. And what was worse, it felt like running from no danger at all. Sharon considered telling Susan what she really thought—which was that no matter who was dead already, the two of them were safe—but decided against it. If she said something like that, Susan would want her to explain it, and Sharon wasn't sure she could.

At this point, Sharon Morrissey wasn't sure she could explain anything.

2

"I THINK it's time I got out of here," Amanda Ballard was saying to Peter Callisher ten minutes later, pacing back and forth across his living-room floor, rubbing every once in a while against the raw patch of skin at the side of her face. The raw patch of skin was a scrape from a brick she'd run into getting out the back way after the—Peter didn't want to call it a riot—and it seemed to nag at her. Timmy was out in the kitchen, drinking coffee full of sugar and cream and looking cold. He would fall asleep where he was sitting and they would have to move him. Amanda kept picking things up and putting them down again. Peter wanted to make her sit still.

"I don't think you're being fair," he told her, wishing his voice didn't sound so tight, wishing he didn't really care. "They're not like that. Not most of the time. You know they're not like that."

"I don't know what they're like."

"This has been a good place for you. I've been a good man for you. I don't see how you can talk about walking out on it all after everything we've been to each other."

"We haven't been anything to each other, Peter. We've just been sleeping together. And sex is only important to men."

"Sex used to be important to you."

"No, it didn't. Not really."

Peter started to argue the point and stopped himself. It was a ludicrous point to argue. It was an argument no man could win. All the woman had to do was say she'd been faking it, and how would the man ever know? Peter got up and went to the window. He could see Main Street and the town park. He could see streets filled with tourists and the bleacher tents like giant blobs blocking his view. It had all gone back to normal in no time at all.

"It's as if it never happened," he said, watching a cluster of bright silver balls tied to a fire hydrant bounce in the wind. "It's all back to normal. And it's going to stay back to normal. It was some kind of catharsis."

"It was the next best thing to a lynching."

"They would never have lynched anybody."

"You would never have lynched anybody," Amanda said. "You're you. They're them. I'm sorry, Peter. It's my fault, really. I didn't realize what I was doing. I didn't understand it could work out this way."

"I don't see why it's your fault."

"I have to get Timmy out of here."

"He didn't come with you to begin with. I wish I understood you, Amanda. I wish I knew what you wanted out of life."

"I want what everybody wants," Amanda said. "I want to be left alone."

Peter didn't think that was what everybody wanted, but Amanda was on her way to the bedroom and he was following her. She went to the big oak wardrobe he'd bought in Burlington and began to take her sweaters down from its high shelf. He stood in the doorway with his arms folded over his chest and felt the sweat come pouring down his forehead into his eyes.

"Amanda," he said.

Amanda unhooked an empty felt Christmas stocking with her name on it from the wardrobe's upper molding and tossed it on the bed.

"Don't tell me how much I mean to you, because we'll both know it won't be true. I was never anything more to you than a convenience."

"A convenience," Peter repeated.

"That's why I like Timmy," Amanda told him. "He gets angry and sad and happy and horny, but he never tries to cover it up by saying it's something else."

Peter didn't have an answer to that. He didn't know where to begin to look for an answer to that. He hadn't even figured out what to think about tonight. He did tell himself that the right thing to do right this second would be to get her to stop, to prove through force and ardor that he hadn't felt about her as she assumed he had felt about her, that nothing was the way she thought it to be, but for some reason he felt paralyzed, and the paralysis translated into visions of Gregor Demarkian, going off to talk to Kelley Grey while the crowd melted away into the night.

Maybe Amanda was right. Maybe she had been only a convenience. Maybe putting up with Timmy had been the coin of the realm.

3

WHEN IT WAS over, the first thing Stuart Ketchum wanted to do was to drive out to Rose Hill Cemetery and visit his mother's grave. He hadn't been there since the funeral and didn't intend to go again. He went once to any grave that concerned him and then left it alone. That was what he'd done with the boys he'd known in Nam who hadn't come home. If he found out where they were buried he went to see their markers, once, and then he walked away. It made sense. It made the only sense Stuart could think of, when it came to death. It had never ceased to surprise him just how final dying was.

He never made it to the cemetery. He stood in the middle of Main

Street, watching it empty out, thinking of these people he had known all his life. He thought of himself holding that pistol in the air, that pistol he'd only had with him because he was going to go down to Burlington tonight and talk to his dealer about selling it off. He had started collecting guns of every type and only settled on rifles after a time. What would have happened if he hadn't had it with him? What would have happened if he'd had one of the rifles instead, so that he was out there in the middle of that circle looking like an ad for the United States Marines? What would his friends and neighbors have done then? Minute by minute, he had a harder and harder time thinking of these people as "his friends and neighbors." They were like the pod people from the remake of *Invasion of the Body Snatchers,* the ones that opened their mouths and made a horrible noise.

He looked around in the empty street and saw Gregor Demarkian standing by himself, his hands in the pockets of his long city coat, his head bare. Stuart's head was bare, too, and he could guess how Demarkian felt. Stuart thought his own ears were frozen solid and about to drop off. He went down the pavement and stopped just close enough to make conversation possible. Demarkian was staring into the gutter with a frown on his face. It was one of the things Stuart had noticed. Demarkian was the kind of man who looked intelligently at inanimate objects, as if they could tell him something.

The dwarf evergreen bushes that lined the walk to the front door of the Green Mountain Inn on the other side of the street had been decked out with gold Christmas balls. Stuart hadn't seen them there the last time he'd been in. He moved a little closer to Demarkian and said, "Where did Franklin go? Did he disappear with the riot?"

"Chief Morrison was called away on an errand. By Kelley Grey."

"What about you?" Stuart said.

"I am waiting here for no good reason, and in a moment I'll go back to the Inn and get changed for the performance. I suppose it's getting late."

"Getting."

Demarkian rocked back and forth on his heels. "Would you mind telling me something? If I asked you a question?"

"You can *ask* me anything."

"Meaning you don't have to answer."

"Exactly."

"This is a very little question," Demarkian said. "I have heard, from a number of people, that your mother was having her portrait painted by Jan-Mark Verek."

"That's right."

"And that she was very excited about this, and that she talked about it and about the times she spent at the Verek house. That she talked to quite a few people."

"Definitely. She was tickled pink, to put it the way she would have herself."

"That's what I thought. Did she mention anything at all in particular about that house? Did she go only in Jan-Mark's studio or did she go into the other rooms? Did she ever say she'd seen anything—"

"You mean in Tisha's office?" Stuart laughed. "Of course she'd seen Tisha's office. Jan-Mark shows people Tisha's office. Haven't you had a chance to talk to Cara Hutchinson?"

"Who's Cara Hutchinson?"

"High-school girl, plays Elizabeth in the Nativity play this year. She's the new portrait subject, the one Jan-Mark picked on after my mother died. I don't know why he needs subjects, though, it's all found objects and collages. Anyway, first day she was there, he gave her a tour."

"He gave your mother a tour also, when she was alive?"

"No," Stuart said, "it was Tisha who gave my mother the tour, at least as I understood it. Does this have something to do with why she died?"

"Why she was killed?" Gregor asked. "Yes. Yes, it does. It also confirms something for me."

"Which is what?"

"Which is that that entire alarm nonsense we went through today was staged for the purpose of letting Mr. Jan-Mark Verek get a look at me, and incidentally to find out what we were doing, which wasn't much."

"You mean you don't think he was robbed?"

"Of the photographs?" Demarkian smiled. "Maybe he was and maybe he wasn't. He certainly wasn't robbed of them today."

"Why not?"

"Because this Cara Hutchinson person of yours is not dead. I take it nothing you've heard of has happened so that she's just narrowly escaped death? No one has shot at her? She wasn't the person originally intended for Gemma Bury's seat?"

"She's in the play, like I told you. And you know what this town is like. If something really odd had happened, you'd have heard yourself by now. You've been in the paper so much, you're practically a resident."

"Fine," Gregor said. "Then the photos weren't stolen today, if they were stolen at all. They would have had to have been removed before this Cara Hutchinson first saw Tisha Verek's office. Is there a place in the Verek house where it might be possible to see into your yard?"

"Not into my yard," Stuart said, "because the Verek place is in a hollow. But you know what he can see? The road and the notches in the woods where the stone walls come out."

"Meaning he probably saw Franklin and me wandering in and out when we were using the stone walls. All right. That will do."

"Why did the pictures have to be taken before Cara Hutchinson saw Tisha Verek's office?"

Gregor Demarkian got a surprised look on his face that Stuart remembered from grade school. It was the look of a teacher whose prize pupil has just asked a monumentally stupid question.

"Because one of those photos was recognizable, of course," Demarkian said. "That's what all this has been about from the beginning. One of those photographs was recognizable." Demarkian turned toward the Inn and frowned again. "It's really too bad, in a way," he said, "because I don't think Tisha Verek would ever have picked it up on her own. Not from what I've heard of her, anyway. I think the first recognition came with your mother. I don't know. I'm making this up. From what I've heard of Tisha Verek, she wasn't a woman I would have liked. So I'm trying to give your mother all the insight. Maybe I'm wrong."

"If it's because the picture was recognizable," Stuart asked, "why hasn't someone tried to kill Jan-Mark Verek?"

"Because the picture's only recognizable to someone who's seen the person herself. And Jan-Mark Verek does not see many people in this town. Not if he can help it."

"That's true," Stuart admitted. "What about Gemma Bury? Did she see the picture?"

"No. She was looking through a window on the third floor of the Episcopalian rectory when Tisha Verek was killed. Those windows look directly down into the Verek driveway."

"You mean she saw Tisha killed?"

"I mean she saw Tisha's killer, although I don't think she realized it at the time."

"What happens now?" Stuart asked. "Do you get all the suspects into a large room and reveal the solution? Who are the suspects?"

"Right now I go over and get changed, just like I told you I was going to do. Then I make a phone call. After that, I don't know what anybody could do. Have a good evening, Mr. Ketchum."

"Oh, I will," Stuart Ketchum said. "Soon as I can get my adrenaline down."

"Work on it," Demarkian told him. Then he turned away and walked rapidly across the street.

Stuart watched him go, a big, tall, middle-aged man totally out of place on this country Main Street, a man of long coats and hard leather shoes in a world made for parkas and cleated boots. He should have looked ridiculous, but he did not. Stuart thought he looked a lot like salvation. Before they had begun talking, Stuart had been ready to walk out—into what, or where, he had no idea, but out, away from here, away from the kind of people who could shoot rifles at women sitting in half-filled bleachers and threaten a man for no other reason than that he was mentally retarded. Now Stuart felt as if it all fit into something larger, a western movie with common sense in the white hat and hysteria in the black, and if he just put his mind to it, he could be part of it. It was silly, of course, but that was the way Demarkian made him feel. Stuart had had a sergeant like that in the army.

Sometimes, Stuart had a terrible feeling he was that sort of man himself.

4

KELLEY GREY had gotten hold of Franklin Morrison, and now Candy George could see them both standing just inside the entrance to the dressing-room tent, talking to each other. That was all well and good, but it didn't solve Candy's problem, which was what to do about Reggie, who was not back home in the basement where she had left him. Candy hadn't really expected him to be. She had told Kelley Grey all about it, and all about where the basement windows were and how strong Reggie was and also how the doors wouldn't hold him, but Kelley was one of that alien breed, a woman who had never known a man like this. She had no idea what could happen. She had no idea what someone like Reggie could do.

Candy had a very detailed idea of what Reggie could do, and that was why she was watching him now, staying out of sight behind the flap to the dressing room she shared with Cara Hutchinson and Mrs. Johnson. He was going in and out of the dressing rooms on the other side of the corridor, the ones that belonged to the men. He was calling out to people he knew and laughing hard, as if he didn't care who was around who might hear. He had been here before and nobody thought anything of the fact that he was here again. Kelley and Franklin didn't know he was anywhere near them. There was a lot of noise in this tent, and they were so close to the flap they were probably hearing sounds from outside. The animals were kept back there. Every once in a while, Candy heard the donkey braying.

There were five dressing rooms on either side of the corridor, all of them tiny, all of them cold. It was a blessing nobody really had to do any dressing in any of them. Since there were no costume changes, actors came dressed for their parts every night and used the "dressing rooms" just to dress, or to repair make-up when it became necessary. Candy didn't repair make-up because she didn't use any. She had always used a great deal, ever since she was ten or eleven years old, because her friends had used it and because her stepfather had liked to see her in it—*just like Lolita,* he used to say, *just like Lolita*—but here in this place that was hers she didn't like it. It helped that the distance between the gazebo where she spent most of her time and the stands was such that not having any on made no real difference. Cara Hutchinson was always slathering her face with foundation and rouge, but Candy couldn't see that anyone in the bleachers would be able to tell. Or that it would do much good even if they could.

Reggie had reached the third dressing room on the other side. Candy's was the last on this one. She retreated behind the flap and counted to ten in her head. Then she bent over and very carefully put on the shoes she had brought with her for just this occasion. The shoes had been a risk. She had had to go back to the house and get them, moving very quietly so that Reggie didn't hear. He had still been in the basement then and still bellowing. She'd had to sneak into the bedroom and get them out of her closet and get back into the car again. She's done it just before she'd gone to see Kelley Grey. When it was over, her chest felt so tight, she didn't think she would ever be able to breathe again.

The shoes were one of the three pairs Reggie had bought for her special. Candy didn't wear shoes like these for herself, because the heels were too high and too pointy and she didn't walk well in them, and because the toes came to so sharp a point they made her own toes ache. These were made of pink patent leather and had little straps instead of heels at the backs.

Cara Hutchinson saw her putting them on and said, "You can't wear those on stage. They wouldn't look right."

"I'm not going to wear them on stage," Candy said, whispering instead of talking.

"You should speak up," Cara told her. "I swear, I don't understand how anyone hears a thing you say out there. You're always such a little mouse. You have to learn to project."

Candy's private opinion was that the thing she'd most like to project at the moment was Cara Hutchinson's rear end, right out into the snow, but she didn't have time for that now. There was serious business to take care of. She leaned toward the flap and looked out again. Kelley and Chief Morrison were still talking, still blocking the front entrance to the dressing-room tent. They should have realized that Reggie would come in from the back, the way most of the actors did.

Reggie got to the fourth of the dressing rooms on that side. Candy let the flap fall in front of her face and held her breath again and counted to ten again and tried to remember how to pray. It had been such a long time, all she could remember was "Now I lay me . . ." and then everything went blank. Reggie said hello to Evan Underwood in a false hearty voice that recognized how little he and Evan got along. He moved on to the fifth of the dressing rooms, and in that dressing room somebody did what Candy had been expecting all along. Somebody told Reggie where she was.

"Right across the aisle," she heard Reggie say.

Candy stepped back into the tiny room and positioned herself so that she was facing the slit at the center of the flaps. She looked around and saw that Cara Hutchinson was absorbed in her make-up but Mrs. Johnson was quiet and watchful, alert, ready for something to happen. Just don't get in my way, Candy told the old lady, silently, in the back of her mind, while she was still not breathing. And then the canvas flaps opened and he was there.

"Candy," he said, the smile starting to spread across his face, the smile she knew so well. They all had smiles like that. That was the odd thing. They all had smiles that were exactly alike. Reggie filled the flap opening now, the canvas pulled back above his shoulders, his legs spread wide so that she wouldn't have room to pass. It was beyond his comprehension that she might not want to pass.

Years ago, when she was still in junior high school and still naïve, Candy had worked very hard to make the cheerleading squad. She had practiced for months doing splits and kicks. She had worked up dance routines and learned to jump three feet in the air. That was before she realized that girls like her never did become cheerleaders, no matter how good they were; they had reputations instead, and it didn't matter how they'd gotten those reputations in the first place. She had thought that the only thing that mattered was being the best, and for the only time in her life she had worked herself to death, singlemindedly, to be the best. And it had worked. She hadn't made the cheerleading squad, but on the day of the tryouts she had done the cleanest split, jumped the highest jump and turned cartwheels with her body so straight she looked like a spinning snowflake. She had also done the highest and fastest and most elegant kick in the history of cheerleading in Bethlehem, Vermont.

"Candy," Reggie said again.

That was when Candy did it again, high and hard, as high and as hard as she had that day back in junior high school, but this time in a pair of spike-heeled shoes with the stiff sharp tips of the toes aimed straight at the one thing Reggie George had ever given a damn about in his life. He saw what she was doing and stepped back, more surprised than angry, but not fast enough. She caught him squarely in the center underneath and he screamed.

My God, Candy thought, as the scream went on and on, higher and higher. I think I've killed him.

She hadn't killed him. He was lying on the floor, hunched into a fetal ball, screaming and crying, but he was alive enough. Franklin Morrison came rushing up and grabbed him by the shoulder. Candy kicked the shoes off her feet and turned away.

"I want to have him arrested," she said. "He tried to kill me. I want to have him arrested for attempted murder."

"It's true," Mrs. Johnson piped up, her round little matron's face thrusting itself toward Franklin Morrison's stunned one, her look of innocence so perfect that only Candy knew she had to be lying. "It's true," Mrs. Johnson said again. "He went for her throat. And I'll testify to that in court."

Candy George closed her eyes and told herself:
Your name is Candace Elizabeth Spear.
And you are going to be all right.

s i x

1

GREGOR DEMARKIAN knew that there were people in town who were afraid the killings would have the wrong effect on the Celebration. They worried that people would get nervous and leave in droves, destroying any hopes Bethlehem had of having a happy new year. He wasn't worried. He'd spent over twenty years of his life officially involved with murder. He knew what people were like. The bleachers around the seats he shared with Bennis and Father Tibor were sparsely populated for that night's performance, but all the other bleachers were crammed full, even fuller than they'd been the night before. The vast American public was irresistibly drawn to other people's danger. That was why network television was full of series about violent detectives.

The second night of the Bethlehem Nativity play was full of donkeys and camels, although why that was so, Gregor was not able to explain. This was a night of imagination, where a lot of events had been added that appeared in none of the ordinary accounts of Christ's birth. At one point, the audience was treated to at least part of a Jewish wedding. Gregor thought that whatever the writers and producers had done might be of some scholarly interest, since Tibor was intent throughout, but since Gregor had no scholarly interests of his own, he couldn't have said. He contented himself with waiting, and being happy that Bennis seemed to have given in and decided to munch her way through one of Tibor's brown paper bakery bags, and thinking about what he was going to have to do. He was sorry Kelley Grey was not in the seat beside him, although he'd have been surprised if she'd come, even if he hadn't known she had something else to do for the evening. Bennis noticed her being gone, too, and remarked on it, both at the intermission and when the play was over.

"If I was that woman, I'd never sit in bleachers again," she said. "Gregor, what are you up to? You've been halfway to Mars all night."

"I'm not up to anything. Is Tibor falling asleep?"

Bennis leaned over, to find Tibor peering suspiciously at his program and not asleep at all. All the other bleachers were emptying out. Their own, already mostly empty, was the scene of a few last-minute scrambles. Tibor was ignoring it all.

"He's trying to find out what source they used," Bennis sighed, "and he keeps expecting to come up with someone like Raymond Brown—"

"Not Raymond Brown, Bennis, please, he's always looking for natural explanations for miracles—"

"Whichever," Bennis said. "Some hot biblical scholar, at any rate. And I keep telling him he's not going to find it. Whoever wrote this play just made all that stuff up."

"You do not make up events in the life of Christ and His Mother," Tibor said.

"Sure you do. Think about Nikos Kazantzakis. Think about Martin Scorsese. Think about—"

"I have enough to think about, Bennis. Have you finished your muffins?"

Bennis fished around inside the bag and came up with a muffin. "Pumpkin bread," she said solemnly. "Tibor got them for me special. I've already had six."

"What was the alternative?" Gregor asked her.

"Death by hanging." She put the muffin back in the bag. "Gregor, are you sure you're all right? Are you sure you're not up to something dangerous?"

"If you mean something you can help me with, no. I have to go talk to Franklin Morrison for a moment. I'd have talked to him before this but he had to take a young man to jail. Franklin'll be free by now. Then I'm going to come right home."

"And you don't want to tell me what this is about?"

"He doesn't need to tell you what this is about," Tibor said, "he needs only to let you eat. Eat all the muffins, Bennis, you are looking much too thin. It could be bad for you."

"Right," Bennis said. "Gregor."

The loudspeakers that had been used to amplify the voices of the actors in and around the gazebo were now being used to broadcast Christmas carols. The first one of the night was, as Gregor suspected it always was, "O Little Town of Bethlehem." Gregor put his coat on and got his gloves out of the pockets.

"Maybe you should start making him eat," Bennis said to Tibor. "I think he's become addled from malnutrition."

Tibor clucked. Gregor backed away from both of them. "I have to go talk to Franklin Morrison. You two go back to the Inn and relax."

"We two ought to follow him," Bennis said. "He's up to something."

And that, Gregor thought, as he turned his back on the both of them and hurried out of the park, was true enough. On the other hand, he was always up to something, and he had told Bennis and Tibor the literal truth. He did have to talk to Franklin Morrison.

He stopped to look back at the park and sighed. It had all been so much easier in the FBI. You got a warrant. You made an arrest. You let some Federal prosecutor figure out how to prove your case in court in a day and age when it was impossible to prove much of anything in court. You certainly didn't wander around small towns in Vermont, wishing you could get your act together well enough to know what you were supposed to do next.

Or if what you'd decided to do next would work.

2

SHE HAD HAD to wait until the end of the Nativity play, because until then Kelley Grey was otherwise engaged. "Otherwise engaged" was a phrase she liked very much, because it reminded her of one of the doctors in that place they'd sent her to, the one who was so afraid of her he wouldn't sit down when she was in the room. They were all afraid of her in that place, really. It surprised her. After a while, she thought it might be because they knew she wasn't crazy. That was the so hard to get people to understand. They said, "You murdered some-one." They said, "You were only a child." They said, "You must have been crazy." It was like those syllogisms she had found in the book about logic she had taken out of the library, thinking that if she could prove that she was logical she could make them see she didn't belong in an institution. All men are mortal. Socrates is a man. Socrates is mortal. It was like that. But it wasn't true. Murder was sometimes the sanest possible solution. It was sane even when resorted to by a child. It was what everybody would do if they had the chance and the weapon, if they understood what life was all about.

The phone call had come at the very last minute, just before she was getting ready to go out, and then she'd had to stop and think about it all again, about the logistics. She couldn't go back out to the Ketchum farm. Someone might be home. Someone might spot her driving along in the dark like that, when nobody and nothing else was on the road. She couldn't go back to Eddie Folier's place, either, because the police had been there earlier today and Eddie had been called back from Canada. The place was at least locked up. She wouldn't put it past them to have it guarded. She'd had to think long and hard about it after that. She knew half the guns in town—it was the kind of information she was always careful to put together, whenever she arrived in a new place—but stealing one wasn't so easy in the middle of the night. In the end she opted for the gun club at the American Legion because the back-door lock was easy to break. The guns on the walls were .22s, and they weren't locked into their racks, either. Maybe she should have used one of those and not Eddie Folier's when she killed Dinah Ketchum. It was a tough one to call.

The gun club kept its ammunition in big metal drawers built into one wall of the meeting room. She rifled through the boxes until she found one full of clips for the Remington Model 552 Speedmaster she had chosen. She wished she had something else to choose. This weighed over five pounds. It wasn't the heaviest gun she had ever held, but it was heavier than she liked. She thought about standing in the trees at the side of the Delaford Road and firing at Dinah Ketchum, thought about the gun jerking to the right as it always did, thought about the fact that that gun had been heavy, too. If women ever got real equal rights, they would start making guns for themselves that didn't pull and didn't kick so much. She supposed that in the long run it didn't matter. They were both dead, the really evil one and the one who was just like a sick animal, dangerous but without guilt. That was how she thought about Dinah Ketchum. Tisha Verek was like a picture of the devil in an illustrated Fundamentalist Bible. She threatened and laughed. Dinah Ketchum just sat in the car saying, ''Oh, I'm so sorry dear, I just noticed and I was just trying to tell you that if you don't want people to know you should—''

You should what?

She loaded the rifle and wrapped it into her coat. She'd worn her long coat instead of her parka for just this purpose. She could carry it pressed to her left side without looking too strange on the street. It was very cold and people who saw her passing would think she was simply stiff with cold. Besides, nobody was really looking at anybody right now, not after what they had done to Timmy Hall. They had all gone back home to be ashamed of themselves.

She got the rifle early and went over to the park. It would have been a three-block walk if she had been in the city, maybe a third of a mile. She went into the tent they used as a dressing room and looked around, being careful not to be seen. It wasn't hard. It was the last fifteen minutes of the play, with everybody in the cast for the night either out at the gazebo or waiting in the passage to take a bow. She thought Kelley must have gone out there, too, since Kelley was nowhere around. It was too bad. She believed in her luck—or at least, she believed in her luck with rifles—but she also knew you could push luck only so far. She'd been pushing hers straight off the cliff these last few weeks.

''Listen,'' Kelley Grey had said on the telephone. ''I think we have to talk.''

''Who is it?'' a voice said from the other room, and she had held her breath and crossed her fingers.

''It's for me.''

''Listen,'' Kelley Grey said again. ''Gemma had this manuscript. That Tisha Verek wrote, you know. And last night I read it.''

''So?''

''So there's something in it you have to see.''

''What?''

''A picture.''

''I don't want to see any pictures.''

''Yes, you do,'' Kelley Grey insisted. ''You have to see this one. You should come up to the rectory tonight after the play and let me show it to you.''

Once there had been a voice on the phone that said: *I saw you walking on the stone walls Monday morning. What were you doing on the stone walls?*

That voice had belonged to Gemma Bury, and the next time she had heard it Gemma had been on her way to do what she had threatened to do, on her way to talk to Peter Callisher about the story and to get it all put in the newspaper and make it . . . make it what?

There were people who said it was safer to kill in emptiness, but she knew it wasn't true. She could go out to the rectory. She could shoot Kelley Grey there. She could rid herself of all the restrictions imposed by being in this tent and having so many other people to take into account. She could do all that, but if she did she would have a whole new set of problems and one she liked less. To be seen, even by one person, would be death. To make a mistake, no matter how minor, would be disaster. Besides, Kelley would be ready for her up there, waiting for her, taking precautions. She couldn't have that.

There was a place at the end of the tent farthest from the passage to the park "stage" where the flaps came together and made a kind of curtain. She checked it out, decided it would do, and folded herself into it. Her feet were exposed, but she didn't think anyone would notice. They would be coming back in after taking their bows and concentrating on going home. She backed up against the tent's corner and tried to look out. She could see the flap of the two dressing rooms diagonally across from where she was. She would have to hope that Kelley came in on her own or stayed later than the others, or most of the others. If Kelley didn't do that, she would have to go on up to the rectory after all. She got the rifle out from under her coat and felt its weight in her arms.

In the place where she had been they had long wide rooms full of tables to eat at, but if you had been good you got to sit in the smaller room where the tables were round. It was not a prize she had ever valued much—if there had been waiters and waitresses in the round-tabled room she might have felt differently—but she had always been so conscientious about working for prizes and playing to win games and being good, that she had worked at that, too. Then she would get there and it would all begin to seem so awful and terrible, so much a part of the lie that that place was, she wouldn't be able to stand it anymore. She would stand up and start throwing things, forks and spoons, there were never any knives, furniture. She would shout and scream and tell them all to go to hell, she didn't belong in a crazy place, and then they would sit her down in some doctor's room and tell her: If you could behave for three months straight, we'd be more than willing to let you out of here.

But it wasn't true.

It wasn't true.

The whole world was a cage.

That was true.

The whole world was a cage and there was only one way to keep yourself out of it.

That first time she had stood behind the door with the sweat pouring down her face and her heart hammering and she had seen him coming up the walk, coming up as if there was nothing wrong at all, nothing he had done, nothing he ought to be ashamed of. There were people on the street behind him, walking down the sidewalk, walking dogs, carrying packages. She saw an old lady with a hat with a flower on it and a mother with two small children who looked frazzled in the heat. It had been very hot for days and it was going to get hotter. It was ten o'clock in the morning and already so thick with humidity the air felt wet. She watched him coming up toward her and decided it didn't matter. As long as she killed him it didn't matter what else happened because nothing else would. Nothing else ever would. She was alone on top of a high place and very calm. She could aim her father's rifle out the front door and down the front walk and right out into the street and the bullet would be magic. It wouldn't go to the right or to the left. It would hit him in the heart just as surely as if it had been drawn there with a magnet.

Safe, she thought now. Safe, safe, safe. She was always safe.

The flap at the far end of the tent opened and she could hear someone moving down the center aisle, humming and shuffling along. She tensed against the long stock of the rifle and waited. The voice sounded right but she couldn't be sure. If it turned out to be right she would be luckier than she had ever imagined. She held her breath and waited. She brought the rifle up a little higher and waited. She listened to the humming get louder and realized it was "The First Noel."

"Bugger," Kelley Grey said, interrupting her music, banging her leg into a metal folding chair that had been left out to no good purpose. Kelley moved the chair and then pulled back the flap on the dressing room at the very end of the row on the far side. She made the flap secure, went into the cubicle, and sat down on a bench with her back to the corridor. She was dressed in a bright red sweater that seemed to sparkle and pulse in the dim light.

Behind the curtain flaps in the corner, she waited, barely able to breathe.

3

"BUGGER, BUGGER, bugger," Kelley Grey said, to the air, to nothing at all. It was cold and she was colder. It had been a long night and she wanted it to end. Reggie George was in jail but she still had Candy to take care of. The play was almost over for the night, but she had Candy's things to pack up before the tent could be taken down. Her head ached and she began to wonder what she really wanted to do with her life. Last week, she would have answered that with: Grow up. Now she wasn't so sure. Growing up was all about responsibility. She'd had enough responsibility tonight to last her forever.

Candy had left her few pieces of jewelry in a small box on one of the tables. She didn't think it was right for Mary to wear jewelry even if it couldn't be seen. Kelley checked through the box to make sure it contained a pair of gold earrings, an ivory ring in the shape of a daisy and a tiny locket on a chain. Then she put the box into her pocket and went looking for a change purse. The change purse was supposed to be red plastic and not to have anything in it but a New York City subway token Candy said she kept for luck.

Kelley found the change purse and the subway token on the floor, next to one of the spike-heeled shoes. She didn't know if it was the shoe Candy had used to kick Reggie or not. Even if it wasn't, it looked lethal. She picked it up and turned it over in her hand.

"I wonder if she wants these," she said, to nobody at all.

Then she got off the bench and dropped to the floor, to see if she could find the other one.

4

W H E N   K E L L E Y   G R E Y dropped to the floor, she had just brought the rifle up to her shoulder. She was in the process of adjusting it against the padding of her coat. Then all of a sudden, Kelley was out of sight. She was talking to herself and moving around on the ground. If it went on very much longer, the actors would be in from the play, and then what would she do? There was nothing to say Kelley would stick around until most of the rest of them were gone. She would have to go out to the rectory, and she really didn't want that.

"Shoes," Kelley Grey said. "Stupid shoes."

She was moving around much too much.

If you stay calm it will work no matter what, she told herself, watching Kelley move, hearing Kelley swear.

Just remember.

Her body is a magnet.

Her body is a magnet for the bullets from this gun.

Your hands are steady.

All you have to do is fire.

5

"D A M N E D   S T U P I D shoes," Kelley Grey said to herself again, and then it went past her, hard air moving fast, and the next thing she heard was wood splintering and metal whining in complaint.

"What the hell," she said.

6

THE FIRST ONE missed but it didn't matter. It didn't matter because she was absolutely calm. She was always absolutely calm at times like this. She steadied the rifle against her shoulder and fired again, felt the pull again, saw the bullet miss again. She didn't panic because there was nothing to panic about. There was nobody and nothing in the universe but herself and this rifle and Kelley Grey.

All she had to do was go on firing.

7

THE SECOND ONE hit the back of the bench she had been sitting on when she came in, and with that Kelley knew what was happening. She was being shot at. There was somebody else in the tent with her and she was being shot at. She was supposed to be shot at, but not yet, not here, and where was Gregor Demarkian when you needed him? That was the question. That and what the hell it was she was supposed to do.

There sure as hell wasn't anyplace she was going to be able to hide.

She whipped around and looked in the direction she thought the bullet must have come from. She could see nothing or nobody and it made her afraid. That was what she had to do. She had to bring it all out into the open.

She grabbed the metal folding chair, collapsed it into a shield and held it out in front of her, or at least what she hoped was in front of her, between herself and where she was sure the bullet must have come from.

"Come out of there," she said, as loud as she could. "Come out of there right this minute. Amanda, for God's sake."

8

MY NAME IS NOT Amanda, Amanda Ballard thought. My name has never been Amanda. It was only supposed to be.

Kelley Grey had the metal folding chair up over her head.

Amanda knew no one could hold onto metal when the metal had been hit by a bullet.

The bullet made the metal vibrate and the metal stung.

She raised the rifle to firing height again and positioned it ever more carefully against her shoulder. She had never been able to take the kick very well and now her shoulder ached.

She fired at the metal folding chair and hit it.

She heard Kelley cry out and then the clatter of the chair falling to the ground.

She took aim and fired again.

9

"FOR GOD'S SAKE," Gregor Demarkian said. "Franklin, I told you, you were supposed to leave somebody here."

10

GREGOR DEMARKIAN was coming in from the back end of the tent. As soon as she saw him, she knew it had finally gone wrong. Getting caught didn't make it go wrong. Only missing made it go wrong. Getting caught didn't do anything to her at all.

She gave it one more try. She had the rifle in position. She sighted as best she could with this big man bearing down on her and pulled the trigger.

11

G R E G O R   G O T his hands on the barrel of the gun just in time. He felt the barrel rock as he held it, the heat searing his hands, the bullet racing through, the redirected rifle sending sparks into the tent ceiling as the bullet crashed through and into the air. He sent up a little prayer that nobody was out there, in the wrong place at the wrong time, and then heard the splintering of wood that meant the bullet had hit a tree. He let himself relax.

"Get up," he said to Kelley Grey. "It's over now."

"It's over and I'm going to sue you," Kelley said. "What did you think you were doing? Weren't you at least having her watched?"

"I didn't know where she was to start having her watched from," Franklin Morrison said, struggling into the tent himself.

A lot of other people were struggling into the tent, too, actors in costume, animal handlers looking for a nip from the bottle that floated around the dressing room most nights. Gregor saw Candy George, who played Mary, looking from Kelley to Amanda and back again in mild, but not very curious, confusion.

In the end, he turned his attention to Amanda Ballard, who was really Amy Jo Bickerel, and who now looked like nobody in particular at all. Her hair was back and he could see the ear without the earlobe clearly. It made her look not quite finished.

Other than that, she simply looked tired.

EPILOGUE

Hurray for the fun
Is the pudding done?
Hurray for
the pumpkin pie ...

1

I T   W A S Christmas Day, and to Donna Moradanyan's son Tommy,
who was eighteen months old, the purpose of such a day was strikingly
and unquestionably clear. It wasn't presents. Tommy had gotten about
seven million presents at his grandmother's out in Ardmore last night,
and a couple of dozen more in his own apartment this morning, but
although he liked to rip paper off packages, what was inside the packages
didn't make much sense to him yet. It wasn't going to church, either,
although he liked that. The sound of the cantor's voice always put him
to sleep, and he climbed into his mother's arms—or Gregor Demarkian's—and closed his eyes. Tommy Moradanyan liked Gregor Demarkian
about as much as he liked anyone, except he liked his mother better.
But Gregor Demarkian was good. Gregor Demarkian wore ties that
always seemed to be fraying and unraveling along the edges, and if
Tommy was very quiet and very serious, he could take them apart into
threads in no time at all.

What Tommy Moradanyan really liked about Christmas Day was
the food. His grandmother at Ardmore was good at food. His mother
was good at food. His mother's best friend Bennis Hannaford was good
at buying cotton candy from the back of Ohanian's Middle Eastern Food
Store and sneaking it to him when his mother wasn't looking. Nobody
was as good at food as Mrs. Arkmanian. Of course, he didn't call Mrs.
Arkmanian Mrs. Arkmanian, even though his mother wanted him to.
He called her Nana Lida, and every time he did, she smiled at him and
let him take bulgar-covered meatballs from the big bowl she kept in the

refrigerator or stuffed grape leaves from the plastic-wrapped bundle in the vegetable crisper. Tommy Moradanyan's mother was very stern about Eating Vegetables and Having Regular Meals, but Nana Lida was not. Nana Lida just liked to see him eat.

Nana Lida's living room took up the entire second floor of her townhouse. It was a big room to begin with, and it had been made bigger by the removal of almost all the furniture from its center and the repositioning of its chairs along the outer walls. Under the tall narrow windows that looked out on Cavanaugh Street, tables had been set with just about everything Tommy Moradanyan could think of to call wonderful.

Old George Tekemanian had been given the only armchair allowed onto the scene and the job of keeping Tommy out of trouble while Tommy's mother finished helping with the silverware. Tommy sat patiently in old George's lap for a good twenty-five seconds, and then saw something that interested him across the room. Alex Oumoudian, who had come from Armenia just a few months ago and who was only two years older than Tommy himself, had made his way to the grilled shrimp and begun to eat. If he went on eating like that, all the grilled shrimp would be gone. Never mind the grilled peppers that went with it. All across America, small boys were refusing to eat anything that didn't come in a McDonald's wrapper. Tommy Moradanyan would have considered them all nuts. He ate grilled peppers. He ate big thick anchovies imported from Italy. He ate escargot. He ate anything you put in front of him and ninety-nine times out of a hundred he liked it. The world was full of wonderful food. His mother was always saying she hoped he'd gotten his father's metabolism, because if he had he could eat like that forever and still be thin. Tommy didn't know what a metabolism was, and he had only vague ideas about fathers, except for his Father in Heaven, whom he thought of as a priest like Father Tibor. The father his mother was always talking about was someone he'd never met.

Alex Oumoudian had gone from the shrimp to the stuffed grape leaves, and that was really too much. Stuffed grape leaves were Tommy Moradanyan's favorite thing. Old George Tekemanian was humming to himself, not paying attention. Tommy's mother was in the middle of the room, holding a plate of something and talking to Gregor Demarkian and Bennis Hannaford. There was nothing to stop him. Tommy slid to the floor and took off, head down.

When he put his mind to it, he could run faster than a grown man.

2

"W H O O S H ," Donna Moradanyan said, when Tommy came barreling into her legs, not watching where he was going, legs pumping like pistons to get him where he was going. "You're supposed to be with George."

"Eat," Tommy said emphatically.

"You've been eating for a week," Donna said.

"Eat," Tommy said again.

Then he wriggled out of her arms and jumped away. She watched him go to the food tables and shook her head. "Well, at least he's healthy. And he's not fat. The doctor keeps telling me that. How can he not be fat?"

"He's building bones," Bennis said. "What I want to know is why I'm not fat. I've had Mrs. Alvoudian in my apartment all week and all she does is cook. And clean. She threw out my cleaning lady."

"It will only be a couple of weeks," Donna soothed. "Hannah Krekorian has a place for Mrs. Alvoudian opening up next month, and while the three of you were away the committee got up the rest of the price, so we're going to be able to buy that building on Debberfield Street after all. That'll take a couple of months to fix up properly—"

"By which time seventeen more Armenian refugee families will have landed in Philadelphia," Bennis said.

"—but it will help. It really is better than it was even at Thanksgiving, Bennis, you know that."

"At Thanksgiving," Gregor Demarkian said, "I was sleeping in my bathtub."

Donna Moradanyan and Bennis Hannaford both looked him up and down, as if he'd just landed from Mars, and Gregor thought that was all right. He felt as if he'd just landed from Mars. There were more people in this room speaking Armenian than speaking English.

"I'd better go and get Tommy under control," Donna said. "Or maybe it's Father Tibor I should get under control. He's feeding Tommy something and he knows how I feel about it."

"Give it up," Bennis said. "It's like refighting Waterloo on Napoleon's side."

"Maybe it is, but I've got to do something. He's become Cavanaugh Street's official neighborhood grandchild. He's going to be spoiled rotten before he ever gets to school."

"Right," Bennis said.

Donna Moradanyan hurried off in the direction of the food tables, and Bennis looked after her, sighing.

"Sometimes I think they're all right," she told Gregor. "About getting married and having a child, I mean. Donna's, what, fifteen years younger than I am? More? I'm thirty-six years old."

"You date drummers in rock bands who wear Stars of David in their pierced noses. These are not exactly prime husband material, Bennis."

"There was only one of those and he was prime husband material, at least in some senses. He would have been a good provider. That band you're so superior to makes a couple of million dollars a year."

"Big time Mafiosi make a couple of million dollars a year."

"Tell me about Bethlehem," Bennis sighed. "It's got to be better than listening to another lecture."

3

GREGOR DIDN'T KNOW if it would be better than listening to another lecture or not, but he did know that he'd been dying to explain this to somebody, especially since the Philadelphia *Inquirer* had come out with a mangled story that made it sound as if Amanda Ballard had been picked up during an incident that resembled the shoot-out at the O.K. Corral. This was not the *Inquirer's* fault. The original mess of a story had appeared in the *Bethlehem News and Mail*, written by a reporter manqué who had suddenly found himself in charge of a pencil while Peter Callisher was indisposed. Peter Callisher had spent a great deal of time indisposed after Amanda Ballard was arrested. Gregor hadn't been able to blame him. It had to come as a shock that the woman you had been living with had just killed three people and tried to kill a fourth. It had to come as even more of a shock that she had killed one more before she ever met you. That was the sort of shock that came from that most universal of human failings, the delusion each and every one of us has that we are good judges of character.

"It was very simple," he said, and Bennis shot him a look.

"If you start telling me it was elementary, my dear Watson, I'm going to kick you in the shin. It wasn't simple to me."

"Well, the physical procedure was just a matter of logistics," Gregor pointed out. "I explained all that back in Bethlehem."

"Did you ever find out whose gun it was?" Bennis asked him. "That she stole, I mean. To kill Dinah Ketchum."

"It was Mr. Folier's. I'd suspected as much after I found out that Folier's house was so close to the offices of the *News and Mail*. But Dinah Ketchum was the key all along. She was what had to be explained. There had to be two dozen people who would have been more than happy to kill Tisha Verek, and the situation with Gemma Bury was almost as bad. So that left us with Dinah Ketchum, and Tisha Verek's office, and the only thing it could have been, which is that Dinah saw something there."

"And the something had to be those pictures?" Bennis asked. "I don't see why, Gregor, I really don't. I mean, okay, Jan-Mark Verek gave tours of the house and pointed out all the things in his wife's office, but why would Dinah Ketchum have paid particular attention?"

"Probably because Tisha Verek pointed it out to her," Gregor said. "My point here, however, is that it had to be something like that, and something like that was ready to hand in Tisha's research and in the pictures, one of which probably showed Amy Jo Bickerel with her deformed ear clearly in view."

"How did you know it was Amy Jo Bickerel? You never saw the pictures."

"I didn't have to," Gregor said patiently. "Amy Jo Bickerel had two things speaking for her in this case. In the first place, she had done it before—done murder, that is, in exactly the way we were seeing it done in Bethlehem. When Amy Jo Bickerel killed her uncle, she stood behind the front door of her house and aimed a rifle at him as he came up the walk, at ten o'clock on a weekday morning, on a busy street. When Amanda Ballard killed Tisha Verek, she aimed a rifle at her while Tisha was standing in her own driveway and a car was pulling in—almost anybody else would have backed off and waited for another chance. And then there was Gemma Bury—"

"Like she gets so intent on what she's after, she doesn't see what's around her," Bennis said. "All right. But then Dinah Ketchum—"

"Was killed in the only way Amanda could manage it, and right away because she was afraid that Tisha Verek's death might start Dinah talking. Remember, the Bickerel case wasn't some remote report of true crime. It happened right in that area of Vermont, and it was an enormous sensation while it was going on. Dinah might not have remembered the deformed ear before she saw the picture, she might not even have known about it, but she would have remembered it as soon as she heard how Tisha Verek died. So Amanda did what she thought she had to do. That's what Amy Jo Bickerel has always done. What she thought she had to do.''

"What was the second reason?" Bennis asked.

"The second reason was motive," Gregor said. "The rest of the people on that list of missing pictures had been released from the institutions they'd been remanded to, but Amy Jo Bickerel had not. I checked that out afterward, by the way. It turns out she hadn't been released, because every time they got close she seemed to go wild, violent and hallucinatory. She's been doing it for years. But if she hadn't been released, she must have escaped. And if she had escaped—"

"If she'd escaped, wouldn't that have been big news in that part of Vermont?"

"Not in that part of Vermont, no," Gregor said. "Up around Riverton, there it would have been big news. The Bickerel case was old, you have to remember that. The people who remembered it most clearly were old, too. It wasn't Stuart Ketchum or Peter Callisher who talked to us about Amy Jo Bickerel, even though Stuart was with us when we discussed the missing Bickerel picture in Tisha Verek's office. It was Franklin Morrison who remembered—and he's over seventy."

"All right," Bennis said patiently. "So that's why you figured it had to be Amy Jo Bickerel. And you figured Amy Jo Bickerel had to be Amanda Ballard because Amanda was the only one with something physically odd about her that would have been picked up in a picture and made instantly recognizable—"

"Well," Gregor said, "there was this other young woman, just about the right age, named Sharon Morrissey. She had a white streak in her hair she told me she'd had from birth. I dismissed her because I figured all she had to do to disguise that was to dye her hair."

"Fair enough."

"And then there was all that about Riverton and Timmy Hall," Gregor said. "Amanda Ballard had known Timmy Hall when he was at Riverton. She made no secret of that. Everybody assumed that she'd been up there working with retarded children or in the library or the cafeteria or something, but she never actually said that. In the end, all anybody really knew was that Amanda Ballard and Timmy Hall had both spent a fair amount of time at Riverton, background details unknown."

"I suppose we ought to be grateful she didn't kill Timmy."

"She wouldn't have killed Timmy," Gregor said. "She had nothing to fear from Timmy. He was devoted to her—he still is. He wasn't going to give her secret away. And then, of course, there was the obvious. Since Amanda was the one who worked in the *News and Mail* office, she was the one most likely to have heard Peter Callisher giving Gemma Bury tickets to the Nativity play and to know where those tickets were. Since Amanda lived with Peter Callisher and Peter Callisher was Stuart Ketchum's best friend, the chances were she had been at the Ketchum farm often enough to know the layout and be able to steal a gun with the smallest possible fuss. Since Kelley Grey had seen her within inches of that stand of bushes just minutes before Gemma Bury must have been killed, she was in the right place at the right time—"

"All that still bothers me."

"It shouldn't. On any other night—on any night when there was going to be a serious use of animals—it would have been impossible, but on that first night it was easy. We did it out there together. It's simple to disappear behind that stand."

"But how did she get out of there?" Bennis protested. "Kelley Grey saw her at intermission, that's fine, but then she must have gone into the bushes and waited for Gemma Bury and then pressed the trigger, but if she came right out she might have been seen—"

"She didn't come right out. She waited until the play was over."

"What?"

"If Gemma's death had been discovered immediately, or if the silencer hadn't worked, she probably would have come right out, because it would have been best to mingle with the crowd. But when nothing happened at all, she waited until the play was over. That was why Kelley Grey saw her at intermission, and Peter Callisher said she'd gone home sick in the middle of it all, but Stuart Ketchum saw her just outside the bleachers *after* the performance was over. Do you mean to tell me you didn't pick that up?"

"Don't do this to me, Gregor."

"I'm not doing anything to you. I'm just telling you what happened. I will say something else, though."

"What?"

"This is why I get so nervous about the expansion of the right to self-defense. I'm not totally against it, mind you. I have read some cases where I think it made perfect sense. There was that woman in Michigan with the husband who beat her. She divorced him. She moved out of town. She contacted police departments and got court orders. He followed her around, showed up on her doorstep and beat her bloody whenever he wanted to, and the police were very negligent in giving that woman protection. So the fact that she waited for him to pass out from vodka before she blew his head off doesn't bother me at all. I am in full agreement with the acquittal. But."

"But?"

"Well," Gregor said, "the problem with instituting such a principle in law is that you don't know what you're unleashing. You may have a woman like that woman in Michigan, who is protecting herself in the only way she can. You may, however, have someone like Amy Jo Bickerel."

"Maybe Amy Jo Bickerel was Amy Jo Bickerel because of what her uncle did to her."

"Maybe," Gregor agreed, "but there are two arguments from that premise. In the first place, you have to be careful with it, because in most cases adolescent girls who have been abused do not become violent to other people. They tear at themselves. The other thing has been known to happen, however, so we'll let that slide. Then you have to look at this: No matter how Amy Jo Bickerel got to be Amy Jo Bickerel, she's still dangerous. She won't go to jail even now. She'll be sent straight back to a mental institution, with any luck one with more stringent security procedures. Whether you're going to blame her for what she did is not the point."

"Abuse," Bennis said pensively.

"What is it?"

"I don't know, exactly. I got a call from Kelley Grey right before I left for church this morning. I think she was trying to find you and you were out somewhere—"

"I was at Ararat having breakfast in peace."

"Whatever. She said something about you'd want to know, she got Candy George a place in a program in Boston, and if Candy sticks with it she never has to let Reggie beat her up again, although who all these people are—"

"Candy is the girl who played Mary in the nativity play. Reggie is her husband that Gemma Bury said beat her—beat Candy—and also

Reggie is one of the people with the guns Stuart Ketchum was talking about—''

"Does any of this make actual sense to you?''

"No, Bennis, none of this makes actual sense to me, but I'm used to that. I live on Cavanaugh Street.''

"Right,'' Bennis said.

Over at the windows, Lida Arkmanian was standing in front of the grilled shrimp, clapping her hands and dodging Tommy Moradanyan, who seemed to want something that was right behind her.

"The food is all out,'' she called. "It is time for all of you to eat. There are tables set up downstairs if you want to sit at tables. There is punch in the punch bowl. Green punch is for children and old people. Red punch is for adults.''

"Green punch, red punch,'' old George Tekemanian said, coming up to Gregor and Bennis. "I have brought my rum just in case they try to make me listen to the doctor, who is somebody I don't need because if I've survived this long I have to know more than some boy about how to stay alive. Hello, Krekor, Merry Christmas.''

"Where's Martin?'' Gregor asked.

Old George gestured vaguely into the crowd. "Out there some-where. With my granddaughter-in-law, who is a very sweet girl but terrible about this health business. It's all right. I've brought my own alcohol. I can get my own cholesterol. I will see you later, Krekor.''

"Just remember not to stuff butter in your pockets this time,'' Gregor said. "It melts.''

"You think she'd give up,'' Bennis said, meaning old George's granddaughter-in-law. "She never wins an argument and he's already eighty-something. And he seems healthy as a horse.''

"He probably is healthy as a horse,'' Gregor said. "What about you?''

"What about me?''

"Are you healthy as a horse?''

"I'm going to quit smoking for New Year's,'' Bennis said. "I know I do it every New Year's, but at least—''

"That's not what I meant,'' Gregor told her. "I meant the diet.''

"What diet?''

"The diet you keep trying to go on. What I mean to say is, if you have to go on a diet, do you think you could save me a lot of headaches and go on it in such a way that Tibor couldn't tell?''

"Gregor, what are you talking about? I'm not on a diet. I couldn't go on a diet. They wouldn't let me go on a diet. I'd have to secede from Cavanaugh Street."

"What about those diet books you were reading in Vermont?"

"Oh," Bennis said, "those."

"Yes," Gregor said, "those."

"I have to go talk to Donna Moradanyan about something," Bennis said. "I'll be right back."

4

A FEW MINUTES later, Father Tibor Kasparian sidled up to Gregor's side and pulled on the sleeve of his sweater. Gregor stopped in the middle of eating a piece of *yaprak sarma* Hannah Krekorian had gotten for him and looked down at the small priest's head. He still looked tired, but he also looked healthy, which was an improvement from the days before they went to Vermont. That he also looked old was something that Gregor had long ago given up worrying about, in spite of the fact that Tibor was four years younger than he was himself.

"Krekor," Tibor said in a hiss. "Have you asked her? Do you know now why she is on a diet?"

"She says she isn't on a diet," Gregor said.

"If she isn't on a diet, why is she reading these books about how to be on a diet?"

"She didn't say."

"This will not do, Krekor, it will not do. This is an emergency. We have to take action."

"No we don't," Gregor said reasonably. "She's over at the food table, eating through everything in sight."

"Did you ask her if she was on a diet?"

"Of course I did. You told me to."

"I told you to find out if she was on a diet, Krekor, not to come right out and ask. You have probably now committed a disaster. You have probably now made her think you think she ought to go on a diet."

"I think she ought to gain twenty pounds and she knows it. And I'm hungry. I'm going to go back and get something to eat."

"Always you think about food, Krekor. This is life and death."

Actually, on Cavanaugh Street, as far as Gregor could tell, everything was life and death—but at least the life part had *yaprak sarma* in it, and flatbread you could dip into thick yogurt sauces, and lots of fresh dill. If Tibor hadn't looked so worried, Gregor would have left him to stew where he was and done some serious immediate damage to the food supply. Instead, he felt called upon to offer reassurance.

"Don't worry," he said, "I'm taking Bennis out for dinner on New Year's Eve. I've got that sweater I bought that I showed you, with the reindeer on it. I'm going to give it to her. It'll soften her up. Maybe I'll get her to talk."

"You are taking Bennis to a restaurant on New Year's Eve?" Tibor looked interested. "Just the two of you? Alone?"

Gregor Demarkian nearly choked. "Now Tibor," he warned. "Behave yourself."

"I do not know what you are talking about, Krekor. I am a priest. I always behave myself."

"Tibor—"

"I think this is a very good thing," Tibor said. "You and Bennis, alone in a restaurant, on New Year's Eve. If you are intelligent, Krekor, you will pick one with not much light and a great many candles."

"*Tibor.*"

But it was too late. Tibor had disappeared in the direction of the food, and in the direction of the gossip, too, if Gregor was any judge. Tibor was grabbing Lida Arkmanian's arm and whispering excitedly into her ear.

Oh, well, Gregor thought.

Sweater or no sweater, when Bennis Hannaford heard about this, she was going to kill him.